Praise f[or]
USA TO[DAY]
[...]

"Brenda Jackso[...] characters you fall in love with."
—*New York Times* and *USA TODAY*
bestselling author Lori Foster

"Jackson's trademark ability to weave multiple characters and side stories together makes shocking truths all the more exciting."
—*Publishers Weekly*

"There is no getting away from the sex appeal and charm of Jackson's Westmoreland family."
—*RT Book Reviews* on *Feeling the Heat*

"Jackson's characters are wonderful, strong, colorful and hot enough to burn the pages."
—*RT Book Reviews* on *Westmoreland's Way*

"The kind of sizzling, heart-tugging story Brenda Jackson is famous for."
—*RT Book Reviews* on *Spencer's Forbidden Passion*

"This is entertainment at its best."
—*RT Book Reviews* on *Star of His Heart*

Dear Readers,

I introduced Rico Claiborne in my seventh Westmoreland novel, *The Chase is On,* as the brother to my heroine, Jessica Claiborne. And you met him again in *A Durango Affair* as the brother of Savannah Claiborne, the heroine in that novel. Your e-mails began pouring in requesting that I write Rico's story. I put him on my "To Do" list until I thought I had the perfect heroine. Someone who was worthy of his heart.

I found her in Megan Westmoreland.

Texas Wild is Megan and Rico's story as they join forces in search of information about the patriarch of the Denver Westmorelands, Raphel. Their journey takes them from the mountains of Denver to the plains of Texas where the heat they encounter is blazing and wild—and is mainly for each other.

It's time to get to know Rico, up close and personal, in a love story that will leave you breathless and tempt you to get wild.

Happy reading!

Brenda Jackson

TEXAS WILD

BY
BRENDA JACKSON

Published in Great Britain 2012
by Mills & Boon, an imprint of Harlequin (UK) Limited,
Eton House, 18-24 Paradise Road, Richmond, Surrey TW9 1SR

© Brenda Streater Jackson 2012

ISBN: 978 0 263 89348 9
ebook ISBN: 978 1 408 97212 0

51-1212

Harlequin (UK) policy is to use papers that are natural, renewable and recyclable products and made from wood grown in sustainable forests. The logging and manufacturing processes conform to the legal environmental regulations of the country of origin.

Printed and bound in Spain
by Blackprint CPI, Barcelona

To Gerald Jackson, Sr. My one and only. My everything. Happy 40th Anniversary!!

To my readers who asked for Rico Claiborne's story,
Texas Wild is especially for you!

To my Heavenly Father. How Great Thou Art.

Though your beginning was small, yet your
latter end would increase abundantly.
—Job 8:7

Brenda Jackson is a die "heart" romantic who married her childhood sweetheart and still proudly wears
the "going steady" ring he gave her when she was fifteen. Because she believes in the power of love, Brenda's
stories always have happy endings. In her real-life love
story, Brenda and her husband of forty years live in Jacksonville, Florida, and have two sons.

A *New York Times* bestselling author of more than
seventy-five romance titles, Brenda is a recent retiree
who now divides her time between family, writing
and traveling with Gerald. You may write to Brenda at
PO Box 28267, Jacksonville, Florida 32226, USA, by
e-mail at WriterBJackson@aol.com or visit her website,
www.brendajackson.net.

THE DENVER WEST MORELAND FAMILY TREE

Raphel and Gemma Westmoreland

Stern Westmoreland (Paula Bailey)

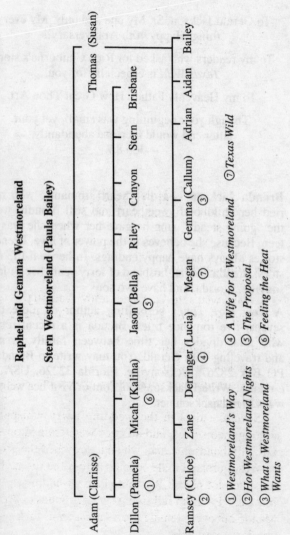

Thomas (Susan)

Adam (Clarisse)

Dillon (Pamela) ①

Micah (Kalina) ⑥

Zane

Derringer (Lucia) ④

Jason (Bella) ⑤

Riley

Canyon

Gemma (Callum) ③

Stern

Adrian

Brisbane

Aidan

Bailey

Ramsey (Chloe) ②

Megan ⑦

① Westmoreland's Way

② Hot Westmoreland Nights

③ What a Westmoreland Wants

④ A Wife for a Westmoreland

⑤ The Proposal

⑥ Feeling the Heat

⑦ Texas Wild

Prologue

A beautiful June day

"OMG, who's the latecomer to the wedding?"

"Don't know, but I'm glad he made it to the reception."

"Look at that body."

"Look at that walk."

"He should come with a warning sign that says Extremely Hot."

Several ladies in the wedding party whispered among themselves, and all eyes were trained on the tall, ultrahandsome man who'd approached the group of Westmoreland male cousins across the room. The reception for Micah Westmoreland's wedding to Kalina Daniels was in full swing on the grounds of Micah Manor, but every female in attendance was looking at one particular male.

The man who'd just arrived.

"For crying out loud, will someone please tell me who he is?" Vickie Morrow, a good friend of Kalina's, pleaded in a low voice. She looked over at Megan Westmoreland. "Most of the good-looking men here are related to you in some way, so tell us. Is he another Westmoreland cousin?"

Megan was checking out the man just as thoroughly as all the other women were. "No, he's no kin of mine. I've never seen him before," she said. She hadn't seen the full view yet, either, just his profile, but even that was impressive—he had handsome features, a deep tan and silky straight hair that brushed against the collar of his suit. He was both well dressed and good-looking.

"Yes, he definitely is one fine specimen of a man and is probably some Hollywood friend of my cousins, since he seems to know them."

"Well, I want to be around when the introductions are made," Marla Ford, another friend of Kalina's, leaned over and whispered in Megan's ear. "Make that happen."

Megan laughed. "I'll see what I can do."

"Hey, don't look now, ladies, but he's turned this way and is looking over here," Marla said. "In fact, Megan, your brother Zane is pointing out one of us to him...and I hope it's me." Seconds later, Marla said in a disappointed voice, "It's *you,* Megan."

Marla had to be mistaken. Why would Zane point her out to that man?

"Yeah, look how the hottie is checking you out," Vickie whispered to Megan. "It's like the rest of us don't even exist. *Lordy, I do declare.* I wish some man would look at me that way."

Megan met the stranger's gaze. Everyone was right.

He was concentrated solely on her. And the moment their eyes connected, something happened. It was as if heat transmitted from his look was burning her skin, flaming her blood, scorching her all over. She'd never felt anything so powerful in her life.

Instant attraction.

Her heart pounded like crazy, and she shivered as everything and everyone around her seemed to fade into the background…everything except for the sound of the soft music from the orchestra that pulled her and this stranger into a cocoon. It was as if no one existed but the two of them.

Her hand, which was holding a glass of wine, suddenly felt moist, and something fired up within her that had never been lit before. Desire. As potent as it could get. How could a stranger affect her this way? For the first time in her adult life, at the age of twenty-seven, Megan knew what it meant to be attracted to someone in a way that affected all her vital signs.

And, as an anesthesiologist, she knew all about the workings of the human body. But up until now she'd never given much thought to her own body or how it would react to a man. At least, not to how it would react to this particular man…whomever he was. She found her own reaction as interesting as she found it disconcerting.

"That guy's hot for you, Megan."

Vickie's words reminded Megan that she had an audience. Breaking eye contact with the stranger, she glanced over at Vickie, swallowing deeply. "No, he's not. He doesn't know me, and I don't know him."

"Doesn't matter who knows who. What just happened between you two is called instant sexual attraction. I felt it. We all did. You would have to be dead not to have felt it. That was some kind of heat emitting between the two of you just now."

Megan drew in a deep breath when the other women around her nodded and agreed with what Vickie had said. She glanced back over at the stranger. He was still staring and held her gaze until her cousin Riley tapped him on the shoulder to claim his attention. And when Savannah and Jessica, who were married to Megan's cousins Durango and Chase, respectively, walked up to him, she saw how his face split in a smile before he pulled both women into his arms for a huge hug.

That's when it hit her just who the stranger was. He was Jessica and Savannah's brother, the private investigator who lived in Philadelphia, Rico Claiborne. The man Megan had hired a few months ago to probe into her great-grandfather's past.

Rico Claiborne was glad to see his sisters, but the woman Zane had pointed out to him, the same one who had hired him over the phone a few months ago, was still holding his attention, although he was pretending otherwise.

Dr. Megan Westmoreland.

She had gone back to talking to her friends, not looking his way. That was fine for now since he needed to get his bearings. What in the hell had that been all about? What had made him concentrate solely on her as if all those other women standing with her didn't exist? There was something about her that made her stand out, even before Zane had told him the one in the pastel pink was his sister Megan.

The woman was hot, and when she had looked at him, every cell in his body had responded to that look. It wasn't one of those I'm-interested-in-you-too kind of looks. It was one of those looks that questioned the power of what was going on between them. It was quite obvious she was just as confused as he was. Never had he reacted so fiercely to a woman before. And the fact that she was the one who had hired him to research Raphel Westmoreland made things even more complicated.

That had been two months ago. He'd agreed to take the case, but had explained he couldn't begin until he'd wrapped up the other cases he was working on. She'd understood. Today, he'd figured he could kill two birds with one stone. He'd attend Micah's wedding and finally get to meet Micah's cousin Megan. But he hadn't counted on feeling such a strong attraction to her, one that still had heat thrumming all through him.

His sisters' husbands, as well as the newlyweds, walked up to join him. And as Rico listened to the conversations swirling around him, he couldn't help but steal glances over at Megan. He should have known it would be just a matter of time before one of his sisters noticed where his attention had strayed.

"You've met Megan, right? I know she hired you to investigate Raphel's history," Savannah said with a curious gleam in her eyes. He knew that look. If given the chance she would stick that pretty nose of hers where it didn't belong.

"No, Megan and I haven't officially met, although we've talked on the phone a number of times," he said, grabbing a drink off the tray of a passing waiter. He needed it to cool off. Megan Westmoreland was so freaking hot he could feel his toes beginning to burn. "But I know which one she is. Zane pointed her out to me a few minutes ago," he added, hoping that would appease his sister's curiosity.

He saw it didn't when she smiled and said, "Then let me introduce you."

Rico took a quick sip of his drink. He started to tell Savannah that he would rather be introduced to Megan later, but then decided he might as well get it over with. "All right."

As his sister led him over to where the group of women stood, all staring at him with interest in their eyes, his gaze was locked on just one. And he knew she felt the strong attraction flowing between them as much as he did. There was no way she could not.

It was a good thing they wouldn't be working together closely. His job was just to make sure she received periodic updates on how the investigation was going, which was simple enough.

Yes, he decided, as he got closer to her, with the way his entire body was reacting to her, the more distance he put between himself and Megan the better.

One

Three months later

"Dr. Westmoreland, there's someone here to see you."

Megan Westmoreland's brow arched as she glanced at her watch. She was due in surgery in an hour and had hoped to grab a sandwich and a drink from the deli downstairs before then. "Who is it, Grace?" she asked, speaking into the intercom system on her desk. Grace Elsberry was a student in the college's work-study program and worked part-time as an administrative assistant for the anesthesiology department at the University of Colorado Hospital.

"He's hot. A Brad Cooper look-alike with a dark tan," Grace whispered into the phone.

Megan's breath caught and warm sensations oozed through her bloodstream. She had an idea who her visitor was and braced herself for Grace to confirm her suspicions. "Says his name is Rico Claiborne." Lowering her voice even more, Grace added, "But I prefer calling him Mr. Yummy…if you know what I mean."

Yes, she knew exactly what Grace meant. The man was so incredibly handsome he should be arrested for being a menace to society. "Please send Mr. Claiborne in."

"Send him in? Are you kidding? I will take the pleasure of *escorting* him into your office, Dr. Westmoreland."

Megan shook her head. She couldn't remember the last time Grace had taken the time to escort anyone into her office. The door opened, and Grace, wearing the biggest of grins, escorted Rico Claiborne in. He moved with a masculine grace that exerted power, strength and confidence, and he looked like a model, even while wearing jeans and a pullover sweater.

Megan moved from behind her desk to properly greet him. Rico was tall, probably a good six-four, with dark brown hair and a gorgeous pair of hazel eyes. They had talked on the phone a number of times, but they had only met once, three months ago, at her cousin Micah's wedding. He had made such an impact on her feminine senses that she'd found it hard to stop thinking about him ever since. Now that he had completed that case he'd been working on, hopefully he was ready to start work on hers.

"Rico, good seeing you again," Megan said, smiling, extending her hand to him. Grace was right, he did look like Brad Cooper, and his interracial features made his skin tone appear as if he'd gotten the perfect tan.

"Good seeing you again as well, Megan," he said, taking her hand in his.

The warm sensation Megan had felt earlier intensified with the touch of his hand on hers, but she fought to ignore it. "So, what brings you to Denver?"

He placed his hands in the pockets of his jeans. "I arrived this morning to appear in court on a case I handled last year, and figured since I was here I'd give you an update. I actually started work on your case a few weeks ago. I don't like just dropping in like this, but I tried calling you when I first got to town and couldn't reach you on your cell phone."

"She was in surgery all morning."

They both turned to note Grace was still in the room. She stood in the doorway smiling, eyeing Rico up and down with a look of pure female appreciation on her face. Megan wouldn't have been surprised if Grace started licking her lips.

"Thanks, and that will be all Grace," Megan said.

Grace actually looked disappointed. "You sure?"

"Yes, I'm positive. I'll call you if I need you," Megan said, forcing back a grin.

"Oh, all right."

It was only when Grace had closed the door behind her that Megan glanced back at Rico to find him staring at her. A shiver of nervousness slithered down her spine. She shouldn't feel uncomfortable around him. But she had discovered upon meeting Rico that she had a strong attraction to him, something she'd never had for a man before. For the past three months, out of sight had meant out of mind where he was concerned—on her good days. But with him standing in the middle of her office she was forced to remember why she'd been so taken with him at her cousin's wedding.

The man was hot.

"Would you like to take a seat? This sounds important," she said, returning to the chair behind her desk, eager to hear what he had to say and just as anxious to downplay the emotional reaction he was causing.

A few years ago, her family had learned that her great-grandfather, Raphel Stern Westmoreland, who they'd assumed was an only child, had actually had a twin brother, Reginald Scott Westmoreland. It all started when an older man living in Atlanta by the name of James Westmoreland—a grandson of Reginald—began genealogy research on his family. His research revealed a connection to the Westmorelands living in Denver—her family. Once that information had been uncovered, her family had begun to wonder what else they didn't know about their ancestor.

They had discovered that Raphel, at twenty-two, had become the black sheep of the family after running off with the preacher's wife, never to be heard from again. He had passed through various states, including Texas, Wyoming, Kansas and Nebraska, before settling down in Colorado. It was found that he had taken up with a number of women along the way. Everyone was curious about what happened to those women, since it appeared he had been married to each one of them at some point. If that was true, there were possibly even more Westmorelands out there that Megan and her family didn't know about. That was why her oldest cousin, Dillon, had taken it upon himself to investigate her great-grandfather's other wives.

Dillon's investigation had led him to Gamble, Wyoming, where he'd not only met his future wife, but he'd also found out the first two women connected with Raphel hadn't been the man's wives, but were women he had helped out in some way. Since that first investigation, Dillon had married and was the father of one child, with another on the way. With a growing family, he was too busy to chase information about Raphel's third and fourth wives. Megan had decided to resume the search, which was the reason she had hired Rico, who had, of course, come highly recommended by her brothers and cousins.

Megan watched Rico take a seat, thinking the man was way too sexy for words. She was used to being surrounded by good-looking men. Case in point, her five brothers and slew of cousins were all gorgeous. But there was something about Rico that pulled at her in a way she found most troublesome.

"I think it's important, and it's the first break I've had," he responded. "I was finally able to find something on Clarice Riggins."

A glimmer of hope spread through Megan. Clarice was rumored to have been her great-grandfather's third wife. Megan leaned forward in her chair. "How? Where?"

"I was able to trace what I've pieced together to a small town in Texas, on the other side of Austin, called Forbes."

"Forbes, Texas?"

"Yes. I plan to leave Thursday morning. I had thought of leaving later today, after this meeting, but your brothers and cousins talked me out of it. They want me to hang out with them for a couple of days."

Megan wasn't surprised. Although the Westmorelands were mostly divided among four states—Colorado, Georgia, Montana and Texas—the males in the family usually got together often, either to go hunting, check on the various mutual business interests or just for a poker game getaway. Since Rico was the brother-in-law to two of her cousins, he often joined those trips.

"So you haven't been able to find out anything about her?" she asked.

"No, not yet, but I did discover something interesting."

Megan lifted a brow. "What?"

"It's recorded that she gave birth to a child. We can't say whether the baby was male or female, but it was a live birth."

Megan couldn't stop the flow of excitement that seeped into her veins. If Clarice had given birth, that could mean more Westmoreland cousins out there somewhere. Anyone living in Denver knew how important family was to the Westmorelands.

"That could be big. Really major," she said, thinking. "Have you mentioned it to anyone else?"

He shook his head, smiling. "No, you're the one who hired me, so anything I discover I bring to you first."

She nodded. "Don't say anything just yet. I don't want to get anyone's hopes up. You can say you're going to Texas on a lead, but nothing else for now."

Presently, there were fifteen Denver Westmorelands. Twelve males and three females. Megan's parents, as well as her aunt and uncle, had been killed in a plane crash years ago, leaving Dillon and her oldest brother, Ramsey, in charge. It hadn't been easy, but now all of the Westmorelands were self-supporting individuals. All of them had graduated from college except for the two youngest—Bane and Bailey. Bane was in the U.S. Navy, and Bailey, who'd fought the idea of any education past high school, was now in college with less than a year to go to get her degree.

There had never been any doubt in Megan's mind that she would go to college to become an anesthesiologist. She loved her job. She had known this was the career she wanted ever since she'd had her tonsils removed at six and had met the nice man who put her to sleep. He had come by to check on her after the surgery. He'd visited with her, ate ice cream with her and told her all about his job. At the time, she couldn't even pronounce it, but she'd known that was her calling.

Yet everyone needed a break from their job every once in a while, and she was getting burned out. Budget cuts required doing more with less, and she'd known for a while that it was time she went somewhere to chill. Bailey had left that morning for Charlotte to visit their cousin Quade, his wife Cheyenne and their triplets. Megan had been tempted to go with her, since she had a lot of vacation time that she rarely used. She also thought about going to Montana, where other Westmorelands lived. One nice thing about having a large family so spread out was that you always had somewhere to go.

Suddenly, a thought popped into Megan's head, and she glanced over at Rico again to find him staring at her. Their gazes held for a moment longer than necessary before she broke eye contact and looked down at the calendar on her desk while releasing a slow breath. For some reason she had a feeling he was on the verge of finding out something major. She wanted to be there when he did. More than anything she wanted to be present when he found out about Clarice's child. If she was in Denver while he was in Texas, she would go nuts waiting for him to contact her with any information he discovered. Once she'd gotten her thoughts and plans together, she glanced back up at him.

"You're leaving for Texas in two days, right?"

He lifted a brow. "Yes. That's my plan."

Megan leaned back in her chair. "I've just made a decision about something."

"About what?"

Megan smiled. "I've decided to go with you."

Rico figured there were a lot of things in life he didn't know. But the one thing he did know was that there was no way Megan Westmoreland was going anywhere with him. Being alone with her in this office was bad enough. The thought of them sitting together on a plane or in a car was too close for comfort. It was arousing him just thinking about it.

He was attracted to her big-time and had been from the moment he'd seen her at Micah's wedding. He had arrived late because of a case he'd been handling and had shown up at the reception just moments before the bride and groom were to leave for their honeymoon. Megan had hired him a month earlier, even though they'd never met in person. Because of that, the first thing Rico did when he arrived at the reception was to ask Zane to point her out.

The moment his and Megan's gazes locked he had felt desire rush through him to a degree that had never happened before. It had shocked the hell out of him. His gaze had moved over her, taking in every single thing he saw, every inch of what he'd liked. And he'd liked it all. Way too much. From the abundance of dark curls on her head to the creamy smoothness of her mahogany skin, from the shapely body in a bridesmaid gown to the pair of silver stilettos on her feet. She had looked totally beautiful.

At the age of thirty-six, he'd figured he was way too old to be *that* attracted to any woman. After all, he'd dated quite a few women in his day. And by just looking at Megan, he could tell she was young, that she hadn't turned thirty yet. But her age hadn't stopped him from staring and staring and staring...until one of her cousins had reclaimed his attention. But still, he had thought about her more than he should have since then.

"Well, with that settled, I'll notify my superiors so they can find a replacement for me while I'm gone," she said, breaking into his thoughts. "There are only a few surgeries scheduled for tomorrow, and I figure we'll be back in a week or so."

Evidently she thought that since he hadn't said anything, he was okay with the idea of her accompanying him to Texas. Boy, was she wrong. "Sorry, Megan, there's no way I'll let you come with me. I have a rule about working alone."

He could tell by the mutinous expression on her face that he was in for a fight. That didn't bother him. He had two younger sisters to deal with so he knew well how to handle a stubborn female.

"Surely you can break that rule this one time."

He shook his head. "Sorry, I can't."

She crossed her arms over her chest. "Other than the fact that you prefer working alone, give me another reason I can't go with you."

He crossed his arms over his own chest. "I don't need another reason. Like I said, I work alone." He did have a reason, but he wouldn't be sharing it with her. All he had to do was recall what had almost happened the last time he'd worked a case with a woman.

"Why are you being difficult?"

"Why are you?" he countered.

"I'm not," she said, throwing her head back and gritting out her words. "This is my great-grandfather we're talking about."

"I'm fully aware of who he was. You and I talked extensively before I agreed to take on this case, and I recall telling you that I would get you the information you wanted…doing things my way."

He watched as she began nibbling on her bottom lip. Okay, so now she was remembering. Good. For some reason, he couldn't stop looking into her eyes, meeting her fiery gaze head on, thinking her eyes resembled two beautiful dark orbs.

"As the client, I demand that you take me," she said, sharply interrupting his thoughts.

He narrowed his gaze. "You can demand all you want, but you're not going to Texas with me."

"And why not?"

"I've told you my reasons, now can we move on to something else, please?"

She stood up. "No, we can't move on to something else."

He stood, as well. "Now you're acting like a spoiled child."

Megan's jaw dropped. "A spoiled child? I've never acted like a spoiled child in my entire life. And as for going to Texas, I will be going since there's no reason that I shouldn't."

He didn't say anything for a moment. "Okay, there is another reason I won't take you with me. One that you'd do well to consider," he said in a calm, barely controlled tone. She had pushed him, and he didn't like being pushed.

"Fine, let's hear it," she snapped furiously.

He placed his hands in the pockets of his jeans, stood with his legs braced apart and leveled his gaze on her when he spoke in a deep, husky voice. "I want you,

Megan. Bad. And if you go anywhere with me, I'm going to have you."

He then turned and walked out of her office.

Shocked, Megan dropped back down in her chair. "Gracious!"

Three surgeries later, back in her office, Megan paced the floor. Although Rico's parting statement had taken her by surprise, she was still furious. Typical man. Why did they think everything began and ended in the bedroom? So, he was attracted to her. Big deal. Little did he know, but she was attracted to him as well, and she had no qualms about going to Texas with him. For crying out loud, hadn't he ever heard of self-control?

She was sister to Zane and Derringer and cousin to Riley and Canyon—three were womanizers to the core. And before marrying Lucia, Derringer had all but worn his penis on his sleeve and Zane, Lord help him, wore his anywhere there was a free spot on his body. She couldn't count the number of times she'd unexpectedly shown up at Zane's place at the wrong time or how many pairs of panties she'd discovered left behind at Riley's. And wasn't it just yesterday she'd seen a woman leave Canyon's place before dawn?

Besides that, Rico Claiborne honestly thought all he had to do was decide he wanted her and he would have her? Wouldn't she have some kind of say-so in the matter? Evidently he didn't think so, which meant he really didn't know whom he was dealing with. The doctors at the hospital, who thought she was cold and incapable of being seduced, called her "Iceberg Megan."

So, okay, Rico had thawed her out a little when she'd seen him at the wedding three months ago. And she would admit he'd made her heart flutter upon seeing him today. But he was definitely under a false assumption if he thought all he had to do was snap his fingers, strut that sexy walk and she would automatically fall into any bed with him.

She scowled. The more she thought about it, the madder she got. He should know from all the conversations they'd shared over the phone that this investigation was important to her. Family was everything to her, and if there were other Westmorelands out there, she wanted to know about them. She wanted to be in the thick of things when he uncovered the truth as to where those Westmorelands were and how quickly they could be reached.

Megan moved to the window and looked out. September clouds were settling in, and the forecasters had predicted the first snowfall of the year by the end of the week. But that was fine since she had no intention of being here in Denver when the snow started. Ignoring what Rico had said about her not going to Texas with him, she had cleared her calendar for not only the rest of the week, but also for the next month. She had the vacation time, and if she didn't use it by the end of the year she would end up losing it anyway.

First, she would go to Texas. And then, before returning to work, she would take off for Australia and spend time with her sister Gemma and her family. Megan enjoyed international travel and recalled the first time she'd left the country to visit her cousin Delaney in the Middle East. That had been quite an enjoyable experience.

But remembering the trip to visit her cousin couldn't keep her thoughts from shifting back to Rico, and she felt an unwelcoming jolt of desire as she recalled him standing in her office, right in this very spot, and saying what he'd said, without as much as blinking an eye.

If he, for one minute, thought he had the ability to tell her what to do, he had another thought coming. If he was *that* attracted to her then he needed to put a cap on it. They were adults and would act accordingly. The mere thought that once alone they would tear each other's clothes off in some sort of heated lust was total rubbish. Although she was attracted to him, she knew how to handle herself. It *was* going to be hard to keep her hands to herself.

But no matter what, she would.

"You sure I'm not putting you out, Riley? I can certainly get a room at the hotel in town."

"I won't hear of it," Riley Westmoreland said, smiling. "Hell, you're practically family."

Rico threw his luggage on the bed, thinking he certainly hadn't felt like family earlier when he'd been alone with Megan. He still couldn't get over her wanting to go to Texas with him. Surely she had felt the sexual tension that seemed to surround them whenever they were within a few feet of each other.

"So how are things going with that investigation you're doing for Megan?" Riley asked, breaking into Rico's thoughts.

"Fine. In fact, I'm on my way to Texas to poke around a new lead."

Riley's brow lifted. "Really? Does Megan know yet?"

"Yes. I met with her at the hospital earlier today."

Riley chuckled. "I bet she was happy about that. We're all interested in uncovering the truth about Poppa Raphel, but I honestly think Megan is obsessed with it

and has been ever since Dillon and Pam shared those
journals with her. Now that Dillon has made Megan
the keeper of the journals she is determined to uncover
everything. She's convinced we have more relatives out
there somewhere."

Rico had read those journals and had found them
quite interesting. The journals, written by Raphel himself, had documented his early life after splitting from
his family.

"And it's dinner tonight over at the big house. Pam
called earlier to make sure I brought you. I hope you're
up for it. You know how testy pregnant women can get
at times."

Rico chuckled. Yes, he knew. In fact, he had noted
the number of pregnant women in the Westmoreland
family. Enough to look like there was some sort of ep-
idemic. In addition to Pam, Derringer's wife, Lucia,
was expecting and so was Micah's wife, Kalina. There
were a number of Atlanta Westmorelands expecting
babies, as well.

Case in point, his own sisters. Jessica was pregnant
again, and Savannah had given birth to her second child
earlier that year. They were both happily married, and
he was happy for them. Even his mother had decided to
make another go of marriage, which had surprised him
after what she'd gone through with his father. But he
liked Brad Richman, and Rico knew Brad truly loved
his mother.

"Well, I'll let you unpack. We'll leave for Dillon's
place in about an hour. I hope you're hungry because
there will be plenty of food. The women are cooking,
and we just show up hungry and ready to eat," Riley
said, laughing.

A half hour later Rico had unpacked all the items

he needed. Everything else would remain in his luggage since he would be leaving for Texas the day after tomorrow. Sighing, he rubbed a hand down his face, noting his stubble-roughened jaw. Before he went out anywhere, he definitely needed to shave. And yes, he was hungry since he hadn't eaten since that morning, but dinner at Dillon's meant most of the Denver Westmorelands who were in town would be there. That included Megan. Damn. He wasn't all that sure he was ready to see her again. He was known as a cool and in-control kind of guy. But those elements of his personality took a flying leap around Megan Westmoreland.

Why did he like the way she said his name? To pronounce it was simple enough, but there was something about the way she said it, in a sultry tone that soothed and aroused.

Getting aroused was the last thing he needed to think about. It had been way too long since he'd had bedroom time with a woman. So he was in far worse shape than he'd realized. Seeing Megan today hadn't helped matters. The woman was way too beautiful for her own good.

Grabbing his shaving bag off the bed, Rico went into the guest bath that was conveniently connected to his room. Moments later, after lathering his face with shaving cream, he stared into the mirror as he slowly swiped a razor across his face. The familiar actions allowed his mind to wander, right back to Megan.

The first thing he'd noticed when he'd walked into her office was that she'd cut her hair. She still had a lot of curls, but instead of flowing to her shoulders, her hair crowned her face like a cap. He liked the style on her. It gave her a sexier look...not that she needed it.

He could just imagine being wheeled into surgery

only to discover she would be the doctor to administer
the drug to knock you out. Counting backward while
lying flat on your back and staring up into her face
would guarantee plenty of hot dreams during whatever
surgery you were having.

He jolted when he nicked himself. Damn. He needed
to concentrate on shaving and rid his mind of Megan.
At least he didn't have to worry about that foolishness
of hers, about wanting to go with him to Texas. He felt
certain, with the way her eyes had nearly popped out
of the sockets and her jaw had dropped after what he'd
said, that she had changed her mind.

He hadn't wanted to be so blatantly honest with her,
but it couldn't be helped. Like he told her, he preferred
working alone. The last time he had taken a woman
with him on a case had almost cost him his life. He remembered it like it was yesterday. An FBI sting operation and his female partner had ended up being more
hindrance than help. The woman blatantly refused to
follow orders.

Granted, there was no real danger involved with Megan's case per se. In fact, the only danger he could think
of was keeping his hands to himself where Megan was
concerned. That was a risk he couldn't afford. And he
had felt the need to be blunt and spell it out to her.
Now that he had, he was convinced they had an understanding.

He would go to Texas, delve into whatever he could
discover about Clarice Riggins and bring his report
back to her. Megan was paying him a pretty hefty fee
for his services, and he intended to deliver. But he
would have to admit that her great-grandfather had
covered his tracks well, which made Rico wonder what
all the old man had gotten into during his younger days.

It didn't matter, because Rico intended to uncover it all. And like he'd told Megan, Clarice Riggins had given birth, but there was nothing to indicate that she and Raphel had married. It had been a stroke of luck that he'd found anything at all on Clarice, since there had been various spellings of the woman's name.

He was walking out of the bathroom when his cell phone rang, and he pulled it off the clip. He checked and saw it was a New York number. He had several associates there and couldn't help wondering which one was calling.

"This is Rico."

There was a slight pause and then... "Hello, son. This is your father."

Rico flinched, drew in a sharp breath and fought for control of his anger, which had come quick...as soon as he'd recognized the voice. "You must have the wrong number because I don't have a father."

Without giving the man a chance to say anything else, he clicked off the phone. As far as he was concerned, Jeff Claiborne could go to hell. Why on earth would the man be calling Rico after all this time? What had it been? Eighteen years? Rico had been happy with his father being out of sight and out of mind.

To be quite honest, he wished he could wash the man's memory away completely. He could never forget the lives that man had damaged by his selfishness. No, Jeff Claiborne had no reason to call him. No reason at all.

Two

Megan tried to downplay her nervousness as she continued to cut up the bell pepper and celery for the potato salad. According to Pam, Rico had been invited to dinner and would probably arrive any minute.

"Has Rico found anything out yet?"

Megan glanced over at her cousin-in-law. She liked Pam and thought she was perfect for Dillon. The two women were alone for now. Chloe and Bella had gone to check on the babies, and Lucia, who was in the dining room, was putting icing on the cake.

"Yes, there's a lead in Texas he'll follow up on when he leaves here," Megan said. She didn't want to mention anything about Clarice. The last thing she wanted to do was get anyone's hopes up.

"How exciting," Pam said as she fried the chicken, turning pieces over in the huge skillet every so often. "I'm sure you're happy about that."

Megan would be a lot happier if Rico would let her go to Texas with him, but, in a way, she had solved that problem and couldn't wait to see the expression on his face when he found out how. Chances were, he thought he'd had the last word.

She sighed, knowing if she lived to be a hundred years old she wouldn't be able to figure out men. Whenever they wanted a woman they assumed a woman would just naturally want them in return. How crazy was that bit of logic?

There was so much Megan didn't know when it came to men, although she had lived most of her life surrounded by them. Oh, she knew some things, but this man-woman stuff—when it came to wants and desires—just went over her head. Until she'd met Rico, there hadn't been a man who'd made her give him a second look. Of course, Idris Elba didn't count.

She lifted her gaze from the vegetables to look over at Pam. Megan knew Pam and Dillon had a pretty good marriage, a real close one. Pam, Chloe, Lucia and Bella were the older sisters she'd never had, and, at the moment, she needed some advice.

"Pam?"

"Hmm?"

"How would you react if a man told you he wanted you?"

Pam glanced her way and smiled. "It depends on who the man is. Had your brother told me that, I would have kicked my fiancé to the curb a lot sooner. The first thing I thought when I saw Dillon was that he was hot."

That was the same thing Megan had thought when she'd seen Rico. "So you would not have gotten upset had he said he wanted you?"

"Again, it depends on who the man is. If it's a man I

had the hots for, then no, I wouldn't have gotten upset. Why would I have? That would mean we were of the same accord and could move on to the next phase."

Megan raised a brow. "The next phase?"

"Yes, the I-want-to-get-to-know-you-better phase." Pam looked over at her. "So tell me. Was this a hypothetical question or is there a man out there who told you he wants you?"

Megan nervously nibbled on her bottom lip. She must have taken too long to answer because Pam grinned and said, "I guess I got my answer."

Pam took the last of the chicken out of the skillet, turned off the stove and joined Megan at the table. "Like I said, Megan, the question you should ask yourself is…if he's someone you want, too. Forget about what he wants for the moment. The question is what do *you* want?"

Megan sighed. Rico was definitely a looker, a man any woman would want. But what did she really know about him, other than that he was Jessica and Savannah's older brother, and they thought the world of him?

"He doesn't want to mix business with pleasure, not that I would have, mind you. Besides, I never told him that I wanted him."

"Most women don't tell a man. What they do is send out vibes. Men can pick up on vibes real quick, and depending on what those vibes are, a man might take them as a signal."

Megan looked perplexed. "I don't think I sent out anything."

Pam laughed. "I hate to say this, but Jillian can probably size a man up better than you can. Your brothers and cousins sheltered you too much from the harsh realities of life." Jillian was Pam's sister, who was a sophomore in college.

Megan shook her head. "It's not that they sheltered me, I just never met anyone I was interested in."

"Until now?"

Megan lifted her chin. "I'm really not interested in him, but I want us to work closer together, and he doesn't…because he wants me."

"Well, I'm sure there will be times at the hospital when the two of you will have no choice but to work together."

Pam thought the person they were discussing was another doctor. Megan wondered what Pam's reaction would be if she found out the person they were talking about was one of her dinner guests.

Megan heard loud male voices and recognized all of them. One stood out, the sound a deep, husky timbre she'd come to know.

Rico had arrived.

Rico paused in his conversation with Dillon and Ramsey when Megan walked into the room to place a huge bowl on the dining room table. She called out to him. "Hello, Rico."

"Megan."

If his gaze was full of male appreciation, it couldn't be helped. She had changed out of the scrubs he'd seen her in earlier and into a cute V-neck blue pullover sweater and a pair of hip-hugging jeans. She looked both comfortable and beautiful. She had spoken, which was a good indication that he hadn't offended her by what he'd told her. He was a firm believer that the truth never hurt, but he'd known more than one occasion when it had pissed people off.

"So, you're on your way to Texas, I hear." Dillon Westmoreland's question penetrated Rico's thoughts.

He looked at Dillon and saw the man's questioning gaze and knew he'd been caught ogling Megan. Rico's throat suddenly felt dry, and he took a sip of his wine before answering. "Yes. I might have a new lead. Don't want to say what it is just yet, until I'm certain it is one."

Dillon nodded. "I understand, trust me. When I took that time off to track down information on Raphel, it was like putting together pieces of a very complicated puzzle. But that woman," he said, inclining his head toward Pam when she entered the room, "made it all worthwhile."

Rico glanced over to where Pam was talking to Megan. He could see how Pam could have made Dillon feel that way. She was a beautiful woman. Rico had heard the story from his sisters, about how Dillon had met Pam while in Wyoming searching for leads on his great-grandfather's history. Pam had been engaged to marry a man who Dillon had exposed as nothing more than a lying, manipulating, arrogant SOB.

Rico couldn't help keeping his eye on Megan as her brother Ramsey and her cousins Dillon and Riley carried on conversations around him. Thoughts of her had haunted him ever since they'd met back in June. Even now, he lay awake with thoughts of her on his mind. How could one woman make such an impression on him, he would never know. But like he told her, he wanted her, so it was best that they keep their distance, considering his relationship with the Westmoreland family.

"So when are you leaving, Rico?"

He turned to meet Ramsey Westmoreland's inquisitive gaze. The man was sharp and, like Dillon, had probably caught Rico eyeing Megan. The hand holding Rico's wineglass tensed. He liked all the Westmore-lands and appreciated how the guys included him in a number of their all-male get-togethers. The last thing he wanted was to lose their friendship because he couldn't keep his eyes off their sister and cousin.

"I'm leaving on Thursday. Why do you ask?"

Ramsey shrugged. "Just curious."

Rico couldn't shake the feeling that the man was more than just curious. He frowned and stared down at his drink. It was either that or risk the wrath of one of the Westmorelands if he continued to stare at Megan, who was busy setting the table.

Dillon spoke up and intruded into Rico's thoughts when he said, "Pam just gave me the nod that dinner is ready."

Everyone moved in the direction of the dining room. Rico turned to follow the others, but Ramsey touched his arm. "Wait for a minute."

Rico nodded. He wondered why Ramsey had de-tained him. Had Megan gone running to her brother and reported what Rico had said to her earlier? Or was Ramsey about to call him out on the carpet for the interest in Megan that he couldn't hide? In either of those scenarios, how could he explain his intense desire for Megan when he didn't understand it himself? He'd wanted women before, but never with this intensity.

When the two of them were left alone, Ramsey turned to him and Rico braced himself for whatever the man had to say. Rico was older brother to two sis-ters of his own so he knew how protective brothers could be. He hadn't liked either Chase or Durango in the beginning only because he'd known something was going on between them and his sisters.

Ramsey was silent for a moment, doing nothing more than slowly sipping his wine, so Rico decided to speak up. "Was there something you wanted to discuss with me, Ramsey?" There were a couple of years' difference in their ages, but at the moment Rico felt like it was a hell of a lot more than that.

"Yes," Ramsey replied. "It's about Megan."

Rico met Ramsey's gaze. "What about her?"

"Just a warning."

Rico tensed. "I think I know what you're going to say."

Ramsey shook his head, chuckling. "No. I don't think that you do."

Rico was confused at Ramsey's amusement. Hell, maybe he didn't know after all. "Then how about telling me. What's the warning regarding Megan?"

Ramsey took another sip of his drink and said, "She's strong-willed. She has self-control of steel and when she sets her mind to do something, she does it, often without thinking it through. And…if you tell her no, you might as well have said yes."

Rico was silent for a moment and then asked, "Is there a reason you're telling me this?"

Ramsey's mouth curved into a smile. "Yes, and you'll find out that reason soon enough. Now come on, they won't start dinner without us."

Megan tried drowning out all the conversation going on around her. As usual, whenever the Westmorelands got together, they had a lot to talk about.

She was grateful Pam hadn't figured out the identity of the man they'd been discussing and seated them beside each other. Instead, Rico was sitting at the other end of the table, across from Ramsey and next to Riley.

If she had to look at him, it would be quite obvious she was doing so.

Riley said something and everyone chuckled. That gave her an excuse to look down the table. Rico was leaning back against the chair and holding a half-filled glass of wine in his hand, smiling at whatever the joke was about. Why did he have to look so darn irresistible when he smiled?

He must have felt her staring because he shifted his gaze to meet hers. For a moment she forgot to breathe. The intensity of his penetrating stare almost made her lips tremble. Something gripped her stomach in a tight squeeze and sent stirrings all through her nerve endings.

At that moment, one thought resonated through her mind. The same one Pam had reiterated earlier. *It doesn't matter if he wants you. The main question is whether or not you want him.*

Megan immediately broke eye contact and breathed in slowly, taking a sip of her wine. She fought to get her mind back on track and regain the senses she'd almost lost just now. She could control this. She had to. Desire and lust were things she didn't have time for. The only reason she wanted to go to Texas with Rico was to be there when he discovered the truth about Raphel.

Thinking it was time to make her announcement, she picked up her spoon and tapped it lightly against her glass, but loud enough to get everyone's attention. When all eyes swung her way she smiled and said, "I have an announcement to make. Most of you know I rarely take vacation time, but today I asked for an entire month off, starting tomorrow."

Surprised gazes stared back at her…except one. She

saw a look of suspicion in Rico's eyes and noted the way his jaw tightened.

"What's wrong? You're missing Bailey already and plan to follow her to North Carolina?" her cousin Stern asked, grinning.

Megan returned his grin and shook her head. "Although I miss Bailey, I'm not going to North Carolina."

"Let me guess. You're either going to visit Gemma in Australia or Delaney in Tehran," Chloe said, smiling.

Again Megan shook her head. "Those are on my to-do list for later, but not now," she said.

When others joined in, trying to guess where she was headed, she held up her hand. "Please, it's not that big of a deal."

"It's a big deal if you're taking time off. You like working."

"I don't like working, but I like the job I do. There is a difference. And to appease everyone's curiosity, I talked to Clint and Alyssa today, and I'm visiting them in Texas for a while."

"Texas?"

She glanced down the table at Riley, which allowed her to look at Rico again, as well. He was staring at her, and it didn't take a rocket scientist to see he wasn't pleased with her announcement. Too bad, too glad. She couldn't force him to take her to Texas, but she could certainly go there on her own. "Yes, Riley, I'm going to Texas."

"When are you leaving?" her brother Zane asked. "I need to, ah, get that box from you before you leave."

She nodded, seeing the tense expression in Zane's features. She wondered about the reason for it. She was very much aware that he had a lock box in her hall closet. Although she'd been tempted, she'd never sat-

isfied her curiosity by toying with the lock and looking inside. "That will be fine, Zane. I'm not leaving
until Friday."

She took another quick glance at Rico before resum-
ing dinner. He hadn't said anything, and it was just as
well. There really wasn't anything he could say. Although they would end up in the same state and within
mere miles from each other, they would not be together.

Since he didn't want her to accompany him, she
would do a little investigating on her own.

Three

The next morning Rico was still furious.

Now he knew what Ramsey's warning had been about. The little minx was going to Texas, pretty damn close to where he would be. He would have confronted her last night, but he'd been too upset to do so. Now here he was—at breakfast time—and instead of joining Zane, Riley, Canyon and Stern at one of the local cafés that boasted hotcakes to die for, he was parked outside Megan's home so he could try and talk some sense into her.

Did she not know what red-hot desire was about? Did she not understand how it was when a man really wanted a woman to the point where self-control took a backseat to longing and urges? Did she not comprehend there was temptation even when she tried acting cool and indifferent?

Just being around her last night had been hard

enough, and now she was placing herself in a position where they would be around each other in Texas without any family members as buffers. Oh, he knew the story she was telling her family, that she would be visiting Clint in Austin. Chances were, she would—for a minute. He was friends with Clint and Alyssa and had planned to visit them as well, during the same time she planned to be there. Since Forbes wasn't that far from Austin, Clint had offered Rico the use of one of their cabins on the Golden Glade Ranch as his headquarters, if needed.

But now Megan had interfered with his plans. She couldn't convince Rico that she didn't have ulterior motives and that she didn't intend to show up in Forbes. She intended to do some snooping, with or without him. So what the hell was she paying him for if she was going to do things her way? He got out of the car and glanced around, seeing her SUV parked at the side of her house. She had a real nice spread, and she'd kept most of it in its natural state. In the background, you could see rolling hills and meadows, mountains and the Whisper Creek Canyon. It was a beautiful view. And there was a lake named after her grandmother Gemma. Gemma Lake was huge and, according to Riley, the fish were biting all the time. If Megan hadn't been throwing him for a loop, Rico would have loved to find a fishing pole while he was here to see if the man's claim was true.

Megan's home was smaller than those owned by her brothers and male cousins. Their homes were two or three stories, but hers was a single story, modest in size, but eye-catching just the same. It reminded him of a vacation cabin with its cedar frame, wraparound porch and oversize windows. It had been built in the perfect location to take advantage of both lake and canyon.

He'd heard the story of how the main house and the three hundred acres on which it sat had been willed to Dillon, since he was the oldest cousin. The remaining Denver Westmorelands got a hundred acres each once they reached their twenty-fifth birthdays. They had come up with pet names for their particular spreads. There was Ramsey's Web, Derringer's Dungeon, Zane's Hideout and Gemma's Gem. Now, he was here at Megan's Meadows.

According to Riley, Megan's property was prime land, perfect for grazing. She had agreed to let a portion of her land be used by Ramsey for the raising of his sheep, and the other by Zane and Derringer for their horse training business.

If Riley suspected anything because of all the questions Rico had asked last night about Megan, he didn't let on. And it could have been that the man was too preoccupied to notice, since Riley had his little black book in front of him, checking off the numbers of women he intended to call.

It was early, and Rico wondered if Megan was up yet. He would find out soon enough. Regardless, he intended to have his say. She could pretend she hadn't recognized the strong attraction between them, that sexual chemistry that kept him awake at night, but he wasn't buying it. However, just in case she didn't have a clue, he intended to tell her. Again. There was no need for her to go to Texas, and to pretend she was going just to visit relatives was a crock.

The weather was cold. Tightening his leather jacket around him, he moved quickly, walking up onto the porch. Knocking on the door loudly, he waited a minute and then knocked again. When there was no answer, he was about to turn around, thinking that perhaps she'd gone up to the main house for breakfast, when suddenly the door was snatched open. His jaw almost dropped. The only thing he could say when he saw her, standing there wearing the cutest baby-doll gown, was *wow*.

Megan stared at Rico, surprised to see him. "What are you doing here?"

He leaned in the doorway. "I came to talk to you. And what are you doing coming to the door without first asking who it is?"

She rolled her eyes. "I thought you were one of my brothers. Usually they are the only ones who drop by without notice."

"Is that why you came to the door dressed like that?"

"Yes, what do you want to talk to me about? You're letting cold air in."

"Your trip to Texas."

Megan stared at him, her lips tight. "Fine," she said, taking a step back. "Come in and excuse me while I grab my robe."

He watched her walk away, thinking the woman looked pretty damn good in a nightgown. Her shapely backside filled it out quite nicely and showed what a gorgeous pair of legs she had.

Thinking that the last thing he needed to be thinking about was her legs, he removed his jacket and placed it on the coatrack by the door before moving into the living room. He glanced around. Her house was nice and cozy. Rustic. Quaint. The interior walls, as well as the ceiling and floors, were cedar like the outside. The furniture was nice, appropriate for the setting and comfortable-looking. From where he stood, he could see an eat-in kitchen surrounded by floor-to-ceiling windows where you could dine and enjoy a view of the mountains and lake. He could even see the pier at her brother Micah's place that led to the lake and where the sailboat docked.

"Before we start talking about anything, I need my coffee."

Rico turned when she came back into the room, moving past him and heading toward the kitchen. He nodded, understanding. For him, it was basically the same, which was why he had drunk two cups already. "Fine. Take your time," he said. "I'm not going anywhere because I know what you're doing."

She didn't respond until she had the coffeemaker going. Then she turned and leaned back against a counter to ask, "And just what am I doing?"

"You're going to Texas for a reason."

"Yes, and I explained why. I need a break from work."

"Why Texas?"

She lifted her chin. "Why not Texas? It's a great state, and I haven't been there in a while. I missed that ball Clint, Cole and Casey do every year for their uncle. It will be good to see them, especially since Alyssa is expecting again."

"But that's not why you're going to Texas and you know it, Megan. Can you look me in the eyes and say you don't plan to set one foot in Forbes?"

She tilted her head to look at him. "No. I can't say that because I do."

"Why?"

Megan wondered how she could get him to understand. "Why not? These are my relatives."

"You are paying me to handle this investigation," he countered.

She tried not to notice how he filled the entrance to her kitchen. It suddenly looked small, as if there was barely any space. "Yes, and I asked to go to Forbes with you. It's important for me to be there when you find out if I have more relatives, but you have this stupid rule about working alone."

"Dammit, Megan, when you hired me you never told me you would get involved."

She crossed her arms over her chest. "I hadn't planned on getting involved. However, knowing I might have more kin out there changes everything. Why can't you understand that?"

Rico ran a frustrated hand down his face. In a way, he did. He would never forget that summer day when his mother had brought a fifteen-year-old girl into their home and introduced her as Jessica—their sister. Savannah had been sixteen, and he had been nineteen, a sophomore in college. It hadn't mattered to him that he hadn't known about Jessica before that time. Just the announcement that he had another sister had kicked his brotherly instincts into gear.

"I do understand, Megan," he said in a calm voice. "But still, there are things that I need to handle. Things I need to check out before anyone else can become involved."

She lifted a brow. "Things like what?"

Rico drew in a deep breath. Maybe he should have leveled with her yesterday, but there were things that had come up in his report on Raphel that he needed to confirm were fact or fiction. So far, everything negative about Raphel had turned out not to be true in Dillon's investigation. Rico wanted his final report to be as factual as possible, and he needed to do more research of the town's records.

She poured a cup of coffee for herself and one for him, as well. "What's wrong, Rico? Is there something you're not telling me?"

He saw the worry in her eyes as he accepted his coffee. "Look, this is my investigation. I told you that I was able to track down information on Clarice and the fact that she might have given birth to a child. That's all I know for now, Megan. Anything else is hearsay."

"Hearsay like what?"

"I'd rather not say."

After taking a sip of coffee, she said, "You're being evasive.

He narrowed his gaze. "I'm being thorough. If you want to go to Texas to visit Clint and Alyssa, then fine. But what I *don't* need is you turning up where you don't need to be."

"Where I don't need to be?" she growled.

"Yes. I have a job to do, and I won't be able to do it with you close by. I won't be able to concentrate."

"Men!" Megan said, stiffening her spine. "Do you all think it's all about you? I have brothers and male cousins, plenty of them. I know how you operate. You want one woman one day and another woman the next. Get over it already. Please."

Rico just stared at her. "And you think it's that simple?"

"*Yesss.* I'm Zane and Derringer's sister, Riley, Canyon and Stern's cousin. I see them. I watch them. I know their M.O. Derringer has been taken out of the mix by marrying Lucia, thank goodness. But the rest of them, and now the twins…oh, my God…are following in their footsteps.

"You see. You want. You do. But not me. *You,* Rico Claiborne, assume just because you want me that you're going to get me. What was your warning? If we go somewhere together alone, that you're going to *have* me. Who are you supposed to be? Don't I have a say-so in this matter? What if I told you that I *don't* want you?"

Rico just stared at her. "Then I would say you're lying to yourself. You want me. You might not realize it, but you want me. I see it every time you look at me. Damn, Megan, admit there's a strong attraction between us."

She rolled her eyes. "Okay, I find you attractive. But I find a lot of men attractive. No big deal."

"And are you sending out the same vibes to them that you're sending to me?" he asked in a deep, husky voice.

Megan recalled that Pam had said something about vibes. Was she sending them out to him without realizing she was doing so? No, she couldn't be. Because right now she wasn't feeling desire for him, she was feeling anger at him for standing there and making such an outlandish claim.

But still, she would have to admit that her heart was pounding furiously in her chest, and parts of her were quivering inside. So, could he be right about those vibes? Naw, she refused to believe it. Like she'd told him, she'd seen men in operation. Zane probably had a long list of women he wanted who he imagined were sending out vibes.

From the first, Rico had come across as a man who knew how to control any given situation, which was why she figured he was the perfect person for the job she'd hired him to do. So what was his problem now?

If he did want her, then surely the man could control his urges.

"Look, I assure you, I can handle myself, and I can handle you, Rico," she said, "All of my senses are intact, and you can be certain lust won't make me lose control. And nothing you or any man can say or do will place me in a position where I will lose my self-control." The men who thought so didn't call her "Iceberg Megan" for nothing.

"You don't think so?" Rico challenged her. "You aren't made of stone. You have feelings. I can tell that you're a very passionate woman, so consider your words carefully."

She chuckled as if what he'd said was a joke. "Passionate? Me?"

"Yes, you. When I first looked at you at the wedding reception and our gazes connected, the air between us was bristling with so much sexual energy I'm sure others felt it," he said silkily. "Are you going to stand there and claim you didn't feel it?"

Megan gazed down into her coffee and erased her smile. Oh, she remembered that day. Yes, she'd felt it. It had been like a surge of sexual, electrical currents that had consumed the space between them. It had happened again, too, every time she saw him looking at her. Until now, she'd assumed she had imagined it, but his words confirmed he had felt the connection, as well.

After that night at the wedding, she'd gone to bed thinking about him and had thought of him several nights after that. What she'd felt had bothered her, and she had talked to Gemma about it. Some of the things her married sister had shared with her she hadn't wanted to hear, mainly because Megan was a firm believer in self-control. Everybody had it, and everybody could manage it. Regardless of how attracted she was to Rico, she had self-control down pat. Hers was unshakable.

She'd had to learn self-control from the day she was told she would never see her parents again. She would never forget how Dillon and Ramsey had sat her down at the age of twelve and told her that not only her parents, but also her aunt and uncle, whom she'd adored, had been killed in a plane crash.

Dillon and Ramsey had assured her that they would keep the family together and take care of everyone, although the youngest—Bane and Bailey—were both under nine at the time. On that day, Ramsey had asked her to stay strong and in control. As the oldest girl in the Denver Westmoreland family, they had depended on her to help Gemma and Bailey through their grief. That didn't mean she'd needed to put her own grief aside, but it had meant that in spite of her grief, she'd had to be strong for the others. And she had. When the younger ones would come to her crying, she was the one who would comfort them, regardless of the circumstances or her emotions.

The ability to become emotionally detached, to stay in control, was how she'd known being an anesthesiologist was her calling. She went into surgery knowing some patients wouldn't make it through. Although she assured the patient of her skill in putting them to sleep, she never promised they would pull through. That decision was out of her hands. Some of the surgeons had lost patients and, in a way, she felt she'd lost them, as well. But no matter what, she remained in control.

Drawing in a deep breath, she eyed Rico. "You might have a problem with control, but I don't. I admit I find you desirable, but I can regulate my emotions. I can turn them on and off when I need to, Rico. Don't worry that I'll lose control one day and jump your bones, because it won't happen. There's not that much desire in the world."

Rico shook his head. "You honestly believe that, don't you?"

She placed her coffee cup on the counter. "Honestly believe what?"

"That you can control a desire as intense as ours."

"Yes, why wouldn't I?"

"I agree that certain desires can be controlled, Megan. But I'm trying to tell you, what you refuse to acknowledge or accept—desire as intense as ours can't always be controlled. What we have isn't normal."

She bunched her forehead. "Not normal? That's preposterous."

Rico knew then that she really didn't have a clue. This was no act. He could stand here until he was blue in the face and she still wouldn't understand. "What I'm trying to say, Megan," he said slowly, trying not to let frustration get the best of him, "is that I feel a degree of desire for you that I've never felt for any woman before."

She crossed her arms over her chest and glared at him. "Should I get excited or feel flattered about it?"

He gritted his teeth. "Look, Megan…"

"No, *you* look, Rico," she said, crossing the room to stand in front of him. "I don't know what to tell you. Honestly, I don't. I admitted that I'm attracted to you, as well. Okay, I'll admit it again. But on that same note, I'm also telling you I won't lose control over it. For crying out loud, there're more important things in life than sexual attraction, desire and passion. It's not about all of that."

"Isn't it?" He paused a moment, trying to keep his vexation in check. And it wasn't helping matters that she was there, standing right in front of him, with a stubborn expression on her face and looking as beautiful as any woman could. And he picked up her scent, which made him fight to keep a grip on his lust. The woman was driving him mad in so many ways.

"Let me ask you something, Megan," he said in a voice he was fighting to keep calm. "When was the last time you were with a man you desired?"

Rico's question surprised Megan, and she didn't say anything. Hell, she'd never been with a man she truly desired because she'd never been with a man period. She had dated guys in high school, college, and even doctors at the hospital. Unfortunately, they'd all had one thing in common. They had reminded her too much of her player-card-toting brothers and cousins, even hitting on her using some of the same lines she'd heard her family use. And a few bold ones had even had the nerve to issue ultimatums. She had retaliated by dropping those men like hot potatoes, just to show she really didn't give a royal damn. They said she was cold and couldn't be thawed and that's when they'd started calling her Iceberg Megan. Didn't bother her any because none of those men had gotten beyond the first boring kiss. She was who she was and no man—coming or going—would change it.

"I'm waiting on an answer," Rico said, interrupting her thoughts.

She gazed up at him and frowned. "Wait on. I don't intend to give you an answer because it's none of your business."

He nodded. "All right. You claim you can control the passion between us, right?"

"Yes."

"Then I want to see how you control this."

The next thing Megan knew, Rico had reached out, pulled her into his embrace and swooped his mouth down onto hers.

Desire that had been lingering on the edges was now producing talons that were digging deep into Megan's skin and sending heated lust all through her veins—and making her act totally out of control. He parted her lips with his tongue and instead of immediately going after her tongue, he rolled the tip around, as if on a tasting expedition. Then he gradually tasted more of it until he had captured it all. And when she became greedy, he pulled back and gave her just the tip again. Then they played the tongue game over and over again.

She felt something stir within her that had never stirred before while kissing a man. But then no man had ever kissed her like this. Or played mouth games with her this way.

He was electrifying her cells, muddling her brain as even more desire skittered up her spine. She tried steadying her emotions, regaining control when she felt heat flooding between her thighs, but she couldn't help but release a staggering moan.

Instead of unlocking their mouths, he intensified the kiss, as his tongue, holding hers in a dominant grip, began exploring every part of her mouth with strokes so sensual her stomach began doing somersaults. She felt her senses tossed in a number of wild spins, and surprised herself when she wrapped her arms around his neck and began running her fingers through the softness of his hair, absently curling a strand around her finger.

She could taste the hunger in his kiss, the passion and the desire. Her emotions were smoldering, and blocking every single thought from her already chaotic mind. The man was lapping up her mouth, and each stroke was getting hotter and hotter, filling her with emotions she had pushed aside for years. Was he ever going to let go of her mouth? Apparently no time soon.

This kiss was making her want to do things she'd never done before. Touch a man, run her hands all over him, check out that huge erection pressing against her belly.

She felt his hands rest on her backside, urging her closer to his front. And she shifted her hips to accommodate what he wanted. She felt the nipples of her breasts harden and knew her robe was no barrier against the heat coming from his body.

No telling how long they would have stood in the middle of her kitchen engaged in one hell of a feverish kiss if his cell phone hadn't gone off. They broke apart, and she drew in a much needed breath and watched him get his phone out of the back pocket of his jeans.

She took note of the angry look on his face while he talked and heard him say to the caller, "I don't want you calling me." He then clicked off the line without giving the person a chance to respond.

She tensed at the thought that the person he'd just given the brush-off was a woman. Megan lifted her chin. "Maybe you should have taken that call."

He glanced over at her while stuffing his phone back into the pocket of his jeans. She watched as his hazel eyes became a frosty green. "I will never take *that* call."

She released a slow, steady breath, feeling his anger as if it were a personal thing. She was glad it wasn't directed at her. She wondered what the woman had done to deserve such animosity from him. At the moment, Megan didn't care because she had her own problems. Rico Claiborne had made her lose control. He had kissed her, and she had kissed him back.

And rather enjoyed it.

Dread had her belly quaking and her throat tightening when she realized she wasn't an iceberg after all. Rico had effectively thawed her.

She drew in a deep breath, furious with herself for letting things get out of hand when she'd boasted and bragged about the control she had. All it had taken was one blazing kiss to make a liar out of her. It was a fluke, it had to be. He had caught her off guard. She didn't enjoy kissing him as much as she wanted to think she did.

Then why was she licking her lips and liking the taste he'd left behind? She glanced over and saw he'd been watching her and was following the movement of her tongue. Her fingers knotted into a fist at her side, and she narrowed her gaze. "I think you need to leave."

"No problem, now that I've proven my point. You're as passionate as you are beautiful, Megan. Nothing's changed. I still want you, and now that I've gotten a taste, I want you even more. So take my warning, don't come to Texas."

A part of Megan knew that if she was smart, she would take his warning. But the stubborn part of her refused to do so. "I'm going to Texas, Rico."

He didn't say anything for a long moment, just stood there and held her gaze. Finally, he said, "Then I guess I'll be seeing you at some point while you're there. Don't say I didn't warn you."

Rico strode away and, before opening the door to leave, he grabbed his jacket off the coatrack. He turned, smiled at her, winked and then opened the door and walked out.

Megan took a deep breath to calm her racing heart. She had a feeling that her life, as she'd always known it, would never, ever be the same. Heaven help her, she had tasted passion and already she was craving more.

Four

Upon arriving at Megan's place early Friday morning, Ramsey glanced down at the two overpacked traveling bags that sat in the middle of her living room. "Hey, you're planning on coming back, aren't you?" he asked, chuckling.

Megan smiled and tapped a finger to her chin. "Umm, I guess I will eventually. And those bags aren't *that* bad."

"They aren't? I bet I'll strain my back carrying them out to the truck. And how much you want to bet they're both overweight and you'll pay plenty when you check them in at the airport."

"Probably, but that's fine. A lot of it is baby stuff I bought for Alyssa. She's having a girl and you know how I like buying all that frilly stuff." He would know since his two-year-old daughter, Susan, had been the first female born to the Denver Westmorelands since

Bailey. Megan simply adored her niece and would miss her while away in Texas.

She looked up at Ramsey, her oldest brother, the one she most admired along with her cousin Dillon. "Ram?"

He looked over at her after taking a sip of the coffee she'd handed him as soon he had walked through the door. "Yes?"

"I was a good kid while growing up, wasn't I? I didn't give you and Dillon any trouble, right?"

He grinned, reached out and pulled one of her curls. "No, sport, you didn't give us any trouble. You were easier to handle than Bailey, the twins and Bane. But everyone was easier than those four."

He paused a moment and added, "And unlike a lot of men with sisters, I never once had to worry about guys getting their way with the three of you. You, Gemma and Bail did a good job of keeping the men in line yourselves. If a guy became a nuisance, you three would make them haul ass the other way. Dillon and I got a chuckle out of it, each and every time. Especially you. I think you enjoyed giving the guys a hard time."

She playfully jabbed him in the ribs. "I did not."

He laughed. "Could have fooled us." He grabbed her close for a brotherly hug. "At one time we thought you were sweet on Charlie Bristol when you were a senior in high school. We knew for a fact he was sweet on you. But according to Riley, he was too scared to ask you out."

Megan smiled over at him as she led him to the kitchen. She remembered Charlie Bristol. He used to spend the summers with one of his aunts who lived nearby. "He was nice, and cute."

"But you wouldn't give him the time of day," he said, sitting down at the table.

Ramsey was right, she hadn't. She recalled having a crush on Charlie for a quick second but she'd been too busy helping out with Gemma and Bailey to think about boys.

"I'm going to miss you, sport," Ramsey said, breaking into her thoughts.

Megan smiled over at him as she joined him at the table. "And I'm going to miss you, as well. Other than being with Gemma during the time she was giving birth to CJ, and visiting Delaney those two weeks in Tehran, this is the first real vacation I've taken, and the longest. I'll be away from the hospital for a full month."

"How will they make it without you? Ramsey teased.

"I'm sure they'll find a way." Even while attending college, she had stayed pretty close to home, not wanting to go too far away. For some reason, she'd felt she was needed. But then, she'd also felt helpless during Bailey's years of defiance. She had tried talking to her baby sister, but it hadn't done any good. She'd known that Bailey's, the twins' and Bane's acts of rebellion were their way of handling the grief of losing their parents. But still, at the time, she'd wished she could do more.

"Ram, can I ask you something?"

He chuckled. "Another question?" He faked a look of pain before saying, "Okay, I guess one more wouldn't hurt."

"Do you think having control of your emotions is a bad thing?" She swallowed tightly as she waited for his answer.

He smiled at her. "Having too much self-control isn't healthy, and it can lead to stress. Everyone needs to know how to let loose, release steam and let their hair down every once in a while."

Megan nodded. Releasing steam wasn't what she was dealing with. Letting go of a buildup of sexual energy was the problem. And that kiss the other day hadn't helped matters any.

She hadn't seen Rico since then, and she knew he'd already left for Texas. She'd been able to get that much out of Riley when he'd dropped by yesterday. "So it's okay to…"

"Get a little wild every once in a while?" He chuckled. "Yes, I think it is, as long as you're not hurting anyone."

He paused a second and then asked, "You're planning to enjoy yourself while you're in Texas, right?"

"Yes. But as you know, it won't be all fun, Ram." Ramsey and Dillon were the only ones she'd told the real reason why she was going to Texas. They also knew she had asked Rico to take her with him, and he'd refused. Of course, she hadn't told them what he'd told her as the reason behind his refusal. She'd only told them Rico claimed he preferred working alone and didn't need her help in the investigation. Neither Dillon nor Ramsey had given their opinions about anything, because she hadn't asked for them. The "don't ask—don't tell" rule was one Dillon and Ramsey implemented for the Westmorelands who were independent adults.

"You can do me a favor, though, sport," he said in a serious tone.

She lifted an eyebrow. "What?"

"Don't be too hard on Rico for not wanting to take you along. You're paying him to do a job, and he wants to do it."

Megan rolled her eyes. "And he will. But I want to be there. I could help."

"Evidently he doesn't want your help."

Yes, but he does want something else, Megan thought. She could just imagine what her brother would think if he knew the real reason Rico didn't want her in Texas. But then, Ramsey was so laid-back it probably wouldn't faze him. He'd known for years how Callum had felt about Gemma. But he'd also known his sisters could handle their business without any interference from their big brother unless it became absolutely necessary.

"But what if there are other Westmorelands somewhere?" she implored. "I told you what Rico said about Clarice having a baby."

"Then Rico will find out information and give it to you to bring to us, Megan. Let him do his job. And another thing."

"Yes?"

"Rico is a good guy. I like him. So do the rest of the Westmorelands. I judge a man by a lot of things and one is how he treats his family. He evidently is doing something right because Jessica and Savannah think the world of their brother."

Megan leaned back in her chair and frowned. "Is there a reason you're telling me that?"

Ramsey was silent for a moment as he stared at her. Then a slow smile touched his lips. "I'll let you figure that one out, Megan."

She nodded and returned his smile. "Fair enough. And about that self-control we were discussing earlier?"

"Yes, what about it?" he asked.

"It *is* essential at times," she said.

"I agree, it is. At times."

"But I'm finding out I might not have as much as I thought. That's not a bad thing, right, Ram?"

Ramsey chuckled. "No, sport, it's just a part of being human."

Rico had just finished eating his dinner at one of the restaurants in Forbes when his cell phone vibrated. Standing, he pulled it out of his back pocket. "This is Rico."

"Our father called me."

Rico tensed when he heard Savannah's voice. He sat back down and leaned back in his chair. "He called me as well, but I didn't give him a chance to say anything," he said, trying to keep his anger in check.

"Same here. I wonder what he wants, and I hope he doesn't try contacting Jessica. How long has it been now? Close to eighteen years?"

"Just about. I couldn't reach Jessica today, but I did talk to Chase. He said Jess hadn't mentioned anything about getting a call from Jeff Claiborne, and I think if she had, she would have told him," said Rico.

"Well, I don't want him upsetting her. She's pregnant."

"And you have a lot on your hands with a new baby," he reminded her.

"Yes, but I can handle the likes of Jeff regardless. But, I'm not sure Jessica can, though. It wasn't our mother who committed suicide because of him."

"I agree."

"Where are you?" Savannah asked him.

"Forbes, Texas. Nice town."

"Are you on a work assignment?"

"Yes, for Megan," he replied, taking a sip of his beer.

"Is she there with you?"

Rico's eyebrows shot up. "No. Should she be?"

"Just asking. Well, I'll be talking with—"

"Savannah?" he said in that particular tone when he knew she was up to something. "Why would you think Megan was here with me? I don't work that way."

"Yes, but I know the two of you are attracted to each other."

He took another sip of his beer. "Are we?"

"Yes. I noticed at Micah's wedding. I think everyone did."

"Did they?"

"Yes, Rico, and you're being evasive."

He laughed. "And you're being nosy. Where's Durango?" he asked, changing the subject.

"Outside giving Sarah her riding lessons."

"Tell him I said hello and give my niece a hug."

"I will…and Rico?"

"Yes?"

"I like Megan. Jess does, too."

Rico didn't say anything for a long moment. He took another sip of his beer as he remembered the kiss they'd shared a couple of days ago. "Good to hear because I like her, too. Now, goodbye."

He clicked off the phone before his sister could grill him. Glancing around the restaurant, he saw it had gotten crowded. The hotel had recommended this place, and he was glad they had. They had served good Southern food, the tastiest. But nothing he ate, no matter how spicy, could eradicate Megan's taste from his tongue. And personally, he had no problem with that because what he'd said to Savannah was true. He liked Megan. A capricious smile touched his lips. Probably, too damn much.

He was about to signal the waitress for his check

when his phone rang. He hoped it wasn't Savannah calling back being nosy. He sighed in relief when he saw it was Martin Felder, a friend who'd once worked with the FBI years ago but was now doing freelance detective work. He was an ace when it came to internet research. "Sorry, I meant to call you earlier, Rico, but I needed to sing Anna to sleep."

Rico nodded, understanding. Martin had become a single father last year when his wife, Marcia, had died from pancreatic cancer. He had pretty much taken early retirement from the Bureau to work from home. He had been the one to discover information about Clarice's pregnancy.

"No problem, and I can't tell you enough about what a great job you're doing with Anna."

"Thanks, Rico. I needed to hear that. She celebrated her third birthday last week, and I wished Marcia could have been here to see what a beautiful little girl we made together. She looks more and more like her mom every day."

Martin paused a minute and then said, "I was on the internet earlier today and picked up this story of a woman celebrating her one-hundredth birthday in Forbes. They were saying how sharp her memory was for someone her age."

"What's her name?" Rico asked, sitting up straight in his chair.

"Fanny Banks. She's someone you might want to talk to while in town to see if she remembers anything about Clarice Riggins. I'll send the info over to you."

"That's a good idea. Thanks." Rico hung up the phone and signaled for the waitress.

A few moments later, back in his rental car, he was reviewing the information Martin had sent to his iPhone. The woman's family was giving her a birthday party tomorrow so the earliest he would be able to talk to her would be Saturday.

His thoughts shifted to Megan and the look in her eyes when she'd tried explaining why it was so important for her to be there when he found out information on Raphel. Maybe he *was* being hard-nosed about not letting her help him. And he had given her fair warning about how much he wanted her. They'd kissed, and if she hadn't realized the intensity of their attraction before, that kiss should have cinched it and definitely opened her eyes.

It had definitely opened his, but that's not all it had done. If he'd thought he wanted her before then he was doubly certain of it now. He hadn't slept worth a damn since that kiss and sometimes he could swear her scent was in the air even when she wasn't around. He had this intense physical desire for her that he just couldn't kick. Now he had begun to crave her and that wasn't good. But it was something he just couldn't help. The woman was a full-blown addiction to his libido.

He put his phone away, thinking Megan should have arrived at Clint's place by now. It was too late to make a trip to Austin tonight, but he'd head that way early tomorrow…unless he could talk himself out of it overnight.

And he doubted that would happen.

Five

"I can't eat a single thing more," Megan said, as she looked at all the food Alyssa had placed on the table for breakfast. It wouldn't be so bad if she hadn't arrived yesterday at dinnertime to a whopping spread by Chester, Clint's cook, housekeeper and all-around ranch hand.

Megan had met Chester the last time she'd been here, and every meal she'd eaten was to die for. But like she'd said, she couldn't eat a single thing more and would need to do some physical activities to burn off the calories.

Clint chuckled as helped his wife up from the table. Alyssa said the doctor claimed she wasn't having twins but Megan wasn't too sure.

"Is there anything you need me to do?" she asked Alyssa when Clint had gotten her settled in her favorite recliner in the living room.

Alyssa waved off Megan's offer. "I'm fine. Clint is doing great with Cain," she said of her three-year-old son, who was the spitting image of his father. "And Aunt Claudine will arrive this weekend."

"How long do you think your aunt will visit this time?" Megan asked as she took the love seat across from Alyssa.

"If I have anything to do with it, she won't be leaving," Chester hollered out as he cleared off the kitchen table.

Megan glanced over at Clint, and Alyssa only laughed. Then Clint said, "Chester is sweet on Aunt Claudine, but hasn't convinced her to stay here and not return to Waco."

"But I think he might have worn her down," Alyssa said, whispering so Chester wouldn't hear. "She mentioned she's decided to put her house up for sale. She told me not to tell Chester because she wants to surprise him."

Megan couldn't help but smile. She thought Chester and Alyssa's aunt Claudine, both in their sixties, would make a nice couple. She bet it was simply wonderful finding love at that age. It would be grand to do so at any age…if you were looking for it or interested in getting it. She wasn't.

"If it's okay, I'd like to go riding around the Golden Glade, especially the south ridge. I love it there."

Clint smiled. "Most people do." He looked lovingly at Alyssa. "We've discovered it's one of our most favorite places on the ranch."

Megan watched as Alyssa exchanged another loving look with Clint. She knew the two were sharing a private moment that involved the south ridge in some way. They made a beautiful couple, she thought. Like all the other Westmoreland males, Clint was too hand-some for his own good, and Alyssa, who was even more beautiful while pregnant, was his perfect mate.

Seeing the love radiating between the couple—the same she'd witnessed between her cousins and their wives, as well as between her brothers and their wives—made a warm feeling flow through Megan. It was one she'd never felt before. She drew in a deep breath, thinking that feeling such a thing was outright foolish, but she couldn't deny what she'd felt just now.

As if remembering Megan was in the room, Clint turned to her, smiled and said, "Just let Marty know that you want to go riding, and he'll have one of the men prepare a horse for you."

"Thanks." Megan decided it was best to give Clint and Alyssa some alone time. Cain was taking a nap, and Megan could make herself scarce real fast. "I'll change into something comfortable for riding."

After saying she would see them later, she quickly headed toward the guest room.

One part of Rico's mind was putting up one hell of an argument as to why he shouldn't be driving to Austin for Megan. Too bad the other part refused to listen. Right now, the only thing that particular part of his brain understood was his erection throbbing some-thing fierce behind the zipper of his pants. Okay, he knew it shouldn't be just a sexual thing. He shouldn't be allowing all this lust to be eating away at him, prac-tically nipping at his balls, but hell, he couldn't help it. He wanted her. Plain and simple.

Although there was really nothing plain and simple about it, anticipation made him drive faster than he should. *Slow down, Claiborne. Are you willing to get a speeding ticket just because you want to see her again? Yes.*

He drew in a sharp breath, not understanding it. So he continued driving and when he finally saw Austin's city-limits marker, he felt a strong dose of adrenaline rush through his veins. It didn't matter that he still had a good twenty minutes to go before reaching the Golden Glade Ranch. Nor did it matter that Megan would be surprised to see him, and even more surprised that he would be taking her back with him to Forbes to be there when he talked to Fanny Banks.

But he would explain that taking her to meet Fanny would be all he'd let her do. He would return Megan to the Golden Glade while he finished up with the investigation. Nothing had changed on that front. Like he'd told her, he preferred working alone.

He checked the clock on the car's dashboard. Breakfast would be over by the time he reached the ranch. Alyssa might be resting, and if Clint wasn't around then he was probably out riding the range.

Rico glanced up at the sky. Clear, blue, and the sun was shining. It was a beautiful day in late September, and he planned to enjoy it. He pressed down on the accelerator. Although he probably didn't need to be in a hurry, he was in one anyway.

A short while later he released a sigh of anticipation when he saw the marker to the Golden Glade Ranch. Smiling, he made a turn down the long, winding driveway toward the huge ranch house.

Megan was convinced that the south-ridge pasture of the Golden Glade was the most beautiful land she'd ever seen. The Westmorelands owned beautiful prop-

erty back in Denver, but this here was just too mag-
nificent for words.

She dismounted her horse and, after tying him to
a hitching post, she gazed down in the valley where it
seemed as though thousands upon thousands of wild
horses were running free.

The triplets, Clint, Cole and Casey, had lived on
this land with their Uncle Sid while growing up. Sid
Roberts had been a legend in his day. First as a rodeo
star and then later as a renowned horse trainer. Megan
even remembered studying about him in school. In
their uncle's memory, the triplets had dedicated over
three thousand acres of this land along the south ridge
as a reserve. Hundreds of wild horses were saved from
slaughter by being shipped here from Nevada. Some
were left to roam free for the rest of their days, and
others were shipped either to Montana, where Casey
had followed in her uncle's footsteps as a horse trainer,
or to Denver, where some of her cousins and brothers
were partners in the operation.

Megan could recall when Zane, Derringer and Jason
had decided to join the partnership that included Clint,
their cousin Durango, Casey and her husband, McKin-
non. All of the Westmorelands involved in the partnership loved horses and were experts in handling them.

Megan glanced across the way and saw a cabin nestled among the trees. She knew it hadn't been here
the last time she'd visited. She smiled, thinking it was
probably a lovers' hideaway for Clint and Alyssa and
was probably the reason for the secretive smile they'd
shared this morning.

Going back to the horse, she unhooked a blanket
she'd brought and the backpack that contained a book
to read and a Ziploc bag filled with the fruit Chester

had packed. It didn't take long to find the perfect spot to spread the blanket on the ground and stretch out. She looked up at the sky, thinking it was a gorgeous day and it was nice to be out in it. She enjoyed her job at the hospital, but there was nothing like being out under the wide-open sky.

She had finished one chapter of the suspense thriller that her cousin Stone Westmoreland, aka Rock Mason, had written. She was so engrossed in the book that it was a while before she heard the sound of another horse approaching. Thinking it was probably Clint or one of the ranch hands coming to check on her, to make sure she was okay, she'd gotten to her feet by the time a horse and rider came around the bend.

Suddenly she felt it—heat sizzling down her spine, fire stirring in her stomach. Her heart began thumping hard in her chest. She'd known that she would eventually run in to Rico, but she'd thought it would be when she made an appearance in Forbes. He had been so adamant about her not coming to Texas with him that she'd figured she would have to be the one to seek him out and not the other way around.

Her breasts began tingling, and she could feel her nipples harden against her cotton shirt when he brought his horse to a stop beside hers. Nothing, she thought, was more of a turn-on than seeing a man, especially this particular man, dismount from his horse…with such masculine ease and virile precision, and she wondered if he slid between a woman's legs the same way.

She could feel her cheeks redden with such brazen thoughts, and her throat tightened when he began walking toward her. Since it seemed he didn't have anything to say, she figured she would acknowledge his presence. "Rico."

He tilted his hat to her. She thought he looked good in his jeans, chambray shirt and the Stetson. "Megan."

She drew in a deep breath as he moved toward her. His advance was just as lethal, just as stealthy, as a hunter who'd cornered his prey. "Do you know why I'm here?" he asked her in a deep, husky voice.

Megan she shook her head. "No. You said you wanted to work alone."

He smiled, and she could tell it didn't quite reach his eyes. "But you're here, which means you didn't intend on letting me do that."

She lifted her chin. "Just pretend I'm not here, and when you see me in Forbes, you can pretend I'm not there."

"Not possible," he said throatily, coming to a stop in front of her. Up close, she could see smoldering desire in the depths of his eyes. That should have jarred some sense into her, but it didn't. Instead it had just the opposite effect.

Megan tilted her head back to look up at him and what she saw almost took her breath away again—hazel eyes that were roaming all over her, as if they were savoring her. There was no way she could miss the hunger that flared in their depths, making her breath come out in quick gulps.

"I think I need to get back to the ranch," she said.

A sexy smile touched his lips. "What's the rush?"

There was so much heat staring at her that she knew any minute she was bound to go up in flames. "I asked why you're here, Rico."

Instead of answering, he reached out and gently cradled her face between his hands and brought his mouth so close to hers that she couldn't keep her lips from quivering. "My answer is simple, Megan. I came for you."

He paused a moment and then added, "I haven't been able to forget that kiss and how our tongues tangled while I became enmeshed in your taste. Nothing has changed other than I think you've become an addiction, and I want you more than before."

And then he lowered his mouth to hers.

He knew the instant she began to lose control because she started kissing him back with a degree of hunger and intimacy that astounded him.

He wrapped his arms around her waist while they stood there, letting their tongues tangle in a way that was sending all kinds of sensual pulses through his veins. This is what had kept him up nights, had made him drive almost like a madman through several cities to get here. He had known this would be what awaited him. Never had a single kiss ignited so much sexual pressure within him, made him feel as if he was ready to explode at any moment.

She shifted her body closer, settling as intimately as a woman still wearing clothes could get, at the juncture of his legs. The moment she felt his hard erection pressing against her, she shifted her stance to cradle his engorged shaft between her thighs.

If he didn't slow her down, he would be hauling her off to that blanket she'd spread on the ground. Thoughts of making love to her here, in such a beautiful spot and under such a stunning blue sky, were going through his mind. But he knew she wasn't ready for that. She especially wasn't ready to take it to the level he wanted to take it.

His thoughts were interrupted when he felt her hand touch the sides of his belt, trying to ease his shirt out of his pants. She wanted to touch some skin, and he had no problems letting her do so. He shifted again, a deliberate move on his part to give her better access to what she wanted, although what she wanted to do was way too dangerous to his peace of mind. It wouldn't take much to push him over the edge.

When he felt her tugging at his shirt, pulling it out of his jeans, he deepened the kiss, plunging his tongue farther into her mouth and then flicking it around with masterful strokes. He wasn't a man who took advantage of women, but then he was never one who took them too seriously, either, even while maintaining a level of respect for any female he was involved with.

But with Megan that respect went up more than a notch. She was a Westmoreland. So were his sisters. That was definitely a game changer. Although he wanted Megan and intended to have her, he needed to be careful how he handled her. He had to do things decently and in the right order. As much as he could.

But doing anything decently and in the right order was not on his mind as he continued to kiss her, as his tongue explored inside her mouth with a hunger that had his erection throbbing.

And when she inched her hand beneath his shirt to touch his skin, he snatched his mouth from hers to draw in a deep breath. He held her gaze, staring down at her as the silence between them extended. Her touch had nearly scorched him it had been so hot. He hadn't been prepared for it. Nor had he expected such a reaction to it.

He might have reeled in his senses and moved away from her if she hadn't swiped her tongue across her lips. That movement was his downfall, and he felt fire roaring through his veins. He leaned in closer and began licking her mouth from corner to corner. And when she let out a breathless moan, he slid his tongue back inside to savor her some more.

Their tongues tangled and dueled and he held on to her, needing the taste as intense desire tore through him. He knew he had to end the kiss or it could go on forever. And when her hips began moving against him, rotating against his huge arousal, he knew where things might lead if he didn't end the kiss here and now.

He slowly pulled back and let out a breath as his gaze seized her moistened lips. He watched the eyes staring back at him darken to a degree that would have grown hair on his chest, if he didn't have any already.

"Rico?"

Heat was still simmering in his veins, and it didn't help him calm down when she said his name like that. "Yes?"

"You did it again."

He lifted a brow. "What did I do?"

"You kissed me."

He couldn't help but smile. "Yes, and you kissed me back."

She nodded and didn't deny it. "We're going to have to come to some kind of understanding. About what we can or cannot do when we're alone."

His smile deepened. *That would be interesting.* "Okay, you make out that list, and we can discuss it."

She tilted her head back to look at him. "I'm serious."

"So am I, and make sure it's a pretty detailed list because if something's not on there, I'll be tempted to try it."

When she didn't say anything, he chuckled and told

her she was being too serious. "You'll feel better after getting dinner. You missed lunch."

She shook her head as he led her over to the horses. "I wasn't hungry."

He licked his mouth, smiled and said, "Mmm, baby, you could have fooled me."

Six

Once they had gotten back to the ranch and dismounted, Rico told the ranch hand who'd come to handle the horses not to bother, that he would take care of them.

"You're from Philadelphia, but you act as if you've been around horses all your life," she said, watching him remove the saddles from the animals' back.

He smiled over at her across the back of the horse she'd been riding. "In a way, I have. My maternal grandparents own horses, and they made sure Savannah and I took riding lessons and that we knew how to care for one."

She nodded. "What about Jessica?"

He didn't say anything for a minute and then said, "Jessica, Savannah and I share the same father. We didn't know about Jess until I was in college."

"Oh." Megan didn't know the full story, but it was

obvious from Rico and Savannah's interracial features that the three siblings shared the same father and not the same mother. She had met Rico and Savannah's mother at one of Jessica's baby showers and thought she was beautiful as well as kind. But then Megan had seen the interaction between the three siblings and could tell their relationship was a close one.

"You, Jessica and Savannah are close, I can tell. It's also obvious the three of you get along well."

He smiled. "Yes, we do, especially since I'm no longer trying to boss them around. Now I gladly leave them in the hands of Chase and Durango and have to admit your cousins seem to be doing a good job of keeping my sisters happy."

Megan would have to agree. But then she would say that all the Westmorelands had selected mates that complemented them, and they all seemed so happy together, so well connected. Even Gemma and Callum. She had visited her sister around the time Gemma's baby was due to be born and Megan had easily felt the love radiating between Gemma and her husband. And Megan knew Callum Junior, or CJ as everyone called him, was an extension of that love.

"We'll be leaving first thing in the morning, Megan."

She glanced back over at Rico, remembering what he'd said when he'd first arrived. He had come for her. "And just where are we supposed to be going?"

She couldn't help noticing how a beam of light that was shining in through the open barn door was hitting him at an angle that seemed to highlight his entire body. And as weird as it sounded, it seemed like there was a halo over his head. She knew it was a figment of her imagination because the man was no angel.

"I'm taking you back to Forbes with me," he said,

leading both horses to their stalls. "You did say you wanted to be included when I uncover information about Clarice."

She felt a sudden tingling of excitement in her stomach. Her face lit up. "Yes," she said, following him. "You found out something?"

"Nothing more than what I told you before. However, my man who's doing internet research came across a recent news article. There's a woman living in Forbes who'll be celebrating her one-hundredth birthday today. And she's lived in the same house for more than seventy of those years. Her address just happens to be within ten miles of the last known address we have for Clarice. We're hoping she might remember her."

Megan nodded. "But the key word is *remember*. How well do you think a one-hundred-year-old person will be able to remember?"

Rico smiled. "According to the article, she credits home remedies for her good health. I understand she still has a sharp memory."

"Then I can't wait for us to talk to her."

Rico closed the gate behind the horses and turned to face her. "Although I'm taking you along, Megan, I'm still the one handling this investigation."

"Of course," she said, looking away, trying her best not to get rattled by his insistence on being in charge. But upon remembering what Ramsey had said about letting Rico do his job without any interference from her, she decided not to make a big deal of it. The important thing was that Rico was including her.

He began walking toward the ranch house, and she fell in step beside him. "What made you change your mind about including me?" she asked as she tilted her head up.

He looked over at her. "You would have shown up in Forbes eventually, and I decided I'm going to like having you around."

Megan stopped walking and frowned up at him. "It's not going to be that kind of party, Rico."

She watched how his lips curved in a smile so sensuous that she had to remind herself to breathe. Her gaze was drawn to the muscular expanse of his chest and how the shirt looked covering it. She bet he would look even better shirtless.

Her frown deepened. She should not be thinking about Rico without a shirt. It was bad enough that she had shared two heated kisses with him.

"What kind of party do you think I'm having, Megan?"

She crossed her arms over her chest. "I don't know, you tell me."

He chuckled. "That's easy because I'm not having a party. You'll get your own hotel room, and I'll have mine. I said I wanted you. I also said eventually I'd have you if you came with me. But I'll let you decide when."

"It won't happen. Just because we shared two enjoyable kisses and—"

"So you did enjoy them, huh?"

She wished she could swipe that smirk off his face. She shrugged. "They were okay."

He threw his head back and laughed. "Just okay? Then I guess I better improve my technique the next time."

She nibbled on her bottom lip, thinking if he got any better she would be in big trouble.

"Don't do that."

She raised a brow. "Don't do what?"

"Nibble on your lip that way. Or else I'm tempted to improve my technique right here and now."

Megan swallowed, and as she stood there and stared up at him, she was reminded of how his kisses could send electrical currents racing through her with just a flick of his tongue.

"I like it when you do that."

"Do what?"

"Blush. I guess guys didn't ever talk to you that way, telling you what they wanted to do to you."

She figured she might as well be honest with him. "No."

"Then may I make a suggestion, Megan?"

She liked hearing the sound of her name from his lips. "What?"

"Get used to it."

Rico sat on a bar stool in the kitchen while talking to Clint. However, he was keeping Megan in his peripheral vision. When they'd gotten back to the house, Clint had been eager to show Rico a beauty of a new stallion he was about to send to his sister Casey to train, and Alyssa wanted to show Megan how she'd finished decorating the baby's room that morning.

Cain was awake, and, like most three-year-olds, he wanted to be the life of the party and hold everyone's attention. He was doing so without any problems. He spoke well for a child his age and was already riding a horse like a pro.

Rico had admired the time Clint had spent with his son and could see the bond between them. He thought about all the times he had wished his father could have been home more and hadn't been. Luckily, his grandfather had been there to fill the void when his father had been living a double life.

Megan had gone upstairs to take a nap, and by the time he'd seen her again it had been time for dinner. She had showered and changed, and the moment she had come down the stairs it had taken everything he had to keep from staring at her. She was dressed in a printed flowing skirt and a blouse that showed what a nice pair of shoulders she had. He thought she looked refreshed and simply breathtaking. And his reaction upon seeing her reminded him of how it had been the first time he'd seen her, that day three months ago.

"Rico?" Clint said, snapping his fingers in front of his face.

Rico blinked. "Sorry. My mind wandered there for a minute."

"Evidently," Clint said, grinning. "How about if we go outside where we can talk without your mind wandering so much?"

Rico chuckled, knowing Clint knew full well where his concentration had been. "Fine," he said, grabbing his beer off the counter.

Moments later, while sitting in rocking chairs on the wraparound porch, Clint had brought Rico up to date on the horse breeding and training business. Several of the horses would be running in the Kentucky Derby and Preakness in the coming year.

"So how are things going with the investigation?" Clint asked when there was a lull in conversation. "Megan mentioned to Alyssa something about an old lady in Forbes who might have known Clarice."

"Yes, I'm making plans to interview her in a few days, and Megan wants to be there when I do." Rico spent the next few minutes telling Clint what the news article had said about the woman.

"Well, I hope things work out," Clint said. "I know how it is when you discover you have family you never knew about, and I guess Megan is feeling the same way. If it hadn't been for my mother's deathbed confession, Cole, Casey and I would not have known that our father was alive. Even now, I regret the years I missed by not knowing."

Clint stood and stretched. "Well, I'm off to bed now. Will you and Megan at least stay for breakfast before taking off tomorrow?"

Rico stood, as well. "Yes. Nothing like getting on the road with a full stomach, and I'm sure Chester is going to make certain we have that."

Clint chuckled. "Yes, I'm certain, as well. Good night."

By the time they went back into the house, it was quiet and dark, which meant Alyssa and Megan had gone to bed. Rico hadn't been aware that he and Clint had talked for so long. It was close to midnight.

Clint's ranch house was huge. What Rico liked most about it was that it had four wings jutting off from the living room—north, south, east and west. He noted that he and Megan had been given their own private wing—the west wing—and he couldn't help wondering if that had been intentional.

He slowed his pace when he walked past the guest room Megan was using. The door was closed but he could see light filtering out from the bottom, which meant she was still up. He stopped and started to knock and then decided against it. It was late, and he had no reason to want to seek her out at this hour.

"Of course I can think of several reasons," he muttered, smiling as he entered the guest room he was using. He wasn't feeling tired or sleepy so he decided to work awhile on his laptop.

Rico wasn't sure how long he had been sitting at the desk, going through several online sites, piecing together more information about Fanny Banks, when he heard the opening and closing of the door across the hall, in the room Megan was using. He figured she had gotten up to get a cup of milk or tea. But when moments passed and he didn't hear her return to her room, he decided to find out where she'd gone and what she was doing.

Deciding not to turn on any lights, he walked down the hall in darkness. When he reached the living room, he glanced around before heading for the kitchen. There, he found her standing in the dark and looking out the window. From the moonlight coming in through the glass, he could tell she was wearing a bathrobe.

Deciding he didn't want to startle her, he made his presence known. "Couldn't you sleep?"

She swung around. "What are you doing up?"

He leaned in the doorway with his shoulder propped against a wall. "I was basically asking you the same thing."

She paused a moment and didn't say anything and then said, "I tried sleeping but couldn't. I kept thinking about my dad."

His brows furrowed. "Your dad?"

"Yes. This Saturday would have been his birthday. And I'm proud to say I was a daddy's girl," she said, smiling.

"Were you?"

She grinned. "Yes. Big-time. I remember our last conversation. It was right before he and Mom got ready to leave for the airport. As usual, the plan was for Mrs. Jones to stay at the house and keep us until my parents returned. He asked that I make sure to help take care of Gemma, Bailey and the twins. Ramsey was away at college, Zane was about to leave for college and Derringer was in high school. I was twelve."

She moved away from the window to sit at the table. "The only thing was, they never returned, and I didn't do a good job of taking care of Bailey and the twins. Gemma was no problem."

Rico nodded. Since getting to know the Denver Westmorelands, he had heard the stories about what bad-asses Bailey, the twins and Bane were. And each time he heard those stories, his respect and admiration for Dillon and Ramsey went up a notch. He knew it could not have been easy to keep the family together the way they had. "I hope you're not blaming yourself for all that stupid stuff they did back then."

She shook her head. "No, but a part of me wishes I could have done more to help Ramsey with the younger ones."

Rico moved to join her at the table, figuring the best thing to do was to keep the conversation going. Otherwise, he would be tempted to pull her out of that chair and kiss her again. Electricity had begun popping the moment their gazes had connected. "You were only twelve, and you did what you could, I'm sure," he said, responding to what she'd said. "Everybody did. But people grieve in different ways. I couldn't imagine losing a parent that young."

"It wasn't easy."

"I bet, and then to lose an aunt and uncle at the same time. I have to admire all of you for being strong during that time, considering what all of you were going through."

"Yes, but think of how much easier it would have been had we known the Atlanta, Montana and Texas Westmorelands back then. There would have been others, and Dillon and Ramsey wouldn't have had to do it alone. Oh, they would have still fought to keep us together, but they would have had some kind of support system. You know what they say…it takes a village to raise a child."

Yes, he'd heard that.

"That's one of the reasons family is important to me, Rico. You never know when you will need the closeness and support a family gives to each other." Silence lingered between them for a minute and then she asked, "What about you? Were you close to your parents…your father…while growing up?"

He didn't say anything for a while. Instead, he got up and walked over to the refrigerator. To answer her question, he needed a beer. He opened the refrigerator and glanced over his shoulder. "I'm having a beer. Want one?"

"No, but I'll take a soda."

He nodded and grabbed a soda and a beer out of the refrigerator and then closed the door. Returning to the table, he turned the chair around and straddled it. "Yes. Although my father traveled a lot as a salesman, we were close, and I thought the world of him."

He popped the top on his beer, took a huge swig and then added, "But that was before I found out what a two-bit, lying con artist he was. He was married to my mother, who was living in Philly, while he was involved with another woman out in California, stringing both of them along and lying through his teeth. Making promises he knew he couldn't keep."

Rico took another swig of his beer. "Jessica's grandfather found out Jeff Claiborne was an imposter and told Jessica's mother and my mother. Hurt and humiliated that she'd given fifteen years to a man who'd lied to her, Jessica's mother committed suicide. My mother filed for a divorce. I was in my first year of college. He came to see me, tried to make me think it was all Mom's fault and said, as males, he and I needed to stick together, and that Mom wouldn't divorce him if I put in a good word for him."

Rico stared into his beer bottle, remembering that time, but more importantly, remembering that day. He glanced back at her. "That day he stopped being my hero and the man I admired most. It was bad enough that he'd done wrong and wouldn't admit to it, but to involve me and try to pit me against Mom was unacceptable."

Rico took another swig of his beer. A long one this time. He rarely talked about that time in his life. Most people who knew his family knew the story, and chances were that Megan knew it already since she was friends with both of his sisters.

She reached out and took his hand in hers, and he felt a deep stirring in his groin as they stared at each other, while the air surrounding them became charged with a sexual current that sent sparks of desire through his body. He knew she felt it, as well.

"I know that must have been a bad time for you, but that just goes to show how a bad situation can turn into a good one. That's what happened for you, Savannah and Jessica once the three of you found out about each other, right?"

Yes, that part of the situation had turned out well, because he couldn't imagine not having Jessica and Savannah in his life. But still, whenever he thought of how Jessica had lost her mother, he would get angry all over again. Yet he said, "Yes, you're right."

She smiled and released his hand. "I've been known to be right a few times."

For some reason, he felt at ease with her, more at ease than he'd felt with any other woman. Why they were sitting here in the dark he wasn't sure. In addition to the sexual current in the room, there was also a degree of intimacy to this conversation that was ramping up his libido, reminding him of how long it had been since he'd slept with a woman. And when she had reached out and touched his hand that hadn't helped matters.

He studied her while she sipped on her soda. Even with the sliver of light shining through the window from the outside, he could see the smooth skin of her face, a beautiful shade of mocha.

She glanced over at him, caught him staring, and he felt thrumming need escalate all through him. He'd kissed her twice now and could kiss her a dozen more times and be just as satisfied. But at some point he would want more. He intended to get more. She had been warned, and she hadn't heeded his warning. The attraction between them was too great.

He wouldn't make love to her here. But they would make love, that was a given.

However, he *would* take another kiss. One that would let her know what was to come.

She stood. "I think I'll go back to bed and try to sleep. You did say we were leaving early, right?" she asked, walking over to the garbage with her soda can.

"Yes, right after breakfast." He didn't say anything but his gaze couldn't help latching on to her backside. Even with her bathrobe on, he could tell her behind was a shapely one. He'd admired it in jeans earlier that day.

On impulse, he asked, "Do you want to go for a ride?"

She turned around. "A ride?"

"Yes. It's a beautiful night outside."

A frown tugged at her brow. "A ride where?"

"The south ridge. There's a full moon, and the last time I went there at night with Clint while rounding up horses under a full moon, the view of the canyon was breathtaking."

"And you want us to saddle horses and—"

"No," he chuckled. "We'll take my truck."

She stared at him like he couldn't be thinking clearly. "Do you know what time it is?"

He nodded slowly as he held her gaze. "Yes, a time when everyone else is sleeping, and we're probably the only two people still awake."

She tilted her head and her gaze narrowed. "Why do you want me to take a ride with you at this hour, Rico?"

He decided to be honest. "Because I want to take you someplace where I can kiss you all over."

Seven

The lower part of Megan's stomach quivered, and she released a slow breath. What he was asking her, and pretty darn blatantly, was to go riding with him to the south ridge where they could park and make out. They were too old for that sort of thing, weren't they? Evidently he didn't think so, and he was a lot older than she was.

And what had he said about kissing her all over? Did he truly know what he was asking of her? She needed to be sure. "Do you know what you're asking me when you ask me to go riding with you?"

A smile that was so sexy it could be patented touched his lips. "Yeah."

Well, she had gotten her answer. He had kissed her twice, and now wanted to move to the next level. What had she really expected from a man who'd told her he wanted her and intended to have her? In that case,

she had news for him: two kisses didn't mean a thing.
She had let her guard down and released a little of her
emotional control, but that didn't mean she would release any more. Whenever he kissed her, she couldn't
think straight, and she considered doing things that
weren't like her.

She stood there and watched his hazel eyes travel all
over her, roaming up and down. When his gaze moved
upward and snagged hers, the very air between them
crackled with an electrical charge that had certain parts
of her tingling.

"Are you afraid of me, Megan?" he asked softly.

Their gazes held for one searing moment. No, she
wasn't afraid of him per se, but she was afraid of the
things he had the ability to make her feel, afraid of the
desires he could stir in her, afraid of how she could
lose control around him. How could she make him
understand that being in control was a part of her that
she wasn't ready to let go of yet?

She shook her head. "No, I'm not afraid of you,
Rico. But you say things and do things I'm not used
to. You once insinuated that my brothers and cousins
might have sheltered me from the realities of life, and
I didn't agree with you. I still don't, but I will say that
I, of my own choosing, decided not to take part in a lot
of things other girls were probably into. I like being my
own person and not following the crowd."

He nodded, and she could tell he was trying to follow her so she wasn't surprised when he asked, "And?"

"And I've never gone parking with a guy before."
There, she'd said it. Now he knew what he was up
against. But when she saw the unmistakable look of
deep hunger in his eyes, her heart began pounding,
fast and furious.

Then he asked, "Are you saying no guy has ever taken you to lover's lane?"

Why did his question have to sound so seductive, and why did she feel like her nerve endings were being scorched? "Yes, that's what I'm saying, and it was my decision and not theirs."

He smiled. "I can believe that."

"I saw it as a waste of time." She broke eye contact with him to look at his feet. They were bare. She'd seen men's feet before, plenty of times. With as many cousins and brothers as she had she couldn't miss seeing them. But Rico's were different. They were beautiful but manly.

"Did you?"

She glanced back up at him. "Yes, it was a waste of time because I wasn't into that sort of thing."

"You weren't?"

She shook her head. "No. I'm too in control of my emotions."

"Yet you let go a little when we kissed," he reminded her.

And she wished she hadn't. "Yes, but I can't do that too often."

He got up from the table, and she swallowed deeply while watching him cross the floor and walk over to her on those beautiful but manly bare feet. He came to a stop in front of her, reached out and took her hand. She immediately felt that same sexual charge she'd felt when she'd taken his hand earlier.

"Yet you did let go with me."

Yes, and that's what worried her. Why with him and only him? Why not with Dr. Thad Miller, Dr. Otis Wells or any of the other doctors who'd been trying

for years to engage her in serious—or not so serious—
affairs?

"Megan?"

"Yes?"

"Would you believe me if I were to say I would never
intentionally hurt you?"

"Yes." She could believe that.

"And would it help matters if I let you set the pace?"
he asked huskily in a voice that stirred things inside
of her.

"What do you mean?"

"You stay in control, and I'll only do what you allow
me to do and nothing more."

She suddenly felt a bit disoriented. What he evidently didn't quite yet understand was that he was a
threat to her self-imposed control. But then, hadn't
Ramsey said that she should let loose, be wild, release
steam and let her hair down every once in a while? But
did that necessarily mean being reckless?

"Megan?"

She stared up at him, studying his well-defined features. Handsome, masculine. Refined. Strong. Controlled. But was he really controlled? His features were
solid, unmovable. The idea that perhaps he shared
something in common with her was a lot to think about.
In the meantime…

Taking a ride with him couldn't hurt anything. She
couldn't sleep, and perhaps getting out and letting the
wind hit her face would do her some good. He did say
he would let her be in control, and she believed him. Although he had a tendency to speak his mind, he didn't
come across as the type of man who would force himself on any woman. Besides, he knew her brothers and
cousins, and was friends with them. His sisters were

married to Westmorelands, and he wouldn't dare do anything to jeopardize those relationships.

"Okay, I'll go riding with you, Rico. Give me a minute to change clothes."

Rico smiled the moment he and Megan stepped outside. He hadn't lied. It was a beautiful night. He'd always said if he ever relocated from Philadelphia, he would consider moving to Texas. It wasn't too hot and it wasn't too cold, most of the time. He had fallen in love with the Lone Star state that first time he'd gone hunting and fishing with his grandfather. His grandparents had never approved of his mother's marriage, but that hadn't stopped them from forging a relationship with their grandchildren.

"There's a full moon tonight," Megan said when he opened the SUV's door for her.

"Yes, and you know what they say about a full moon, don't you?"

She rolled her eyes. "If you're trying to scare me, please don't. I've been known to watch scary movies and then be too afraid to stay at my own place. I've crashed over at Ramsey's or Dillon's at times because I was afraid to go home."

He wanted to tell her that if she got scared tonight, she could knock on his bedroom door and join him there at any time, but he bit back the words. "Well, then I won't scare you," he said, grinning as he leaned over to buckle her seat belt. She had changed into a pretty dress that buttoned up the front. There were a lot of buttons, and his fingers itched to tackle every last one of them.

And he thought she smelled good. Something sweet and sensual with an allure that had him wanting to do more than buckle her seat belt. He pulled back. "Is that too tight?"

"No, it's fine."

He heard the throatiness in her voice and wondered if she was trying to downplay the very thing he was trying to highlight. "All right." He closed the door and then moved around the front of the truck to get in the driver's side.

"If it wasn't for that full moon it would be pitch-black out here."

He smiled. "Yes, you won't be able to see much, but what I'm going to show you is beautiful. That's why Clint had that cabin built near there. It's a stunning view of the canyon at night, and whenever there's a full moon the glow reflects off certain boulders, which makes the canyon appear to light up."

"I can't wait to see it."

And I can't wait to taste you again, he thought, as he kept his hand firmly on the steering wheel or else he'd be tempted to reach across, lift the hem of her dress and stroke her thigh. When it came to women, his manners were usually impeccable. However, around Megan he was tempted to touch, feel and savor.

He glanced over at her when he steered the truck around a bend. She was gnawing on her bottom lip, which meant she was nervous. This was a good time to get her talking, about anything. So he decided to let the conversation be about work. Hers.

"So you think they can do without you for thirty days?"

She glanced over at him and smiled. "That's the same thing Ramsey asked. No one is irreplaceable, you know."

"What about all those doctors who're pining for you?"

She rolled her eyes. "Evidently you didn't believe me when I said I don't date much. Maybe I shouldn't tell you this, but they call me Iceberg Megan behind my back."

He jerked his eyes from the road to glance over at her. "Really?"

"Yes."

"Does it bother you?"

"Not really. They prefer a willing woman in their beds, and I'm not willing and their beds are the last places I'd want to be. I don't hesitate to let them know it."

"Ouch."

"Whatever," she said, waving her hand in the air. "I don't intend to get in any man's bed anytime soon."

He wondered if she was issuing a warning, and he decided to stay away from that topic. "Why did you decide to become an anesthesiologist?"

She leaned back in the seat, getting comfortable. He liked that. "When I got my tonsils out, this man came around to talk to me, saying he would be the one putting me to sleep. He told me all about the wonderful dreams I would have."

"And did you?"

She looked confused. "Did I what?"

"Have wonderful dreams?"

"Yes, if you consider dreaming about a promised trip to Disney World a wonderful dream."

He started to chuckle and then he felt the rumble in his stomach when he laughed. She was priceless. Wonderful company. Fun to have around. "Did you get that trip to Disney World?"

"Yes!" she said with excitement in her voice. "It was the best ever, and the first of many trips our family took together. There was the time…"

He continued driving, paying attention to both the rugged roads and to her. He liked the sound of her voice, and he noticed that more than anything else, she liked talking about her family. She had adored her parents, her uncle and aunt. And she thought the world of her brothers, cousins and sisters. There were already a lot of Westmorelands. Yet she was hoping there were still more.

His mother had been an only child, and he hadn't known anything about his father's family. Jeff Claiborne had claimed he didn't have any. Now Rico wondered if that had been a lie like everything else.

She gasped. He glanced over at her and followed her gaze through the windshield to look up at the sky. He brought the truck to a stop. "What?"

"A shooting star. I saw it."

"Did you?"

She nodded and continued to stare up at the sky. "Yes."

He shifted his gaze to stare back at her. "Hurry and make a wish."

She closed her eyes. A few minutes later she re-opened them and smiled over at him. "Done."

He turned the key in the ignition to start the truck back up. "I'm glad."

"Thanks for taking the time to let me do that. Most men would have thought it was silly and not even suggested a wish."

He grinned. "I'm not like most men."

"I'm beginning to see that, Mr. Claiborne."

He smiled as he kept driving, deciding not to tell her that if the truth be known, she hadn't seen anything yet.

Eight

"I think this is a good spot," Rico said, bringing the car to a stop.

Megan glanced around, not sure just what it was a good spot for, but decided not to ask. She looked over at him and watched as he unbuckled his seat belt and eased his seat back to accommodate his long legs. She decided to do the same—not that her legs were as long as his, mind you. He was probably six foot four to her five foot five.

When she felt his gaze on her, she suddenly felt heated. She rolled down her window and breathed in the deep scent of bluebonnets, poppies and, of all things, wild pumpkin. But there was another scent she couldn't ignore. The scent of man. Namely, the man sitting in the truck with her.

"Lean toward the dash and look out of the windshield."

Slowly, she shifted in her seat and did as he instructed. She leaned forward and looked down and what she saw almost took her breath away. The canyon appeared lit, and she could still see horses moving around. Herds of them. Beautiful stallions with their bands of mares. Since she and Rico were high up and had the help of moonlight, she saw a portion of the lake.

"So what do you think of this place, Megan?"

She glanced over at him. "It's beautiful. Quiet." *And secluded,* she thought, realizing just how alone they were.

"It didn't take you long to change clothes," he said.

She chuckled. "A habit you inherit when you have impatient brothers. Zane drove me, Gemma and Bailey to school every day when he was around. And when he wasn't, the duty fell on Derringer."

Rico seemed to be listening so she kept on talking, telling him bits and pieces about her family, fun times she'd encountered while growing up. She knew they were killing time and figured he was trying to make sure she was comfortable and not nervous with him. He wanted her to be at ease. For what, she wasn't sure, although he'd told her what he wanted to do and she'd come anyway. They had kissed twice so she knew what to expect, but he'd also said he would let her stay in control of the situation.

"You're hot?"

She figured he was asking because she'd rolled down the window. "I was, but the air is cooler outside than I thought," she said, rolling it back up. She took a deep, steadying breath and leaned forward again, trying to downplay the sexual energy seeping through her bones. He hadn't said much. He'd mainly let her talk and listened to what she'd said. But as she stared down at the canyon again she felt his presence in an intense way.

"Megan?"

Her pulse jumped when he said her name. With a deliberate slowness, she glanced over at him. "Yes?"

"I want you over here, closer to me."

She swallowed and then took note that she was sort of hugging the door. The truck had bench seats, and there was a lot of unused space separating them. Another body could sit between them comfortably. "I thought you'd want your space."

"I don't. What I want is you."

It was what he said as well as how he'd said it that sent all kinds of sensations oozing through her. His voice had a deep, drugging timbre that made her feel as if her skin were being caressed.

Without saying anything, she slid across the seat toward him, and he curved his arms across the back of the seat. "A little closer won't hurt," he said huskily.

She glanced up at him. "If I get any closer, I'll end up in your lap."

"That's the idea."

Megan's brows furrowed. He wanted her in his lap? He had to be joking, right? She studied his gaze and saw he was dead serious. Her stomach quivered as they stared at each other. The intensity in the hazel eyes that held her within their scope flooded her with all kinds of feelings, and she was breathless again.

"Do you recall the first time we kissed, Megan?"

She nodded. "Yes." How on earth could she forget it?

"Afterward, I lay awake at night remembering how it had been."

She was surprised a man would do that. She thought

since kisses came by the dozen, they didn't remember one from the next. "You did?"

"Yes. You tasted good."

She swallowed and felt her bottom lips began to tremble. "Did I?"

He reached out and traced a fingertip across her trembling lips. "Yes. And do you know what else I remembered?"

"No, what?"

"How your body felt pressed against mine, even with clothes on. And of course that made me think of you without any clothes on."

Desire filtered through her body. If he was saying these things to weaken her, break down her defenses, corrode her self-control, it was working. "Do you say this to all the girls?" she asked—a part of her wanted to know. Needed to know.

He frowned. "No. And in a way, that's what bothers me."

She knew she shouldn't ask but couldn't stop herself from doing so. "Bothers you how?"

He hesitated for a moment, broke eye contact with her to look straight ahead, out the window. Slowly, methodically, he returned his gaze back to her. "I usually don't let women get next to me. But for some reason I'm allowing you to be the exception."

He didn't sound too happy about it, either, she concluded. But then, wasn't she doing the same thing? She had let him kiss her twice, where most men hadn't made it as far as the first. And then she was here at two in the morning, sitting in a parked truck with him in Texas. If that wasn't wild, she didn't know what was.

"You have such warm lips."

He could say some of the most overwhelming

words…or maybe to her they were overwhelming because no other man had said them to her before. "Thanks."

"You don't have to thank me for compliments. Everything I say is true. I will never lie to you, Megan."

For some reason, she believed him. But if she wasn't supposed to thank him, what was she supposed to say? She tilted her head back to look at him and wished she hadn't. The intense look in his gaze had deepened, and she felt a stirring inside of her, making her want things she'd never had before.

He must have seen something in her eyes, because he whispered, "Come here." And then he lifted her into his arms, twisted his body to stretch his legs out on the seat and sat her in his lap. Immediately, she felt the thick, hard erection outlined against his zipper and pressed into her backside. That set off a barrage of sensations escalating through her, but nothing was as intense as the sensual strokes she felt at the juncture of her thighs.

And then, before she could take her next breath, he leaned down and captured her lips in his.

Rico wasn't sure just what there was about Megan that made him want to do this over and over again— mate his mouth with hers in a way that was sending him over the edge, creating more memories that would keep him awake at night. All he knew was that he needed to taste her again like he needed to breathe.

In the most primal way, blood was surging through his veins and desire was slamming through him, scorching his senses and filling him with needs that only she could satisfy. He couldn't help but feel his erection pressing against her and wishing he could be skin-to-skin with her, but he knew this wasn't the time or the place. But kissing her here, now, was essential.

His tongue continued to explore her mouth with an intensity that had her trembling in his arms. But he wouldn't let up. It couldn't be helped. There was something between them that he couldn't explain. It was wild and, for him, unprecedented. First there had been that instant attraction, then the crackling of sexual chemistry. Then, later, after their first kiss, that greedy addiction that had him in a parked truck, kissing her senseless at two in the morning.

He slowly released her mouth to stare down at her and saw the glazed look in her eyes. Then he slowly began unbuttoning her shirt dress. The first sign of her bra had him drawing in a deep breath of air—which only pulled her scent into his nostrils, a sensuous blend of jasmine and lavender.

Her bra had a front clasp and as soon as his fingers released it, her breasts sprang free. Seeing them made him throb. As he stared down at them, he saw the nipples harden before his eyes, making hunger take over his senses. Releasing a guttural moan, he leaned down and swooped a nipple between his lips and began sucking on it. Earnestly.

Megan gasped at the contact of his wet mouth on her breast, but then, when the sucking motion of his mouth made her sex clench, she threw her head back and moaned. His tongue was doing the same things to her breasts that it had done inside her mouth, and she wasn't sure she could take it. The strokes were so keen and strong, she could actually feel them between her legs.

She reached out and grabbed at his shoulder and when she couldn't get a firm grip there, she went for his hair, wrapping some of the silky strands around her finger as his mouth continued to work her breasts, sending exquisite sensations ramming through her.

But what really pushed her over the edge was when his hand slid underneath her dress to touch her thigh. No man had ever placed his hand underneath her dress. Such a thing could get one killed. If not by her, then surely by her brothers. But her brothers weren't here. She was a grown woman.

And when Rico slid his hands higher, touching her in places she'd never been touched, his fingertips making their way to her center, she shamelessly lifted her hips and shifted her legs wider to give him better access. Where was her self-control? It had taken a freaking hike the moment he had touched his mouth to hers.

Then he was kissing her mouth again, but she was fully aware of his hand easing up her thigh, easing inside the crotch of her panties to touch her.

She almost shot out of his lap at the contact, but he held her tight and continued kissing her as his fingers stroked her, inching toward her pulsating core.

He broke off the kiss and whispered, "You feel good here. Hot. Wet. I like my fingers here, touching you this way."

She bit down on her lips to keep from saying that she liked his fingers touching her that way, as well. Whether intentional or not, he was tormenting her, driving her over the edge with every stroke. She was feeling light-headed, sensually intoxicated. He was inciting her to lose control, and she couldn't resist. The really sad thing was that a part of her didn't want to resist.

"And do you know what's better than touching you here?" he asked.

She couldn't imagine. Already she had been reduced to a trembling mess as he continued to stroke her. She gripped his hair tighter and hoped she wasn't causing him any pain. "No, I can't imagine," she whispered, struggling to get the words out. Forcing anything from her lungs was complicated at the moment.

"Then let me show you, baby."

Her mind had been so focused on his term of endearment that she hadn't realized he had quickly shifted their bodies so her head was away from him, closer to the passenger door. The next thing she knew he had pushed the rest of her dress aside, eased off her panties and lifted her hips to place her thighs over his shoulders.

He met her gaze once, but it was enough for her to see the smoldering heat in his eyes just seconds before he lowered his head between her legs. Shock made her realize what he was about to do, and she called out his name. "Rico!"

But the sound was lost and became irrelevant the moment his mouth touched her core and his tongue slid between the folds. And when he began stroking her, tasting her, she couldn't help but cry out his name again. "Rico."

He didn't let up as firm hands held her hips steady and a determined mouth licked her like she was a meal he just had to have. She continued to moan as blood gushed through her veins. His mouth was devouring her, driving her over the edge, kicking what self-control remained right out the window. The raw hunger he was exhibiting was sending her senses scurrying in all directions. She closed her eyes as moan after moan after moan tore from her lips. The feelings were intense. Their magnitude was resplendent and stunning. Plea-

sure coiled within her then slowly spread open as desire sharpened its claws on her. Making her feel things
she had never felt before. Sensations she hadn't known
were possible. And the feel of his stubble-roughened
jaw on her skin wasn't helping her regain control.

"Rico," she whispered. "I—I need…" She couldn't
finish her thought because she didn't have a clue what
she needed. She'd never been with a man like this before, and neither had Gemma before Callum. All her
sister had told Megan was that it was something well
worth the wait. But if this was the prologue, the wait
just might kill her.

And then he did something, she wasn't sure what,
with his tongue. Some kind of wiggly formation followed by a fierce jab that allowed his mouth to actually lock down on her.

Sensations blasted through her, and she flung back
her head and let out a high-pitched scream. But he
wouldn't let go. He continued to taste and savor her as
if she was not only his flavor of the day, but also his
flavor of all time. She pushed the foolish thought from
her mind as she continued to be bombarded with feelings that were ripping her apart.

She gasped for breath before screaming again when
her entire body spiraled into another orgasm. She
whimpered through it and held tight to his hair as she
clutched his shoulders. He kept his mouth locked on her
until the very last moan had flowed from her lips. She
collapsed back on the car seat, feeling totally drained.

Only then did he pull back, adjusting their bodies
to bring her up to him. He tightened his hold when she
collapsed weakly against his chest. Then he lowered
his head and kissed her, their lips locked together intensely. At that moment, she was craving this contact,

this closeness, this very intimate connection. Moments later, when he released her mouth, he pulled her closer to him, tucking her head beneath his jaw, and whispered, "This is only the beginning, baby. Only the beginning."

Nine

The next morning, Rico and Megan left the Golden Glade Ranch after breakfast to head out to Forbes. He had been driving now for a little more than a half hour and his GPS indicated they had less than a hundred miles to go. He glanced up at the skies, saw the gray clouds and was certain it would rain before they reached their destination.

Rico then glanced over at Megan and saw she was still sleeping soundly and had been since he'd hit the interstate. Good. He had a feeling she hadn't gotten much sleep last night.

She had pretty much remained quiet on the drive back to the ranch from the south ridge, and once there, she quickly said good-night and rushed off to her room, closing the door behind her. And then this morning at breakfast, she hadn't been very talkative. Several times he had caught her barely able to keep her eyes open.

If Clint and Alyssa had found her drowsiness strange, neither had commented on it.

Rico remembered every single thing about last night, and, if truth be told, he hadn't thought of much of anything else since. Megan Westmoreland had more passion in her little finger than most women had in their entire bodies. And just the thought that no other man had tempted her to release all that passion was simply mind-boggling to him.

Ramsey had warned him that she was strong-willed. However, even the most strong-willed person couldn't fight a well-orchestrated seduction. But then, being overcome with passion wasn't a surrender. He saw it as her acceptance that nothing was wrong with enjoying her healthy sexuality.

I like being my own person and not following the crowd. Those were the words she had spoken last night. He remembered them and had both admired and respected her for taking that stance. His sisters had basically been the same and had handled their own business. Even when Savannah had gotten pregnant by Durango, she had been prepared to go at it alone had he not wanted to claim the child as his. And knowing his sister, marriage had not been on her mind when she'd gone out to Montana to tell Durango he was going to be a father. Thanks to Jeff Claiborne, a bad taste had been left in Savannah's mouth where marriage was concerned. That same bad taste had been left in Rico's, as well.

But Savannah had married Durango and was happy and so were Jess and Chase. Rico was happy for them, and with them married off, he had turned his time and attention to other things. His investigation business mainly. And now, he thought, glancing over at Megan

again, to her. She was the first woman in years who
had garnered any real attention from him.

What he'd told her last night was true. What they'd
started was just the beginning. She hadn't responded
to what he'd said one way or the other, but he hadn't
really expected her to. He had been tempted to ask if
she'd wanted to talk about last night but she had dozed
off before he could do so.

But before he had a conversation with her about
anything, it would be wise to have one with himself.
When it came to her, he was still in a quandary as to
why he was as attracted to her as he was. What was
there about her that he wanted to claim?

He would let her sleep, and when she woke up, they
would talk.

The sound of rain and thunder woke Megan. She
first glanced out the windshield and saw how hard it
was raining, before looking over at Rico as he maneu-
vered the truck through the downpour. His concentration was on his driving, and she decided to allow her
concentration to be on him.

Her gaze moved to the hands that gripped the steering wheel. They were big and strong. Masculine hands.
Even down to his fingertips. They were hands that had
touched her in places no other man would have dared.
But he had. And what had happened as a result still
had certain parts of her body tingling.

She started to shift in her seat but then decided to
stay put. She wasn't ready for him to know she was
awake. She needed time to think. To ponder. To pull
herself together. She was still a little rattled from last
night when she had literally come unglued. Ramsey
had said that everyone needed to let loose and let her

hair down every once in a while, and she had definitely taken her brother's suggestion.

She didn't have any regrets, as much as she wished she did. The experience had been simply amazing. With Rico's hands, mouth and tongue, she had felt things she had never felt before. He had deliberately pushed her over the edge, given her pleasure in a way she'd never received it before and wouldn't again.

This is only the beginning.

He had said that. She remembered his words clearly. She hadn't quite recovered from the barrage of pleasurable sensations that had overtaken her, not once but twice, when he had whispered that very statement to her. Even now she couldn't believe she had let him do all those things to her, touch her all over, touch her in all those places.

He'd said he would let her stay in control, but she had forgotten all about control from the first moment he had kissed her. Instead, her thoughts had been on something else altogether. Like taking every single thing he was giving, with a greed and a hunger that astounded her.

"You're awake."

She blinked and moved her gaze from his hands to his face. He'd shaven, but she could clearly remember the feel of his unshaven jaw between her legs. She felt a tingling sensation in that very spot. Maybe, on second thought, she should forget it.

She pulled up in her seat and stared straight ahead. "Yes, I'm awake."

Before she realized what he was doing, he had pulled the car over to the shoulder of the road, unleashed his seat belt and leaned over. His mouth took hers in a deep, languid and provocative kiss that whooshed the very air from her lungs. It was way too passionate and too roastingly raw to be a morning kiss, one taken on the side of the road amidst rush-hour traffic. But he was doing so, boldly, and with a deliberate ease that stirred everything within her. She was reminded of last night and how easily she had succumbed to the passion he'd stirred, the lust he had provoked.

He released her mouth, but not before one final swipe of his tongue from corner to corner. Her nipples hardened in response and pressed tightly against her blouse. Her mouth suddenly felt hot. Taken. Devoured.

"Hello, Megan," he said, against her lips.

"Hello." If this was how he would wake her up after a nap, then she would be tempted to doze off on him anytime.

"Did you get a good nap?"

"Yes, if you want to call it that."

He chuckled and straightened in his seat and resnapped his seat belt. "I would. You've been sleeping for over an hour."

She glanced back at him. "An hour?"

"Yes, I stopped for gas, and you slept through it."

She stretched her shoulders. "I was tired."

"I understand."

Yes, he would, she thought, refusing to look over at him as he moved back into traffic. She licked her lips and could still taste him there. Her senses felt short-circuited. Overwhelmed. She had been forewarned, but she hadn't taken heed.

"You feel like talking?"

Suddenly her senses were on full alert. She did look at him then. "What about?"

"Last night."

She didn't say anything. Was that the protocol with a man and a woman? To use the morning after to discuss the night before? She didn't know. "Is that how things are done?"

He lifted a brow. "What things?"

"The morning-after party where you rehash things. Say what you regret, what you wished never happened, and make promises it won't happen again."

She saw the crinkling of a smile touch the corners of his lips. "Not on my watch. Besides, I told you it will happen again. Last night was just the beginning."

"And do I have a say in the matter?"

"Yes." He glanced over at her. "All you have to say is that you don't want my hands on you, and I'll keep them to myself. I've never forced myself on any woman, Megan."

She could believe that. In fact, she could very well imagine women forcing themselves on him. She began nibbling at her bottom lip. She wished it could be that simple, just tell him to keep his hands to himself, but the truth of the matter was…she liked his hands on her. And she had thoroughly enjoyed his mouth and tongue on her, as well. Maybe a little too much.

Looking over at him, she said. "And if I *don't* tell you to keep your hands to yourself?"

"Then the outcome is inevitable," he said quietly, with a calmness that stirred her insides. She knew he meant it. From the beginning, he had given her fair warning. "Okay, let's talk," she said softly.

He pulled to the side of the road again, which had her wondering if they would ever reach their destination. He unfastened his seat belt and turned to her. "It's like this, Megan. I want you. I've made no secret of that. The degree of my attraction to you is one that I can't figure out. Not that I find the thought annoying, just confusing, because I've never been attracted to a woman to this magnitude before."

Welcome to the club, she thought. She hadn't ever been this attracted to a man before, either.

"This should be a business trip, one to find the answers about your family's history. Now that you're here, it has turned into more."

She lifted a brow. "What has it turned into now?"

"A fact-finding mission regarding us. Maybe constantly being around you will help me understand why you've gotten so deeply under my skin."

Megan's heart beat wildly in her chest. He wanted to explore the reason why they were so intensely attracted to each other? Did there need to be any other reason than that he was man and she was woman? With his looks, any woman in her right mind would be attracted to him, no matter the age. He had certainly done a number on Grace, without even trying. But Megan had been around good-looking men before and hadn't reacted the way she had with him.

"I won't crowd you, and when we get to Forbes you will have your own hotel room if you want."

He paused a moment and then added, "I'm not going to assume anything in this relationship, Megan. But you best believe I plan to seduce the hell out of you. I'm not like those other guys who never made it to first base. I plan on getting in the game and hitting a home run."

You are definitely in the game already, Rico Claiborne. She broke eye contact with him to gaze out the window. If nothing else, last night should have solidified the knowledge that her resistance was at an all-time low around him. Her self-control had taken a direct hit, and since he was on a fact-finding mission, maybe she needed to be on one, as well. Why was she willing to let him go further than any man had before?

"If you think I'm going to sit here and say I regret anything about last night, then you don't have anything to worry about, Rico."

He lifted a brow. "I don't?"

"No."

She wouldn't tell him that he had opened her eyes about a few things. That didn't mean she regretted not engaging in any sort of sexual activity before, because she didn't. What it meant was that there was a reason Rico was the man who'd given her her first orgasm. She just didn't know what that reason was yet, which was why she wanted to find out. She needed to know why he and he alone had been able to make her act in a way no other man before him had been capable of making her act.

"So we have an understanding?" he asked.

"Sort of."

He raised a brow. "Sort of?" He started the ignition and rejoined traffic again. It had stopped raining, and the sun was peeking out from beneath the clouds.

"Yes, there's still a lot about you that I don't know."

He nodded. "Okay, then ask away. Anything you want."

"Anything?"

A corner of his mouth eased into a smile. "Yes, anything, as long I don't think it's private and privileged information."

"That's fair." She considered the best way to ask her first question, then decided to just come out with it. "Have you ever been in love?"

He chuckled softly. "Not since Mrs. Tolbert."

"Mrs. Tolbert?"

"Yes, my third-grade teacher."

"You've got to be kidding me."

He glanced over at her and laughed at her surprised expression. "Kidding you about what? Being in love with Mrs. Tolbert or that she was my third-grade teacher?"

"Neither. You want me to believe that other than Mrs. Tolbert, no other woman has interested you?"

"I didn't say that. I'm a man, so women interest me. You asked if I've ever been in love, and I told you yes, with Mrs. Tolbert. Why are you questioning my answer?"

"No reason. So you're like Zane and Riley," she said.

"Maybe you need to explain that."

"Zane and Riley like women. Both claim they have never been in love and neither wants their names associated with the word."

"Then I'm not like Zane and Riley in that respect. Like I said, women interest me. I am a man with certain needs on occasion. However, falling in love doesn't scare me and it's not out of the realm of possibility. But I haven't been in a serious relationship since college."

She was tempted to ask him about that phone call he'd refused to take at her place the other day. Apparently, some woman was serious even if he wasn't. "But you have been in a serious relationship before?"

"Yes."

Her brow arched. "But you weren't in love?"

"No."

"Then why were you in the relationship?"

He didn't say anything for a minute. "My maternal grandparents are from old money and thought that as their grandson the woman I marry should be connected to old money, as well. They introduced me to Roselyn.

We dated during my first year of college. She was nice, at least I thought she was, until she tried making me choose between her and Jessica."

Megan's eyes widened. "Your sister?"

"Yes. Roselyn said she could accept me as being interracial since it wasn't quite as obvious, but there was no way she could accept Jessica as my sister."

Megan felt her anger boiling. "Boy, she had some nerve."

"Yes, she did. I had just met Jessica for the first time a month before and she felt that since Jessica and I didn't have a bond yet, she could make such an ultimatum. But she failed to realize something."

"What?"

"Jessica was my sister, whether Roselyn liked it or not, and I was not going to turn my back on Jessica or deny her just because Roselyn had a problem with it. So I broke things off."

Good for you, Megan thought. "How did your grandparents feel about you ending things?"

"They weren't happy about it, at least until I told them why. They weren't willing to make the same mistake twice. They were pretty damn vocal against my mother marrying my father, and they almost lost her when Mom stopped speaking to them for nearly two years. There was no way they would risk losing me with that same foolishness."

"You're close to your grandparents?"

"Yes, very close."

"And your father? I take it the two of you are no longer close."

She saw how his jaw tightened and knew the answer before he spoke a single word. "That's right. What he did was unforgivable, and neither Jess, Savannah or I have seen him in almost eighteen years."

"That's sad."

"Yes, it is," he said quietly.

Megan wondered if the separation had been his father's decision or his but decided not to pry. However, there was another question—a very pressing one—that she needed answered right away. "Uh, do you plan to stop again anytime soon?" She recalled he'd said he had stopped for gas while she was asleep. Now she was awake, and she had needs to take care of.

He chuckled. "You have to go to the little girl's room, do you?"

She grinned. "Yes, you can say that."

"No problem, I'll get off at the next exit."

"Thanks."

He smiled over at her, and she immediately felt her pulse thud and the area between her thighs clench. The man was too irresistible, too darn sexy, for his own good. Maybe she should have taken heed of his warning and not come to Texas. She had a feeling things were going to get pretty darn wild now that they were alone together. Real wild.

Ten

Rico stopped in front of Megan and handed her the key. "This is for your room. Mine is right next door if you need me for anything. No matter how late it is, just knock on the connecting door. Anytime you want."

She grinned at his not-so-subtle, seductive-as-sin hint as she took the key from him. "Thanks, I'll keep that in mind."

She glanced around. Forbes, Texas, wasn't what she'd imagined. It was really a nice place. Upon arriving to town, Rico had taken her to one of the restaurants for lunch. It was owned by a Mexican family. In fact, most of the townspeople were Mexican, descended from the settlers who had founded the town back in the early 1800s. She had been tempted to throw Raphel's name out there to see if any of them had ever heard of him but had decided not to. She had promised Rico she would let him handle the investigation, and she intended to keep her word.

"You can rest up while I make a few calls. I want to contact Fanny Banks's family to see if we can visit in a day or so."

"That would be nice," she said as they stepped on the elevator together. The lady at the front desk had told them the original interior of the hotel had caught fire ten years ago and had been rebuilt, which was why everything inside was pretty modern, including the elevator. From the outside, it looked like a historical hotel.

They were the only ones on the elevator, and Rico stood against the panel wall and stared over at her. "Hey, come over here for a minute."

She swallowed, and her nipples pressed hard against her shirt. "Why?"

"Come over here and find out."

He looked good standing over there, and the slow, lazy smile curving his mouth had her feeling hot all over. "Come here, Megan. I promise I won't bite."

She wasn't worried about him taking a bite out of her, but there were other things he could do that were just as lethal and they both knew it. She decided two could play his game. "No, you come over here."

"No problem."

When he made a move toward her, she retreated and stopped when her back touched the wall. "I was just kidding."

"But I kid you not," he said, reaching her and caging her with hands braced against the wall on either side of her. "Open up for me."

"B-but, what if this elevator stops to let more people on? We'll be on our floor any minute."

He reached out and pushed the elevator stop button. "Now we won't." Then he leaned in and plied her mouth with a deep and possessively passionate kiss.

She did as he'd asked. She opened up for him, letting him slide his tongue inside her mouth. He settled the middle of himself against her, in a way that let her feel his solid erection right in the juncture of her thighs. The sensations that swamped her were unreal, and she returned his kiss with just as much hunger as he was showing.

Then, just as quickly as he'd begun, he pulled his mouth away. Drawing in a deep breath, she angled her head back to gaze up at him. "What was that for?"

"No reason other than I want you."

"You told me. Several times," she murmured, trying to get her heart to stop racing and her body to cease tingling. She glanced up at him—the elevator wasn't that big and he was filling it, looking tall, dark and handsome as ever. He was looking her up and down, letting his gaze stroke over her as if it wouldn't take much to strip her naked then and there.

"And I intend to tell you several more times. I plan to keep reminding you every chance I get."

"Why?" Was it some power game he wanted to play? She was certain he had figured out that her experience with men was limited. She had all but told him it was, so what was he trying to prove? Was this just one of the ways he intended to carry out his fact-finding mission? If that was the case, then she might have to come up with a few techniques of her own.

He pushed the button to restart the elevator, and she couldn't help wondering just where her self-control was when she needed it.

* * *

Rico entered his hotel room alone and tossed his keys on the desk. Never before had he mixed business with pleasure, but he was doing so now without much thought. He shook his head. No, that wasn't true, because he was giving it a lot of thought. And still none of it made much sense.

He was about to pull off his jacket when his phone rang. He pulled his cell out of his jeans pocket and frowned when he recognized the number. Jeff Claiborne. Couldn't the man understand plain English? He started to let the call go to voice mail but impulsively decided not to.

Rico clicked on the phone. "What part of *do not call me back* did you not understand?"

"I need your help, Ricardo."

Rico gritted his teeth. "My help? The last thing you'll get from me is my help."

"But if I don't get it, I could die. They've threatened to kill me."

Rico heard the desperation in his father's voice. "Who are they?"

"A guy I owe a gambling debt. Morris Cotton."

Rico released an expletive. His grandfather had told Rico a few years ago that he'd heard Jeff Claiborne was into some pretty shady stuff. "Sounds like you have a problem. And I give a damn, why? And please don't say because you're my father."

There was a pause. "Because I'm a human being who needs help."

Rico tilted his head back and stared up at the ceiling. "You say you're in trouble? Your life is threatened?"

"Yes."

"Then go to the police."

"Don't you understand? I can't go to the police. They will kill me unless…"

"Unless what?"

"I come up with one hundred thousand dollars."

Rico's blood boiled with rage. "And you thought you could call the son and daughter you hadn't talked to in close to eighteen years to bail you out? Trust me, there's no love lost here."

"You can't say I wasn't a good father!"

"You honestly think that I can't? You were an imposter, living two lives, and in the end an innocent woman took her life because of you."

"I didn't force her to take those pills."

Rico couldn't believe that even after all this time his father was still making excuses and refusing to take ownership of his actions. "Let me say this once again. You won't get a penny out of me, Jessica or Savannah. We don't owe you a penny. You need money, work for it."

"Work? How am I supposed to work for that much money?"

"You used to be a salesman, so I'm sure you'll think of something."

"I'll call your mother. I heard she remarried, and the man is loaded. Maybe she—"

"I wouldn't advise you to do that," Rico interrupted to warn him. "She's not the woman you made a fool of years ago."

"She was my only wife."

"Yes, but what about Jessica's mother and the lies you told to her? What about how she ended her life because of you?"

There was a pause and then… "I loved them both."

Not for the first time, Rico thought his father was

truly pitiful. "No, you were greedy as hell and used them both. They were good women, and they suffered because of you."

There was another pause. "Think about helping me, Ricardo."

"There's nothing to think about. Don't call me back." Rico clicked off the phone and released a deep breath. He then called a friend who happened to be a high-ranking detective in the NYPD.

"Stuart Dunn."

"Stuart, this is Rico. I want you to check out something for me."

A short while later Rico had showered and re-dressed, putting on khakis instead of jeans and a Western-style shirt he had picked up during his first day in Forbes. He knew one surefire way to get information from shop owners was to be a buying customer. Most of the people he'd talked to in town had been too young to remember Clarice. But he had gone over to the *Forbes Daily Times* to do a little research, since the town hadn't yet digitally archived their oldest records.

Unfortunately, the day he'd gone to the paper's office, he'd been told he would have to get the permission of the paper's owner before he could view any documents from the year he wanted. He'd found that odd, but hadn't put up an argument. His mind had been too centered on heading to Austin to get Megan.

Now that he had her—and right next door—he could think of a number of things he wanted to do with her, and, as far as he was concerned, every one of them was fair game. But would acting on those things be a smart move? After all, she was cousin-in-law to his sisters. But he *had* warned her, not once but several times. However, just to clear his mind of any guilt, he would try rattling her to the point where she might decide to leave. He would give her one last chance.

And if that didn't work, he would have no regrets, no guilty conscience and no being a nice, keep-your-hands-to-yourself kind of guy. He would look forward to putting his hands—his mouth, tongue, whatever he desired—all over her. And he desired plenty. He would mix work with pleasure in a way it had never been done before.

Suddenly, his nostrils flared as he picked up her scent. Seconds later, there was a knock at his hotel room door. Amazing that he had actually smelled her through that hard oak. He'd discovered that Megan had an incredible scent that was exclusively hers.

He crossed the room and opened the door. There she was, looking so beautiful he felt the reaction in his groin. She had showered and changed clothes, as well. Now she was wearing a pair of jeans and a pullover sweater. She looked spectacular.

"I'm ready to go snooping."

He lifted a brow. "Snooping?"

"Yes, I'm anxious to find out about Raphel, and you mentioned you were going back to the town's newspaper office."

Yes, he had said that in way of conversation during their drive. He figured they had needed to switch their topic back to business or else he would have been tempted to pull to the side of the road and tear away at her mouth again.

"I'm ready," he said, stepping out into the hall and closing his hotel room door behind him. "I thought you would be taking a nap while I checked out things myself."

"I'm too excited to rest. Besides, I slept a lot in the car. Now I'm raring to go."

He saw she was. Her eyes were bright, and he could see excitement written all over her face. "Just keep in mind that this is my investigation. If I come across something I think is of interest I might mention it or I might not."

She frowned up at him as they made their way toward the elevator. "Why wouldn't you share anything you find with me?"

Yes, why wouldn't he? There was still that article Martin Felder had come across. Rico had been barely able to read it from the scan Martin had found on the internet, but what he'd read had made Rico come to Forbes himself to check out things.

"That's just the way I work, Megan. Take it or leave it. I don't have to explain the way I operate to you as long as the results are what you paid me to get."

"I know, but—"

"No buts." He stopped walking, causing her to stop, as well. He placed a stern look on his face. "We either do things my way or you can stay here until I get back." He could tell by the fire that lit her eyes at that moment that he'd succeeded in rattling her.

She crossed her arms over her chest and tilted her head back to glare up at him. "Fine, but your final report better be good."

He bent slowly and brushed a kiss across her lips. "Haven't you figured out yet that everything about me is good?" he whispered huskily.

"Arrogant ass."

He chuckled as he continued brushing kisses across her lips. "Hmm, I like it when you have a foul mouth."

She angrily pushed him away. "I think I'll take the stairs."

He smiled. "And I think I'll take you. Later."

She stormed off toward the door that led to the stairwell. He stared after her. "You're really going to take the stairs?"

"Watch me." She threw the words over her shoulder.

"I am watching you, and I'm rather enjoying the sight of that cute backside of yours right now."

She turned and stalked back over to him. The indignant look on her face indicated he might have pushed her too far. She came to a stop right in front of him and placed her hands on her hips. "You think you're the only one who can do this?"

He intentionally looked innocent. "Do what?"

"Annoy the hell out of someone. Trust me, Rico. You don't want to be around me when I am truly annoyed."

He had a feeling that he really wouldn't. "Why are you getting annoyed about anything? I meant what I said about making love to you later."

She looked up at the ceiling and slowly counted to ten before returning her gaze back to him. "And you think that decision is all yours to make?"

"No, it will be ours. By the time I finish with you, you'll want it as much as I do. I guarantee it."

She shook her head, held up her hand and looked as if she was about to say something that would probably blister his ears. But she seemed to think better of wasting her time doing so, because she tightened her lips together and slowly backed up as if she was trying to retain her control. "I'll meet you downstairs." She'd all but snarled out the words.

He watched her leave, taking the stairs.

Rico rubbed his hand over his jaw. Megan had had

a particular look in her eyes that set him on edge. She had every reason to be ticked off with him since he had intentionally pushed her buttons. And now he had a feeling she would make him pay.

The nerve of the man, Megan thought as she took the stairs down to the lobby. When she had decided to take this route she had forgotten that they were on the eighth floor. If she needed to blow off steam, this was certainly one way to do it.

Rico had deliberately been a jerk, and he had never acted that way before. If she didn't know better she would think it had been intentional. Her eyes narrowed suspiciously, and she suddenly slowed her pace. Had it been intentional? Did he assume that if he was rude to her she would pack up and go running back to Denver?

Well, if that's what he thought, she had news for him. It wouldn't happen. Now that she was here in Forbes, she intended to stay, and he would find out that two could play his game.

Not surprisingly, he was waiting for her in the lobby when she finally made it down. Deciding to have it out with him, here and now, she walked over and stared up at him. "I'm ready to take you on, Rico Claiborne."

He smiled. "Think you can?"

"I'm going to try." She continued to hold his gaze, refusing to back down. She felt the hot, explosive chemistry igniting between them and knew he felt it, too.

"I don't think you know what you're asking for, Megan."

Oh, she knew, and if the other night was a sample, she was ready to let loose and let her hair down again. "Trust me, I know."

His smile was replaced with a frown. "Fine. Let's go."

They were on their way out the revolving doors when his cell phone rang. They stopped and he checked his caller ID, hoping it wasn't Jeff Claiborne again, and answered it quickly when he saw it was Fanny Banks's granddaughter returning his call. Moments later, after ending the call, he said to Megan, "Change in plans. We'll go to the newspaper office later. That was Dorothy Banks, and her grandmother can see us now."

Eleven

"Yes, may I help you?"

"Yes, I'm Rico Claiborne and this is Megan Westmoreland. You were expecting us."

The woman, who appeared to be in her early fifties, smiled. "Yes, I'm Dorothy Banks, the one you spoke to on the phone. Please come in."

Rico stepped aside to let Megan enter before him and followed her over the threshold, admiring the huge home. "Nice place you have here."

If the house wasn't a historical landmark of some sort then it should be. He figured it had to have been built in the early 1900s. The huge two-story Victorian sat on what appeared to be ten acres of land. The structure of the house included two huge columns, a wrap-around porch with spindles, and leaded glass windows. More windows than he thought it needed, but if you were a person who liked seeing what was happening outside, then it would definitely work. The inside was just as impressive. The house seemed to have retained the original hardwood floors and inside walls. The furniture seemed to have been selected to complement the original era of the house. Because of all the windows, the room had a lot of light from the afternoon sunshine.

"You mentioned something about Ms. Westmoreland being a descendant of Raphel Westmoreland?" the woman asked.

"Yes. I'm helping her trace her family roots, and in our research, the name Clarice Riggins came up. The research indicated she was a close friend of Raphel. Since Ms. Banks was living in the area at the time, around the early nineteen hundreds, we thought that maybe we could question her to see if she recalls anyone by that name."

Dorothy smiled. "Well, I can tell you that, and the answer is yes. Clarice Riggins and my grandmother were childhood friends. Although Clarice died way before I was born, I remember Gramma Fanny speaking of her from time to time when she would share fond memories with us."

Megan had reached out and touched his hand. Rico could tell she had gotten excited at the thought that the Bankses knew something about Clarice.

"But my grandmother is the one you should talk to," Dorothy added.

"We would love to," Megan said excitedly. "Are you sure we won't be disturbing her?

The woman stood and waved her hand. "I'm positive. My grandmother likes talking about the past." She chuckled. "I've heard most of it more times than I can count. I think she would really appreciate a new set of ears. Excuse me while I go get her. She's sitting on the back porch. The highlight of her day is watching the sun go down."

"And you're sure we won't be disrupting her day?" Megan asked.

"I'm positive. Although I've heard the name Clarice, I don't recall hearing the name of Raphel Westmoreland before. Gramma Fanny will have to tell you if she has."

Megan turned enthusiastic eyes to Rico. "We might be finding out something at last."

"Possibly. But don't get your hopes up, okay?"

"Okay." She glanced around. "This is a nice place. Big and spacious. I bet it's the family home and has been around since the early nineteen hundreds."

"Those were my thoughts."

"It reminds me of our family home and—"

Megan stopped talking when Dorothy returned, walking with an older woman using a cane. Both Megan and Rico stood. Fanny Banks was old, but she didn't look a year past eighty. To think the woman had just celebrated her one-hundredth birthday was amazing.

Introductions were made. Megan thought she might have been mistaken, but she swore she'd seen a hint of distress in Fanny's gaze. Why? In an attempt to assure the woman, Megan took her hand and gently tightened her hold and said, "It's an honor to meet you. Happy belated birthday. I can't believe you're a hundred. You are beautiful, Mrs. Banks."

Happiness beamed in Fanny Banks's eyes. "Thank you. I understand you have questions for me. And call me Ms. Fanny. Mrs. Banks makes me feel old."

"All right," Megan said, laughing at the teasing. She looked over at Rico and knew he would do a better job of explaining things than she would. The last thing she wanted was for him to think she was trying to take over his job.

They continued to stand until Dorothy got Ms. Fanny settled into an old rocking chair. Understandably, she moved at a slow pace.

"Okay, now what do you want to ask me about Clarice?" Ms. Fanny asked in a quiet tone.

"The person we really want information about is Raphel Westmoreland, who we believe was an acquaintance of Clarice's."

Megan saw that sudden flash of distress again, which let her know she hadn't imagined it earlier. Ms. Fanny nodded slowly as she looked over at Megan. "And Raphel Westmoreland was your grandfather?"

Megan shook her head. "No, he was my great-grandfather, and a few years ago we discovered he had a twin brother we hadn't known anything about."

She then told Ms. Fanny about the Denver Westmorelands and how they had lost Raphel's only two grandsons and their wives in a plane crash, leaving fifteen of them without parents. She then told Fanny how, a few years ago, they discovered Raphel had a twin named Reginald, and how they had begun a quest to determine if there were more Westmorelands they didn't know about, which had brought them here.

Ms. Fanny looked down at her feeble hands as if studying them…or trying to make up her mind about something. She then lifted her gaze and zeroed in on Megan with her old eyes. She then said, "I'm so sorry to find out about your loss. That must have been a difficult time for everyone."

She then looked down at her hands again. Moments later, she looked up and glanced back and forth between Rico and Megan. "The two of you are forcing me to

break a promise I made several years ago, but I think
you deserve to know the truth."

Nervous tension flowed through Megan. She
glanced over at Rico, who gazed back at her before
he turned his attention back to Ms. Fanny and asked,
"And what truth is that?"

The woman looked over at her granddaughter, who
only nodded for her to continue. She then looked at
Megan. "The man your family knew as Raphel Westmoreland was an imposter. The real Raphel Westmoreland died in a fire."

Megan gasped. "No." And then she turned and collapsed in Rico's arms.

"Megan," Rico whispered softly as he stroked the
side of her face with his fingertips. She'd fainted, and
poor Ms. Fanny had become nervous that she'd done
the wrong thing, while her granddaughter had rushed
off to get a warm facecloth, which he was using to try
to bring Megan back around.

He watched as she slowly opened her eyes and
looked at him. He recognized what he saw in her gaze.
A mixture of fear and confusion. "She's wrong, Rico.
She has to be. There's no way my great-grandfather
was not who he said he was."

Rico was tempted to ask why was she so certain
but didn't want to upset her any more than she already
was. "Then come on, sit up so we can listen to her tell
the rest of it and see, shall we?"

Megan nodded and pulled herself up to find she was
still on the sofa. There was no doubt in her mind that
both Ms. Fanny and Dorothy had heard what she'd just
said. Manners prompted her to apologize. "I'm sorry,
but what you said, Ms. Fanny, is overwhelming. My

great-grandfather died before I was born so I never knew him, but all those who knew him said he was a good and honest person."

Ms. Fanny nodded. "I didn't say that he wasn't, dear. What I said is that he wasn't the real Raphel."

Tightening his hand on Megan's, Rico asked, "If he wasn't Raphel, then who was he?"

Ms. Fanny met Rico's gaze. "An ex-convict by the name of Stephen Mitchelson."

"An ex-convict!" Megan exclaimed, louder than she'd intended to.

"Yes."

Megan was confused. "B-but how? Why?"

It took Ms. Fanny a while before she answered then she said, "It's a long story."

"We have time to listen," Rico said, glancing over at Megan. He was beginning to worry about her. Finding out upsetting news like this was one of the reasons he hadn't wanted her here, yet he had gone and brought her anyway.

"According to Clarice, she met Raphel when she was visiting an aunt in Wyoming. He was a drifter moving from place to place. She told him about her home here and told him if he ever needed steady work to come here and her father would hire him to work on their ranch."

She paused a moment and then said, "While in Wyoming, she met another drifter who was an ex-con by the name of Stephen Mitchelson. She and Stephen became involved, and she became pregnant. But she knew her family would never accept him, and she thought she would never see him again."

Ms. Fanny took a sip of water from the glass her granddaughter handed her. "Only the man who showed up later, here in Texas, wasn't Raphel but Stephen. He told her Raphel had died in a fire. To get a fresh start, he was going to take Raphel's identity and start a new life elsewhere. And she let him go, without even telling him she was pregnant with his child. She loved him that much. She wanted to give him a new beginning."

Ms. Fanny was quiet for a moment. "I was there the day she made that decision. I was there when he drove away and never looked back. I was also there when she gave birth to their child. Alone."

The room was silent and then Megan spoke softly. "What happened to her and the baby?"

"She left here by train to go stay with extended family in Virginia. Her father couldn't accept she had a baby out of wedlock. But she never made it to her destination. The train she was riding on derailed, killing her and the baby."

"My God," Megan said, covering her hands with her face. "How awful," she said. A woman who had given up so much had suffered such a tragic ending.

She drew in a deep breath and wondered how on earth she was going to return home to Denver and tell her family that they weren't Westmorelands after all.

Several hours later, back in his hotel room, Rico sat on the love seat and watched as Megan paced the floor. After leaving the Bankses' house, they had gone to the local newspaper office, and the newspaper articles they'd read hadn't helped matters, nor had their visit to the courthouse. The newspapers had verified the train wreck and that Clarice and her child had been killed. There was also a mention of the fire in Wyoming and that several men had been burned beyond recognition.

There were a lot of unanswered questions zigzagging through Rico's mind but he pushed them aside to concentrate on Megan. At the moment, she was his main concern. He leaned forward and rested his arms on his thighs. "If you're trying to walk a hole in the floor, you're doing a good job of it."

She stopped, and when he saw the sheen of tears in her eyes, he was out of his seat in a flash. He was unsure of what he would say, but he knew he had to say something. "Hey, none of that," he whispered quietly, pulling her into his arms. "We're going to figure this out, Megan."

She shook her head and pushed away from him. "This is all my fault. In my eagerness to find out everything about Raphel, I may have caused the family more harm than good. You heard Fanny Banks. The man everyone thought was Raphel was some ex-convict named Stephen Mitchelson. What am I going home to say? We're not really Westmorelands, we're Mitchelsons?"

He could tell by the sound of her voice she was really torn up over what Fanny Banks had said. "But there might be more to what she said, Megan."

"But Fanny Banks was there, Rico," she countered. "I always said there was a lot about my great-grandfather that we didn't know. He went to his grave without telling anyone anything about having a twin brother or if he had family somewhere. Now I know why. He probably didn't know any of Raphel's history. He could never claim anyone. I don't know how the fourth woman named Isabelle fits in, but I do know Raphel—Stephen—finally settled down with my great-grandmother Gemma. From the diary she left behind, the one that Dillon let me read, I know they had a good marriage, and she always said he was a kind-hearted man. He certainly didn't sound like the kind who would have been an ex-con. The only thing I ever heard about Raphel was that he was a kind, loving and honorable man."

"That still might be the case, Megan."

As if she hadn't heard him, she said, "I have to face the possibility that the man my father and uncle idolized, the man they thought was the best grandfather in the entire world, was nothing but a convict who wasn't Raphel Westmoreland and—"

"Shh, Megan," he whispered, breaking in and pulling her closer into his arms. "Until we find out everything, I don't want you getting upset or thinking the worst. We'll go to the courthouse tomorrow and dig around some more."

Sighing deeply, she pulled away from him, swiped at more tears and tilted her head back to look up at him. "I need to be alone for a while so I'm going to my room. Thanks for the shoulder to cry on."

Rico shoved his hands into the pockets of his khakis. "What about dinner?"

"I'm not hungry. I'll order room service later."

"You sure?"

She shrugged. "Right now, Rico, I'm not sure about anything. That's why I need to take a shower and relax."

He nodded. "Are you going to call Dillon or Ramsey and tell them the latest developments?"

She shook her head. "Not yet. It's something I wouldn't be able to tell them over the phone anyway." She headed for the door. "Good night. I'll see you in the morning."

"Try to get some sleep," he called out to her. She nodded but kept walking and didn't look back. She opened the connecting door and then closed it behind her.

Rico rubbed his hand down his face, feeling frustration and anger all rolled into one. He glanced at his watch and pulled his cell phone out of his back pocket. A few moments later a voice came on the line. "Hello."

"This is Rico. A few things came up that I want you to check out." He spent the next twenty minutes bringing Martin up to date on what they'd found out from Fanny Banks.

"And you're actually questioning the honesty of a one-hundred-year-old woman?"

"Yes."

Martin moaned. "Ah, man, she's one hundred."

"I know."

"All right. In that case, I'll get on it right away. If the man was an imposter then I'll find out," Martin said. "But we are looking back during a time when people took on new identities all the time."

That's the last thing Rico wanted to hear.

After hanging up the phone he stared across the room at the door separating him from Megan. Deciding to do something with his time, before he opened the connecting door, he grabbed his jacket and left to get something to eat.

An hour later, Megan had showered, slipped into a pair of pajamas and was lounging across her bed when she heard the sound of Rico returning next door. When she'd knocked on the connecting door earlier and hadn't gotten a response, she figured he had gone to get something to eat. She had ordered room service and had wanted to know if he wanted to share since the hotel had brought her plenty.

Now she felt fed and relaxed and more in control of her emotions. And what she appreciated more than anything was that when she had needed him the most,

Rico had been there. Even while in the basement of
the newspaper office, going through microfilm of old
newspapers and toiling over all those books to locate
the information they wanted, he had been there, ready
to give her a shoulder to cry on if she needed one. And
when she had needed one, after everything had gotten
too emotional for her, she'd taken him up on his offer.

He had been in his room for no more than ten minutes when she heard a soft knock on the connecting
door. "Come in."

He slowly opened the door, and when he appeared
in her room the force of his presence was so powerful
she had to snatch her gaze away from his and train it
back on the television screen.

"I was letting you know I had returned," he said.

"I heard you moving around," she said, her fingers
tightening around the remote.

"You've had dinner?" he asked her.

From out of the corner of her eye, she could see him
leaning in the doorway, nearly filling it completely.
"Yes, and it was good."

"What did you have?"

"A grilled chicken salad. It was huge." *Just like you,*
she thought and immediately felt the blush spread into
her features.

"Why are you blushing?"

Did the man not miss anything? "No reason."

"Then why aren't you looking at me?"

Yes, why wasn't she looking at him? Forcing herself
to look away from the television, she slid her eyes over
to his and immediately their gazes clung. That was the
moment she knew why it had been so easy to let her
guard down around him, why it had been so effortless
to lose her control and why, even now, she was filled

with a deep longing and the kind of desire a woman had for the man she loved.

She had fallen in love with Rico.

A part of her trembled inside with that admission. She hadn't known something like this could happen this way, so quickly, completely and deeply. He had gotten to her in ways no other man had. Around him she had let go of her control and had been willing to let emotions flow. Her love hadn't allowed her to hold anything back. And when she had needed his strength, he'd given it. Unselfishly. He had an honorable and loyal spirit that had touched her in ways she'd never been touched before. Yes, she loved him, with every part of her being.

She sucked in a deep breath because she also knew that what she saw in his eyes was nothing more than pent-up sexual energy that needed to be released. And as she continued to watch him, his lips curved into a smile.

Now it was her time to ask all the questions. "Why are you smiling?"

"I don't think you want to know," he said, doing away with his Eastern accent and replacing it with a deep Texas drawl.

"Trust me, I do." Tonight she needed to think about something other than her grandfather's guilt or innocence, something other than how, in trying to find out about him, she might have exposed her family to the risk of losing everything.

"Since you really want to know," he said, straightening his stance and slowly coming toward her. "I was thinking of all the things I'd just love to do to you."

His words made her nipples harden into peaks, and

she felt them press hard against her pajama top. "Why just think about it, Rico?"

He stopped at the edge of the bed. "Don't tempt me, Megan."

She tilted her head to gaze up at him. "And don't tempt me, Rico."

"What do you know about temptation?"

She became caught up by the deep, sensuous look in his eyes. In one instant, she felt the need to look away, and then, in another instant, she felt the need to be the object of his stare. She decided to answer him the best way she knew how. "I know it's something I've just recently been introduced to," she said, remembering the first time she'd felt this powerful attraction, at Micah's wedding.

"And I know just how strong it was the first time I saw you. Something new for me. Then I remember our first kiss, and how the temptation to explore more was the reason I hadn't wanted it to end," she whispered softly.

"But I really discovered what temptation was the night you used your mouth on me," she said, not believing they were having this sort of conversation or that she was actually saying these things. "I've never known that kind of pleasure before, or the kind of satisfaction I experienced when you were finished, and it tempted me to do some things to you, to touch you and taste you."

She saw the darkening of his eyes, and the very air became heated, sensuously so. He reached out, extending his hand to hers, and she took it. He gently pulled her up off the bed. The feel of the hard, masculine body pressed against hers, especially the outline of his arousal through his khakis, made her shiver with desire. When his hand began roaming all over her, she drew in a deep breath.

"I want to make love to you, Megan," he said, lowering his head to whisper in her ear. "I've never wanted a woman as much as I want you."

For some reason she believed him. Maybe it was because she wanted to believe. Or it could be that she wanted the feeling of being in his arms. The feeling of him inside her while making love. She wanted to be the woman who could satisfy him as much as he could satisfy her.

He tilted her chin up so their gazes could meet again. She was getting caught up in every sexy thing about him, even his chin, which looked like it needed a shave, and his hair, which seemed to have grown an inch and touched his shoulders. And then he leaned down and captured her mouth in one long, drugging kiss. Pleasure shot to all parts of her body, and her nerve endings were bombarded with all sorts of sensations while he feasted on her mouth like it was the last morsel he would ever taste.

At that moment, she knew what she wanted. She wanted to lose control in a way she'd never lost it before. She wanted to get downright wild with it.

She pulled back from the kiss and immediately went for his shirt, nearly tearing off the buttons in her haste. "Easy, baby. What are you doing?"

"I need to touch you," she said softly.

"Then here, let me help," he said, easing his shirt from his shoulders. A breathless moan slipped from her throat. The man was so perfectly made she could feel her womb convulsing, clinching with a need she was beginning to understand.

Her hand went to his belt buckle and within seconds

she had slid it out of the loops to toss it on the floor. On instinct, she practically licked her lips as she eased down his zipper. Never had she been this bold with a man, never this brazen. But something was driving her to touch him, to taste him, the same way he had done to her last night.

All she could register in her mind was that this scenario was one she had played out several times in her dreams. The only thing was, all the other times she would wake up. But this was reality at its best.

"Let me help you with this, as well," he whispered.

And then she watched as he eased his jeans and briefs down his legs and revealed an engorged erection. He was huge, and on instinct, her hand reached out and her fingers curled around the head. She heard how his breathing changed. How he was forcing air into his lungs.

When she began moving her fingers, getting to know this part of him, she felt rippling muscles on every inch of him. The thick length of his aroused shaft filled her hand and then some. This was definitely a fine work of art. Perfect in every way. Thick. Hard. With large veins running along the side.

"Do you have what you want?" he asked in a deep, husky tone.

"Almost." And that was the last word she spoke before easing down to her knees and taking him into her mouth.

A breathless groan escaped from between Rico's lips. He gripped the curls on Megan's head and threw his head back as her mouth did a number on him. He felt his muscles rippling as her tongue tortured him in ways he didn't know were possible. Her head, resting against his belly, shifted each time her mouth moved and sent pleasurable quivers all through him.

He felt his brain shutting down as she licked him from one end to the other, but before it did, he had to know something. "Who taught you this?"

The words were wrenched from his throat, and he had to breathe hard. She paused a moment to look up at him. "I'll tell you later."

She then returned to what she was doing, killing him softly and thoroughly. What was she trying to do? Lick him dry and swallow him whole? Damn, it felt like it. Every lick of her tongue was causing him to inhale, and every long powerful suck was forcing him to exhale. Over and over again. He felt on the edge of exploding, but forced himself not to. He wanted it to be just like in his dreams. He wanted to spill inside of her.

"Megan." He gently tugged on a section of her hair, while backing up to pull out of her mouth.

And before she could say anything, he had whipped her from her knees and placed her on the bed, while removing her pajama top and bottoms in the process. He wanted her, and he wanted her now.

Picking up his jeans off the floor, he retrieved a condom packet from his wallet and didn't waste any time while putting it on. He glanced at her, saw her watching and saw how her gaze roamed over his entire body. "Got another question for you, Megan, and you can't put off the answer until later. I need to know now."

She shifted her gaze from below his waist up to face. "All right. What's your question?"

"How is your energy level?"

She lifted a brow. "My energy level?"

"Yes."

"Why do you want to know?"

"Because," he said, slowly moving toward the bed.
"I plan to make love to you all night."

Twelve

All night?

Before Megan had time to digest Rico's proclamation, he had crawled on the bed with her and proceeded to pull her into his arms and seize her mouth. They needed to talk. There were other things he needed to know besides her energy level; things she wanted to tell him. She wanted to share with him what was in her heart but considering what they were sharing was only temporary, it wouldn't be a good idea. The last thing she wanted was for him to feel guilty about not reciprocating her feelings. And then there was the issue of her virginity. He didn't have a clue right now, but pretty soon he would, she thought as he slid his tongue between her lips.

His skin, pressed next to hers, felt warm, intoxicating, and he was kissing her with a passion and greed that surpassed anything she'd ever known. There was no time for talking. Just time to absorb this, take it all in and enjoy. A shiver ran through her when he released her mouth and lowered his head to aim for her breasts, sucking a nipple.

He really thought they could survive an all-nighter? she asked herself. No way. And when he reached down to slide his fingers between her legs and stroked her there, she moaned out his name. "Rico."

He paid her no mind, but continued to let his mouth lick her hardened nipple, while his hand massaged her clit, arousing her to the point where jolts of pleasure were running through her body.

She knew from his earlier question that he assumed she was experienced with this sort of thing. Little did he know she was as green as a cucumber. Again she thought, he needed to be told, but not now. Instead, she reached out to grip his shoulders as his fingers circled inside of her, teasing her mercilessly and spreading her scent in the air.

Then he leaned up, leaving her breasts. Grabbing a lock of her hair with his free hand, he tugged, pulling her face to his and kissing her hard on the mouth, sending her passion skyrocketing while shock waves of pleasure rammed through her.

He pulled his mouth from hers and whispered against her moist lips. "You're ready for me now. You're so wet I can't wait any longer," he said, nibbling on her earlobe and running his tongue around the rim of her ear, so close that she could feel his hot breath.

He moved to slide between her legs and straddle her thighs, looked down at her and whispered, "I'm going to make it good for you, baby. The best you've ever had."

She opened her mouth to tell him not only would it

be the best, but that it would also be the first she ever had when his tongue again slid between her lips. That's when she felt him pressing hard against her, trying to make an entry into her.

"You're tight, baby. Relax," he whispered against her cheek as he reached down and grabbed his penis, guiding it into her. He let the head stroke back and forth along her folds. She started moaning and couldn't stop. "There, you're letting go. Now I can get inside you," he whispered huskily.

"It's not going to be easy," she whispered back.

He glanced down at her. "Why do you say that?" he asked as he continued to stroke her gently, sliding back and forth through her wetness.

Megan knew he deserved an answer. "I'm tight down there for a reason, Rico."

"What reason is that?"

"Because I've never made love with a man before."

His hand went still. "Are you saying—"

"Yes, that's what I'm saying. But I've never wanted any man before." *Never loved one before you,* she wanted to say, but didn't. "Don't let that stop you from making love to me tonight, Rico."

He leaned in and gently kissed her lips. "Nothing can stop me from making love to you, sweetheart. I couldn't stop making love to you tonight even if my life depended on it."

And then he was kissing her again, this time with a furor that had her trembling. Using his knees, he spread her legs wider, and she felt the soft fabric against her skin when he grabbed a pillow to ease under her backside. He pulled back from the kiss. "I wish I could tell you it's not going to hurt. But…"

"Don't worry about it. Just do it."

He looked down at her. "Just do it?"

"Yes, and please do it now. I can't wait any longer. I've waited twenty-seven years for this, Rico." *And for you.*

She looked dead center into his eyes. She felt the head of him right there at her mound. He reached out and gently stroked the side of her face and whispered, "I want to be looking at you when I go inside of you."

Their gazes locked. She felt the pressure of him entering her and then he grabbed her hips, whispered for her to hold on and pushed deeper with a powerful thrust.

"Rico!" she cried out, but he was there, lowering his head and taking her mouth while he pushed even farther inside her, not stopping until he was buried deep. And then, as if on instinct, her inner muscles began clenching him hard.

He threw his head back and released a guttural moan. "What are you doing to me?"

He would ask her that. "I don't know. It just feels right" was the only reply she could give him. In response, he kissed her again while his lower body began moving. Slowly at first, as if giving her body time to adjust. And then he changed the rhythm, while leaning down to suck on her tongue.

Megan thought she was going to go out of her mind. Never had she thought, assumed, believed—until now. He was moving at a vigorous pace, and she cried out, not in pain but in sensations so pleasurable they made her respond out loud.

Her insides quivered, and she went after his tongue with speed and hunger. She cried out, screamed, just like she'd done that night at the south ridge. That only made him thrust harder and penetrate deeper. Then they both ignited in one hell of an explosion that sent sparks flying all through her body, and especially to the area where their bodies were joined.

He shook, she shook and the bed shook almost off the hinges as he continued to pound into her...making her first time a time she would always remember. It seemed as if it took forever for them to come down off their orgasmic high. When they did, he shifted his weight off hers and pulled her to him.

"We'll rest up a bit," he said silkily. "How do you feel?"

She knew her eyes were filled with wonderment at what they'd done. "I feel good." And she meant it.

Her heart was beating fast, and her pulse was off the charts. She had totally and completely lost control. But all that was fine because she had gotten the one thing she'd wanted. A piece of Rico Claiborne.

Rico pulled her closer to him, tucked her body into the curve of his while he stroked a finger across her cheek. He'd only left the bed to dispose of the condom and get another. Now he was back and needed the feel of her in his arms. She had slept for a while, but now she was awake and he had questions.

"I think it's time to tell me how someone who can work their mouth on a man the way you do has managed to remain a virgin. I can think of one possibility, but I want to hear it from you."

She smiled up at him. "What? That I prefer oral sex to the real thing?" She shook her head. "That's not it, and just to set the record straight, I've never gone down on a man until you."

He leaned back and lifted a brow. "Are you saying that—"

"Yes. What I did to you tonight was another first for me."

He chuckled. "Hell, you could have fooled me."

Excitement danced in her eyes. "Really? I was that good?"

"Yeah," he said, running a finger across her cheek again. "Baby, you were that good. So, if I was your first, how did you know what to do?"

She snuggled closer to him. "I was snooping over at Zane's place one day, looking for a pair of shoes I figured I'd left there, and came across this box under his bed. I was curious enough to look inside and discovered a bunch of DVDs marked with *X*s. So of course I had to see what was on them."

Rico chuckled again. "Is that the box he mentioned he would get from you after dinner the other night?"

She smiled. "No, that's another box altogether, a lock box. So he would know if I had tampered with it. Those videos were in a shoe box, and to this day I've never told Zane about it. I was only seventeen at the time, but I found watching them pretty darn fascinating. I was curious about how a woman could give a man pleasure that way, with her mouth."

"But not curious enough to try it on anyone until now?"

There was amusement in his voice, but to her it wasn't amusing, not even a little bit, because what he'd said was true. She hadn't had any desire to try it out on any other man but him. "Yes."

"I'm glad. I'm also surprised you've never been curious enough to sleep with anyone."

"I couldn't see myself sharing a bed with a man just for the sake of curiosity. Had I been in a serious relationship things might have been different, but most of my life has been filled with either going to school or working. I never had time for serious relationships. And the few times that a man wanted to make it serious, I just wasn't feeling it."

But she hadn't had a problem feeling him. She had wanted him. Had wanted to taste him the way he had tasted her. Had wanted to put her mouth on him the same way he'd put his on her. And she didn't regret doing so.

But nothing had prepared her for when he had shed his pants and briefs and shown his body to her. He was so magnificently made, with a masculine torso and rippling muscles. What had captured her attention more than anything else was the engorged erection he had revealed. Seeing it had aroused her senses and escalated her desires.

But for her, last night had been about more than just sex. She loved him. She wasn't certain just how she felt being in a one-sided love affair, but she wouldn't worry about it for now. She had let her hair down and was enjoying the situation tremendously. She had been in control of her emotions for so long, and she'd thought that was the best way to be, but now she was seeing a more positive side of being out of control. She knew what it felt like to be filled with a need that only one man could take care of. She knew how it felt to be wild.

And she wanted to experience more of it.

She pulled away from Rico and shifted her body to straddle his.

"Hey, what do you think you're doing?" he asked, trying to pull her back into his arms.

She shook her head. "Taking care of this," she whispered. "You said I can have control so I'm claiming ownership. You also told me you wanted me, and you told me what would happen if we were together. It did happen, and now I want to show you how much I want you."

"But you're sore."

She chuckled. "And I'll probably be sore for a long time. You aren't a small man, you know. But I can handle it, and I can handle you. I want to handle you, Rico, so let me."

He held her gaze, and the heat radiating between them filled the room with desire. His hands lifted and stroked her face, touched her lips that had covered his shaft, and she understood the degree of hunger reflected in his eyes. There was no fighting the intense passion they seemed to generate. No fighting it, and no excusing it.

"Then you are going to handle it, baby. You are the only woman who can," she heard him whisper.

Pleased by what he said, she lowered her head, and he snagged her mouth by nibbling at her lips, stroking them with his tongue. She gripped his shoulders, and his erection stood straight up, aimed right for her womanly core like it had a mind of its own and knew what it wanted.

The need to play around with his mouth drove her to allow his tongue inside her lips. And then she toyed with his tongue, sucked on it and explored every aspect of his mouth. The way his hand was digging into her scalp made her tongue lash out even more, and she felt him tremble beneath her. The thought that she could make him feel this way, give him this much pleasure, sent her blood rushing through her veins.

She eased the lower part of her body down but deliberately did it in a way that had his penis under her and not inside of her. Then she moved her thighs to grind herself against his pubic bone.

"Oh, hell." The words rushed from his lips, and she closed her eyes, liking the feel of giving him such an intimate massage. Moving back and forth, around in circular motions, christening his flesh with her feminine essence.

"I need you now, Megan. I can't take any more." His voice was filled with torment. Deciding to put him out of his misery, she leaned up and positioned her body so he could slide inside of her.

Megan shuddered when she felt the head of his shaft pierce through her wetness, pushing all the way until it could go no more. She held his gaze as she began to ride him. She'd always heard that she was good at riding a horse, and she figured riding a man couldn't be much different. So she rode him. Easing lower then easing back up, she repeated the steps until they became a sensual cycle. She heard his growl of pleasure, and the sound drove her to ride him hard.

Grabbing her hips, he lifted his own off the bed to push deeper inside of her. "Aw, hell, you feel so damn good, Megan." His shaft got even larger inside of her, burying deeper.

His words triggered a need within her, a need that was followed by satisfaction when her body exploded. She screamed and continued coming apart until she felt his body explode, as well. Pleasure was ripping through her, making it hard to breathe. He was rock-solid, engorged, even after releasing inside of her. He wouldn't go down. It was as if he wasn't through with her yet.

He shifted their bodies, pulling her beneath him with her back to him. "Let me get inside you this way, baby. I want to ride you from behind."

Pulling in as much energy as she could, she eased up on all fours, and no sooner had she done so than she felt the head of his erection slide into her. And then he began moving, slowly at first, taking long, leisurely strokes. Each one sent bristles of pleasure brushing over her. But then he increased the rhythm and made the strokes deeper, harder, a lot more provocative as he rode her from the back. She moved her hips against him, felt his stomach on the cheeks of her backside while his hand caressed her breasts.

She glanced over her shoulder, their gazes connected, and she saw the heated look in his eyes. It fueled even more desire within her, making her moan and groan his name aloud.

"Rico."

"That sounds good, baby. Now I want to hear you say 'Ricardo.'"

As spasms of pleasure ripped through her, she whispered in a low, sultry voice. "Ricardo."

Hearing her say his birth name made something savage inside of Rico snap. He grabbed her hips as unadulterated pleasure rammed through him, making him ride her harder, his testicles beating against her backside. The sound of flesh against flesh echoed loudly through the room and mingled with their moans and groans.

And then it happened. The moment he felt her inner muscles clamp down on him, felt her come all over him, he exploded. He wouldn't be surprised if the damn condom didn't break from the load. But, at that moment, the only thing he wanted to do was fill her with his essence. Only her. No other woman.

He continued to shudder, locked tight inside of her. He threw his head back and let out a fierce, primal growl. The same sound a male animal made when he found his true mate. As pleasure continued to rip through him, he knew, without a shadow of a doubt, that he had found his.

He lowered his head and slipped his tongue inside her mouth, needing the connection as waves of pleasure continued to pound into him. It seemed to take forever before the last spasm left his body. But he couldn't move. Didn't want to. He just wanted to lie there and stay intimately connected to her.

But he knew being on all fours probably wasn't a comfortable position for her, so he eased their bodies down in a way that spooned his body against hers but kept him locked inside of her. He needed this moment of just lying with her, being inside of her while holding her in his arms.

She was so damn perfect. What they'd just shared had been so out-of-this-world right. He felt fulfilled in a way he had never felt before, in a way he hadn't thought he was capable of feeling.

"Anything else you think I ought to know?" he asked, wrapping his arms around her, liking the feel of her snuggled tightly to him.

"There is this thing about you using a condom."

"Mmm, what about it?"

"You can make it optional if you want. I take birth control injections, to stay regulated, so I'm good."

He had news for her. She was better than good. "Thanks for telling me."

"And I'm healthy so I'm safe that way, as well," she added.

"So am I," he assured her softly, gently rubbing her stomach, liking the knowledge that the next time they made love they could be skin-to-skin.

"Rico."

He looked down at her. She had tilted her head back to see him.

"Yes?"

"I like letting go with you. I like getting wild."

He lowered his head to brush a kiss across her lips. "And I like letting go and getting wild with you, too."

And he meant it in a way he wasn't ready to explain quite yet. Right now, he wanted to do the job she had hired him to do. He hadn't accepted everything Ms. Fanny and her daughter had said, although the newspapers and those documents somewhat supported their claims, especially the details of the fire and the train wreck. There was still a gut feeling that just wouldn't go away.

Something wasn't adding up, but he couldn't pinpoint what it was. He had been too concerned about the impact of their words on Megan to take the time to dissect everything. He hadn't been on top of his A-game, which is one of the reasons he hadn't wanted her here. He tended to focus more on her than on what he was supposed to be doing.

But now, as he replayed everything that had transpired over the past fourteen hours in his mind, a lot of questions were beginning to form. In the morning, he would talk to Megan over breakfast. Right now, he just wanted to hold her in his arms for a while, catch a little sleep and then make love to her again.

If he had thought he was addicted to her before, he knew he was even more so now.

Thirteen

"I think Fanny Banks's story isn't true."

Megan peered across the breakfast table at Rico. It took a few seconds for his words to fully sink in. "You do?"

"Yes. Someone is trying to hide something."

Serious doubt appeared in her gaze. "I don't know, Rico. What could they be trying to hide? Besides, we saw the articles in the newspapers, which substantiated what she said."

"Did they?"

Megan placed her fork down and leaned back in her chair. "Look, I admit I was upset by what I learned, and I wish more than anything that Fanny Banks might have gotten her information wrong or that at one hundred years old she couldn't possible remember anything. But her memory is still sharp."

"Too sharp."

Megan leaned forward, wondering why he suddenly had a doubtful attitude. "Okay, why the change of heart? You seemed ready to accept what she said."

"Yes, I was too ready. I was too quick to believe it because, like you, I thought it made sense, especially after reading those newspaper articles. But last night while you slept, I lay there and put things together in my mind and there's one thing that you and I can't deny that we didn't give much thought to."

She lifted a brow. "And what is that?"

"It's no coincidence that the Westmorelands of Atlanta and the Denver Westmorelands favor. And I don't mean a little bit. If you put them in a room with a hundred other people and asked someone to pick out family members, I'd bet ninety-eight percent of all the Westmorelands in the room would get grouped together."

Megan opened her mouth to say something and then decided there was nothing she could say because he was right. The first time the two groups had gotten together, and Dare Westmoreland—one of the Atlanta Westmorelands who was a sheriff in the metro area—had walked into the room, every member of the Denver Westmorelands' jaws had dropped. He and Dillon favored so much it was uncanny.

"And that level of similarity in looks can only come from the same genes," Rico added. "If push comes to shove, I'll have DNA testing done."

She picked up her fork. "You still haven't given me a reason for Ms. Banks to make up such a story."

Rico tossed down his napkin. "I don't have a reason, Megan, just a gut feeling."

He reached across the table and took her hand in his. "I saw yesterday that what she said took a toll on you and that became my main concern. I got caught up in your hurt and pain. I felt it, and I didn't want that for you."

She understood what he meant. Last night, making love to him had been an eye opener. She had felt connected to him in a way she'd never been connected to a man. She was in tune to her emotions and a part of her felt in tune to his, as well. Their time together had been so special that even now the memories gave her pause. "If your theory is true, how do we prove it?" she asked him.

"We don't. We visit them again and ask questions we didn't ask yesterday when our minds were too numb to do so."

He gently tightened his hold on her hand. "I need you to trust me on this. Will you do that?"

She nodded. "Yes, I will trust you."

After making a call to the Banks ladies after breakfast, they discovered they would have to put their visit on hold for a while. Dorothy Banks's daughter advised them that her mother and great-grandmother weren't at home and had gone on a day trip to Brownwood and wouldn't be returning until that evening.

So Rico and Megan went back to their hotel. The moment they walked into the room he gently grabbed her wrist and tugged her to him. "You okay? How is the soreness?"

He found it odd to ask her that since he'd never asked a woman that question before. But then he couldn't recall ever being any woman's first.

She rested her palms on his chest and smiled up at him. "My body is fine. Remember, I do own a horse that I ride every day, and I think that might have helped some." She paused and then asked, "What about you?"

He raised a brow. "Me?"

"Yes," she said, smiling. "I rode you pretty darn hard."

Yes, she had. The memory of her doing so made his erection thicken against her. "Yes, but making love with you was amazing," he said, already feeling the air crackling with sexual energy. "Simply incredible. I enjoyed it tremendously."

Her smile widened, as if she was pleased. "Did you?"

"Yes. I can't really put it into words."

She leaned closer and ran the tip of her tongue alongside his lips. Tempting him. Seducing him, slowly and deliberately. "Then show me, Rico. Show me how much you enjoyed it. Let's get wild again."

He was already moving into action, tugging off his shirt and bending down to remove his shoes and socks. She wanted wild, he would give her wild. Texas wild. Following his lead, she began stripping off her clothes. He lowered his jeans and briefs while watching her ease her own jeans down her thighs. He discovered last night that she wore the cutest panties. Colorful. Sexy. No thongs or bikinis. They were hip-huggers, and she had the shapely hips for them. They looked great on her. Even better off her.

He stood there totally nude while she eased her panties down. She was about to toss them aside when he said, "Give them to me."

She lifted a brow as she tossed them over to him. He caught them with one hand and then raised them to his nose. He inhaled her womanly scent. His erection throbbed and his mouth watered, making him groan. He tossed her panties aside and looked at her, watching her nipples harden before his eyes.

He lowered his gaze to her sex. She kept things simple, natural. Some men liked bikini or Brazilian, but he preferred natural. She was beautiful there, her womanly core covered with dark curls.

His tongue felt thick in his mouth, and he knew where he wanted it to be. He moved across the room and dropped to his knees in front of her. Grabbing her thighs he rested his head against her stomach and inhaled before he began kissing around her belly button and along her inner and outer thighs. He tasted her skin, licking it all over and branding it as his. And then he came face-to-face with the core of her and saw her glistening folds. With the tip of his tongue, he began lapping her up.

She grabbed hold of his shoulders, dug her fingernails into the blades, but he didn't feel any pain. He felt only pleasure as he continued to feast on her. Savoring every inch of her.

"Rico."

He heard her whimper his name, but instead of letting up, he penetrated her with his tongue, tightened his hold on her hips and consumed her.

He liked having his tongue in her sex, tasting her honeyed juices, sucking her and pushing her into the kind of pleasure only he had ever given her. Only him.

"Rico!"

She called out his name a little more forcefully this time, and he knew why. She removed her hands from his shoulders to dig into his hair as she released another high-pitched scream that almost shook the room. If hotel security came to investigate, it would be all her fault.

Moments later, she finished off her orgasm with an intense moan and would have collapsed to the floor had he not been holding her thighs. He stood. "That was just an appetizer, baby. Now for the meal."

Picking her up in his arms he carried her to the bedroom, but instead of placing her on the bed, he grabbed one of the pillows and moved toward the huge chair. He sat and positioned her in his lap, facing him. Easing up he placed the pillows under his knees.

"Now, this is going to work nicely. You want wild, I'm about to give you wild," he whispered, adjusting her body so that she was straddling him with her legs raised all the way to his shoulders. He lifted her hips just enough so he could ease into her, liking the feel of being skin-to-skin with her. The wetness that welcomed him as he eased inside made him throb even more, and he knew he must be leaking already, mingling with her wetness.

"You feel so good," he said in a guttural tone. They were almost on eye level, and he saw the deep desire in the depths of her gaze. She moved, gyrating her hips in his lap. Her movement caused him to moan, and then he began moving, setting the rhythm, rocking in place, grasping her hips tightly to receive his upward thrusts. And she met his demands, tilting her hips and pushing forward to meet him.

He could feel heat building between them, sensations overtaking them so intensely that he rocked harder, faster. His thrusts were longer, deeper, even more intense as they worked the chair and each other.

He knew the moment she came. He felt it gush all around him, triggering his own orgasm. He shuddered uncontrollably, as his body did one hell of a blast inside of her. She stared into his face and the look in her eyes told him she had felt his hot release shooting inside of her. And he knew that was another new experience for her. The thought was arousing, and he could only groan raggedly. "Oh, baby, I love coming inside of you. It feels so good."

"You feel good," she countered. And then she was kissing him with a passion that was like nothing he'd ever experienced before. No woman had ever put this much into her kiss. It was raw, but there was something else, something he couldn't define at the moment. It was more than just tongues tangling and mating aggressively. There were emotions beneath their actions. He felt them in every part of his body.

He would have given it further thought if she hadn't moved her mouth away to scream out another orgasm. As she sobbed his name, he felt his body explode again, as well. He cried out her name over and over as he came, increasing the rocking of the chair until he was convinced it would collapse beneath them.

But it didn't. It held up. Probably better than they did, he thought, as they fought for air and the power to breathe again. Megan's head fell to his chest and he rubbed her back gently. Passion had his vision so blurred he could barely see. But he could feel, and what he was feeling went beyond satisfying his lust for her. It was much deeper than that. With her naked body connected so tightly to his, he knew why they had been so in tune with each other from the first. He understood why the attraction had been so powerful that he hadn't been able to sleep a single night since without dreaming of her.

He loved her.

There was no other way to explain what he was feeling, no other way to explain why spending the rest of his life without her was something he couldn't do. He pulled in a deep breath before kissing her shoulder blades. When he felt her shiver, his erection began hardening inside of her all over again.

She felt it and lifted her head to stare at him with languid eyes, raising both brows. "You're kidding, right? You've just got to be."

He smiled and combed his hands through the thick curls on her head. "You said you wanted wild," he murmured softly.

She smiled and wrapped her hands around his neck, touching her own legs, which were still on his shoulders. "I did say that, didn't I?" she purred, beginning to rotate her hips in his lap.

He eased out of the chair with their bodies still locked together. "Yes, and now I'm going to take you against the wall."

"Hey, you awake over there?" Rico asked when he came to a traffic light. He glanced across the truck seat at Megan. She lifted her head and sighed. Never had she felt so satiated in her life. For a minute, she'd thought he would have to carry her out of the hotel room and down to the truck.

They had made love a couple more times after the chair episode. First against the wall like he'd said, and then later, after their nap, they'd made out in the shower. Both times had indeed been wild, and such rewarding experiences. Now she was bone-tired. She knew she would have to perk up before they got to the Bankses' place.

"I'm awake, but barely."

"You wanted it wild," he reminded her.

She smiled drowsily. "Yes, and you definitely know how to deliver."

He chuckled. "Thanks. And that's Texas wild. Wait

until I make love to you in Denver and show you Colorado wild."

She wondered if he realized what he'd insinuated. It sounded pretty much like he had every intention of continuing their affair. And since he didn't live in Denver did that mean he planned to come visit her at some point for pleasure rather than business?

Before she could ask him about what he'd said, his cell phone rang. After he checked the ID, Megan heard him let out a low curse. "I thought I told you not to call me."

"You didn't say you would sic the cops on me," Jeffery Claiborne accused.

"I didn't sic the cops on you. I wanted to check out your story. I have, and you lied. You need money for other things, and I'm not buying." He then clicked off the phone.

Megan had listened to the conversation. That was the second time he'd received a similar phone call in her presence. The thought that he was still connected to some woman in some way, even if he didn't want to be bothered, annoyed her. She tried pushing it from her mind and discovered she couldn't. A believer in speaking her mind, she said, "Evidently someone didn't understand your rule about not getting serious."

He glanced over at her. His gaze penetrated hers. "What are you talking about?"

"That call. That's the second time she's called while I was with you."

"She?"

"Yes, I assume it's a female," she said, knowing she really didn't have any right to assume anything.

He said nothing for a minute and then. "No, that

wasn't a female. That was the man who used to be my father."

She turned around in her seat. "Your father?" she asked, confirming what he'd said.

"Yes. He's called several times trying to borrow money from me. He's even called Savannah. Claims his life is in jeopardy because he owes a gambling debt. But I found out differently. Seems he has a drug problem, and he was fired from his last job a few months ago because of it."

Now it was her time to pause. Then she said, "So what are you going to do?"

He raised his brow and looked over at her. "What am I going to do?"

"Yes."

"Nothing. That man hurt my mother and because of him Jess lost hers."

Megan swallowed tightly, telling herself it wasn't any of her business, but she couldn't help interfering. "But he's your father, Rico."

"And a piss-poor one at that. I could never understand why he wasn't around for all the times that were important to me while growing up. His excuse was always that as a traveling salesman he had to be away. It never dawned on me, until later, that he really wasn't contributing to the household since we were mostly living off my mother's trust fund."

He stopped at another traffic light and said, "It was only later that we found out why he spent so much time in California. He was living another life with another family. He's never apologized for the pain he caused all of us, and he places the blame on everyone but himself. So, as far as me doing anything for him, the answer is

I don't plan on doing a single thing, and I meant what I just told him. I don't want him to call me."

Megan bit down on her lips to keep from saying anything else. It seemed his mind was pretty made up.

"Megan?"

She glanced over at him. "Yes?"

"I know family means a lot to you, and, believe it or not, it means a lot to me, too. But some things you learn to do without...especially if they are no good. Jeff Claiborne is bad news."

"Sounds like he needs help, like drug rehab or something."

"Yes, but it won't be my money paying for it."

His statement sounded final, and Megan had a problem with it. It was just her luck to fall in love with a man who had serious issues with his father. What had the man done to make Rico feel this way? Should she ask him about it? She immediately decided not to. She had enough brothers and male cousins to know when to butt out of their business...until it was a safe time to bring it back up again. And she would.

Fourteen

"Mr. Claiborne, Ms. Westmoreland," Dorothy said, reluctantly opening the door to let them in. "My daughter told me you called. We've told you everything, and I'm not sure it will be good on my grandmother to have to talk about it again."

Rico stared at her. "Just the other day you were saying you thought it would be good for her to talk about it."

"Yes, but that was before I saw what discussing it did to her," she said "Please have a seat."

"Thanks," he said, and he and Megan sat down on the sofa. "If your grandmother isn't available then perhaps you won't mind answering a few questions for us."

"I really don't know anything other than what Gramma Fanny told me over the years," she said, taking the chair across from them. "But I'll try my best because my grandmother hasn't been herself since your visit. She had trouble sleeping last night and that's not like her. I guess breaking a vow to keep a promise is weighing heavily on her conscience."

For some reason Rico felt it went deeper than that. "Thanks for agreeing to talk to us." He and Megan had decided that he would be the one asking the questions. "Everybody says your grandmother's memory is sharp as a tack. Is there any reason she would intentionally get certain facts confused?"

The woman seemed taken back. "What are you trying to say, Mr. Claiborne?"

Rico sighed deeply. He hadn't told Megan everything yet, especially about the recent report he'd gotten from Martin while she'd been sleeping. "Stephen Mitchelson was not the one who survived that fire, and I'd like to know why your grandmother would want us to think that he was."

The woman look surprised. "I don't know, but you seem absolutely certain my grandmother was wrong."

He wasn't absolutely certain, but he was sure enough, thanks to the information Martin had dug up on Mitchelson, especially the man's prison photo, which looked nothing like the photographs of Raphel that the Westmorelands had hanging on their wall at the main house in Denver.

He knew Megan was just as surprised by his assertion as Ms. Banks's granddaughter. But there was that gut feeling that wouldn't go away. "It could be that Clarice lied to her about everything," he suggested, although he knew that probably wasn't the case.

"Possibly."

"But that isn't the case, and you know it, don't you, Mr. Claiborne?"

Rico turned when he heard Fanny Banks's frail voice. She was standing in the doorway with her cane.

"Gramma Fanny, I thought you were still sleeping," Dorothy said, rushing over to assist her grandmother.

"I heard the doorbell."

"Well, Mr. Claiborne and Ms. Westmoreland are back to ask you more questions. They think that perhaps you were confused about a few things," Dorothy said, leading her grandmother over to a chair.

"I wasn't confused," the older woman said, settling in her chair. "Just desperate, child."

Confusion settled on Dorothy's face. "I don't understand."

Fanny Banks didn't say anything for a minute. She then looked over at Rico and Megan. "I'm glad you came back. The other day, I thought it would be easier to tell another lie, but I'm tired of lying. I want to tell the truth...no matter who it hurts."

Rico nodded. "And what is the truth, Ms. Fanny?"

"That it was me and not Clarice who went to Wyoming that year and got pregnant. And Clarice, bless her soul, wanted to help me out of my predicament. She came up with this plan. Both she and I were single women, but she had a nice aunt in the East who wanted children, so we were going to pretend to go there for a visit for six months, and I would have the baby there and give my baby to her aunt and uncle. It was the perfect plan."

She paused for a minute. "But a few weeks before we were to leave, Raphel showed up to deliver the news that Stephen had died in a fire, and Raphel wanted me to have the belongings that Stephen left behind. While he was here, he saw Clarice. I could see that they were instantly attracted to each other."

Rico glanced over at Megan. They knew firsthand just how that instant-attraction stuff worked. "Please go on, Ms. Fanny."

"I panicked. I could see Clarice was starting something with Raphel, which could result in her changing our plans about going out East. Especially when Raphel was hired on by Clarice's father to do odds and ends around their place. And when she confided in me that she had fallen in love with Raphel, I knew I had to do something. So I told her that Raphel was really my Stephen, basically the same story I told the two of you. She believed it and was upset with me for not telling him about the baby and for allowing him to just walk away and start a new life elsewhere. She had no idea I'd lied. Not telling him what she knew, she convinced her father Raphel was not safe to have around their place. Her father fired him."

She paused and rubbed her feeble hands together nervously. "My selfishness cost my best friend her happiness with Raphel. He never understood why she began rebuffing his advances, or why she had him fired. The day we caught the train for Virginia is the day he left Forbes. Standing upstairs in my bedroom packing, we watched him get in his old truck and drive off. I denied my best friend the one happiness she could have had."

Rico drew in a deep breath when he saw the tears fall from the woman's eyes. "What about the baby? Did Clarice have a baby?"

Ms. Fanny nodded. "Yes. I didn't find out until we reached her aunt and uncle's place that Clarice had gotten pregnant."

Megan gasped. "From Raphel?"

"Yes. She thought she'd betrayed me and that we

were having babies from the same man. Even then I never told her the truth. She believed her parents would accept her child out of wedlock and intended to keep it. She had returned to Texas after giving birth only to find out differently. Her parents didn't accept her, and she was returning to Virginia to make a life for her and her baby when the train derailed."

"So it's true, both her and the baby died," Megan said sadly.

"No."

"No?" Rico, Megan and Dorothy asked simultaneously.

"Clarice didn't die immediately, and her son was able to survive with minor cuts and bruises."

"Son?" Megan whispered softly.

"Yes, she'd given birth to a son, a child Raphel never knew about…because of me. The baby survived because Clarice used her body as a shield during the accident."

Fanny didn't say anything for a minute. "We got to the hospital before she died, and she told us about a woman she'd met on the train, a woman who had lost her baby a year earlier…and now the woman had lost her husband in the train wreck. He was killed immediately, although the woman was able to walk away with only a few scratches."

Dorothy passed her grandmother a tissue so she could wipe away her tears. Through those tears, she added, "Clarice, my best friend, who was always willing to make sacrifices for others, who knew she would not live to see the next day, made yet another sacrifice by giving her child to that woman." Ms. Fanny's aged voice trembled as she fought back more tears. "Because she believed my lie, she wasn't certain she could leave her baby with me to raise because I would be constantly reminded of his father's betrayal. And her aunt couldn't afford to take on another child after she'd taken on mine. So Clarice made sure she found her baby a good home before she died."

Megan wiped tears away from her own eyes, looked over at Rico and said softly, "So there might be more Westmorelands out there somewhere after all."

Rico nodded and took her hand and entwined their fingers. "Yes, and if there are, I'm sure they will be found."

Rico glanced back at Fanny, who was crying profusely, and he knew the woman had carried the guilt of what she'd done for years. Now, maybe she would be able to move on with what life she had left.

Standing, Rico extended his hand to Megan. "We have our answers, now it's time for us to go."

Megan nodded and then hugged the older woman. "Thanks for telling us the truth. I think it's time for you to forgive yourself, and my prayer is that you will."

Rico knew then that he loved Megan as deeply as any man could love a woman. Even now, through her own pain, she was able to forgive the woman who had betrayed not only her great-grandfather, but also the woman who'd given birth to his child…a child he hadn't known about.

Taking Megan's hand in his, he bid both Banks women goodbye and together he and Megan walked out the door.

Rico pulled Megan into his arms the moment the hotel room door closed behind them, taking her mouth with a hunger and greed she felt in every portion of his body. The kiss was long, deep and possessive. In response, she wrapped her arms around his neck and returned the kiss with just as much vigor as he was putting into it. Never had she been kissed with so much punch, so much vitality, want and need. She couldn't do anything but melt in his arms.

"I want you, Megan." He pulled back from the kiss to whisper across her lips, his hot breath making her shudder with need.

"And I want you, too," she whispered back, then outlined his lips with the tip of her tongue. She saw the flame that had ignited in his eyes, felt his hard erection pressed against her and knew this man who had captured her heart would have her love forever.

Megan wanted to forget about Ms. Fanny's deceit, her betrayal of Clarice, a woman who would have done anything for her. She didn't want to think about the child Clarice gave up before she died, the child her great-grandfather had never known about. And she didn't want to think of her great-grandfather and how confused he must have been when the woman he had fallen in love with—at first sight—had suddenly not wanted anything to do with him.

She felt herself being lifted up in Rico's arms and carried into the bedroom, where he placed her on the bed. He leaned down and kissed her again, and she couldn't help but moan deeply. When he released her mouth, she whispered, "Let's get wild again."

They reached for each other at the same time, tearing at each other's clothes as desire, as keen as it could get, rammed through her from every direction. They kissed intermittently while undressing, and when all their clothes lay scattered, Rico lifted her in his arms. Instinctively, she wrapped her legs around him. The thickness of him pressed against her, letting her know

he was willing, ready and able, and she was eager for
the feel of him inside of her.

He leaned forward and took her mouth again. His
tongue tasted her as if he intended to savor her until
the end of time.

He continued to kiss her, to stimulate her to sensual
madness as he walked with her over to the sofa. Once
there, he broke off the kiss and stood her up on the
sofa, facing him. Sliding his hands between her legs,
he spread her thighs wide.

"You still want wild, I'm going to give you wild," he
whispered against her lips. "Squat a little for me, baby.
I want to make sure I can slide inside you just right."

She bent her knees as he reached out and grabbed
her hips. His arousal was hard, firm and aimed right
at her, as if it knew just where it should go. To prove
that point, his erection unerringly slid between her wet
folds.

"Mercy," he said. He inched closer, and their pel-
vises fused. He leaned forward, drew in a deep breath
and touched his forehead to hers. "Don't move," he
murmured huskily, holding her hips as he continued
to ease inside of her, going deep, feeling how her inner
muscles clenched him, trying to pull everything out of
him. "I wish our bodies could stay locked together like
this forever," he whispered.

She chuckled softly, feeling how deeply inside of
her he was, how closely they were connected. "Don't
know how housekeeping is going to handle it when
they come in our room tomorrow to clean and find us
in this position."

She felt his forehead move when he chuckled. His
feet were planted firmly on the floor, and she was
standing on the sofa. But their bodies were joined in a

way that had tingling sensations moving all over her naked skin.

He then pulled his forehead back to look at her. "Ready?"

She nodded. "Yes, I'm ready."

"Okay, then let's rock."

With his hands holding her hips and her arms holding firm to his shoulders, they began moving, rocking their bodies together to a rhythm they both understood. Her nipples felt hard as they caressed his chest, and the way he was stroking her insides made her groan out loud.

"Feel that?" he asked, hitting her at an angle that touched her G-spot and caused all kinds of extraordinary sensations to rip through her. She released a shuddering moan.

"Yes, I feel it."

"Mmm, what about this?" he asked, tilting her hips a little to stroke her from another angle.

"Oh, yes." More sensations cascaded through her.

"And now what about this?" He tightened his hold on her hips, widened her legs even more and began thrusting hard within her. She watched his features and saw how they contorted with pleasure. His eyes glistened with a need and hunger that she intended to satisfy.

As he continued to rock into her, she continued to rock with him. He penetrated her with long, deep strokes. His mouth was busy at her breasts, sucking the nipples into his mouth, nipping them between his teeth. And then he did something below—she wasn't sure what—but he touched something inside of her that made her release a deep scream. He immediately silenced her by covering her mouth with his, still thrusting inside of her and gripping her hips tight. This was definitely wild.

She felt him. Hot molten liquid shot inside of her, and she let out another scream as she was thrown into another intense orgasm. She closed her eyes as the explosion took its toll.

"Wrap your legs around me now, baby."

She did so, and he began walking them toward the bed, where they collapsed together. He pulled her into his arms and gazed down at her. "I love you," he whispered softly.

She sucked in a deep breath and reached out to cup his jaw in her hand. "And I love you, too. I think I fell in love with you the moment you looked at me at the wedding reception."

He chuckled, pulling her closer. "Same here. Besides wanting you extremely badly, another reason I didn't want you to come to Texas with me was because I knew how much finding out about Clarice and Raphel meant to you. I didn't want to disappoint you."

"You could never disappoint me, but you will have to admit that we make a good team."

Rico leaned down and kissed her lips. "We most certainly do. I think it's time to take the Rico and Megan show on the road, don't you?"

She lifted a brow. "On the road?"

"Yes, make it permanent." When she still had a confused look on her face, he smiled and said, "You know. Marriage. That's what two people do when they discover they love each other, right?"

Joy spread through Megan, and she fought back her tears. "Yes."

"So is that a yes, that you will marry me?"

"Did you ask?"

He untangled their limbs to ease off the bed to get down on his knees. He reached out for her hand. "Megan Westmoreland, will you be my wife so I can have the right to love you forever?"

"Can we get wild anytime we want?"

"Yes, anytime we want."

"Then yes, Ricardo Claiborne, I will marry you."

"We can set a date later, but I intend to put an engagement ring on your finger before leaving Texas."

"Oh, Rico. I love you."

"And I love you, too. I'm not perfect, Megan, but I'll always try to be the man you need." He eased back in bed with a huge masculine smile on his face. "We're going to have a good life together. And one day I believe those other Westmorelands will be found. It's just so sad Fanny Banks has lived with that guilt for so many years."

"Yes, and she wasn't planning on telling us the truth until we confronted her again. Why was that?" Megan asked.

"Who knows? Maybe she was prepared to take her secret to the grave. I only regret Raphel never knew about his child. And there's still that fourth woman linked to his name. Isabelle Connors."

"Once I get back to Denver and tell the family everything, I'm sure someone will be interested in finding out about Isabelle as well as finding out what happened to Clarice and Raphel's child."

"You're anxious to find out as well, right?"

"Yes. But I've learned to let go. Finding out if there are any more Westmorelands is still important to me, but it isn't the most important thing in my life anymore. You are."

Megan sighed as she snuggled more deeply into Rico's arms. She had gotten the answers she sought, but there were more pieces to the puzzle that needed to be found. And eventually they would be. At the moment, she didn't have to be the one to find them. She felt cherished and loved.

But there were a couple of things she needed to discuss with Rico. "Rico?"

"Yes, baby?"

"Where will we live? Philly or Denver?"

He reached out and caressed the side of her face gently. "Wherever you want to live. My home, my life is with you. Modern technology makes it possible for me to work from practically anywhere."

She nodded, knowing her home and life was with him as well and she would go wherever he was. "And do you want children?"

He chuckled. "Most certainly. I intend to be a good father."

She smiled. "You'll be the best. There are good fathers and there are some who could do better...who should have done better. But they are fathers nonetheless."

She pulled back and looked up at him. "Like your father. At some point you're going to have to find it in your heart to forgive him, Rico."

"And why do you figure that?" She could tell from the tone of his voice and the expression on his face that he definitely didn't think so.

"Because," she said, leaning close and brushing a kiss across his lips. "Your father is the only grandfather our children will have."

"Not true. My mother has remarried, and he's a good man."

She could tell Rico wanted to be stubborn. "I'm

sure he is, so in that case our children will have two grandfathers. And you know how important family is to me, and to you, as well. No matter what, Jeff Claiborne deserves a second chance. Will you promise me that you'll give him one?"

He held her gaze. "I'll think about it."

She knew when not to push. "Good. Because it would make me very happy. And although I've never met your dad, I believe he can't be all bad."

Rico lifted a brow. "How do you figure that?"

"Because you're from his seed, and you, Rico, are all good. I am honored to be the woman you want as your wife."

She could tell her words touched him, and he pulled her back down to him and kissed her deeply, thoroughly and passionately. "Megan Westmoreland Claiborne," Rico said huskily, finally releasing her lips. "I like the sound of that."

She smiled up at him. "I like the sound of that, as well."

Then she kissed him, deciding it was time to get wild again.

Two weeks later, New York

Rico looked around at the less than desirable apartment complex, knowing the only reason he was here was for closure. He might as well get it over with. The door was opened on the third knock and there stood the one man Rico had grown up loving and admiring— until he'd learned the truth.

He saw his father study Rico's features until recognition set in. Rico was glad his father recognized him because he wasn't sure if he would have recognized his father if he'd passed the old man in the street. It was obvious that drugs and alcohol had taken their toll. Jeff looked ten years older than what Rico knew his age to be. And the man who'd always taken pride in how he looked and dressed appeared as if he was all but homeless.

"Ricardo. It's been a while."

Instead of answering, Rico walked past his father to stand in the middle of the small, cramped apartment. When his father closed the door behind him, Rico decided to get to the point of his visit.

He shoved his hands into his pockets and said, "I'm getting married in a few months to a wonderful woman who believes family is important. She also believes everyone should have the ability to forgive and give others a second chance."

Rico paused a moment and then added, "I talked to Jessica and Savannah and we're willing to do that…to help you. But you have to be willing to help yourself. Together, we're prepared to get you into rehab and pay all the expenses to get you straightened out. But that's as far as our help will go. You have to be willing to get off the drugs and the alcohol. Are you?"

Jeff Claiborne dropped down in a chair that looked like it had seen better days and held his head in his hands. "I know I made a mess of things with you, Jessica and Savannah. And I know how much I hurt your mom…and when I think of what I drove Janice to do…" He drew in a deep breath. "I know what I did, and I know you don't believe me, but I loved them both—in different ways. And I lost them both."

Rico really didn't want to hear all of that, at least not now. He believed a man could and should love only one woman, anything else was just being greedy and without morals. "Are you willing to get help?"

"Are the three of you able to forgive me?"

Rico didn't say anything for a long moment and then said, "I can't speak for Jessica and Savannah, but with me it'll take time."

Jeff nodded. "Is it time you're willing to put in?"

Rico thought long and hard about his father's question. "Only if you're willing to move forward and get yourself straightened out. Calling your children and begging for money to feed your drug habit is unacceptable. Just so you know, Jess and Savannah are married to good men. Chase and Durango are protective of their wives and won't hesitate to kick your ass—father or no father—if you attempt to hurt my sisters."

"I just want to be a part of their lives. I have grandkids I haven't seen," Jeff mumbled.

"And you won't be seeing them if you don't get yourself together. So back to my earlier question, are you willing to go to rehab to get straightened out?"

Jeff Claiborne stood slowly. "Yes, I'm willing."

Rico nodded as he recalled the man his father had been once and the pitiful man he had become. "I'll be back in two days. Be packed and ready to go."

"All right, son."

Rico tried not to cringe when his father referred to him as "son," but the bottom line, which Megan had refused to let him deny, was that he was Jeff Claiborne's son.

Then the old man did something Rico didn't expect. He held his hand out. "I hope you'll be able to forgive me one day, Ricardo."

Rico paused a moment and then he took his father's hand, inhaling deeply. "I hope so, too."

Epilogue

"Beautiful lady, may I have this dance?"

"Of course, handsome sir."

Rico led Megan out to the dance floor and pulled her into his arms. It was their engagement party, and she was filled with so much happiness being surrounded by family and friends. It seemed no one was surprised when they returned from Texas and announced they were engaged. Rico had taken her to a jeweler in Austin to pick out her engagement ring, a three-carat solitaire.

They had decided on a June wedding and were looking forward to the day they would become man and wife. This was the first of several engagement parties for them. Another was planned in Philly and would be given by Rico's grandparents. Megan had met them a few weeks ago, and they had welcomed her to the family. They thought it was time their only grandson decided to settle down.

He pulled her closer and dropped his arms past her waist as their bodies moved in sensual sync with the music. Rico leaned in and hummed the words to the song in her ear. There was no doubt in either of their minds that anyone seeing them could feel the heat between them…and the love.

Rico tightened his arms around her and gazed down at her. "Enjoying yourself?"

"Yes, what about you?"

He chuckled. "Yes." He glanced around. "There are a lot of people here tonight."

"And they are here to celebrate the beginning of our future." She looked over his shoulder and chuckled.

Rico lifted a brow. "What's so funny?"

"Riley. Earlier today, he and Canyon pulled straws to see who would be in charge of Blue Ridge Management's fortieth anniversary Christmas party this year, and I heard he got the short end and isn't happy about it. We have close to a thousand employees at the family's firm and making sure the holiday festivities are top-notch is important…and a lot of work. I guess he figures doing the project will somehow interfere with his playtime, if you know what I mean."

Rico laughed. "Yes, knowing Riley as I do, I have a good idea what you mean."

The music stopped, and Rico took her hand and led her out the French doors and onto the balcony. It was the first week in November, and it had already snowed twice. According to forecasters, it would be snowing again this weekend.

They had made Denver their primary home. However, they planned to make periodic trips to Philly to visit Rico's grandparents, mother and stepfather. They would make occasional trips to New York as well to check on Rico's father, who was still in rehab. Megan had met him and knew it would be a while before he recovered, but at least he was trying.

"You better have a good reason for bringing me out here," she said, shivering. "It's cold, and, as you can see, I'm not wearing much of anything."

He'd noticed. She had gorgeous legs and her dress showed them off. "I'll warm you."

He wrapped his arms around her, pulled her to him and kissed her deeply. He was right; he was warming her. Immediately, he had fired her blood. She melted a little with every stroke of his tongue, which stirred a hunger that could still astound her.

Rico slowly released her mouth and smiled down at her glistening lips. Megan was his key to happiness, and he intended to be hers. She was everything he could possibly want and then some. His goal in life was to make her happy. Always.

* * * * *

"I'm going to be a single mum."

Nick sat back in his seat, looking stunned. "How? Who's going to be the father?"

"I'm going to use a donor."

After a long moment of silence, Nick said, "You really want to do it. Have a baby, I mean."

"I really do."

"What if I had a better way? For both of us."

Both of them? She failed to see how her plan to have a baby could in any way benefit him. "I'm not sure what you mean."

"I know the perfect man to be the father of your baby. Someone who would actually be around. Someone willing to take financial responsibility for the rest of the baby's life."

Whoever this so-called perfect man was, he sounded too good to be true. "Oh, yeah?" she said. "Who?"

He leaned forward, his dark eyes serious. "Me."

Dear Reader,

Welcome to my new series, THE CAROSELLI INHERITANCE! And the next installment of my "Getting to know Michelle" reader letters.

Spring has always been my favorite time of year. For the past twenty-two years, since we bought our first house, it's meant that it's time to plant the vegetable garden. I've had many hobbies over the years—drawing, painting, crafts, crochet—but by far my favorite and most consistent is gardening.

First I have to decide what to plant. Around the middle of February I make a list of what we'll need for the year, then I fire up the lights in the greenhouse in my basement, run to English Gardens for seeds and soil, and get to work. I've been starting my own plants for several years now, although I used to buy them, and though I know it sounds a little silly, each year it continues to amaze me to watch the tender little seedlings sprout, then grow into thriving plants.

Strangely enough, the actual planting is my least favorite part, and I can't say I'm thrilled picking weeds either, but when I bite into that first big, juicy tomato, snap a crisp green bean or slice a tangy clove of fresh garlic, it's worth the work! Though by now most of the plants are probably shriveled and dead—if I'm lucky I may still have a sprig or two of broccoli to pick—that's okay. I get to start it all over again in a few months!

Best,

Michelle

CAROSELLI'S CHRISTMAS BABY

BY
MICHELLE CELMER

Published in Great Britain 2012
by Mills & Boon, an imprint of Harlequin (UK) Limited,
Eton House, 18-24 Paradise Road, Richmond, Surrey TW9 1SR

© Michelle Celmer 2012

ISBN: 978 0 263 89348 9
ebook ISBN: 978 1 408 97213 7

51-1212

Printed and bound in Spain
by Blackprint CPI, Barcelona

Michelle Celmer is a bestselling author of more than thirty books. When she's not writing, she likes to spend time with her husband, kids, grandchildren and a menagerie of animals.

Michelle loves to hear from readers. Visit her website, www.michellecelmer.com, like her on Facebook, or write her at PO Box 300, Clawson, MI 48017, USA.

For Steve, who truly is my hero.

Prologue

"As your attorney, and your friend, I have to say, Giuseppe, that I think this is a really bad idea."

Giuseppe Caroselli sat in his wingback leather chair—the one his wife, Angelica, God rest her saintly soul, had surprised him with for his eighty-fifth birthday—while Marcus Russo eyed him furtively from the sofa. And he was was right. This scheme Giuseppe had concocted had the potential to blow up in his face, and create another rift in a family that already had its share of quarrels. But he was an old man and time was running low. He could sit back and do nothing, but the potential outcome was too heartbreaking to imagine. He had to do *something*.

"It must be done," he told Marcus. "I've waited long enough."

"I can't decide which would be worse," Marcus said, rising from the sofa and walking to the window that boasted a picturesque view of the park across the street, though most of the leaves had already fallen. "If they say no, or they actually say yes."

"They've left me no choice. For the good of the family, it must be done." Carrying on the Caroselli legacy had always been his number one priority. It was the reason he had fled Italy at the height of the Second World War, speaking not a word of English, with a only few dollars in the pocket of his trousers and his *nonni*'s secret family chocolate recipe emblazoned in his memory. He knew the Caroselli name was destined for great things.

He'd worked scrimped and saved until he had the money to start the first Caroselli Chocolate shop in downtown Chicago. In the next sixty years the Caroselli name grew to be recognized throughout the world, yet now it was in danger of dying out forever. Of his eight grandchildren and six great-grandchildren, there wasn't a single heir to carry on the family name. Though his three sons each had a son, they were all still single and seemed to have no desire whatsoever to marry and start families of their own.

Giuseppe had no choice but to take matters into his own hands, and make them an offer they simply could not refuse.

There was a soft rap on the study door, and the butler appeared, tall and wiry and nearly as old as his charge. "They're here, sir."

Right on time, Giuseppe thought with a smile. If there was one thing that could be said about his grandsons, they were unfailingly reliable. They were also as ambitious as Giuseppe had been at their age, which is why he believed this might work. "Thank you, William. Send them in."

The butler nodded and slipped from the room. A few seconds later his grandsons filed in. First Nicolas, charming and affable, with a smile that had been known to get him out of trouble with authority, and into trouble with the ladies. Following him was Nick's cousin Robert, serious, focused and unflinchingly loyal. And last but not least, the oldest of all his grandchildren, ambitious, dependable Antonio Junior.

His joints protesting the movement, Giuseppe rose from his chair. "Thank you for coming, boys." He gestured to the couch. "Please, have a seat."

They did as he asked, all three looking apprehensive.

"You are obviously curious as to why you're here," Giuseppe said, easing back into his chair.

"I'd like to know why we had to keep it a secret," Nick said, his brow furrowed with worry. "And why is Marcus here? Is something wrong?"

"Are you ill?" Tony asked.

"Fit as a fiddle," Giuseppe said. Or as fit as an arthritic man of ninety-two could be. "There is a matter of great importance we must discuss."

"Is the business in trouble?" Rob asked. For him, the company always came first, which was both a blessing and a curse. Had he not been so career-focused, he could be married with children by now. They all could.

"This isn't about the business," he told them. "At least, not directly. This is about the Caroselli family name, which will die unless the three of you marry and have sons."

That earned him a collective eye roll from all three boys.

"*Nonno,* we've been through this before," Nick said. "I for one am not ready to settle down. And I think I speak for all of us when I say that another lecture isn't going to change that."

"I know, that's why this time I've decided to offer an incentive."

That got their attention. Tony leaned forward slightly and asked, "What sort of incentive?"

"In a trust I have placed the sum of thirty million dollars to be split three ways when each of you marries and produces a male heir."

Three jaws dropped in unison.

Nick was the first to recover. "You're seriously going to give us each ten *million* dollars to get hitched and have a kid?"

"A *son*. And there are conditions."

"If you're going to try to force us into arranged marriages with nice Italian girls from the homeland, forget it," Rob said.

If only he could be so lucky. And while he would love to see each of them marry a nice Italian girl, he was in no position to be picky. "You're free to marry whomever you please."

"So what's the catch?" Tony asked.

"First, you cannot tell a soul about the arrangement. Not your parents or your siblings, not even your intended. If you do, you forfeit your third of the trust and it will be split between the other two."

"And?" Nick said.

"If I should join your *nonni,* God rest her saintly soul, by the end of the second year and before a male heir is born to any one of you, the trust will be rolled back into my estate."

"So the clock is ticking," Nick said.

"Maybe. Of course, I could live to be one hundred. My doctor tells me that I'm in excellent health. But is that a chance any of you is willing to take? If you agree to my terms, that is."

"What about Jessica?" Nick asked. "She has four children, yet I suspect you've not given her a dime."

"I love your sister, Nick, and all my granddaughters, but their children will never carry the Caroselli name. I owe it to my parents, and my grandparents, and those who lived before them to keep the family name alive for future generations. But I also don't want to see my granddaughters hurt, which is why this must always remain a secret."

"Do you intend to have us sign some sort of contract?" Tony asked, turning to Marcus.

"That was my suggestion," Marcus told him, "but your grandfather refuses."

"No one will be signing anything," Giuseppe said. "You'll just have to trust that my word is good."

"Of course we trust your word, *Nonno*," Nick said, shooting the others a look. "You've never given us any reason not to."

"I feel the same way about the three of you. Which is why I trust you to keep our arrangement private."

Tony frowned. "What if you die? Won't the family learn about it then?"

"They won't suspect a thing. The money is already put aside, separate from the rest of my fortune, and as my attorney and executor to my will, Marcus and Marcus alone will have access to it. He will see that the money is distributed accordingly."

"What if we aren't ready to start families?" Rob asked.

Giuseppe shrugged. "Then you lose out on ten million dollars, and your third will go to your cousins."

All three boys glanced at each other. Knowing how proud and independent they were, there was still the very real possibility that they might deny his request.

"Do you expect an answer today?" Nick asked.

"No, but I would at least like your word that each of you will give my offer serious thought."

Another look was exchanged, then all three nodded.

"Of course we will, *Nonno*," Rob said.

Had he been standing, Giuseppe may have crumpled with relief, and if not for gravity holding him to the earth, the heavy weight lifted from his stooped shoulders surely would have set him aloft. It wasn't a guarantee, but they hadn't outright rejected the idea, either, and that was a start. And given their competitive natures, he was quite positive that if one agreed, the other two would eventually follow suit.

After several minutes of talk about the business and family, Nick, Rob and Tony left.

"So," Marcus asked, as the study door snapped closed behind them, "how do you suppose they'll react when they learn there is no thirty million dollars set aside?"

Giuseppe shrugged. "I think they will be so blissfully happy, and so grateful for my timely intervention, that the money will mean nothing to them."

"You have the money, Giuseppe. Have you considered actually giving it to them if they meet your terms?"

"And alienate my other grandchildren?" he scoffed. "What sort of man do you think I am?"

Marcus shook his head with exasperation. "And if you're wrong? If they do want the money? If they're angry that you lied to them?"

"They won't be." Besides, to carry on the Caroselli name—his legacy—that was a risk he was willing to take.

One

Late again.

Terri Phillips watched with a mix of irritation and amusement as her best friend, Nick Caroselli, walked briskly through the dining room of the bistro to their favorite booth near the bar, where they met every Thursday night for dinner.

With his jet-black hair, smoldering brown eyes, warm olive complexion and lean physique, heads swiveled and forks halted halfway to mouths as he passed. But Nick being Nick, he didn't seem to notice. Not that he was unaware of his effect on women, nor was he innocent of using his charm to get his way when the need arose.

Not that it worked on her anymore.

"Sorry I'm late," he said with that crooked grin he flashed when he was trying to get out of trouble. Fat snowflakes peppered the shoulders of his wool coat and dotted his hair, and his cheeks were rosy from the cold, meaning he'd walked the two blocks from the world head-quarters of Caroselli Chocolate. "Work was crazy today."

"I've only been here a few minutes," she said, even though it had actually been more like twenty. Long enough to have downed two glasses of the champagne they were supposed to be toasting with.

He leaned in to brush a kiss across her cheek, the rasp of his evening stubble rough against her skin. She breathed in the whisper of his sandalwood soap—a birthday gift from her—combined with the sweet scent of chocolate that clung to him every time he spent the day in the company test kitchen.

"Still snowing?" she asked.

"It's practically a blizzard out there." Nick shrugged out of his coat, then stuck his scarf and leather gloves in the sleeve—a habit he'd developed when they were kids, after misplacing endless sets of mittens and scarves—then hung it on the hook behind their booth. "At this rate, we may actually get a white Christmas this year."

"That would be nice." Having spent the first nine years of her life in New Mexico, she'd never even seen snow until she'd moved to Chicago. To this day, she still loved it. Of course, having a home business meant no snowy commute, so she was biased.

"I ordered our usual," she said as Nick slid into his seat.

He loosened his tie, and gestured to the champagne bottle. "Are we celebrating something?"

"You could say that."

He plucked his napkin from the table and draped it across his lap. "What's up?"

"First," she said, "you'll be happy to know that I broke up with Blake."

Nick beamed. "Well, damn, that is a reason to celebrate!"

Nick had never liked her most recent boyfriend—the latest in a long and depressing string of failed relationships. He didn't think Blake had what it took to make Terri happy. Turned out he was right. Even if it did take her four months to see it.

But last week Blake had mentioned offhandedly that his lease was almost up, and it seemed silly that they should both be paying rent when he spent most of his time at her place, anyway. Despite being more than ready to get married and start a family, when she imagined doing it with him, she'd felt…well, not much of anything, actually. Which was definitely not a good way to feel about a potential husband and father of her children. It was proof that, as Nick had warned her, she was settling again.

Nick poured himself a glass of champagne and took a sip. "So, what did he say when you dumped him?"

"That I'll never find anyone else like him."

Nick laughed. "Well, yeah, isn't that the point? He was about as interesting as a paper clip. With half the personality."

She wouldn't deny that he'd been a little, well…bland. His idea of a good time was sitting at the computer, with it's twenty-seven-inch high-def monitor, for hours on end playing *World of Warcraft* while she watched television or read. The truth is, he would probably miss her computer more than her.

"He's an okay guy. He just isn't the guy for me," she told Nick. One day he would meet the game addict of his dreams and they would live a long happy life in cyberspace together.

Their waitress appeared to deliver their meal. A double pepperoni deep-dish pizza and cheesy bread. When she was gone, Nick said, "He's out there, you know. The one for you. You'll find him."

She used to think so, too. But here she was almost thirty with not a single prospect anywhere in her near future. Her life plan had her married with a couple kids already. Which is why she had decided to take matters into her own hands.

"There's something else we're celebrating," she told Nick. "I'm going to have a baby."

He bolted upright and set down his glass so hard she was surprised it didn't shatter against the tiled tabletop. "What? When? Is it Blake's?"

"God, no!" She could just imagine that. The kid would probably be born with a game remote fused to its hands.

Nick leaned forward and hissed under his breath, "Whoever it is, he damn well better be planning to do right by you and the baby."

Always looking out for her, she thought with a shot of affection so intense it burned. When he wasn't getting her into trouble, that is. Although it was usually the other way around. It was typically her making rash decisions, and Nick talking sense into her. This time was different. This time she knew exactly what she was doing.

"There is no *who,*" she told him, dishing them each out a slice of pizza. "I'm not actually pregnant. Yet."

Nick frowned. "Then why did you say you're having a baby?"

"Because I will be, hopefully within the next year. I'm going to be a single mom."

He sat back in his seat, looking stunned. "How? I mean, who's going to be the father?"

"I'm going to use a donor."

"A *donor?*" His dark brows pulled together. "You're not serious."

She shoved down the deep sting of disappointment. She had hoped he would understand, that he would be happy for her. Clearly, he wasn't. "Completely serious. I'm ready. I'm financially sound, and since I work at home, I won't have to put the baby in day care. The timing is perfect."

"Wouldn't it be better if you were married?"

"I've pretty much struck out finding Mr. Right. I always said that I wanted to have my first baby by the time I'm thirty, and I'm almost there. And you know that I've always wanted a family of my own. Since my aunt died, I've got no one."

"You've got me," he said, his expression so earnest her heart melted.

Yes, she had him, not to mention his entire crazy family, but it wasn't the same. When the chips were down, she was still an outsider.

"This doesn't mean we aren't going to be friends still," she said. "In fact, I'll probably need you more than ever. You'll be the baby's only other family. Uncle Nicky."

The sentiment did nothing to erase the disenchantment from his expression. He pushed away his plate, as if he'd suddenly lost his appetite, and said, "You deserve better than a sperm donor."

"I don't exactly have the best luck with men."

"But what about the baby?" Nick said, sounding testier by the second. "Doesn't it deserve to have two parents?"

"As you well know, having two parents doesn't necessarily make for a happy childhood."

His deepening frown said that he knew she was right. Though he didn't like to admit it, his childhood had left deep, indelible scars.

"I was hoping you would understand," she said, and for some stupid reason she felt like crying. And she hardly *ever* cried. At least, not in front of other people. All it had ever earned her from her aunt—who didn't have a sympathetic bone in her body—was a firm lecture.

"I do," Nick said, reaching across the table for her hand. "I just want you to be happy."

"This *will* make me happy."

He smiled and gave her hand a squeeze. "Then I'm happy, too."

She hoped he really meant that. That he wasn't just humoring her. But as they ate their pizza and chatted, Nick seemed distracted, and she began to wonder if telling him about having a baby had been a bad idea, although for the life of her she wasn't sure why it would matter either way to him.

After they finished eating, they put on their coats and were walking to the door when Nick asked, "Did you drive or take the bus?"

"Bus," she said. If she thought she might be drinking, she always opted for public transportation. If the man who had plowed into her father's car had only been as responsible, she wouldn't be an orphan.

"Walk back to the office with me and I'll drive you home."

"Okay."

The snow had stopped, but a prematurely cold wind whipped her hair around her face and the pavement was slippery, which made the two-block hike tricky. It was how she rationalized the fact that he was unusually quiet and there was a deep furrow in his brow.

When they got to the Caroselli Chocolate world headquarters building, it was closed for the night, so Nick used a key card to let them in. With a retail store taking up most of the ground floor, the lobby smelled of the chocolate confections lining the shelves. Everything from standard chocolate bars to gourmet chocolate-covered apples.

Nick felt around in his pockets, then cursed under his breath. "I left my car keys in my office."

"You want me to wait down here?"

"No, you can come up." Then he grinned and said, "Unless you're an industrial spy trying to steal the Caroselli secret recipe."

"Right, because we both know what an accomplished cook I am." If there were a way to burn water, she would figure it out. Meaning she ordered out a lot, and the rest of the time ate microwave dinners.

They walked past the receptionist's desk and he used his key card to activate the elevator. Only authorized personnel and approved visitors were allowed above the ground floor. And no one but the Caroselli family and employees with special clearance were allowed in the test kitchen.

Nick was quiet the entire ride up to the fourth floor, and while they walked down the hall to his office. She had to smile as he opened the door and switched on the light, and she saw the lopsided stacks of papers and memos on the surface of his desk, leaving no space at all to work. She suspected that this was why he spent so much time on the top floor in the kitchen.

He opened the desk drawer and pulled out his car keys, but then he just stood there. Something was definitely bugging him and she needed to know what.

"What's the matter, Nick? And don't tell me nothing. I've known you long enough to know when something is wrong."

"I've just been thinking."

"About me having a baby?"

He nodded.

"It's what I want."

"Then there's something we need to talk about."

"Okay," she said, her heart sinking just the tiniest bit, mostly because he wouldn't look at her. And he must have been anticipating a long discussion because he took off his coat and tossed it over the back of his chair. She did the same, then nudged aside a pile of papers so she could sit beside him on the edge of his desk.

He was quiet for several long seconds, as though he was working something through in his head, then he looked at her and said, "You really want to do it? Have a baby, I mean."

"I really do."

"What if I had a better way?"

"A better way?"

He nodded. "For both of us."

Both of them? She failed to see how her plan to have a baby could in any way benefit him. "I'm not sure what you mean."

"I know the perfect man to be the father of your baby. Someone who would actually be around. Someone willing to take financial responsibility for the rest of the baby's life."

Whoever this so-called perfect man was, he sounded too good to be true. "Oh, yeah?" she said. "Who?"

He leaned forward, his dark eyes serious. "Me."

For a second she was too stunned to speak. Nick wanted to have a baby with her? "Why? You've been pretty adamant about the fact that you don't want children."

"Trust me when I say that it will be a mutually advantageous arrangement."

"Advantageous how?"

"What I'm about to tell you, you have to promise not to repeat to anyone. *Ever*."

"Okay."

"Say, 'I promise.'"

She rolled her eyes. What were they, twelve? *"I promise."*

"Last week my grandfather called me, Rob and Tony to his house for a secret meeting. He offered us ten million dollars each to produce a male heir to carry on the Caroselli name."

"Holy crap."

"That was pretty much my first reaction, too. I wasn't sure I was even going to accept his offer. I'm really not ready to settle down, but then you mentioned your plan…" He shrugged. "I mean, how much more perfect could it be? You get the baby you want and I get the money."

It made sense in a weird way, but her and *Nick?*

"Of course, we would have to get married," he said.

Whoa, wait a minute. *"Married?* Haven't you told me about a million times that you'll *never* get married?"

"You know how traditional *Nonno* is. I don't have a choice. But the minute I have the cash in hand, we can file for a quickie divorce. An ironclad prenup should eliminate any complications…not that I expect there would be any."

"That sounds almost too easy."

"Well, we will have to make it look convincing."

Why did she get the feeling she wasn't going to like this? "What exactly do you mean by *convincing?*"

"You'll have to move into my place."

A fake marriage was one thing, but to *live* together? "I don't think that's a good idea."

"I have lots of space. You can have the spare bedroom and you can turn the den into your office."

Space wasn't the issue. They'd tried the roommate thing right after college, in an apartment more than spacious enough for two people. Between the random girls parading in and out at ridiculous hours—and the fact that Nick never picked up after himself and left the sink filled with his dirty dishes while the dishwasher sat empty, and a couple dozen other annoying quirks and habits he had—after two months she'd reached her limit. Had she stayed even a day longer, it would have either killed their friendship, or she would have killed him.

"Nick, you know I love you, and I value our friendship beyond anything else, but we've tried this before. It didn't work."

"That was almost eight years ago. I'm sure we've both matured since then."

"Have you stopped being a slob, too? Because I loathe the thought of spending the next nine months cleaning up after you."

"You won't have to. I have a cleaning service come in three times a week. And for the record, I'm not particularly looking forward to you nagging me incessantly."

"I do not nag," she said, and he shot her a look. "Okay, maybe I nag a little, but only out of sheer frustration."

"Then we'll just have to make an effort to be more accommodating to each other. I promise to keep on top of the clutter, if you promise not to nag."

That might be easier said than done.

"Think how lucky the kid will be," Nick said. "Most divorced parents hate each other. Mine haven't had a civilized conversation in years. His will be best friends."

He had a good point there. "So that means you'll be a regular part of the baby's life?"

"Of course. And he'll have lots of cousins, and aunts and uncles."

Wasn't a part-time father better than no father at all? And she would never have to worry financially. She knew Nick would take care of the baby. Not that she was hurting for money. If she was careful, the trust her aunt had willed her, combined with her growing web design business, would keep her living comfortably for a very long time. But Nick would see that the baby went to the best schools, and had every advantage, things she couldn't quite afford. And he would be a part of a big, loving, happy family. Which was more than she could say for her own childhood. The baby might even join the Caroselli family business some day.

"And suppose, God forbid, something should happen to you," he said. "Where would the baby go if he was fathered by a donor?"

Having lost her own parents, of course that was a concern. Now that her aunt was gone, there was no family left to take the child if she were in an accident or… Although the baby would probably be better off in foster care than with someone like her aunt. She would have been.

"With me as the father, he'll always have a family," Nick said.

As completely crazy as the idea was, it did make sense. "I think it could work."

He actually looked excited, although who wouldn't be over the prospect of ten million bucks? Why settle for the life of a millionaire when he could be a *multi*millionaire?

"So," he said, "is that an 'I'm still thinking about it,' or is that a definite yes?"

Though she was often guilty for jumping into things without full consideration, maybe in this case overthinking it would be a bad idea. Or maybe she just didn't want the opportunity to talk herself out of it. They would both be getting what they wanted. More or less.

"I just have one more question," she said. "What about women?"

"What about them?"

"Will it be a different girl every other night? Will I have to listen to the moaning and the headboard knocking against the wall? See her traipsing around the next morning in nothing but her underwear and one of your shirts?"

"Of course not. As long as we're married, I wouldn't see anyone else."

"Nick, we're talking at least nine months. Can you even go that long without dating?"

"Do you really mean *dating,* or is that code for sex?"

"Either."

"Can you?"

She could. The real question was, did she want to? But to have a baby, wasn't it worth it?

"Maybe," Nick said, "we don't have to."

"Are you suggesting that we cheat on each other?" Even if it wasn't a real marriage, that could be an obstacle. And while she was sure Nick would have no trouble finding willing participants, with her big belly and swelling ankles, she was fairly certain no men would be fighting for the chance to get into her maternity jeans.

"I'm assuming you plan to use artificial insemination," he said.

She felt a little weird about discussing the particulars, but he was a part of this now. It would be his baby, too. "That or in vitro, which is much more reliable, but crazy expensive. Either way it could take several months."

"Or we could pay nothing at all," he said.

She must have looked thoroughly confused, because he laughed and said, "You have no idea what I'm talking about."

"I guess I don't."

"Think about it." He wiggled his eyebrows and flashed her a suggestive smile.

Wait a minute. He couldn't possibly mean—

"Why pay a doctor to get you pregnant," he said, "when we could just do it the old-fashioned way for free?"

Two

Terri gaped at Nick, her eyes—which were sometimes green and sometimes blue, depending on the light—wide with shock and horror. It took her several seconds to find her voice, and when she did, she said, a full octave higher than her usual range, "That was a joke, right?"

"Actually, I've never been more serious." Nick would be the first to admit it was a pretty radical idea, but on a scale of one to ten, this entire situation had a weird factor of about fifty.

He had given *Nonno*'s offer a lot of thought and had come to the conclusion that he just wasn't ready to settle down yet. It wasn't so much the idea of being a father that put him off—he loved kids—but the marriage end of the deal that gave him the willies. His parents had gone through hell, and put Nick and his two older sisters through it, too. Now with his sister Jessica's marriage in trouble, as well, the idea of marital bliss was nothing

more than a fairy tale to him. And not worth the pain of
the inevitable divorce. Not even for ten million dollars.

It had never occurred to him that the actual marriage
could be a sham. Not to mention so mutually advantageous. And who in his family would question the plau-
sibility that after twenty years of devoted friendship, his
and Terri's relationship had moved to the next level? The
women in his family ate up that kind of romantic garbage.

Terri tucked her long dark hair behind her ears. He'd
only seen her do this when she was nervous or uncomfortable, and that wasn't very often. She was one of the most
centered, secure and confident people he'd ever known.
Sometimes this led to her being a touch impulsive, but in
this instance could only work in his favor.

"The sooner this kid is born, the better," he told her.
"So why would we spend a lot of time and money on pro-
cedures that could take months to work?"

Indecision wrinkled the space between her brows and
she picked at the frayed cuff of her sweatshirt. "Aren't
you worried that it might make things weird between
us?" she asked.

"Maybe a little," he admitted. "But, haven't you ever
been curious?"

"Curious?"

He gave her arm a gentle nudge. "You've never wondered what it might be like if you and I…"

It took an awful lot to embarrass her, but there was a
distinct red hue working its way across her cheekbones.
That was a yes if he'd ever seen one, even if she didn't
want to admit it. And he couldn't deny that he'd thought
about it himself more than a time or two. She was funny
and smart and beautiful, so who could blame him?

"I've never told you this," he said. "But there was a
time when I had a pretty serious crush on you."

She blinked. "You did?"

He nodded. "Yep."

"When?"

"Our junior year of high school."

She looked genuinely stunned. "I—I had no idea."

That's because he'd never said a word about it. Up until then, he'd never viewed her in a sexual way. Nor, it seemed, did many other boys. She had been a late bloomer, a typical tomboy, lanky and tall—taller than all the other girls and even a fair share of the boys—and as far from feminine as a girl could be. But she'd spent the entire summer after their sophomore year in Europe with her aunt and something intriguing had happened. She left Chicago a girl, and returned a woman.

Boys in school began paying attention to her, talking about her in the locker room, and he wouldn't deny that she became the subject of a few of his own teenage fantasies. Not that he would have acted on those feelings. They were, after all, only friends, though that fact did little to erase the jealousy he felt when he saw her with other boys, or would hear the rumors of the things she had done with them. And as much as he liked how she changed, he resented her for it. He wanted the old Terri back. But he got over it, of course. What choice did he have?

"Why didn't you tell me?" she asked.

"Aside from the fact that I thought it would probably freak you out?" He shrugged. "It was a crush. I had them all the time. And our friendship was too important to me to ruin over raging teenage hormones."

"But you would be willing to ruin it now?"

"Maybe if we were sleeping together just for the sake of doing it, but this is different. We have a legitimate reason to have sex."

In his experience, romantic love and friendship occupied opposite sides of the playing field, and he would never let one interfere with the other. Which is why he was so sure that if they approached this situation logically, it would work. And when all was said and done, everyone would get exactly what they wanted.

"It's a means to an end," he said. "It wouldn't *mean anything*."

She shot him a look. "That's just what every girl wants to hear when she's considering sleeping with a man."

"You get my point. And yes, it could potentially change our relationship, but not necessarily for the worse. It might even bring us closer together."

She didn't look convinced. Maybe she was opposed to the idea for an entirely different reason.

"Do you have moral objections?" he asked. "Or is it just that you find the idea of sleeping with me revolting?"

She rolled her eyes. "You are *not* revolting. And though it's embarrassing to admit, I had kind of a crush on you once, too."

If that was true, she'd done one hell of a job hiding it. "When?"

"It pretty much started the day I transferred into Thomas Academy school in fourth grade."

He recalled that day clearly, when she'd walked into his class, bitter, sullen and mad as hell. It was obvious to everyone in the elite private school that she was an outsider. And trouble. A fact she drove home that very first day when she had come up behind Nick on the playground and pushed him off his swing, knocking him face-first in the dirt. He wanted to shove her right back, but he'd had it drilled into him by his mother to respect girls, so he'd walked away instead. Which only seemed to fuel her lust for blood.

For days he'd tolerated kicks in the shin, pinches on

the arm, prods in the cafeteria line and endless ribbing from his buddies for not retaliating. With his parents in the middle of a nasty divorce, he'd had some anger issues of his own, and the unprovoked attacks started to grate on him. A week or so later she tripped him on his way to the lunch table, making him drop his tray and spill his spaghetti and creamed corn all over the cafeteria floor and himself. The other students laughed, and something inside Nick snapped. Before he realized what he was doing, he hauled off and popped her one right in the mouth.

The entire cafeteria went dead silent, everyone watching to see what would happen next, and he'd felt instantly ashamed for hitting a weak, defenseless girl.

He would never forget the way he'd stood watching her, waiting for the tears to start as blood oozed from the corner of her lip and down her chin. And how she balled her fist, took a swing right back at him, clipping him in the jaw. He was so stunned, he just stood there. But she wasn't finished. She launched herself at him, knocking him to the floor, and there was nothing girly about it. No biting or scratching or hair-pulling. She fought like a boy, and her fists were lethal weapons. He had no choice but to fight back. To defend himself. Plus, he had his pride, because to a nine-year-old boy, being accepted meant everything.

It had taken three teachers to pry them apart and haul them to the dean's office, both of them bruised and bloody. They were given a fourteen-day in-school suspension, though that was mild compared to the tirade he'd endured from his father, and the disappointment from his mother, who he knew were miserable enough without any help from him.

He spent the next two weeks holed up in a classroom alone with Terri, and as the black eyes faded and the split lips healed, something weird happened. To this day he wasn't sure whether it was mutual admiration or two lost souls finding solace in each other, but they walked out of that room friends, and had been ever since.

"So, you beat the snot out of me because you *liked* me?" he said.

"It wasn't even a conscious thing. Until I looked back at it years later did I realize why I was so mean to you. But once we became friends, I never thought about you in a romantic way."

"Never?"

"Why would I?" she said, but a hot-pink blush crept up into her cheeks. She pushed herself off his desk and walked over to the window, looking out into the darkness, at the traffic crawling past on icy roads.

If she hadn't, why the embarrassment? Why was she running away from him?

He knew he should probably let it go, but he couldn't. "You never thought about what it might be like if I kissed you?"

With her back to him, she shrugged. "You kiss me all the time."

"Not a real kiss." But now that he'd gotten the idea into his head, he couldn't seem to shake it off. He *wanted* to kiss her.

He pushed off the desk, walked over to the window and stood behind her. He put his hands on her shoulders and she jerked, sucking in a surprised breath. "Nick…"

He turned her so she was facing him. She was so tall they were practically nose to nose. "Come on, aren't you the least bit curious?"

"It's just…it would be weird."

He propped a hand on the windowpane beside her

head, so she was blocked in by his arm on one side and the wall on the other. "How will you know until you try?"

He reached up to run his finger down her cheek, and not only was it crimson, but burning hot.

"Nick," she said, but it came out sounding low and breathy. It was a side of her that he didn't see often. A softer, vulnerable Terri, and he liked it. And it occurred to him, as he leaned in closer, that what he was feeling right now wasn't just curiosity. He was turned-on. And it was no longer the childish fantasies of a teenage boy who knew he wanted something, but wasn't quite sure what it was. This time Nick knew exactly what he wanted.

"One kiss," he told her, coming closer, so his mouth was just inches from hers. "And if it's really that awful, we won't ever do it again."

Heat rolled off her in waves. Her pulse was racing, and as she tentatively laid a hand near the collar of his jacket, he could feel her trembling. Was she afraid, or as sexually charged by this as he was? Or was it a little of both? With her hand strategically placed on his chest, she could either push him away, or grab his lapel and pull him in.

Which would it be?

He leaned in slowly, drawing out the suspense. When his lips were a fraction of an inch away, so near he could feel the flutter of her breath, as her fingers curled around the lapel of his jacket…a loud noise from the hallway startled them both and they jumped apart.

Damn it!

Nick walked to the door and looked out to see a member of the cleaning crew pushing her cart down the hall toward the conference room.

He turned, hoping they could pick up where they left off, only to find Terri yanking on her coat. "What are you doing?"

"I really need to get home."

"Terri—"

"This was a mistake, Nick. I think we're better off using a doctor, like I originally planned."

"If that's what you really want," he said, feeling disappointed, but trying not to let it show.

"I'll cover the cost."

As if he would let her do that. "I insist on paying at least half."

She looked as if she might argue, then seemed to change her mind. She nodded and said, "That sounds fair."

He grabbed his coat and shrugged into it. "I'll drive you home."

She didn't say a word as they walked to the elevator, and rode it to the underground parking garage, but he could practically hear the wheels in her mind moving. As much as he wanted to know what she was thinking, he knew better than to ask. If she wanted him to know, she would talk when she was ready. If he tried to drag it out of her, she would clam up. He'd seen her do it a million times. As close as they were, there was always a small part of herself that she vigilantly guarded from everyone, and could he blame her? His parents' relationship may have been a disaster, but at least he had parents. Despite their dysfunctional marriage, they loved him and his sisters. From the time she moved to Chicago, all Terri ever had was an aunt who only tolerated her presence. If she had loved Terri, she had been unable, or unwilling to let it show.

Though he knew it irked her, Nick opened the passenger door for Terri. Normally she would make a fuss about being completely capable of opening her own door thank-you-very-much, but she didn't say a word this time. Anyone who knew Terri was well aware she always had something to say, or an opinion about pretty much everything. Tonight, she was quiet the entire ride to her condominium complex on the opposite side of town.

Nick pulled up in front of her unit and turned to her, but she was just sitting there, looking out the windshield. "Everything okay?" he asked.

She nodded, but didn't move.

"Are you sure? You can talk to me."

"I know. I just…" She shrugged.

Whatever it was, she wasn't ready to discuss it.

"Well, you know where I am if you need me," he said, even though as long as he'd known her, Terri never truly *needed* anyone. She wrote the handbook on self-sufficiency.

He leaned over to kiss her cheek, the way he always did, but she flung open the car door and jumped out before he had the chance. As he watched her dart into the building without looking back, he couldn't help thinking that in her attempt to keep things between them from changing, they already had.

Three

Though she had hoped getting a good night's sleep would make things clearer, Terri tossed and turned all night, then woke the next morning feeling just as confused as she had been when Nick had dropped her at home.

She didn't want their relationship to change. But what she realized last night while he drove her home was that it already had changed, and it was too late to go back. They had opened a door, and there would be no closing it again until they both stepped through. Unfortunately, she had no idea what was waiting on the other side.

After a long and unproductive workday spent wondering what to do next, how they could pull this off without killing their friendship—if they hadn't already—she realized that she'd made her decision last night in his office. She'd just been too afraid to admit it. Not only to him, but to herself. Which was what led her to his apartment this evening. He hadn't tried to contact her all day, by phone or even email, meaning that he was smart enough to realize she needed time to work this through on her own. He was always there when she needed him, but he also knew when she needed space. She realized it said an awful lot about their relationship.

He opened the door dressed in jeans and a T-shirt, with a chef's apron tied around his waist and smudged with what looked like chocolate batter. The scent of something sweet and delicious reached out into the hallway to greet her.

"Hey," he said, looking not at all surprised to see her.

"Can we talk?"

"Of course." He stepped aside to let her in, and she gazed around the high-rise apartment that would be home for the next nine months or so. It was painted in rich, masculine hues, yet it still managed to feel warm and homey, in large part due to the casual-comfy furnishings and the dozens of framed family photos throughout the space.

Nick may have had an aversion to marriage, but when it came to his family, he couldn't be more devoted. She was also happy to see that most of the clutter that had been there last week was gone.

"Come on into the kitchen," he said. "I'm trying a new cake recipe."

A culinary genius, he spent much of his free time cooking and baking. He'd often said that if it wasn't for Caroselli Chocolate, he would have opened his own restaurant, but he would never leave the family business.

On her way through the living room, Terri dropped her purse and coat on the sofa, then followed Nick into his state-of-the-art kitchen, half of which she wouldn't have the first clue how to use. Nor did she have the desire to learn.

"Whatever it is, it smells delicious," she told Nick as she took a seat on one of the three bar stools at the island.

"Triple chocolate fudge," he said. "Jess wants me to make something special for Angie's birthday party next Saturday."

"She'll be eleven, right?"

"Twelve."

"*Really?* Wow. I remember when she was born, how excited you were to be an uncle. It doesn't seem like twelve years ago."

"It goes by fast," he said, checking the contents of one of the three top-of-the-line wall ovens. Then he untied the apron and draped it over the oven door handle—where it would probably remain until someone else put it in the broom closet where it belonged. He leaned against the edge of the granite countertop, folded his arms and asked, "So, enough of the small talk. What's up?"

That was Nick, always getting right to the point. "First, I want to apologize for the way I acted last night. You just…surprised me."

"It's okay. You were a little overwhelmed. I get it."

"But I've been giving it a lot of thought. In fact, it's about the only thing I *can* think about, and I just have one more question."

"Shoot."

"If we do this, if we make the baby the old-fashioned way, can you promise me that afterward things will go back to the way they were? That nothing will change?"

"No. I can't promise that."

She sighed. Did he have to be so damned honest? Couldn't he just humor her into thinking she was making the right choice? But that wasn't Nick. He was a straight shooter, and the only time he sugarcoated was in the kitchen.

"The best I can do is promise you that I'll always be there for you," he said. "We'll always be friends. Whether we use a doctor or do this conventionally, we're going to have a child together. That alone is bound to change things."

He was right, of course. She'd been so focused on the idea of how sleeping together would affect their relationship, that she hadn't truly grasped the enormity of having a child together. She'd wanted a baby so badly, she hadn't let herself fully consider the consequences. She realized now that *everything* would change. The question was, would it be a good change?

"I guess I didn't think this through completely," she told Nick. "Big surprise, right?"

"And now that you have?"

It scared her half to death. She'd been friends with Nick longer than anyone. Longer than she knew her own father. "I'm still hopelessly confused."

"Then we aren't going to do it. You can stick to your original plan and use a donor."

"And what will you do?" The idea of him entering a fake marriage with someone else, having a baby with her, left a knot in her belly.

"I won't do anything," he said.

"What do you mean?"

"I'll admit, I was sort of excited about the idea of having a baby, but only because I would be having it with you."

"But, what about the money?"

"Terri, our friendship means more to me than any sum of money."

She was too stunned to speak.

Nick laughed. "Why do you look so surprised?"

"It's just…I think that's probably the nicest thing anyone has ever said to me."

"I didn't say it to be nice. I said it because it's the truth."

And she felt ashamed that she hadn't trusted him, that she never realized just how much her friendship meant to him. "Let's do it," she said. "Let's have a baby."

Now he was the one who looked surprised. "Maybe you should take a little more time to consider this."

"I don't need more time."

"Are you sure?"

She couldn't recall ever feeling more sure about anything in her entire life. She didn't know why exactly. She just knew. "I want to do this."

"The wedding, the baby, moving in with me. Everything?"

"Everything."

"I guess the only question now is, how soon can we get started?" he asked.

"Well, I'm due to ovulate in two weeks, give or take a day or two. I'd rather not wait another month. The sooner I get pregnant, the better."

"The question is, can we plan a wedding in fourteen days?"

"I guess it depends on the kind of wedding you want."

"I would be happy to do this in front of a judge with a couple witnesses."

"That works for me," she said. Terri hadn't spent her adolescence dreaming of and planning her wedding. And why drop a lot of money on a marriage that was guaranteed to end in divorce?

"There's only one problem with that," he said.

She knew exactly what he was going to say. "Your family would have a fit." If there was one thing that the

Carosellis loved, it was a party. They would never pass up the opportunity to gather together, overeat and drink too much.

"Exactly," he said.

"So, how big are you thinking?"

"Immediate family only, maybe a few people from work."

"Two weeks would be the Saturday before Thanksgiving. I can guarantee most places will be booked."

Nick considered that for a moment, then his face lit up. "Hey, how about *Nonno's* house? It would definitely be big enough. We could have the ceremony in the great room, in front of the fireplace."

"He wouldn't mind?"

"Are you kidding? He would be thrilled. The whole point of this is to get the three of us married off and making babies as soon as possible."

It seemed like a logical choice to her, too. "Call him and make sure it's okay. On such short notice, I'm thinking we should keep it as simple as possible. Drinks and appetizers will be the best way to go."

"My cousin Joe on my mom's side can get us a good deal on the liquor. Make a list of what you think we'll need, then remember that it's my family and whatever you plan to order, double it. And we should call the caterer we use for business events. The food is great, and their prices are reasonable."

"Email me the number and I'll call them." There was so much to do, and so little time. But she was sure they could pull it off. She knew that as soon as his mom and his sisters heard the news, they would be gunning to help.

"You understand that my family has to believe this marriage is real, that we have to look like two people madly in love?"

"I know."

"That means we'll have to appear comfortable kissing and touching each other."

The thought of kissing and touching Nick, especially in front of his family, made her heart skip a beat.

"Can you do that?" he asked.

Did she have a choice? "I can do it."

"Are you sure? Last night when I touched you, you jumped a mile."

"I was just nervous. And confused."

"And you aren't now?"

"I'm trying to look at it logically. Like we're just two people…conducting a science experiment."

Nick laughed. "That sounds fun. And correct me if I'm wrong, but didn't you almost blow up the science lab in middle school?"

Which had taught her the invaluable lesson that when a teacher said chemicals aren't to be mixed, she actually meant it. That, plus a week of suspension, and a month of summer school to make up the failing grade she'd more than earned in the class, drove the message home.

But what Nick seemed to be forgetting was she'd only done it because he'd *dared* her.

"I didn't think it was supposed to be fun," she said.

He frowned. "You don't think sex should be fun?"

"Not *all* sex. I guess I just thought, because we're friends, we would just sort of…go through the motions."

"There's no reason why we can't enjoy it," Nick said.

"What if we're not compatible?"

"As far as I'm aware, we both have the right parts," he said with a grin. "Unless there's something you haven't told me."

She rolled her eyes. "I don't mean *biologically* compat-

ible. What if we get started and we don't get, you know…
turned-on?"

"Are you saying you find me unattractive?"

"No, but in twenty years, I've never looked at you and
had the uncontrollable urge to jump your bones. I just
don't think of you that way."

"Come here," he said, summoning her around the island with a crooked finger.

"Why?"

"I'm going to kiss you."

Her heart skipped a beat. "Now?"

"Why not now? Before we go through the trouble of
getting married, shouldn't we know for sure? Besides,
what if we wait until our wedding day, and it all goes
horribly wrong? Suppose we bump noses, or we both tilt
our head the same way. And what about our honeymoon?
Are we just going to hop into bed without ever having
touched each other? Doesn't it make more sense for us
to ease into it gradually?"

He definitely had a point. The problem here was that
she was trying to play by a set of rules that didn't exist.
They were making it up as they went along. "I guess that
does make sense."

"So, what are you waiting for?" He tapped his lips with
his index finger. "Lay one on me."

The idea that they were really going to do it, that he
was going to kiss her for real, and not his usual peck on
the cheek, gave her a funny feeling in her head. Her hands
went all warm and tingly, as if all the blood in her body
was pooling somewhere south of her heart.

It's just Nick. She had no reason to be nervous or
scared or whatever it was she was feeling. But as her
feet carried her around the island to where he stood, her
heart was racing.

"Ready?" he asked, and she nodded.

Nick leaned in, but before their lips could meet, a giggle burst up from her chest. Nick drew back, looking exasperated.

"Sorry, I guess I'm a little nervous." She took a deep breath and blew it out, shaking the feeling back into her fingers. "I'm okay now. I promise not to laugh again."

"Good, because you're bruising my fragile ego."

Somehow she doubted that. She'd never met a man more secure in his prowess with women.

"Okay," he said. "Are you ready?"

"Ready."

"*Really* ready?"

She nodded. "Really ready."

Nick leaned in, and she met him halfway, and their lips just barely touched.

She couldn't help it, she giggled again.

Backing away, Nick sighed loudly. "This is not working."

"I am so sorry," she said. "I'm really trying."

Maybe this wasn't going to work. If she couldn't feel comfortable kissing him, what would it be like trying to have sex?

"Close your eyes," he said.

She narrowed them at him instead. "Why?"

"Just close them. And *keep* them closed."

Even though she felt stupid, she did as he asked, and for what felt like a full minute he did nothing, and she started to feel impatient. "Any day now."

"Shush."

Another thirty seconds or so passed and finally she felt him move closer, felt the whisper of his breath on her cheek, then his lips brushed over hers. This time she didn't giggle, and she wasn't so nervous anymore. His lips were soft and his evening stubble felt rough against her chin, but in a sexy way. And though it wasn't exactly passionate, it wasn't merely friendly, either.

This is nice, she thought. Nice enough that she wanted to see what came next, and when Nick started to pull away, before he could get too far, she fisted her hands in the front of his shirt and pulled him back in.

He made a sound, somewhere between surprise and pleasure, and he must have forgotten all about their ease-into-it-gradually plan, because it went from *nice* to *holy-cow-can-this-guy-kiss* in two seconds flat. He must have been sampling the cake batter earlier, because he tasted sweet, like chocolate.

Oh, my gosh, she was kissing *Nick,* her *best friend.* It was Nick's arms circling her, Nick's hand cupping her cheek, sliding under the root of her ponytail and cocking her head to just the right angle.

Her internal thermometer shot into the red zone and her bones began a slow melt, dripping away like icicles in the hot sun. And only when she heard Nick moan, when she felt her fingers sink through the softness of his hair, did she realize that her arms were around his shoulders, that her body was pressed against him, her breasts crushed against the hard wall of his chest. It was thrilling and arousing, and scary as hell, and a couple dozen other emotions all jumbled up together. But more than anything, it just felt...*right.* In a way that no other kiss had before. And all she could think was *more.*

For the second time Nick was the one to pull away, and she had to fight the urge to tighten her arms around his neck and pull him to her again. But instead of letting go completely, he hooked his fingers in the belt loop of her jeans.

"Wow," he said, searching her face, almost as if he were seeing her for the first time. "That was…"

"Wow," she agreed. If she had known kissing Nick would be like that, she might have tried it a long time ago.

"Are you still worried about us being incompatible?" he asked.

"Somehow I don't think that's going to be a problem."

"Do you feel weird?"

"Weird?"

"You said before that you were afraid things might get weird between us."

The only thing she felt right now was turned-on, and ready to kiss him again. "It's difficult to say after one kiss."

"Oh, really?" he said, tugging her closer. "Then I guess we'll just have to do it again."

Four

Their second kiss was even better than the first, and this time when Nick stopped and asked, "Feeling weird yet?" instead of answering, Terri just pulled him in for number three. And she was so wowed by the fact that it was Nick kissing her, Nick touching her, that she didn't really think about *where* he was touching her. Not until his hand slid down over the back pocket of her jeans, then everything came to a screeching halt.

She backed away and looked at him. "Your hand is on my butt."

"I know. I put it there." He paused, then said, "Am I moving too fast?"

Was he? Was it too much too soon? Was there some sort of schedule they were supposed to follow? A handbook for friends who become lovers to have a baby? As long as it felt good, as long as they both wanted it, why stop?

And boy, did it feel good.

"No," she said. "You're not moving too fast. If you were, would I be thinking how much better it would feel if my jeans were off?"

He made a growly noise deep in his chest and kissed her hard, but despite that shameless invitation into her pants, he kept his hands on the outside of her clothes. And no matter where she touched him, how she rubbed up against him, or encouraged him with little moans of pleasure, he didn't seem to be getting the hint that she was ready to proceed.

When he did finally slide his hand under her shirt, she felt like pumping her fist in the air, and shouting, "Yes!" But then he just kept it there. It wasn't that it didn't feel good resting just above the waist of her jeans, but she was sure it would feel a whole lot better eight inches or so higher and slightly to the left.

She pulled back and said, "If you felt the need to touch my breast, or pretty much any other part of my anatomy, I wouldn't stop you."

Looking amused, he said, "It's not often a woman tells me I'm moving too slow."

"I could play coy, but what's the point? We both know we're going to end up in bed tonight."

His brows rose. "We do?"

"Can you think of a reason we shouldn't?"

When most men would have jumped at the offer, he actually took several seconds to think about it. Which for some strange reason made her want it even more. It was crazy to think that on Wednesday she wouldn't have even considered a physical relationship with him, but two days and a couple kisses later, she couldn't wait to get him out of his clothes. And if he turned her down, she was going to be seriously unhappy.

After a brief pause he shrugged and said, "Nothing is coming to mind."

The way she figured it, their friendship had been leading up to this, even if they hadn't realized it. That equated to about twenty years of foreplay. Technically, no one could say they were rushing things. "So why are we still standing in the kitchen?"

He opened his mouth to answer her, when they heard the apartment door open. Terri's first thought was that it was another woman. Someone he was dating that he'd given a key to. Then she heard Nick's mom call, "Yoo-hoo! Nicky, I'm here!"

Nick muttered a curse. And here he thought the days of his mom interrupting while he was with a girl had ended when he moved away from home.

"In the kitchen," he called, then turned to Terri to apologize. But he never got the words out. Her hair was a mess, her clothes disheveled and she had beard burn all over her chin. Unless his mom had forgotten to put her contacts in that morning, it would be obvious that they'd been fooling around. He could hope that she wouldn't notice, but she noticed *everything,* and typically had an opinion she always felt compelled to share. Terri was a lot like her in that way.

Terri's eyes went wide, and she glanced at his crotch, but she didn't have to worry. He'd lost his erection the second he heard the door and remembered that his mom was stopping by.

"I can't believe this weather," his mom said, her voice growing louder as she walked toward the kitchen. "Two days ago we get a blizzard—" she appeared in the kitchen doorway, a five-foot-three-inch, one-hundred-and-two-pound ball of energy dressed in the yoga gear she wore ninety-nine percent of the time "—and today it feels like spring." She stopped short when she saw Terri standing there beside him. Then she smiled and said, "Well, hello there! I didn't know you were—"

Whatever she was going to say never made it out. Instead, she looked from him, to Terri, then back to him again. "Oh, my, it looks as if I've interrupted something."

He could see the wheels in her head spinning, and he knew exactly what she was thinking—that all the while they were posing as friends, he and Terri had been hitting the sheets together. Friends with benefits. And while he didn't care what she thought of him, he didn't want her to think Terri was like that. And he was pretty sure, by the crimson blossoming in Terri's cheeks, she was worried about the same thing.

Terri always said that his mom was the mom she should have had, and his mom said Terri was the third daughter she'd never had. Sometimes Nick could swear that if forced to ever choose, she might actually pick Terri over him.

"It's not what you think," he told his mom.

"Sweetheart, what you do in the privacy of your own home is none of my business."

"But we're not...I mean, we haven't been—"

His mom held up a hand. "No need to explain," she said, but underneath her blasé facade, he could see disappointment lurking there. And he was sure that it was directed as much at him as it was at Terri.

He turned to Terri and said, "So, should we tell her now?"

Terri looked over to his mom. "I don't know, what do you think?"

"Tell me what?" his mom asked.

"Well," Nick said. "She's going to find out eventually."

Terri grinned, enjoying this game as much as he was. There was no better way to drive his mom nuts than to make her think someone had a juicy secret and she'd been left out of the loop.

"I guess that's true," Terri said. "But are we ready to let the news out?"

"What news?" Though she was trying to sound nonchalant, he could see she was practically busting with curiosity.

"Because you know that as soon as we tell her, everyone will know."

"Nicky!" his mom scolded, even though they all knew it was true. She couldn't keep a secret to save her life. And oftentimes she told him things about family, or her "man-friends" as she called them, that he wished he could permanently wipe from his memory.

His mom folded her arms and pouted. "I know someone who's getting a big fat lump of coal in his stocking this year."

"Terri and I are getting married," Nick said.

"Married?"

"Yep."

"Really?"

"Yes, really."

She narrowed her eyes at him. "You're not just saying that because I caught you fooling around?"

He laughed. "We're *really* getting married."

His mom shrieked so loud he was sure the apartment below heard her through the industrial soundproofing. She scurried around the island to pull Terri—not him, but Terri—into a hug.

"Oh, honey! I'm so happy for you. I always hoped. You know I would never interfere, but I did hope."

Curiously, her idea of not interfering was telling him,

after meeting whatever girl he happened to be dating at the time, that "She was nice, but she wasn't Terri."

His mom held Terri at arm's length, tears shimmering in her eyes, looking as if it was the happiest moment of her entire life. Then she turned to Nick, the tears miraculously dried, and said, "It's about damn time."

Yep, she would definitely choose Terri over him.

"Have you set a date? And please don't tell me that this is going to be one of those ten-year engagements so that you can live together and not feel guilty. You know that you'll never hear the end of it from *Nonno*. He put your poor cousin Chrissy through hell when she moved in with David."

"We're getting married in two weeks."

She blinked. "Did you just say *two* weeks?"

"Yep."

She sucked in a breath and turned to Terri, asking in a hushed voice, even though there was no one around but them, "Are you pregnant?"

"No," Terri said, sounding incredibly patient under the circumstances. "I'm not pregnant."

Looking baffled, she shrugged and said, "Then what's the rush?"

"Neither of us sees any point in waiting," Terri said, shooting him a quick sideways glance filled with innuendo. "My plan has always been to be pregnant by the time I'm thirty, and I'm almost there."

"You want kids, Nicky?" his mom asked, beaming with joy.

"We want to try for a baby right away," he told her. "And we figured it would be best to get married first. We both prefer a small wedding, with a ceremony that's short and sweet. Immediate family and close friends *only*."

"You know that your father's family will have something to say about that."

"We'll videotape it and post it on YouTube," Nick said, earning him an elbow in the side from his fiancée. It also reminded him that they would need to hire a photographer, which then had him wondering if the studio that did the company's promotional shoots did weddings, too.

"Nicky, where's your laptop?" his mom asked.

"On my desk. Why?"

"With only two weeks, Terri and I need to start planning this thing right now. We have to pick out your colors and find a florist and I know just the place to get the cake." She exhaled a long-winded sigh. "There's *so much* to do!"

"But Mom…"

Ignoring Nick, she grabbed Terri by the arm and all but dragged her in the direction of Nick's office. Terri looked back over her shoulder, shrugging helplessly. So much for having a little premarital fun.

On the bright side, he doubted that after tonight they would be uncomfortable kissing and touching, so convincing his family that they were crazy about each other would be a breeze. And he was willing to bet that until he got her alone and into his bed, touching her again was all he would be able to think about.

Though Nick would have preferred to announce their engagement himself, his mom called his sisters, and his sisters called their cousins, and after that the news went viral. So it was no surprise when Tony and Rob cornered him as he was on his way to the test kitchen the next Monday morning.

"Is it true?" Rob asked.

"If you're referring to my engagement, then yes, it's true."

Tony gestured them into a room that wasn't much more than a glorified closet.

Oh, boy, here we go, Nick thought, doubting they were there for a friendly chat.

Boxes of old files lined metal shelves on either side and the air smelled musty. Tony switched on the light and shut the door behind them. "This seems awfully convenient, don't you think?"

Nick frowned, playing dumb. "What do you mean?"

"You know exactly what I mean."

"You've been friends with Terri for all these years," Rob said, "and you just happen to pick now to ask her to marry you?"

Nick leaned against a shelf and it shifted slightly under his weight. "What are you suggesting?"

"You know damn well what he's suggesting," Tony said. "And I don't think a marriage of convenience is what *Nonno* had in mind."

"I don't recall him ever saying that."

Rob shot him a look. "It was implied, and you know it. He wants us all to settle down and have big families. Lots of male heirs to carry on the Caroselli name."

"I love Terri," he said, which wasn't a lie. He just wasn't *in* love with her.

"Is she pregnant?" Rob asked.

With such a short engagement, he had the feeling he'd be getting that question a lot. "Not that it's any of your business, but no, she isn't. Not yet."

"Then why the big hurry to get hitched?" Tony said.

Though his family had many good qualities, they sure could be nosy.

"Again, not that it's *any* of your business, but we want

to start a family right away, and we want to be married first," he said, using the explanation Terri had given his mom last night, which was truly brilliant because none of it was untrue. They just left out a few pertinent facts.

Tony didn't look convinced. "Yeah, but two weeks is pretty fast, don't you think?"

"Terri is almost thirty and she has a ticking biological clock. And you know why *I'm* in a hurry."

Tony lowered his voice, even though they were alone. "Does she know about the money?"

Nick grinned. "What's the matter? Are you jealous that I'm going to get my cut of the money first?"

"Don't forget, it has to be a *male* heir," Rob said. "It could take more than one try. You could end up with three or four kids."

Of course, having a girl was a possibility, and whether or not they decided to ride it out and try again would be up to Terri.

"I think I speak for Rob when I say that we've always really liked Terri. And if either of us finds out you only married her so she'll have your offspring, and you hurt her, I will personally kick your ass."

Hurting her was definitely not on the agenda. They both knew exactly what they were getting into. What could go wrong?

"Honestly, Tony, I figured you would be making an announcement soon, too," Nick said. "You and Lucy have been together a long time now."

A nerve in Tony's jaw ticked. "It would have been a year in December."

"*Would* have been?" Rob asked.

"We split up."

"*When?*"

"Last week."

"Dude," Nick said. "Why didn't you say anything?"

Tony shrugged. "It didn't seem worth mentioning."

Nick couldn't say he was surprised. Lucy was never what anyone would consider a devoted girlfriend. In all the time they were together, she had been to no more than two or three family functions, and Tony rarely mentioned her. They seemed to lead very separate lives. "What happened?"

"I honestly don't know. I thought everything was fine, then I stopped by her place after work one night and she was gone. Her roommate said she moved back to Florida."

Rob shook his head in amazement. "Without saying a word?"

Tony shrugged again, but underneath the stoic facade, he was tense. Nick could feel it. "If there was a problem, she never mentioned it to me."

"I'm really sorry, man," Nick said.

"It's her loss."

Though Tony would never come right out and say it, Nick could tell that deep down he was hurting. But neither he nor Rob pushed the subject.

The door to the room opened and all three jumped like little boys caught playing with matches. A woman Nick didn't recognize stood in the open doorway, looking as surprised to see them as they were to see her. She was in her mid-forties, with short, stylish dark hair peppered with gray and striking blue eyes. She was very attractive for a woman her age, and there was something oddly familiar about her.

"I'm sorry, I didn't know anyone was in here," she said, looking nervously at them.

"It's okay," Tony said. "We were just talking."

She retreated a step. "I can come back."

"It's okay," Nick said, shooting his cousins a look. "We're finished."

"Nick, I don't think you've met Rose Goldwyn. Her mom, Phyllis, worked as *Nonno*'s secretary for years, up until he retired."

"For almost twenty years," Rose said.

Nick was struck with a distinct mental picture of a youngish, attractive woman seated outside *Nonno*'s office. That was why she looked familiar.

"I remember your mom," Nick said. "You look like her."

She smiled. "That's what everyone says."

"How is she doing?"

"Unfortunately mom passed away this September," Rose said. "Cancer."

"I'm so sorry. I remember that she was always smiling, and gave me and my sisters candy whenever we visited *Nonno* at his office."

"She always loved working here. Being here makes me feel a little closer to her."

"And we're happy to have you," Tony said.

"I heard this morning that you're getting married soon," she told Nick. "Congratulations."

"Thanks. You should come."

"Me?" she said, looking surprised.

"Sure. At Caroselli Chocolate, we like to think of our employees as extended family. I'll tell my fiancée to put you on the guest list. It's a week from this coming Saturday."

"I'll definitely be there," she said.

"Gentlemen, why don't we get out of her way," Tony said, nodding toward the door.

"Nice to have met you," Nick said, shaking her hand. They headed back down the hall in the direction of the kitchen, and when they turned the corner Nick asked, "When did we hire her?"

"A few weeks ago. We didn't actually need anyone, but because of the family history, they found a place for her in accounting. When she saw the condition of the file room, she offered to scan in the old files and take us completely digital."

"Correct me if I'm wrong," Nick said. "But isn't there a lot of sensitive information in there?"

Tony shrugged. "Mostly old financial records and employee files. Maybe some marketing materials. Nothing top secret."

"No old recipes?"

"Not that I know of. Why, do you think she's a spy?"

Corporate espionage certainly wasn't unheard of, especially with a world-renowned product like Caroselli Chocolate. "Doesn't hurt to be cautious."

Nick's cell phone rang and his mom's number popped up on the screen. "Sorry, I have to take this," he said, then told Tony, "If you need to talk…"

Tony nodded. Enough said.

Even if they weren't buying his story—because in all honesty, if the tables were turned he would have the same suspicions—Nick doubted they would rat him out to *Nonno*. Still, he planned to keep up the charade. If anyone else figured out that the marriage was a sham, it could definitely mean trouble.

"Hey, Mom, what's up?" he answered.

"White lilies or pink roses?"

"Excuse me?"

"Which do you prefer?" she said, sounding impatient, as if he should have known what she meant. "I'm at the florist with Terri and we can't decide between the lilies and the roses."

Not only did he not know the difference, he didn't care, either. "If you like them, why not pick both?"

"That's what I suggested, but she says it would be too expensive."

"And I told her that I didn't care what it costs. To get what she likes."

"Then you talk to her. She won't listen to me."

He heard muffled voices, then Terri came on the line. "Nick, the flowers are going to be really expensive."

He sighed. She was frugal to a fault. "It doesn't matter. Get whatever you want."

She lowered her voice. "For a fake wedding? I already feel horrible about this."

"Why?"

"Because your mom and your sisters are *so* excited. I feel like we're deceiving them."

"We are getting married, aren't we?"

"You know what I mean."

"Well, it's too late to back out now," Nick said.

There was a pause, and he wondered if she actually was reconsidering her decision. Then she said, "I guess you're right."

"And, Terri, get the flowers you want, regardless of the cost, okay? As long as we're married, what's mine is yours."

"Okay. I have to go, I'll call you later," she said. Then the line went dead.

They weren't doing anything wrong, so why did he get the feeling Terri still had doubts?

Five

Terri rummaged through her toiletries bag, checking off in her mind everything she would need for their honeymoon. When she was sure she had all the essentials, she zipped the bag and laid it in her suitcase. If she had forgotten something, she could pick it up when they got to the resort in Aruba.

She never realized just how much planning went into a wedding—even one as small as hers and Nick's—and thank goodness his mom and sisters were more than happy to tend to the details, leaving Terri time to finish up a high-profile web design job that was due to be completed while they were in the middle of their honeymoon. And since they already had to cut their trip short to be home in time for Thanksgiving, she doubted Nick would appreciate her bringing work with her. Which translated into five consecutive eighteen-hour days in front of the computer, until she was sure her eyes would start bleeding.

Nick had been developing a new product—one so top secret he couldn't even tell her about it—that they hoped to have in production before Easter, so he had been just as busy. Other than brief, nightly phone conversations to keep him up-to-date on the wedding progress, in which one or both of them started to doze off, their contact was minimal. They'd even had to skip their weekly Thursday dinner.

They hadn't discussed practicing for their wedding night since that evening in his kitchen, but it was never far from her mind, and she couldn't help but wonder if he'd been thinking about it, as well. Had he been having sex dreams about her, too? Fantasizing about their first time when he was supposed to be working?

When they finally did get a free night together the Wednesday before the wedding it was too late. According to her doctor it was best to refrain from sex at least five days before she ovulated, to keep Nick's sperm count high, which would make conception more likely. So after a short make-out session that only heightened the sexual tension, they decided it would be safer if they kept their hands to themselves until their wedding night. He helped her pack instead, which included dismantling her entire computer system so she could set up an office at his place. Then later, as they were relaxing by the fire, Nick got down on one knee and pretend-proposed—to give her the full experience, he'd said—but the four-carat, princess-cut diamond solitaire he slid on her ring finger was very real and stunningly beautiful, and hers to keep as a token of his affection even after they divorced.

While she thought it was a sweet gesture, it was a little heartbreaking that the best she could do in thirty years was a fake marriage proposal. But she knew he meant well. It wasn't his fault that she had lousy luck with men.

"All packed?" Nick asked from the bedroom doorway, and she turned to find him leaning casually against the jamb, thumbs hooked in the front pockets of his jeans.

"I think I may have over-packed," she said, tugging at the zipper in an effort to close the bulging case.

"You really think I'm going to let you wear clothes?" he said with one of those sizzling grins that made her heart flutter and her face hot. And though she probably wouldn't have noticed a couple weeks ago, in faded jeans that were ripped at the knees and a white T-shirt that enhanced his dark complexion, he looked sexy as hell. When they had first hatched this plan, the idea of sleeping with him wasn't just unusual, it really scared her. She didn't want their relationship to change. But then he'd kissed her, and touched her, and other than the fact that she was itching to get her hands on him and she couldn't wait to jump his bones, she didn't feel any differently about him than she had before. They were friends, and they were going to have sex—simple as that.

According to her temperature she should have started ovulating today, but the test she took this morning was negative. If the test had been positive, she didn't doubt that they would have consummated their marriage tonight, tradition be damned. And if she didn't start ovulating tomorrow? After two weeks of anticipating their first time making love, could they really hold out another day or two? She might have to say to hell with it and jump him, anyway.

"Anything you still need to do for tomorrow?" he asked. He'd already perfected his new recipe that would go through taste testing and marketing and whatever else they did with a new product, so they were free to spend the next five days relaxing and enjoying each other's company.

"I talked to your mom a couple hours ago and it sounds as if they have everything covered. I seriously don't know what I would have done without them. And I can't help feeling guilty."

"Why?"

"If they knew we're going to be getting divorced as soon as we have the baby, do you really think they would have spent all this time, and gone through all this trouble?"

"If we were getting married for real, who's to say it wouldn't end in divorce, anyway? There are no guarantees, Terri."

She knew that, but it still felt underhanded. Their current circumstance aside, she would never marry a man if she thought the relationship might end in divorce. Of course, would anyone? And there were definite advantages to being married, even if it was only pretend. It meant having someone to talk to without picking up the phone, and not eating dinner alone in front of the television watching *Seinfeld* reruns.

The best part, though, was that having Nick's baby meant always having someone to love—and someone to love her—unconditionally. Though her aunt had probably done her best raising Terri, she hadn't been much of a kid person. She'd never had children of her own, much less expected to have a great-niece she'd never even met dumped in her care. It had been a lonely way to grow up, but when the baby was born, Terri would never be lonely again. She would give her child all the love and affection her aunt had failed to show her. Terri would never make her child feel as if he was inconsequential. She wouldn't travel abroad for weeks at a time and leave him in the care of a nanny. She would be a good mom, and she hoped Nick would be a good dad. Either way, she had enough love to give for both of them.

"Are you nervous?" he asked.

She shrugged. "Should I be?"

"I hear that brides often are the day before their wedding."

Well, she wasn't a typical bride. "I'm just hoping everything goes well."

"Did my mom say what the final guest count will be?" Nick asked.

"Forty-eight."

"That's not bad. Maybe we'll get lucky and my dad won't show."

It broke her heart that Nick and his dad were so at odds. He didn't realize how lucky he was to have both his parents, even if they could be trying at times. She would have given anything to have her dad back. Her mom died when Terri was a baby, and it was harder to miss something she never really had, but she still regretted not getting to know her.

"I'm sure he'll behave," she told Nick. Or at least she *hoped* he would. His sister's wedding had been a disaster thanks to Nick's dad, Leo, who got into it with his ex-wife's date. The argument became so heated, shoves were exchanged, and though they never knew for sure who threw the first punch, fists began to fly. Eventually other family members from both sides of the wedding party had gotten into the scuffle, until it became a full-fledged brawl that resulted in a handful of arrests for drunk and disorderly behavior, several people requiring medical attention and an enormous bill for the damage from the banquet hall.

Never a dull moment in the Caroselli family.

But that had been more that thirteen years ago. His parents had been apart now for more years than they had been married, and had each wed and divorced again—in his dad's case twice. Terri would think that any issues they'd had back then would be resolved by now. Yet she couldn't deny worrying about what might happen if she was wrong.

"Everything will be perfect," she told him, hoping she sounded convincing.

"I hope so," Nick said. "I unpacked the last box of books and set up your computer system. I checked it and everything seems to be working correctly."

He had insisted that they get her moved in *before* the wedding, so the impending task wouldn't be in the back of their minds during their trip. She'd felt a little weird moving her things in before they were actually married. What if during their honeymoon something went terribly wrong? Sexually they seemed compatible enough, but suppose after four days in close quarters, they realized that they couldn't stand living together? She would have to fly home and move all her stuff back to her place.

That isn't going to happen, she told herself, but every now and then she thought about when they were roommates and doubt danced around the edge of her subconscious. There was also the question of sex. Not whether it would be good, but how often they would have it. Would they sleep together once, and hope she conceived, or the entire time she was ovulating? Would he be content to go an entire nine months without sex? The truth was that she liked sex. A lot. Even mediocre sex was better than none at all. And while she was perfectly capable of taking care of things herself, it was so much more fun to have a partner. But for her and Nick to have a full-blown affair would be a mistake. They had to keep this in perspective.

"Thanks for all your help today," she said, tugging the case off the bed so she could roll it out to the foyer. It weighed a ton.

"Let me get that," he said, taking it from her. He lifted it with little effort, then carried it to the entranceway and set it beside his own, which she noticed was half the size of hers and not nearly as stuffed. Maybe he really was expecting to spend the majority of their time naked.

This just kept getting better and better.

She looked over at the clock on the mantel, surprised to see that it was already after ten. "I should probably get home."

"Are you sure you don't want to sleep here?"

"In two hours it will be our wedding day, and it's bad luck for the groom to see the bride."

He gazed at her with tired eyes and a wry grin. "You don't really believe that."

Not really, but she'd be damned if she was taking any chances. "I think we should stick to tradition. Just in case."

He laughed. "And how is what we're doing *traditional?*"

"How many couples our age do you think still wait until their wedding night to consummate their relationship? That's a tradition."

"But we're only waiting because we *have* to. And I'd be happy to break that one right now."

Oh, man, so would she. But as much as she wanted to get him naked and put her hands all over him, she wanted to get pregnant even more, which meant they had to do this by the book.

"Everything that I need for tomorrow is at my place. It'll be easier if I stay there. But before I go, there is something I wanted to show you."

His brows rose. "Is it your breasts, because I'd love to see them."

She folded her arms and glared at him.

"That's a no, I guess."

"It's something I picked up at the doctor's office."

He followed into her bedroom and sat down beside her on the bed. She grabbed a manila folder off the nightstand and pulled out printed sheets, handing them to Nick.

He read the first line and his brows rose. "Methods for conceiving a boy?"

"I mentioned to the doctor that we were hoping for a boy and he gave me this. He said it in no way guarantees a baby boy, but there are some parents who swear by it. I highlighted the important parts."

The first couple pages were about ovulation and cervical conditions, and the differences in the mobility of the X and Y sperm.

"The male sperm are smaller and faster, but not as robust as their larger female counterparts," he read, giving her a sideways glance. "While trying to conceive a male, deep penetration from your partner will deposit the sperm closer to the cervix giving the quicker moving 'boy' sperm a head start to fertilizing the egg first. In addition, female orgasm is important as the contractions which accompany orgasm help move the sperm up and into the cervix. It also makes the vaginal environment more alkaline, which is favorable for the boy sperm." He turned to her, looking intrigued. "Deep penetration? How deep?"

"The next page has examples, actually."

Nick turned to the next page, which contained several vividly graphic illustrations depicting the positions they should use for the deepest penetration. His brows rose and he said, "Wow."

Along with a couple of tried-and-true positions, there were several that she was pretty sure only a contortionist could perform. And they had weird names like The Reverse Cowgirl and The Crab on its Back.

Nick narrowed his eyes, cocking his head to one side, then the other. "Huh, it looks like they're playing Twister."

"I admit some of them are a little...adventurous," she said. And not terribly romantic, if that's the mood they were going for. But they did look fun, and he had said himself that it should be fun. She liked to experiment and try new things, but maybe he was more conservative. Maybe his idea of fun was the missionary position. "They're just examples. I understand if you don't want to try them."

He looked at her as if she were nuts. "Are you kidding? Of *course* I want to try them."

Or maybe he *wasn't* conservative.

He pointed to one of the illustrations. "I like this, but do you really think you can get your legs over your head like that?"

She grinned. "I'm *very* flexible."

He cursed under his breath and handed the papers to her. "I think it would be best if I stopped looking at these. Because now I'm picturing you in all those positions."

What a coincidence, because so was she. She slid the papers back into the folder.

"I have to say, I'm a bit surprised by how open you are about this," he said.

"Why?"

"Over the years we've both made off-the-cuff comments about people we've dated, but we really never talked about our sex lives."

"Why do you think that is?"

"In my case, I consider it disrespectful to kiss and tell."

Good answer. While she was aware that he'd dated a lot of women, and *assumed* he'd slept with the majority of them, she really didn't have a clue how many. And frankly didn't want to know.

"In your case," he said, "I figured you were uncomfortable talking about sex."

"Repressed, you mean."

"Just…private. Like it probably took you a while to get to know someone before you would be comfortable being intimate with them. But then the other night, you were so…"

"Slutty?"

He shot her a look. *"Aggressive."*

"You don't like aggressive women?"

"Do I honestly strike you as the type who wouldn't like an aggressive woman?"

She wouldn't have thought so. But his perception of her, and reality, were two very different things.

"First you propositioned me," Nick said, "then you sat me down for a talk about sexual positions. And I'm not suggesting I don't like it. I think it's pretty obvious that I *do.* I'm just surprised. I thought I knew everything about you, but here's this side of you that I didn't even know existed."

It was odd, after all these years, there was still a part of her that he didn't know. But that was her own fault. "So you're seeing me differently than you did before?"

"A little, but in a good way. It makes me feel closer to you."

What she liked about their friendship was that it had always been very straightforward. There were no overblown expectations, and none of the games men and women played when they were physically involved. She didn't want that to change, though she couldn't deny that the idea of someone knowing her that well scared her a little. Especially now that sex was about to be part of the equation.

Six

Though he never thought he would see the day, Nick was a married man.

Legally, anyway.

He gazed down at the polished platinum band on the ring finger of his left hand. It was a brand, a warning to women that he was now taken, a tourniquet placed there to cut off the lifeblood of his single life. And while he'd expected that to bother him on some level, to make him feel caged or smothered, he actually felt okay about it. Maybe because he knew it was only temporary, or he was looking forward to collecting ten million dollars.

Or maybe he was looking forward to the honeymoon.

He'd received a text message from Terri at 6:00 a.m. this morning that read simply: The eagle has landed.

Which he knew was her way of saying that she was ovulating, and right on time.

Aside from the occasional random and fleeting fantasy,

he hadn't really thought about her in a sexual way since high school. The past two weeks, he had barely thought of much else, and after their conversation last night, it was *all* he'd thought about. Since the ceremony, he'd kept one eye on their guests—who were drinking champagne and expensive scotch, snacking on bacon-wrapped sea scallops, artichoke phyllo tartlets and gorgonzola risotto croquettes—and the other eye on the clock.

He heard Terri laugh, and turned to see her by the bar with his cousins, Megan and Elana. He rarely saw her in anything but casual clothes, but for the occasion she wore a calf-length, off-white dress made of some silky-soft material that flowed with her body every time she moved. Her long, dark hair was up in one of those styles that looked salon-perfect, yet messy at the same time.

His sister Jessica stepped up beside him and propped her hand on his shoulder. In three-inch heels, she was still a good eight inches shorter. She had their father's olive complexion and naturally curly hair, and took after their mother in height, but she had been struggling with her weight since she'd had her first of four babies. Right now she was on the heavy side, which usually meant she'd been stress eating, a pretty good indication that her marriage was once again on the rocks.

"She looks gorgeous," Jess said.

"Yes, she does," he agreed.

As if she sensed him watching, Terri looked over. She glanced up at the clock, then back at him and smiled, and he knew exactly what she was thinking. Soon they would be on their way to the airport, and after a five-hour flight, and a short limo ride, they would reach the resort.

It would be late by then, but he figured they could sleep on the flight, then spend the rest of the night making love in a variety of interesting ways.

"So, how does it feel?" Jess asked him.

"How does what feel?"

"To be a married man."

He shrugged. "So far so good."

"I never thought you would do it, but I'm glad you chose Terri."

"Me, too," he said. "And thank you again for everything. You and mom and Mags did an amazing job putting this all together."

With a satisfied smile, she gazed around the room. The decorations were simple yet elegant, and included both the lilies and the roses—even though Terri still insisted that it had been excessively expensive. And in lieu of the typical wedding band or DJ, they'd hired a string quartet.

"Considering you only gave us two weeks to plan it, I think so, too," she said.

"How are things with you and Eddie?"

Her smile slipped away. "Oh, you know, same ol' same ol'. We have good days and bad days. The marriage counseling seems to be helping. When I can get him to go."

Nick heard a screech, then Jessica's seven-year-old twin boys, Tommy and Alex, tore through the room like two wild animals, bumping furniture and plowing into guests.

Jess rolled her eyes and mumbled a curse. "Excuse me, I've got children to beat."

Nick knew that, physically, the worst she'd ever done was give them a quick love-tap to the back of the head, which was a long-running Caroselli family tradition. Only according to his father and his uncles, depending on what they'd done, and how angry they'd made *Nonni* Caroselli, hers were more like whacks, and were anything but loving. Nick still had a hard time picturing his *Nonni* as anything but sweet and gentle and unfailingly patient.

Terri crossed the room to where he stood, sliding her arm through his and hugging herself close to his side. He knew it was only for show, but he liked it. There was something nice about having the freedom to touch her, and be close to her, without having to worry that she would read into it, or take it the wrong way. She wouldn't smother him, or demand more than he was willing to give. He would call it friends with benefits, but that seemed to cheapen it somehow. What he and Terri had transcended a typical friendship. They were soul mates, but the platonic kind.

"So, I just had an interesting conversation with your cousins," she told him.

Uh-oh. "By *interesting* I take it you mean *not good*."

"Well, no one is questioning the validity of our wedding."

"That's good, right?"

"Yes, but only because apparently your *entire* family thinks I'm *pregnant*."

He sort of saw that one coming. "Did you tell them that you aren't?"

"Of course. And the reply I got was, 'Sure you aren't,' wink, wink, nudge, nudge."

"Let them think what they want, in eight months or so, when you don't give birth, they'll know you were telling the truth. Besides, I'm betting not everyone thinks it." His mom and sisters knew she wasn't, as did Rob and Tony.

"The limo will be here soon," she told him. "We should say our goodbyes so we can get upstairs and change."

Nick heard his dad's booming laugh, and turned to see that he and Nick's mom were standing together by the bay window talking. He muttered a curse under his breath.

The last time they had been in the same room, face-to-face, the evening had ended with a 9-1-1 call. And though they seemed to be playing nice, that could change in the span of a heartbeat if tempers flared. At least neither had brought a date, since that was what had set them off last time.

"Brace yourself," he told Terri. "I think there's going to be trouble."

"What's wrong?" Terri asked, following his line of vision until she spotted his parents.

Oh, hell.

Up until just then, their wedding had been perfect. So perfect that when *Nonno* walked her into the great room, and she saw everyone standing there looking so genuinely happy and willing to unconditionally welcome her into the family on a permanent basis, she had never felt so loved and accepted. If she wasn't careful, she could almost let herself believe it was real, that when Nick spoke his vows, he actually meant them. That when he promised to love and keep her, in sickness and in health, till death parted them, he was sincere. That the love in his eyes as he slipped the ring on her finger was genuine. If she never found Mr. Right, never married anyone for real, she still could say that she'd had the wedding of her dreams.

She didn't want his parents to ruin it by starting a brawl.

Her first instinct was to shove Nick over there to run interference, but then she noticed that his parents were both…*smiling.* Okay, that was a little weird.

"Is it me, or do they look as if they're actually getting along?" she said.

"Yeah, but for how long? All it will take is one snarky comment from either of them and the barbs will start flying."

Call her selfish, but she hoped they would wait until

she and Nick left for the airport before they decided to
duke it out.

"Do you think I should go over there?" he asked, but
before she could answer, his uncle, Tony Senior, joined his
parents, then looked over at Nick and Terri and winked.
Clearly they weren't the only ones concerned. And if anyone could keep hotheaded Leo Caroselli in line, it was
his big brother.

"Thank you, Uncle Tony," Nick muttered under his
breath, looking relieved. "Let's get the heck out of here.
If there's going to be an explosion, I don't want to be
around to see it."

Neither did she.

They made the rounds to aunts, uncles, cousins and
friends from work, most of whom Terri knew on a first-
name basis.

When they got to Tony and Rob, who were standing
by the bar, Nick shook their hands and said, "Thank you
for coming today."

"Yes, thank you," Terri said. "It meant so much to us
to have you here."

"Wouldn't have missed it," Rob said, giving Terri a
hug and a peck on the cheek. He smelled expensive, like
scotch and cologne, and as always his suit was tailored to
a perfect fit, his dark hair trimmed and neatly combed,
and his nails buffed to a shine. She would bet her life that
he probably got pedicures, too. He was so serious all the
time, so…uptight. Even when they were kids, she had
often wondered if he ever relaxed and had fun.

Tony was attractive in a dark, brooding sort of way,
with his smoldering eyes and guarded smile. She'd never
told Nick, but when they were in high school she'd had a
short-lived crush on Tony. She was quite sure that, being
six years her senior, he hadn't even noticed she was alive.

But now he kissed her cheek and said, "May you have a long and happy life together."

"We plan to." Terri smiled up at Nick and hugged herself close to his side, laying it on thick, since according to Nick, his cousins both had doubts the marriage was real.

"Think you can keep this guy in line?" Rob asked.

"The question is, can he keep *me* in line?"

Nick grinned. "I'll give it my best shot."

"I suppose you noticed your parents are talking," Tony said.

Nick shot a glance their way. "Yeah, but your dad seems to have it under control for now."

Terri could see that he was still nervous.

"I haven't seen your mom in a couple years," Rob said. "She looks great. Very…hip."

Nick's mom had always had her own unique style, so it was no surprise that she had substituted the typical conservative mother-of-the-groom dress for a long, flowing 1970s–style number that she could have picked up—and very likely *did*—at the vintage resale shop. In contrast, his dad looked like the typical executive in his thousand-dollar Italian suit. It's no wonder their marriage failed. Two people couldn't have been more different.

Terri glanced up at the clock and realized they were on the verge of running late. She gave Nick a nudge and said, "Our ride is going to be here soon."

"Again, gentlemen, thanks for coming," Nick said, and after another round of handshakes and hugs, with his arm firmly around her waist, they walked over to his parents. Tony Senior had left to stand by his wife, Sarah, leaving the two of them alone again.

"There's the happy couple," Nick's mom said with a bright smile as they approached.

"We're getting ready to leave," Nick told them. "We just wanted to say goodbye."

"Can't wait to get the honeymoon started, huh?" Nick's dad said, his booming voice making Terri cringe inwardly, as did his overly enthusiastic hug.

"Dad," Nick said in a tone that stated *back off.* But Leo ignored him. It wasn't that she disliked Nick's dad, she just didn't know him very well. And yes, he intimidated her a little, too. A far as she could tell, Nick had always been his polar opposite—at least in every way that mattered. Which is probably why they didn't get along.

"Thanks, Mr. Caroselli," she said when he let go.

He laughed heartily, drawing the attention of the entire room, and boomed, "You're my daughter now! Call me Dad!"

She actually preferred *Mr. Caroselli,* but didn't want to hurt his feelings.

Nick's mom—whom she had been calling Mom for the better part of twenty years—took Terri by her hands and squeezed them hard. "I know I've said this a dozen times in the past couple weeks, but I am so thrilled for the two of you. You are exactly what this guy needed." She smiled and gave Nick's jacket sleeve a playful tug. "Everyone in the family knew you were prefect for each other. I'm so happy that you both finally figured it out."

Terri braced herself against a jab of guilt. Though she liked everyone in Nick's family, his mom held a very special place in her heart. She had been the surrogate mother that Terri had desperately needed as a young woman.

She had taken Terri for her first bra, explained menstrual cycles and feminine hygiene products. And when Terri was finally asked out on her first date at the geriatric age of sixteen, Nick's mom had talked to her about the virtues of waiting, not necessarily for marriage, to have sex—she was far too progressive for that—but at least be until she was love. Then she took Terri to the clinic for birth control pills six months later when Terri decided she might take the leap sooner rather than later.

Nick's mom kissed him on the cheek, and gave Terri a hug, squeezing so hard it was difficult to breathe for a second. Her hugs were always warm and firm and full of love. She was so petite and fragile-looking, Terri was a little afraid to hug back too hard, for fear that she might crush her. But Terri had never known a tougher woman. Tough enough to stand up to—take no crap from—her brawny, loud and opinionated ex-husband. And when her second husband's dark side had emerged, and he took a swing at her, she swung right back. When all was said and done, she spent a few days in the hospital, but he spent those same days in jail with a broken nose and some deep scratch marks on his face so he would, as she phrased it, always have something to remember her by.

"Thank you so much for your help with the wedding," Terri said. "It was perfect. I couldn't have done it without you and Jess and Mags."

"Oh, honey, it was my pleasure. Any time you need my help, all you have to do is ask. And no pressure, but I throw a mean baby shower."

"We'll get right on that," Nick said, shooting Terri a glance that was so hot and steamy, she could practically feel it sizzle.

"So," Nick said, looking warily between his parents. "This is…different."

"What? That we're talking?" his mom asked.

"That you're not screaming at each other, and no fists are flying."

Another hearty laugh burst from his dad, propelling

his head back. "Water under the bridge, son. No hard feelings, right, Gena!"

Nick's mom smiled. "We were just saying that it's time we put the past behind us. That our whole problem was that we're just two very passionate people."

That was definitely one way to look at it. Although Terri always thought that is was simply that they didn't like each other.

Nick winced. "I have to admit, you're creeping me out a little."

"I would think you'd be happy," his mom said.

"Don't get me wrong. It's not that I don't want to see you bury the hatchet. I'm just afraid it's going to wind up protruding from someone's back."

"Not to worry, son," his dad assured him. "Everything is fine."

"Well, we've got to get upstairs and change," Nick told them. "Thanks again, Mom, for all your help."

"You two have fun on that honeymoon," his dad said with a wink that unsettled Terri more than a little bit.

His mom kissed and hugged them both. "Text me when you get there so I know you're safe. And have a good time."

Terri was forced to endure another overenthusiastic hug from his dad. As they were heading up the stairs Nick said, "Sorry about that. I know he can be obnoxious. And you don't have to call him Dad if you don't want to."

"He means well," she said. She didn't want to hurt his feelings, so she would probably force herself to call him Dad since it was only going to be for a short time.

They were running behind schedule, so Terri was thankful that she'd laid out her travel clothes ahead of time. There was nothing she hated more than being late, a virtue hammered into her by her aunt, who was intolerant of tardiness. Not that being on time had ever earned Terri any love and attention. In fact, back then, bad attention seemed favorable to being ignored, so she had been late a lot as a kid.

As they reached the top of the stairs and turned, a woman Terri had seen downstairs earlier, but hadn't yet met, was walking toward them from either the study or the master suite.

"Oh, thank goodness," she said, looking embarrassed. "I was looking for the bathroom but I must have made a wrong turn."

"It's the other way," Nick said, gesturing in that direction. "Second door on the left."

"Thanks. Your grandfather's house is really beautiful. My mother's descriptions don't do it justice."

"Terri, this is Rose," Nick said. "She was recently hired and her mom used to be *Nonno's* secretary."

"Pleasure to meet you," Terri said, shaking her hand. "Thanks for coming today."

"It was an honor to be invited," she said, but the smile she wore didn't quite reach her eyes. She seemed almost… nervous, as if they had caught her doing something underhanded.

"Well, we have a plane to catch," Nick said.

"Have a great honeymoon and a safe trip," she said, then headed swiftly down the stairs, bypassing the bathroom altogether. Call it intuition, or maybe she was just paranoid, but Terri had the feeling this woman was looking for something. And it wasn't the bathroom.

Nick gestured Terri into the spare bedroom where they'd left their things. She was about to voice her suspicions, but Nick closed the door and the next instant, he had her backed her against it, pinned with the weight of his body, his lips on hers.

Oh, man, could he kiss, and as much as she wanted to keep kissing him, they had to go. After a moment she laid her hands on his chest and gently pushed him away. "You know we don't have time."

"I know," he said. "But getting you naked is pretty much all I've thought about since last night."

His words thrilled her, and she liked the idea of him taking her right here, up against the door.

"Don't you think it would be nice if our first time wasn't rushed?" she asked. "And happened in bed?"

Nick gestured over his shoulder. "There's a bed right there."

"Nick—"

"Okay, okay," he said backing away. "But the second we get to Aruba, Mrs. Caroselli, you're mine."

Seven

Keeping his hands off Terri while she changed into jeans and a T-shirt, seeing her in her bra and panties, was the worst kind of torture, but Nick knew that if they were going to make their flight, the fooling around would have to wait. On sheer will he managed to restrain himself, but the image of her standing there mostly naked was emblazoned in his mind.

They arrived at the airport with an hour to spare, only to find their flight had been delayed due to a line of storms that spanned the entire southeast. As a result, they spent the next four hours stuck in the terminal playing solitaire on their phones, and sharing a less-than-gourmet meal at a fast food restaurant. When their flight was finally called, and they did get in the air, the ride was so bumpy neither of them could sleep. Terri sat beside him the entire five hours, her white-knuckled hold on his hand so tight that he had to let go every few minutes to shake the blood flow back into his fingers.

When they finally landed in Aruba, because of the flight delay, they had to wait another hour for their ride. By the time they reached the resort, and were shown to their suite—which was as luxurious as the description on the website, and about the only thing that had gone right so far—the sun was rising.

After a tour of all the amenities that at the moment Nick didn't give a damn about, he gave the bellboy a generous tip, hung the do not disturb sign on the door, then closed and locked it. "I thought that guy would *never* leave."

"It's official," Terri said, looking as beat as he was feeling. "I've been up for twenty-four hours."

So had he. He'd been known to pull all-nighters at work, then function reasonably well the next day. Maybe the stress of the past two weeks had finally caught up with him, or the miserable flight had worn him out, because his body was shutting down. Though he wouldn't have imagined it possible, he was too exhausted for sex. "Maybe we should take a nap."

Without hesitation Terri walked straight to the bedroom, yanked back the covers on the king-size bed and flopped facedown onto the sheet. She sighed and said in a sleepy voice, "Oh, that's nice."

Nick climbed in next to her and stretched out on his back, felt the mattress conform to his body as he relaxed.

Terri scooted close to him and cuddled up to his side, one arm draped across his chest, her breasts nestled against him. He'd been anticipating this day for two weeks, and now he was too damned tired to move.

"I want to jump you," Terri said, "but I don't have the energy."

"Me, neither," he said. "Can we at least sleep naked?"

She was quiet for a second, then sighed and said, "As nice as that sounds, I don't think I have the strength to take my clothes off."

He imagined all the movement getting undressed would require and said, "Come to think of it, neither do I."

"You know, I never imagined how stressful it could be planning a wedding, even with so much help. It was really nice, but I'm kinda glad it's over."

"I'm sorry if it wasn't your dream wedding."

"I was never one of those girls."

"What kind of girl?"

"The ones who start planning their wedding when they're barely out of diapers. I've always been more interested in finding the perfect *man*."

"Well, I'm sorry I couldn't be that, either." For a fleeting moment, he almost wished he could be. Because for him, she would be as close to the perfect woman as he would ever find. The problem was, he had no desire to be any woman's perfect man.

"You're helping me fulfill my dream of having a child," she said. "That's pretty huge."

If he wasn't so damned tired, he would be helping her fulfill that particular dream right now, but he could feel himself drifting off. She was still talking but the words weren't making it through the fog in his brain. He tried to keep his eyes open, but they refused to cooperate.

He finally gave in and let them close, and when he opened them again he was in bed alone. He looked at the time on his watch, surprised that he'd slept for over four hours.

He sat up, looking around the room, taking in the decor that he'd been too exhausted to notice earlier. The tropical theme was typical for the area, and could be a little too touristy for his taste, but here it was done well. He could smell the ocean, hear the water rushing up to meet the sand.

He rolled out of bed and went searching for Terri. Her bag lay open on the sofa, but she was nowhere in the suite. He opened the French doors that led out onto a small portico, then a narrow stretch of private beach. The air was warm but dry, and the sun so intense he had to shade his eyes. Guests sunned themselves in lawn chairs and swimmers dotted the crystal-clear blue water. Farther out was everything from sailboats and luxury yachts to commercial cruise ships.

He didn't see Terri anywhere, and figured she had probably gone for a walk, or maybe down to the pool.

He stepped back inside, thinking he would call her cell phone, until he noticed it sitting on the table by the couch.

He would take a shower instead, and if she wasn't back by the time he was finished, he would go looking for her.

He grabbed what he needed from his suitcase and stepped into the bathroom. The opened toiletries on the shower shelf, and wet towel hanging on the rack, told him that she'd already been there, and the remnants of moisture still clinging to the tile shower wall said it hadn't been that long ago. Too bad she hadn't woken him; they could have showered together.

He imagined how she would look, all slippery and wet, those long gorgeous legs wrapped around him, pressed against the shower wall. He wondered if that was a position that qualified as deep penetration. And decided right then that they would have to try it and find out.

He had just stepped out of the shower and was toweling off when he heard the suite door open.

"Nick!"

"In here." He fastened the towel around his waist and

exited the bathroom. Terri stood by the bed, dressed in nothing but a white bikini top that seemed to glow against her sun-kissed skin, and a pair of frayed, cutoff denim short shorts that showcased her slender legs, making them look a mile long. Her hair hung loose and damp around her shoulders, and the only makeup she wore was a touch of lip gloss.

It wasn't that he hadn't seen her dressed this way before. But those other times, he hadn't really *seen* her—not the way he was now. He had the feeling it was the same for her, because she hadn't peeled her eyes from his chest since he'd entered the room.

"Good nap?" she asked, her eyes finally lifting to his. They had a hazy quality that said she was already turned on. And knowing she was, thrust his libido into overdrive.

"Yeah. How long did you sleep?"

She shrugged. "A couple hours."

"You should have woken me."

"That's okay. I want you well rested."

He would ask why, but the way she was sizing him up, he was pretty sure he already knew. "So I guess this is the official start of our honeymoon."

"Then I guess it would be a good time to mention that I'm not wearing any underwear."

Damn. "What a coincidence, because neither am I."

Her gaze dropped from his chest to the towel and her tongue darted out to wet her lips. "Show me."

Terri watched as Nick gave the towel a quick tug, then let it drop to the floor. She looked him up and down, shaking her head. There was no getting around it—physically, the guy was perfect. "Wow. That is so not fair."

"What?"

"No one should look that good naked."

"And I'm all yours," he said, walking toward her with no modesty or shame, wearing that I'm-going-to-eat-you-alive look.

Her heart skipped a beat.

"Ready to make a baby?"

A baby. They were going to have sex, and try to make a baby.

Her heart gave a sudden, violent jerk as the reality of what she was doing, and who she was doing it with, hit her hard. Was she really ready for this? "We're going to make a baby," she said.

"Yep." He stopped in front of her and made a twirly gesture with his index finger. "Turn around."

"Together," she added, turning.

"That's the idea," he said, and with a quick tug, untied her bikini top. "Of course, we could do it alone, but that wouldn't be nearly as much fun."

Though she'd never been particularly shy about anyone seeing her naked, as her top fell away, she had to fight the urge to cross her arms over her breasts. What was wrong with her? For two weeks she'd been preparing herself for this, thinking about this exact moment over and over. When it came to sex, she always knew exactly what she wanted, and she'd never been shy about asking for it. So why, now, did she feel like a virgin, about to make love for the first time?

He must have sensed something was wrong, because he asked over her shoulder, "Are you still okay with this?"

"Of course," she said, but it was difficult to sound convincing when her voice was trembling.

"Are you sure? Because you sound a little nervous." His arms slid around her and cupped her breasts in his palms, easing her backward against his wide muscular chest. His skin was still warm and damp from his shower.

And even though it felt amazing, and she wanted more, her heart was in her throat.

"We could stop right now," he said.

Would he really? If she told him that she had changed her mind, that she was scared, he wouldn't be upset?

But she wouldn't get scared. Not about sex of all things. "I don't want to stop."

He ran the backs of his fingers slowly down her stomach to the edge of her shorts, and her skin quivered under his touch. One part of her was saying, *don't stop there,* while another said, *what do you think you're doing, pal? We're* friends. *You aren't supposed to touch me this way.*

"As long as we don't consummate the marriage," Nick said, tugging the snap open on her shorts, "we can still have it annulled."

She wasn't sure if he was serious or teasing her. What if he was serious? What would his family think? How would she explain that they'd gone through all that trouble planning a wedding for a marriage that lasted twenty-four hours?

"Terri?" he said, sounding unsure, his hands dropping away.

She turned, arms folded across her breasts. "What if I said I want to stop? That I thought we were making a mistake?"

He blinked, his expression a mix of confusion and surprise. "You're serious?"

She nodded.

He was quiet for several seconds, then said, "If you really don't want to do this, we won't."

"After everything we've been through the past couple weeks, you wouldn't be mad?"

"I would be disappointed, but our friendship comes first, always."

She could see that they weren't just words. He meant it. She wasn't just another woman he was sleeping with, or a convenient way to make ten million dollars. He really cared about her feelings. And she *knew* that. The truth was, this had nothing to do with him. This was about her insecurities.

When it came to relationships, love—or what she perceived love to be—always managed to elude her. And while sex, if she was lucky, was usually fun, she'd never felt the intense emotional connection that she was experiencing right now, with Nick. The *need* to be closer to him. She never *needed* anyone, and it scared her half to death. What if he let her down?

But this was Nick, the most important person in her life. The man she had barely gone a day or two without speaking with in the past two decades. He would *not* let her down. He wouldn't do anything to hurt her. And she refused to ruin what could very well be one of the most significant days in her entire life, just because she had intimacy issues. It was time she grew up, and let go of the past. Time she really trusted someone.

"Do you want to stop?" he asked. "We can."

"No. I don't want to stop."

He eyed her warily. "You're *sure*. Because once we get started, there's really no going back."

"I want this," she said, and she really did, even though she was scared. "I want *you*."

She dropped her arms, baring herself to him, and the hunger in his eyes as he raked his gaze over her made her heart beat faster.

"You had me worried there for a minute," he said. "Although I have to admit, I sort of like you this way."

"What way?"

"Not so confident. A little vulnerable."

Weirdly enough, she sort of liked it, too. She liked the idea of letting someone else take care of her for a change. Within reason, of course. She didn't want him getting the idea that she was a complete pushover.

She slid her arms around his neck and kissed him, then whispered in his ear, "Lay down."

"Now that's the Terri I know," he said with a grin, climbing into bed, watching as she shoved down her shorts and got in with him, straddling his thighs.

"You're so beautiful." He reached up, cupped her breasts in his palms, watched her nipples pull into tight points as he circled them with his thumbs. "I want to take my time, touch and kiss every inch of your body."

She smiled. "Well, if you have to…"

He pulled her against him, wrapped his arms around her and kissed her…and *kissed* her, disarming her with the rhythm of his tongue, his hands sliding across her skin, kissing and stroking away the last of her reservations, until she couldn't recall why she'd been afraid in the first place. And the more she responded, the bolder his explorations became. Still, she could tell he was taking his time, trying not to push too hard or too fast.

She just wanted to touch him—wanted *him*—and as close as he held her, as intimately as he touched her, it wasn't enough. She ached for something, but she wasn't sure what. She just knew she *needed* more. And though she preferred to have the upper hand, when Nick took control, rolling her over onto her back, she let him. Being so tall, logistics in bed could sometimes be a problem for her, but as he settled between her thighs, she and Nick were an ideal fit.

"That's better," he said, his weight pressing her into the mattress.

This was it, she thought, knowing that she would remember this moment for the rest of her life—the exact second when, with one slow deep thrust, they went from being friends to lovers.

She gazed down between them, to where their bodies were joined, thinking it was the most arousing, erotic thing she had ever seen. "Nick, we're making love," she said. "You're inside me."

He followed her gaze, transfixed for a moment, then he wrapped his arms around her and kissed her, started to move inside her.

She really thought she'd been prepared for this, that because they were friends, she could maintain a level of detachment, or objectivity. That it would be "fun" without those pesky feelings of affection to muddy things up. Boy, had she been wrong.

This wasn't supposed to change things, but deep down she knew they would never be quite the same.

"Deeper," she said. "You have to be deeper."

"I can't," he said, thrusting slow and steady, his shoulders tense, his eyes closed in concentration. "I'll lose it."

As it was, she was barely hanging on, and they needed to do this together, and not just so they would have a boy. She...*needed* it. "Nick, look at me."

He opened his eyes and looked down at her. The instant their eyes met, she was toast, and apparently so was he. With a growl, Nick grabbed her legs and hooked them over his shoulders, bending her in half, groaning as he thrust hard and deep, and her body went electric. It was shock and pleasure and perfection, and watching Nick's face, seeing him lose control, reaching their peak together, was the single most erotic experience of her life.

Afterward, Nick dropped his head against her shoulder, his forehead damp with perspiration. He was breathing hard. *"Wow."*

No kidding.

Nick eased her legs off his shoulders and she winced as her muscles, mostly the ones in her butt, screamed in protest. She stretched out her legs and her left cheek started to cramp up. She winced and said, "Ow! Charley horse!"

"Where?" Nick said, rolling off her.

"Left butt cheek."

"Turn over," he said, and when she did, he straddled her thighs and rubbed the knotted muscle, using his thumbs to really work it loose. "Better?"

"Hmm...that feels good," she said, as the pain subsided. She folded her arms around the pillow and tucked it under her head. "I'm going to have a talk with my personal trainer. All those hours spent in the gym, and I'm not nearly as flexible as I should be."

"I guess we'll just have to work on that," he said.

She sighed and closed her eyes. Though she was typically the one doing the pampering after sex, it was nice to be spoiled a little. Only problem was, she was getting a little *too* relaxed, to the point that her body was shutting down.

"Hey," Nick said. "I hope you're not falling asleep."

"Nope," she lied as the world started to go soft and fuzzy around her.

"We're not finished." He gave her a gentle shake. "Wake up."

"I'm awake," she mumbled, or at least she thought she did. It didn't matter because it was already too late. She gave in to the fatigue and drifted off to sleep.

Eight

Nick gave Terri a poke, then a harder poke, but it was useless. She was out cold.

He sighed. Wasn't it the *guy* who was supposed to roll over and fall asleep after sex? His plan had been for them to spend the entire day in bed, trying out many different positions. But he supposed he should be happy that they'd had sex at all.

It was a little difficult to reconcile the Terri from two weeks ago, who propositioned him in his kitchen, and the one who froze up today when he touched her. He wasn't sure what had happened, why she had suddenly gotten cold feet. At first he thought she was teasing him, playing coy, until he saw her face, then the metaphorical ball came out of left field and smacked him right between the eyes.

Was it something he did? Something he said? Did he hurt her feelings? Or was it something he'd had no control over whatsoever?

Damned if he knew.

She was ovulating, so her hormones were probably out of whack, and he knew from growing up in a house with three females, a hormonal woman could be unpredictable—and at times downright scary. But weren't ovulating women supposed to want sex more, not less?

Or was it possible that she didn't find him as appealing as she said she did? Was she so desperate to get pregnant, she would have told him anything?

Nah, that definitely wasn't it, because when they did finally get the ball rolling, it had been pretty freaking amazing. To put his hands all over that lithe, lean body, to feel those incredible legs wrapped around his waist. Over his shoulders.

Damn.

Even so, when he looked at her now, lying there, naked and gorgeous, she was still just *Terri,* his best friend. And other than wanting to put his hands all over her again, he couldn't say that he felt any differently about her now than he had yesterday. Which was exactly how he'd expected to feel.

He assumed, since she would be ovulating for at least a few more days, there was no reason they couldn't have fun until then, or better yet, for the duration of their honeymoon. But he knew that when they returned to Chicago, they would go back to their previous platonic status. The truth was, they hadn't really talked about it. And that had probably been a mistake. But everything had happened in such a rush, they really hadn't had time.

Terri mumbled something in her sleep, then rolled over onto her side, curling up in a ball, as if she were chilled, so he tugged the covers up over her. As long as he'd known her she'd talked in her sleep. There were times, when they lived together, when he would pass by her room at night and hear her babbling incoherently. He would sometimes stop and listen, catch a random word here or there, but it usually didn't make any sense. If she seemed distressed, as if she were having a nightmare, which had happened often, he would push open her door a crack and peek in on her, just to make sure she was okay.

Sometimes he would hear her say his name, wondering what role he played in her dream. There were even times when he imagined crawling into bed with her. How would she react if he did? He never would have done it, though. She wanted the fairy-tale happy ending. A thing he could never give her, and after all the heartache in her life, she deserved to get exactly what she wanted. Even now he hated that she'd had to settle, that he couldn't give her everything her heart desired. But he just wasn't wired that way. Anyone he dated knew that from the start, although that didn't necessarily stop them from believing that they were different, that they would be the one he fell hopelessly in love with.

But Terri knew better. Didn't she?

He was sure she did. They had agreed this situation would be temporary. So why her mixed feelings today? Maybe it would be in everyone's best interest if they had a serious talk about the situation, and set some boundaries to prevent any future confusion. Just in case.

Nick's stomach growled, and he considered ringing for room service, but then he looked at the empty space beside Terri—and the cool sheets and fluffy pillows called out to him. She had said she wanted him well rested, hadn't she?

He stretched out beside her, his eyes feeling heavy the second his head hit the pillow. He rolled over on his side, draping an arm across her hip, wondering, as he drifted off to sleep, if it would be smooth sailing from here on out. Or would she have a change of heart again?

He got his answer when he woke from what he'd thought was an erotic dream. He opened his eyes, looked down at his crotch, and saw the top of Terri's head.

"I'm toast," Terri said.

She dropped face-first onto the sheets, sweaty and out of breath, and Nick fell on top of her, his weight crushing her against the mattress, making it hard to breathe. She was too exhausted to protest. They had been going at it, on and off, for three hours now, and she was ready for a break.

"Do you feel pregnant yet?" he asked, his voice muffled against her hair, which she was sure was probably a knotted mess.

"I think it takes a couple weeks for that part," she said. If she hadn't conceived the first three times they'd made love, she was pretty sure this last time would have done it. Their position, while slightly awkward at first, gave a whole new meaning to the phrase *deep penetration*. Plus, her thighs had gotten one hell of a workout.

She shifted under his weight, feeling light-headed from lack of oxygen. Gathering all her strength, she elbowed him in the ribs. "Hey, you're squishing me."

"Sorry," he said, rolling onto his back. "So, what do you want to do now?"

"Sleep?"

He looked over at her. *"Again?"*

Or not. "I don't know. What do people usually do on their honeymoon?"

He looked over at her and grinned, wiggling his eyebrows.

Good heavens, the man had stamina.

"Something besides intercourse," she said.

He thought about it for a minute, then said, "Oral sex?"

"Funny," she said giving him a playful poke, and he grinned.

"We could sit in the sand and watch the sunset," he said. "I hear they can be pretty spectacular."

"Which I suppose would necessitate me getting up and putting clothes on."

"Personally, I wouldn't mind if you went out there like this, but the other guests might object." He leaned over and kissed her shoulder. "If I could bring the sunset to you, I would."

Wow, that was probably one of the sweetest, most romantic things a man had ever said to her. She smiled and said, "I appreciate the thought."

"Come on," he said, giving her butt a playful smack as he rolled out of bed. "Get up."

She forced herself to stand and walk on jelly legs to the bathroom. It seemed strange that just this morning she'd been uncomfortable with him seeing her naked, and now it seemed perfectly natural. Not only had he seen it all, but there wasn't an inch that he hadn't touched in one way or another. When he told her that he thought sex should be fun, he wasn't kidding. And boy was he *good* at it. He seemed to take pleasure from giving pleasure, which she knew was rare.

She stepped into the bathroom and cringed at her reflection in the mirror. "I look like a beast. I need to do something with my hair."

He appeared in the doorway dressed in shorts and a T-shirt. "Yikes! You do look like a beast."

She glared at him.

"Kidding," he said, flashing her that disarming grin and planting a kiss on her cheek. "I'll meet you out there."

She wrestled a brush through the knots in her hair and brought it back into a ponytail. Not great, but it would suffice. She pulled a light sundress out of her bag and slipped it on, then stepped outside.

The air felt cooler. A gentle breeze rustled the the palm trees, their branches swaying in time like a tropical nature dance. And Nick was right about the sunset. Red-and-orange streaks above the horizon gave the illusion that the sky was on fire.

Nick was on a blanket in the sand a few yards from the water. He sat with his knees bent, his arms wrapped around them. She walked over and sat down beside him.

He smiled at her, nodding to the sky. "Nice, huh?"

"Beautiful."

He leaned back and looped an arm around her, and she rested her head against his shoulder. It felt…comfortable. She wondered if it would be okay to do this after they went home to Chicago, or if any sort of physical contact would be off limits.

"So," he said. "About earlier today…"

She cringed. It was embarrassing, really, the way she'd acted. And she still wasn't quite sure why. "Can we just forget about that?"

"I wanted to be sure that everything is okay now."

"It is, I promise." That should have been obvious the minute she woke him up from his nap, which was exactly why she'd done it. Well, that and he'd looked really good laying there naked.

"You were pretty freaked out," he said.

So apparently they *were* going to talk about it. "I know. I thought I had worked it all out in my head, but then you asked if I was ready to make a baby, and I guess I thought, *I don't know, am I?* It's a huge step. My entire life will change."

"And you were worried about it changing our relationship." It was a statement, not a question.

"That, too."

"Do you think it has?"

"Sort of. But not in a bad way."

"We never really talked about what will happen after the honeymoon."

Which she took to mean that they should talk about it now. "I just assumed we would go back to the way things were. Aside from the fact that we'll be living together, I mean. And, of course, your family will have to believe that we're…you know…*together*."

"So, no sex after the honeymoon?"

Was that disappointment she heard in his voice? Did he want to keep having sex? Or was she just imagining what she wanted to hear? Because she liked sleeping with him. Liked it too much for either of their own good.

"I think that would be best," she said. "Under the circumstances, an intimate relationship could get complicated. Don't you think? I know you don't want to settle down."

He thought about that for a minute, and her heart picked up speed. Was he going to say he wanted to keep sleeping with her? And how would she respond if he did? Even if she wanted it, too, would it be wise to tempt fate?

"You're right," he finally said. "I think it would be better if we went back to the way things were."

She was a little disappointed, but not surprised. And she was sure, when things went back to normal, they would be just as happy being friends.

"What if you don't get pregnant?" Nick asked.

"We try again next month. But not until I'm ovulating."

He nodded, as if that made sense to him, too. "And

if you don't get pregnant then? I mean, for all I know, I could be sterile."

"That's highly unlikely. And it would be fairly easy to determine."

"Even if we're both fine, it could still take months, right?"

"So what you're asking is, how long do we keep this up before we call it quits?"

He nodded.

"As long as we're both comfortable with it, I suppose."

An older couple, who looked to be close to Nick's parents' age, walked by, holding hands. Something about the way they moved together, the way they smiled at one another, made Terri think they had probably been married a long time, and were probably still deeply in love.

They smiled and said hello as they passed, and Terri actually felt a twinge of jealousy. As much as she wanted that for herself, and while most of her friends from college were already happily married and starting families, she had begun to believe that, for her, it would probably never happen. That maybe she was just meant for different things. The only thing she did know for sure was that until she became a mother, she would never feel truly complete. So whatever she had to do to make that happen, wasn't it worth the risk?

Terri woke the next morning to the sound of rain against the windows. Through the filmy curtains, she could see lightning slash across the sky. She glanced over her shoulder at Nick, who was curled up behind her, his arm draped across her hip. Though he was still asleep, certain parts were wide awake and pressed against her. She grabbed her phone and checked her weather app, which called for scattered thunderstorms all day. So much for their plans to rent a car and drive to Arikok National Park.

"Is that rain I hear?" Nick mumbled behind her.

"Yeah. It's supposed to rain on and off all day."

"Darn." Nick slid his arm around her, cupping her breast. "Guess we'll have to stay inside today."

She was sure they could find some indoor activity other than sex, but honestly, why would they want to? They only had a few more days before they went back to being just friends. Besides, newlyweds were supposed to have lots of sex on their honeymoon. Right?

They stayed in bed most of the day, and later that evening when the sky finally cleared, they showered together, then attended a party by the pool with the other resort guests. They played the role of the loving newlyweds, even though they would likely never see any of these people again.

They spent the following day in Arikok National Park. They rented a car, and quickly discovered that very few of the roads in Aruba were marked. They got lost a couple times, but it was worth the hassle when they got there.

Their first stop was Boca Prins, which they were told by another guest at the resort was the most beautiful thing in Aruba. With its beach cliffs, dunes and rocky shore, Terri had to agree. Although the sunset that first night definitely rated a close second.

They stopped for lunch at a local cantina, then drove to Fontein Cave and on to Guadirikiri Cave. Nick found her fear of the the lizards scurrying around incredibly amusing.

In the early evening they dropped off the car and took a taxi to downtown Oranjestad. They did a little shopping as they made their way to Fort Zoutman where they stopped to listen to a steel band and browsed the various local craft booths. They bought souvenirs for Nick's niece and nephews, and Terri found a pair of earrings she knew his mom would adore. She liked them so much she got a pair for herself, too.

Without street signs, it took a while to find the restaurant where they had made reservations for dinner, but the food was incredible. They ate and danced until they were exhausted, but not so much that it stopped them from making love when they got back to their room. After all, it was after their last night together.

Wednesday morning they packed and took a taxi to the airport for their flight home. They made it through security without a problem, found their gate and sat down to wait. That was when the reality of the situation hit home, and suddenly she wasn't ready to leave. Wasn't ready for this to be over.

The longer you wait, the harder it will be, she reminded herself. If they didn't end this now, what would they do? Continue on as lovers until the baby was born, or for the rest of their lives, yet never be in a committed relationship? She wasn't naive enough to believe that any friendship, even one as strong as theirs, could survive that. Besides, she wasn't quite ready to give up on the fairy tale. Finding Mr. Right, and living happily ever after.

But as Nick sat silently beside her, reading an issue of *Time* magazine, she couldn't help but wonder what he was thinking—if he was ready for this to be over or if he had regrets, too. Not that it would make a difference. So why was she obsessing about it?

Their flight was called right on time.

"I guess this is it," Nick said, stuffing the magazine into his carry-on bag. "The end of our honeymoon."

"I guess so." She grabbed her bag and started to stand, but Nick wrapped his hand around her arm.

"Terri…wait."

She sat back down, turning to him. "Is something wr—"

Nick hooked a hand behind her neck, pulled her to him and kissed her. It was slow and deep and bittersweet, and packed with so much raw emotion, she knew he was just as sorry to see this end. But like her, he knew they had no choice.

"Sorry," he said, closing his eyes and pressing his forehead to hers. "I just had to do that one more time."

They were doing the right thing, so why did she suddenly feel like crying? She was too choked up to say anything. If she tried, she would probably burst into tears, and where would that get them? It would just make him feel bad, and her feel stupid.

She pressed one last quick kiss to his lips, then stood and said, "We'd better go."

In the past five days she had grown used to touching and kissing Nick whenever she wanted. Now she would just have to get unused to it. Unless they were around his family, since it was necessary to keep up the ruse.

They boarded the plane, stored their bags and took their seats. With any luck, she was pregnant. She couldn't imagine how she wouldn't be, considering all the unprotected sex they'd been having. And though she almost hoped she hadn't conceived, so they could have honeymoon number two in about four weeks, she knew that dragging this out another month or so would only delay the inevitable. That it would probably be even harder next time.

After they were in the air, she reclined her seat and closed her eyes, pretending to sleep. It was easier than trying to make cheerful small talk, when she felt anything but happy. Nick kept himself amused reading his magazine. At some point she must have really fallen asleep, because suddenly Nick was nudging her and saying that the plane was going to land in a few minutes.

They didn't say much to each other during the miserably long wait in customs. What she wanted was to go back to her own place, curl up in her own bed and be miserable all by herself, but her home was at Nick's apartment now.

"You've been awfully quiet," Nick said, when they were in the car and heading for the city. "Is everything okay?"

She looked over at him and forced a smile. "Fine. I'm just tired. And not looking forward to all the work I have waiting for me."

It wasn't a total lie, but not exactly the truth, either.

"You will take tomorrow off, right?"

"Of course." She hadn't missed Thanksgiving with his family in years. "And maybe I'll do some Black Friday shopping with your mom."

"You're sure everything is okay?" he said.

"I'm sure." She pulled out her cell phone and checked her email. Nick took the hint and didn't ask any more questions.

The car dropped them off around dinnertime, and they rode the elevator up in silence. Though she continued to pretend that everything was fine, there was tension in the air, and she knew that he felt it, too.

She hated for their relationship to take this turn. As long as they had been friends, they had barely even had a fight.

It will just take a little time for things to go back to normal, she assured herself. After that, everything would be fine.

The elevator doors opened and sitting in the hallway outside the apartment door, a suitcase at her side, was

Jess, Nick's sister. She looked tired, and her eyes were red and puffy, as if she might have been crying.

"Hi, there," she said with a weak smile. "How was the honeymoon?"

Nine

"Jess, what are you doing here?" Nick asked, but considering the suitcase beside her, he could make an educated guess.

Jess pushed herself to her feet. "Can we go inside and talk?"

"Sure." He unlocked the door and they all rolled their luggage in. When everyone was inside, he shut the door and turned to his sister.

"Eddie and I are taking a break," she said. "Or, I am, anyway."

"What happened?"

"He blew off counseling for the third week in a row. Knowing I have that to look forward to, that it might make things better eventually, is the only thing that's kept me going the last couple months. He obviously doesn't feel the same way. So I left."

"What about the kids?"

"They're spending Thanksgiving in Indiana with Eddie's parents. They'll be there a week. I'm hoping we can work something out by the time they come back."

"What are you doing here?" Nick asked.

"Honestly, I couldn't bear the thought of staying alone in a hotel for the next week, and I know you guys have the extra bedroom." She smiled hopefully.

"What about Mom's place?"

"I didn't want to worry her. Also, I'd like to keep this quiet, and you know how she is. If she knows, *everyone* will know."

Nick was about to make up some excuse about him and Terri being newlyweds and needing their privacy, but before he could, Terri said, "Of course you can stay here."

"Thank you," Jess said, looking as if she were fighting tears. "You have no idea how much this means to me. And I won't get in the way, I promise."

"That's what family is for," Terri said, hugging her. "Just give me a few minutes to clear my clothes out of the spare room."

Jess frowned. "Why are your clothes in the spare room?"

Nick thought for sure Jess had her stumped with that one, but Terri didn't miss a beat.

"Have you ever looked in your brother's closet?" she asked Jess.

"If it looks anything like it did when he was a kid, I see your point."

"There's beer in the fridge," Nick said. "And the hard stuff is in the bar in my office. I'm going to help my wife."

Jess headed to the kitchen, while Nick and Terri walked to what was supposed to be her bedroom. When they were alone, he whispered, "You realize what you just did, right? You really think it's a good idea for us to share a bedroom? And a *bed?*"

"*No,* but what were we supposed to tell her? Sorry, you can't stay because *I'm* sleeping there? How would we explain *that?*"

If she had just given him a minute to think, he would have come up with something.

"Besides, it's only for a week." She opened the closet and grabbed an armful of clothes. "Do you have room for these in your closet?"

"I'll make room," he said, opening one of the drawers. Of course, with his rotten luck, it was full of lingerie. Damn. "And for the record, my closet looks nothing like it did in high school. Or college."

"I don't care how it looks, as long as it doesn't smell like sweaty sports gear."

He opened his mouth to argue, but realized it probably had smelled pretty awful.

"It doesn't," he said, as they dropped her clothes on his bed. "I keep my gym bag in the utility room behind the kitchen."

"I'll be sure to avoid it," she said, sounding annoyed.

She started to walk away and he grabbed her arm, turning her to face him. "Hey, this was *your* idea."

She looked as if she were about to say something snarky, then it seemed as if all the energy leaked out of her instead. "I know. I'm sorry. I just…I don't even know what's wrong. I'm tired, I guess."

"Just try to cut me a little slack, okay? This isn't easy for me, either."

"I know."

Maybe this scenario of pretending to be married wouldn't be quite as simple as they had imagined, or maybe they just needed a few days to adjust. One thing was certain—having Jess around wasn't going to make the transition any smoother.

They got the rest of Terri's clothes moved into his room and put away in his closet—which she made a point of observing was very tidy—and when they walked out to the kitchen, Jess had made them all dinner. After they ate, they put a movie on, but his sister clearly needed to vent. She alternated between complaining about Eddie and apologizing for complaining.

Around eleven Terri started yawning, which set him off. Once they got started it was a vicious cycle.

"You two must be exhausted from your trip, and here I am talking your heads off," Jess said.

"That's what family is for," Terri told her.

"Well, I'm going to stop whining now and let you two get to bed. And I'm sure I could benefit from a good night's sleep."

Nick was skeptical that she would get one, considering the state of her marriage, and he knew he and Terri wouldn't. Not if they were sleeping in the same bed.

Jess hugged them both good-night, thanked them again for letting her vent then went to bed. When Nick heard her bedroom door close, he turned to Terri. "I guess there's no point putting this off."

"I guess not."

He used the bathroom first, and while she took her turn, he undressed and climbed into bed. She came out wearing a nightshirt that hung to her knees, her hair loose. If it were still their honeymoon, she would be naked, and instead of climbing into the opposite side of the bed, she would be climbing on him.

"So how is this going to work?" she said, pulling the covers up to her waist.

He shrugged. "I stay on my side, you stay on yours."

She shot him a skeptical look. "You can do that?"

Did he have a choice? "It's a king-size bed. You won't even know I'm over here."

She still didn't look completely convinced, but she switched off her light, rolled away from him and pulled the covers over her shoulders.

"What, no kiss?" he said.

She glared at him over her shoulder.

"Kidding." The way she was acting one might have thought that letting his sister stay here had been *his* idea.

He turned off his light, settled onto his back and closed his eyes. He was physically exhausted, but his mind was moving about a million miles an hour, which could make for a very long and sleepless night. The last time he looked at the clock, it was one-thirty, but he must have drifted off because before he knew it, he heard Terri say his name, felt her nudging him awake. He didn't want to wake up; he was too content and comfortable curled up against something warm and soft. It took several seconds to realize that the thing he was curled up against was Terri, and she was looking at him over her shoulder.

"What are you doing on my side of the bed?" he asked.

"I'm not."

He let go and sat up. Sure enough, he had invaded her side of the bed by several feet.

He scooted back onto his own side. "Sorry about that."

"Habit," she said. "Not a big deal."

"It won't happen again." He looked over at the clock and saw that it was only two-thirty. He rolled on his side facing away from her, determined to stay that way the rest of the night.

An hour later she woke him again. He was curled up against her like before, but this time his hand was up her nightshirt and cupped around her bare breast, and he was aroused. In fact, he was horny as hell.

"Um, Nick, maybe you should—"

He yanked his hand from inside her shirt and scooted away from her. "Why didn't you stop me?"

"Don't blame me," she snapped, rolling to face him. "I woke up that way."

He took a deep breath and blew it out. "Sorry, I didn't mean to accuse you."

She sat up. "This is not working. Maybe I should sleep on the floor, or in the bathtub."

"You know what the problem is," he said. "I usually sleep hugging a pillow, but you're lying on it, so I'm hugging you instead."

"Do you have a pillow you could hug instead of me?"

He switched on the light and started to get up, then turned back to her and said, "You may want to look the other way."

Her brows rose. "You don't want me to see you in your pajamas?"

"I wouldn't care if I were wearing any."

Her mouth fell open in surprise. "You're *naked?*"

He shrugged. "I've always slept naked. I don't even own pajamas."

"You own underwear, right? I mean, I've seen you wear it."

He sighed. "I'll put some on."

He hadn't slept with anything on since he was fifteen, but he would just have to get used to it, he supposed.

Terri turned away from him as he got out of bed. But he could swear, as he walked to the closet, he could feel her eyes on him, specifically his ass. He tugged on a pair of boxer briefs, grabbed a pillow from the top shelf, switched off the light and walked back to bed. "Got it."

"And you're not naked?"

"Nope." He climbed into bed. With the skivvies on, he was instantly uncomfortable. Fantastic.

"Well, good night," she said.

"Good night." Though it probably wouldn't be. He curled up with the pillow between them, and must have fallen asleep pretty quickly, because when Terri nudged him awake the next time, it felt like minutes, when in reality a couple hours had passed.

"Nick, you're doing it *again*."

She was right. His arms were around her, his hand was back up her shirt and he was as aroused as he had been the last time.

"Sorry," he said scooting away for a third time, feeling around for the pillow. When he couldn't find it, he asked Terri, "Where did the pillow go?"

"I don't have it," she snapped.

And she was clearly annoyed with him. Not that he could blame her. He switched on the light, and Terri grumbled in protest, covering her head with her pillow. As his eyes adjusted, he looked all around the room and discovered it lying on the floor at the foot of the bed. He must have lobbed it in his sleep. "There it is."

"Awesome."

"I said I was sorry." He threw off the covers in frustration and shoved himself out of bed.

"Nick!"

He turned to her and realized she was staring at the front of his…well, not his underwear, because at some point he'd apparently taken it off. And she was getting an eyeful.

She sat up in bed. "You said you put underwear on."

"I did! I guess I must have taken them off again." He pulled back the covers, and sure enough, there they were, kicked down near the foot of the bed. He grabbed them and said, "Got 'em."

"This is ridiculous," Terri said.

"I'll put them on."

"And what, *staple* them in place?"

Preferably no. "No need to get vicious. And keep your voice down. Jess is going to hear you."

"Do you have any idea what it's like to wake up with someone fondling you?"

It sounded pretty good to him, but by her tone, he was guessing that she disagreed.

"Look, I'm doing my best."

She sat there in silence for a few seconds, just staring at him—mostly at his crotch—then shook her head and said, "Screw it."

He thought her next move would be to grab her pillow and a blanket and charge off to sleep in the tub. Instead, she pulled her nightshirt over her head and said, "Get over here."

Confused, he opened his mouth to speak, then closed it again.

"What are you waiting for?" she asked, tugging off her panties.

"But…I thought we weren't supposed to—"

"Hurry, before I change my mind."

He climbed into bed, and she pushed him onto his back, straddling his thighs.

"For the record, this is it," she said. "This is the last time. Got it?"

"Got it," he said, then sucked in a breath as she leaned over and took him in her mouth.

This pretending to be crazy-in-love thing was going to be harder than Terri originally thought, and maybe telling Jess she could stay hadn't been such a hot idea, after all. Nick was curled around her again and sound asleep— from the waist up, at least. Sure, it never should have happened, and they were only delaying the inevitable, but Terri couldn't deny that after she had jumped him, she had slept like a baby the rest of the night. Which technically hadn't been all that long, since it was eight now and they hadn't gone to sleep until five. But it was definitely going to be the last time, even if that meant sleeping on the couch. She would come up with some plausible excuse to tell Jess. Like Nick snored, or…well, she would think of *something*.

She slipped from under Nick's arm and got out of bed. He grumbled for a second, then went right back to sleep. She grabbed her nightshirt from the floor and pulled it over her head, then shrugged into her robe. As she walked to the kitchen, the aroma of freshly brewed coffee met her halfway there.

Jess was sitting on one of the bar stools, dressed in what Nick referred to as her mom-clothes—cotton pants and an oversize men's button-up shirt—sipping coffee and staring off into space, looking tired and sad.

"Good morning," Terri said.

Jess looked over at her and smiled brightly. "Happy Thanksgiving! I made coffee."

"It smells delicious." She crossed the room to the coffeepot and pulled down a cup from the cupboard.

"It's a fresh pot. I made the first when I got up and it was getting a little funky. I forget that not everyone is on a mom schedule."

Terri poured herself a cup and added a pinch of sugar. "When did you get up?"

"Five-thirty."

"Yikes! The earliest I ever manage to get up is seven, but usually it's closer to eight-thirty."

"One of the benefits of working from home," Jess said. "You roll out of bed and you're there. Of course, that will change when you have kids. For the first year, you'll barely sleep at all." She grinned and added, "Not that you seemed to be getting much sleep last night."

"I'm sorry if we woke you."

"Don't apologize. You're newlyweds. It's what you're supposed to do. And I'd be lying if I said I wasn't jealous. I can barely remember the last time Eddie and I had sex. And the last time we had really *good* sex? It's been ages."

Terri couldn't fathom why Jess would stay married if things were so bad. It's no wonder Nick and Maggs were so against tying the knot. First their parents' marriage ended in disaster, now Jess was turning it into a family tradition.

"So, speaking of kids," Jess said. "I noticed you didn't drink wine with dinner last night. Does that mean…?"

"I'm pregnant?" She shrugged. "I hope so, but I won't know for sure for another week and a half. I'm trying to be cautious just in case. Which means I shouldn't be drinking coffee, either, I guess."

"Or you could start drinking decaf. I think it still has a trace of caffeine, though."

Well, then, this would be her last cup of real coffee, she supposed. She would have to remember to pick up some decaf tomorrow.

Terri sat beside her. "So, how are you doing?"

She shrugged. "Everything about this situation sucks. I'm just so tired of dealing with it. Sometimes I wonder if it's even worth fighting anymore. It's not fair to the kids." She laid a hand on Terri's arm. "But you and Nick, you're different. I've never known two people who were more suited for each other. I mean, look how long you've been friends."

If only that were true. If only they loved each other that way. Because if things could stay just like they were now, she could imagine them being happy together. Of course, there was the slight problem of Nick not wanting to be married. "That doesn't necessarily mean we were meant to be married."

"Terri, are you having second thoughts?" Jess whispered, looking concerned.

"No, of course not. I'm just trying to be realistic."

"As long as you don't let your fears get in the way of your happiness. If you convince yourself it won't work, it won't."

"Was there a time when your marriage was good?"

"The first couple years were great. I mean, we had our disagreements, no marriage is perfect, but we were both happy."

"What do you think went wrong?"

"Marriage takes hard work. I think we got lazy. Between work and raising the kids, we forgot how to be a couple. Does that make sense?"

"I think so." Being friends could be a lot of work, too. It required compromise and patience. Twenty-year friendships, the ones as close as hers and Nicks, were probably as rare as twenty-year marriages. In a way it sort of was like a marriage. Just without the sex. And honestly, they probably talked as much as or more than most married couples.

"Plus, we have a few other issues…" Jess started to say, but her brother walked into the kitchen, and she clammed up. Did that mean it was something she didn't want him to know about?

Dressed in jeans and nothing else, his hair mussed

from sleep, Nick looked adorable. But when didn't he, really? Too bad last night—or, technically, this morning—had been the absolute last time.

"Good morning ladies," he said, sounding way too cheerful. He gave his sister a peck on the cheek, then scooped Terri into his arms, dipped her back and planted a slow, deep kiss on her.

"*Ugh,* get a room," Jess teased, walking to the sink to rinse her cup.

Nick grinned and winked at Terri. "How did you sleep, sweetheart?"

She flashed him a stern look, and gave him a not-so-gentle shove. It was one thing to be affectionate with each other, and quite another for him to molest her in front of his sister. Okay, maybe she did hesitate a few seconds before she pushed him away. But still...

He walked around the island to pour himself a cup of coffee. "So, when are we supposed to be at Mom's?"

"Eleven," Jess said, sticking her cup in the dishwasher. "Dinner is at five at *Nonno's*. Would you mind if I tag along with you guys? I get the feeling the only way I'll make it through dinner this year is by consuming copious amounts of alcohol."

"I won't be drinking," Terri said. "I can be the designated driver."

"So I can get hammered, too?" Nick said with a hopeful grin.

She shrugged. "If you really want to."

It didn't matter to her. She'd known guys who were quiet, brooding drunks, reckless and irresponsible drunks, and downright mean drunks. The worst she'd seen Nick do when he was really hammered is act a little goofy and get super-affectionate. Although not creepy, molester affectionate. He would just hug her a lot, and tell her repeatedly what a good friend she was, and how much he loved her.

"In fact, why don't we start right now?" Nick said. "We have almost a case of champagne left over from the wedding. I could go for a mimosa."

"Oh, that sounds good!" Jess said, rubbing her hands together. "I'll get the glasses and the orange juice."

"I'll open the champagne," Nick said.

And I'll watch, Terri thought, feeling left out. But she knew that having a baby would take sacrifice, and as far as sacrifices go, this one would be minor. And if nothing else, it would be an interesting day.

Ten

Nick's sister Maggie called asking if she could tag along with them to their mom's and then *Nonno*'s. She drove over to Nick's place and they all piled into his Mercedes, with Terri driving, since Nick and Jess had already polished off a bottle and a half of champagne. And it was barely ten-thirty.

Nick's mom served Bellinis with brunch, a traditional Italian cocktail made up of white peach puree and prosecco, an Italian sparkling white wine.

Terri lost track of how many pitchers the four of them consumed, but by the time they left for *Nonno*'s house, no one was feeling any pain. At one point Nick leaned over, touched her cheek, gazed at her with a sappy smile and bloodshot eyes and said, "I love you, Terri."

He was rewarded with two exaggerated *awww*'s from the backseat. They didn't realize he meant that he loved her as a friend.

"I love you, too," she said, taking his hand and placing it back on his side of the front seat so she could concentrate on the road. But before she could pull away, he grabbed her hand and held it tight.

"No, I mean I *really* love you."

She pried herself free and patted his hand. "I really love you, too."

"It's not fair," Maggie whined from the backseat. "I want what you guys have."

"Me, too," Jess said.

Nick looked over his shoulder at his sisters. "You've told me a hundred times that you would never *ever* get married, Mags."

"And you actually *believed* me? Every woman wants to be married, moron. I only say I don't to spare myself the humiliation of being thirty-three and still single."

"I'm going to be forty," Jess said.

Nick scoffed. "In *three* years."

"Besides," Maggie said. "You're *married.*"

"But for how long? I keep telling myself things will change, but they never do." Jess sniffed. "He's not even trying anymore."

"So leave him," Maggie said. "You deserve to be happy."

"I can't."

"Why not?" Nick said.

"There are certain things I'm not willing to give up, like private school for the kids. And do you have any idea how much sports programs cost? I would have to take out a third mortgage."

"Third?" Nick said, and Terri didn't have to see his face to know that he was frowning. She glanced back at Jess in the rearview mirror, and it looked as if all the color had drained from her face. Was she going to be sick?

"You know, forget I said anything," Jess said.

"No," Nick said. "That house was a wedding gift, there shouldn't be a mortgage."

"Can we please drop it?" she asked, sounding nervous.

Nick apparently didn't want to drop it. "Why did you mortgage the house, Jess?"

"Raising a family is expensive."

"You both make good money, and you have your trust to fall back on."

When she didn't answer him, Nick said, "Jess, you do still have your trust? Right?"

"I have enough socked away to put the kids through college, but I won't touch that."

"And the rest?" Mags asked.

Her cheeks crimson, she said, "Gone. It's all gone."

"Where?" Nick demanded.

She hesitated, then said, "Bad investments."

"What kind of investments?"

"Well, it depends on the season. Football, basketball…"

Nick cursed again and leaned back against the headrest, staring straight ahead. "Jessica, why didn't you *tell* someone?"

Jess sniffed again. "It was humiliating. I hoped that the marriage counseling might help him work that out, too, but whenever the subject comes up, he gets furious and denies that there's a problem. That's why he stopped going. I'm not sure what to do now. If there's anything I *can* do."

"Maybe he just needs a little persuasion," Nick said.

Jess paled even more. "What are you going to do?"

"He works for Caroselli Chocolate, and if he wants to keep his job, he'll play by our rules. Either he goes to Gamblers Anonymous, or he's out of a job."

"And then where will the kids and I be? We have so much debt, we're barely hanging on as it is."

"If Eddie won't take care of you," Nick said, his jaw tense, "then the family will."

Terri felt so awful for Jess. She couldn't even imagine what it would be like if someone lost all of her money, and to something as careless as gambling. She wouldn't even waste her money on a dollar scratch-off ticket.

The mood in the car was pretty somber the rest of the way to *Nonno's*, and when they got there, Nick and his sisters went straight to the bar. Wishing she could join them, Terri said hello to everyone—trying not to cringe as Nick's dad gave her one of those cloying hugs—then headed upstairs to use the bathroom. As she reached the top of the stairs, she heard voices coming from *Nonno's* study. A man and a woman. Curious, she stopped to listen, but couldn't make out what was being said, only that they both were angry.

She stepped closer, straining to hear, even though it was none of her business. My God, she really was becoming a Caroselli.

"We have to tell him," the man was saying.

The woman, sounding desperate, said, "But we agreed never to say a word."

"He deserves to know the truth."

"No, I won't do that to him."

"I've kept this secret, but I can't do it anymore. The guilt is eating away at me. Either you tell him or I will."

"Demitrio, wait!"

The doorknob turned and Terri gasped, ducking into the spare bedroom, her heart pounding. She hid behind the door and watched through the crack as Nick's Uncle Demitrio, Rob's dad, marched out, followed a second later by Tony's mom, Sarah. Terri had no clue what they could possibly be fighting about, though she could draw several conclusions from the small snippet of conversation she'd heard. Then again, she could be completely misconstruing the conversation. She could ask Nick, but if he told Tony and Rob what she'd heard, and they confronted their parents, all hell could break loose and she didn't want to be responsible.

When she was sure they were both gone, she used the bathroom, then rushed back downstairs before anyone could miss her.

Elana, Tony's younger sister, stopped her in the great room just outside the dining room door. She had been labeled the family genius after graduating high school at sixteen. She earned her masters five years later and passed the CPA exam shortly after that. She worked in the international tax department of Caroselli Chocolate, and according to Nick, would probably take over as CFO some day.

"So, how are you?" she said, shooting a not-so-subtle glance at Terri's stomach.

"Good." *And by the way, I think your mom is having an affair with your uncle.*

"How was Aruba?"

"A lot of fun. I'd like to go back some time." Maybe after the divorce, she and Nick and the baby could go for a non-honeymoon there.

"I see you don't have a drink. Can I get you something?"

"Thanks, but I can't. I'm the designated driver tonight."

"Oh, right," she said, but Terri doubted she believed her. "I did notice that your husband and his sisters seemed to get an early start this Thanksgiving."

By the time the evening was over, the rest of the family would be hammered, too. It was a Caroselli holiday tradition.

She heard Nick laugh, and spotted him, drink in hand, leaning on the bar. "Excuse me, Elana, I need to have a word with my husband."

Elana grinned. "Sure. Say hi to Gena for me when you see her."

"I will," she said, heading in Nick's direction.

"Hey," Nick said, smiling brightly as she approached. "Where'd ya go?"

"Bathroom. How are you?"

"Just standin' here holdin' up the bar," he said, his speech slightly slurred.

"You mean, the bar is holding you up?"

He nodded, his head wobbly on his neck. "Pretty much."

"Maybe you should give me that," she said, gesturing to his drink, and he handed it over without argument. She set it on the bar, out of his reach. "Why don't we go sit down? Before you fall over."

"You know, that's probably a good idea."

He hooked an arm around her neck and she led him to the sofa. If she hadn't been so tall and fit, he probably would have gone down a couple times and taken her with him.

She got him seated on the couch, but before she could sit beside him, he pulled her down onto his lap instead.

"Nick!"

He just grinned, and whispered in her ear, "Everyone needs to believe we're crazy in love, remember?"

Yes, but there were limits.

She thought about what she'd heard upstairs, and curiosity got the best of her. She doubted Nick would remember much of this night, anyway. "So, what's the deal with your Uncle Demitrio and Aunt Sarah?"

"What do you mean?" he asked, fiddling with the bottom edge of her dress.

She moved his hand to the sofa cushion instead. "I saw them talking and it sounded…strained."

"Well, they do have a history."

"They do?"

He laid his hand on her stocking-clad knee instead. "I never told you?"

If he had, she couldn't recall. "Not that I remember."

"They used to date."

Uh-oh. "Seriously?"

"In high school, I think." His hand began a slow slide upward, under the hem of her dress. "But Demitrio enlisted, and dumped Sarah, then Sarah fell in love with Tony instead."

And in light of what she'd heard upstairs, Terri would say it was pretty likely that Sarah and Demitrio had rekindled their romance. But since it was none of her business, she would keep it to herself.

Nick's roaming hand was now pushing the boundaries of decency. She intercepted it halfway up her thigh.

"Behave yourself," she said, and before he had the chance to do it again, Nick's dad announced that dinner was served.

She assumed she would be relatively safe at the dinner table, but thanks to a tablecloth that hung just low enough, she spent a good part of her meal defending herself against his sneak attacks.

She knew he could be affectionate when he drank, but she'd never known him to be so…hands-on. Of course, the last time she saw him this drunk, they weren't sleeping together. And as much as it annoyed her, she liked it, too.

The food was amazing, and the wine flowed freely, but Terri was able to limit Nick to two glasses. Unfortunately no one was keeping an eye on Jess and Mags, and by the time people started to leave for home, they were so toasted, Terri needed the assistance of Rob—whom she'd never seen even the slightest bit intoxicated—to get the girls in the car, and wondered how the hell she would get them in the building and up to Nick's apartment.

When everyone was buckled in and the doors were closed, Rob asked, "You want me to follow you and help get them upstairs?"

"Would you?" she said. "That would be so awesome. Unless his building has a flat-bed cart I could borrow, it would probably take me half the night to get them up to the apartment."

And just in case she had conceived, it would probably be better if she didn't lift anything too heavy.

"Let me go get Tony and we'll swing by Nick's—I mean, your apartment, on our way to Tony's place."

When she climbed in the car, Nick looked over at her, that goofy grin on his face. "Thanks for being designated driver."

"No problem." She buckled up and started the engine.

He let his head fall back against the rest and loll to one side. "I had a lot to drink today."

"You certainly did."

"Are you mad?"

"A little jealous maybe, but not mad."

He closed his eyes as she pulled away from the curb. They hadn't even made it to the corner when, his eyes still closed, he said, "Are we there yet?"

She laughed. "I bet you were a riot as a kid."

He grinned, and must have fallen asleep after that, because he didn't make another sound all the way to his building. Rob and Tony were a few minutes behind her, and they each took a sister while Terri led Nick—who thankfully was able to walk with little assistance—upstairs.

Rob and Tony got the girls into the guest room, and Terri got Nick undressed—all the way down to nothing because he would end up that way eventually—and into bed.

She leaned down to give him a kiss on the cheek, and discovered that even intoxicated, he was lightening fast. He looped an arm around her neck and pulled her in for a kiss. A long, slow, deep one. He smelled so good, felt so nice, that she let it go on longer than she should have.

He looked up at her, brushing her hair back and tucking it behind her ears. "Do you have any idea how long I've wanted to do this?"

"Um, since the last time you kissed me?"

"For years," he said. "And I wanted to do more than just kiss you."

"Uh-huh." That was definitely the alcohol talking.

"Terri, I mean it. When we lived together, I would meet girls and bring them home—"

"I *remember*."

"But what you didn't know was that when I was with them, I would be wishing it was you."

Her heart took a dive, then shot back up into her throat. "Come on, Nick. You did not."

"No, I did," he said, his eyes so earnest she could swear he was actually telling the truth. But he couldn't be. He was only saying it to soften her up, so she would sleep with him again.

"If you wanted me so much, why didn't you tell me?"

"I should have," he said. "I wish I would have."

"No you don't." He was clearly confusing her with some other woman.

"Yes, I *do*. In the car, when I said I love you, I meant it."

"Of course you did. We're best friends. I love you, too."

"No. I mean, I *really* love you."

In a way she wanted to believe it, but she knew it was just the alcohol making him sentimental. She'd seen it happen before.

"I think I always knew it was inevitable," he said, his eyelids heavy.

"What was inevitable?"

"That we would end up together. And Jess was right, we are perfect for each other. Now I can't believe we didn't figure it out a long time ago. Maybe we just weren't ready."

"You should go to sleep," she said. "We can talk about it in the morning, okay?"

"Okay," he said, letting his arm drop from around her neck, his eyelids sinking closed.

She stood up, knowing that despite what she'd said, this was not a conversation they would be continuing. She doubted he would recall a single word of it.

She switched off the light and walked out to the kitchen. Rob sat on one of the bar stools, drinking a bottled water. Tony had helped himself to a beer and leaned against the fridge drinking it.

"What a night," Terri said, sitting beside Rob. "Thanks for helping me."

"So, what's going on?" Tony asked.

"What do you mean?"

"I've seen Nick and his sisters get pretty drunk, but never all of them at the same time. Is everything okay with Gena?"

"Gena is fine."

"Does it have something to do with Eddie not showing up for dinner?"

"Maybe you should ask Jess about that."

"So it is about Eddie," Rob said.

"I can't really say one way or the other." But they would find out soon enough if Nick followed through and gave Eddie that ultimatum.

"You know," Rob said. "You'll never survive in this family if you don't learn to gossip."

Your dad is sleeping with Tony's mom, she wanted to say. How was that for gossip? "Let's just say it's been a tough day for everyone."

"Everything okay with you and Nick?"

"Great. We're great."

"He mentioned that you guys wanted to start a family right away," Rob said. "And I noticed that all you drank tonight was water."

He and half a dozen other people had noticed. And inquired.

"A preemptive precaution," she said.

She was under the distinct impression that she was being pumped for information. Had Rob and Tony agreed to *Nonno*'s offer, too? Would they be making engagement announcements of their own? And if they did, would this turn into some sort of race to the finish line?

Eleven

Last night's overindulgence had taken its toll, and when Terri returned home around eleven the next morning after a few hours of Black Friday shopping with Nick's mom, she encountered a gruesome scene. Jess and Mags were sacked out in the living room, the curtains drawn, the television off, looking miserable.

"Good morning," Terri said, setting her packages on the floor beside the door so she could take off her coat.

"Not really," Jess said weakly, a compress on her forehead, eyes bloodshot and puffy. "Is it physically possible for a head to explode? Because it feels like mine might."

"I don't think so," Terri said.

"Shhh," Maggie scolded. The previous night's makeup was smeared around her eyes, giving her a raccoon appearance. "Do you two really have to talk so loud?"

"Did you guys take anything?" Terri asked, and both nodded. "Are you drinking lots of water?"

"Yes, Mom," Maggie said.

"Hey, I've gotta practice on someone. Where's Nick?"

"He got up and took some ibuprofen then went back to bed," Jess said.

"How did he look?"

"Have you seen the movie *Zombieland?*" Maggie asked.

"That bad, huh?" Terri had been a little jealous last night to be the odd man out, but in the aftermath, she was glad she hadn't been able to let loose. "I'd better go check on him."

Terri hung her coat in the closet and gathered up the other three coats that had been dumped in various spots throughout the room and hung them up, too. Then she tiptoed into the bedroom. The blinds were closed, all the lights off and Nick was sprawled out diagonally, facedown on the mattress naked, as if he had collapsed there and didn't have the strength to move another inch. He may have been hungover, but he sure did look good.

There were two empty water bottles on the bedside table—so at least he'd had the good sense to hydrate—and a pair of jogging pants on the floor. She picked them up and draped them across the foot of the bed. During their honeymoon, he'd been pretty good about picking up after himself. He left an occasional wet towel on the floor, or whiskers in the sink, but so far he was nowhere near as bad as he used to be.

She was about to turn around and leave, when Nick mumbled, "What time is it?"

"After eleven. You okay?"

He lifted his head and gazed up at her. Only one eyelid was raised, as if he just didn't have the energy to open them both. The eye she could see was so puffy and red-rimmed it almost hurt to look at it. "What do you think?"

"Is there anything I can get you?"

"A gun?"

She laughed. "Anything else?"

He sighed and dropped his head down. "Another bottle of water? And a promise that you'll never let me do that again. I must be getting old, because I'm not bouncing back like I used to in college."

"That happens, I guess." The last time she'd overdone it with a pitcher of margaritas, she'd paid severely the following day. "I'll be right back."

She walked to the kitchen for his water, stopping to ask his sisters if they wanted one, too. They both moan-mumbled an affirmative, and she grabbed an armful from the fridge. She set two beside each sister, then returned to the bedroom, where Nick was actually sitting up in bed. She sat on the edge of the mattress beside him and handed over the water.

"Thanks." She watched his Adam's apple bob, the muscles in his neck flexing as he guzzled down the first bottle in one long gulp. He set the second one on the bedside table for later. He sighed, letting his head rest against the headboard. "Thanks."

"No problem."

"How are the girls doing?"

"In a little better shape than you, but not by much."

"Thanks for taking care of us last night."

"You would have done the same for me. And if I recall correctly, you have a time or two."

He slipped down, flat on his back. "Like the time in high school when you broke up with Tommy Malone and you went a little crazy with the peach Schnapps."

"It was peppermint Schnapps, and I didn't break up with him. He dumped me for Alicia Silberman because

I wouldn't put out. And apparently she was more than happy to."

"I did offer to kick his ass for you."

She smiled at the memory. He would have done it, too. "He wasn't worth the trouble."

"So when did you finally do it?" he said.

Confused, she asked, "Do what?"

"Have sex."

The question took her aback. Not that she was ashamed of her past—not all of it, anyway—but it just wasn't something they had ever talked about. "Why do you want to know?"

"Just curious. I was a junior in high school."

"I heard," she said. "With Beth Evans, in her bedroom when her parents were both at work."

"Who told you?"

"I overheard Tony and Rob talking about it a couple years ago. And, of course, there were rumors around school at the time." Which she had rarely put any stock in, but apparently this time they were right. "I hear you gave quite the performance."

Nick laughed. "Not exactly. I was so nervous I couldn't get her bra unhooked, and the actual sex lasted about thirteen seconds."

"That's not the way Rob tells it. He said that you said you had her begging for more."

"I may have exaggerated a tiny bit," he said with a grin. "Sexual prowess is very important to a teenage boy. The truth is, it was a humiliating experience."

"Well, if it's any consolation, you've perfected your methods since then."

He laughed. "Thanks. When was your first time?"

She cringed. "It's embarrassing."

"Why?"

"Because it was so...cliché."

"Tell me it wasn't a teacher."

It was her turn to laugh. "Of course not! It was the night of senior prom."

"You're right, that is cliché." He paused, then said, "Wait a minute, you went to prom with that guy from the math club. Eugene...something."

"Eugene Spenser."

"Wasn't he kind of a...*geek?*"

"A little, but so was I." And that *geek* had moves that she later realized put most college guys to shame. He actually *did* have her begging for more.

"I don't remember you dating him."

"Um...I don't think you could call what we did dating, per se."

His brows rose. "What *would* you call it?"

"Occasionally we would...hook up."

The brows rose higher. *"Hook up?"*

"You know, have sex."

He sat up again, his hangover temporarily forgotten. "Really?"

"Yes, really."

"You would just...have sex. No relationship, no commitment?"

She nodded. "That's about it."

"Were there *other* guys that you 'hooked up' with?"

"A few."

"But they weren't boyfriends."

"They were friends, but not boyfriends."

"And you had sex with them?"

"I had sex with them," she said, unsure why he found the scenario so unbelievable. "What can I say, I liked sex."

"So did I, but..."

"But it's supposedly different for you?"

"Yes."

"Why? Because you're a guy? Or because you were madly in love with every girl you slept with? I'm recalling the parade of females in and out of your room when we lived together, and I can't say I remember seeing the same face more than once or twice." Which made her think about what he'd said last night. How he would be with a girl but think of Terri. But he'd been so drunk he probably hadn't meant it. He probably didn't even know what he was saying.

"Well, we know you didn't sleep with *all* your friends," he said.

"Not any of my girlfriends, if that's what you mean. Although one did invite me into a three-way with her boyfriend once, and I might have if the guy hadn't been such a creep."

"You never slept with *me,* either."

She shrugged. "You never asked."

His brows perked up again. "If I had, would you?"

At first she thought he was teasing, but his eyes said that he was serious. Had he really wanted to sleep with her back then? Were those not just the ramblings of a drunk man last night? And did she really want to know? It's not as if they had any kind of future as a couple now, so what difference did it make?

"No. Our friendship was too important to me."

"And theirs weren't?"

"Not like ours. For me sex was…I don't know. I guess it made me feel in control. And special in a way. Definitive proof of how much my aunt screwed me up, I guess."

"Do you still feel that way?" he asked, looking intrigued.

"No, not anymore." She also didn't like the direction

this conversation was taking. It was too...*something*.
"Well, I should let you get back to sleep."

"I'm feeling better now. I think I'll take a shower instead."

"Are you hungry? I could pick up lunch."

"Something light, maybe? I have soup in the pantry."

As long as he didn't mind her potentially burning down the building. "Sure. It'll be ready when you're done."

"Unless you'd like to join me," he said, wiggling his brows.

"I thought you were hungover."

"Not *that* hungover."

She couldn't help but laugh, and wonder if there would ever be a time before the divorce when he would stop coming on to her. Or a time when she stopped wanting to say yes. "Well, the answer is no."

He shrugged. "Thought it couldn't hurt to ask."

He rolled out of bed, deliciously naked, and walked to the bathroom. Terri watched him, trying her best not to drool, noting that he'd left the door wide-open.

It was a good thing he didn't realize how little persuasion it would take to change her mind, or she would be joining him.

She heard the shower turn on and before she could even be tempted, or think how good he looked naked and soapy, how his body felt all slippery and warm against hers, she hightailed it to the kitchen, stopping to see if Jess and Mags were hungry.

"I can barely choke down saltines," Jess said. "But thanks."

"I'll pass, too," Maggie said. "I need to get home soon, anyway."

"Let me know if you change your minds."

In the kitchen she opened the door to the walk-in pantry, which was remarkably well organized for a man who used to leave his canned goods in the bag on the kitchen table for days after a trip to the store.

There was an entire shelf dedicated to a dozen brands and types of soup, but she didn't have a clue what he would prefer. Under normal circumstances he liked tomato, but she wondered if that might upset his stomach.

Crap. That meant she would have to go ask him. She would stand outside the bathroom and shout to him, so she wouldn't have to see him through the clear glass shower doors. It would just be easier that way.

That was exactly what she did, and Nick did in fact want tomato, but as she started to walk away, he called, "Hey, Terri, would you grab a washcloth from the cabinet for me?"

Crap.

"Okay," she called. She planned to just throw it over the top of the shower door and run, but before she could, Nick swung open the door. Of course he was wet and soapy, and sexy as hell.

She held out the cloth to him, but he grabbed her wrist instead, tugging her, fully clothed, into the shower and under the hot spray.

"Nick!" she shrieked, trying to pull away, but he wouldn't let go.

"Well, gosh," he said as water saturated her sweatshirt and jeans, her hair. "Looks like now you *need* a shower."

Water leaked out of her hair and into her eyes and her wet clothes were weighing her down. She wanted to be mad, wanted to feel like slugging him, but all she could manage was a laugh.

His hand slid down to cup her behind and he wedged one thigh intimately between hers. A moan slipped out and her head tilted against the tile, giving Nick access to her throat, which he promptly began to devour.

She should be telling him no right now, but damn it, she didn't *want* to. Instead, she said, "This is it," as he kissed his way upward, nibbling the shell of her ear. "This is the *last* time."

He pulled back, eyes black with desire. "Take off your clothes."

Terri pushed her cart through the produce section of the grocery store, dropping in the items on the list Nick had put together last night for her. When she lived alone, she did the majority of her shopping in the frozen food section, so the gourmet meals Nick had been making every night were pretty cool. They also made up for the fact that, although he'd improved a lot, Nick hadn't quite lost all his slob tendencies. He often left newspapers or magazines on the coffee table, or dirty clothes on the bedroom floor, and he never seemed to clean up after himself after using the bathroom in the morning.

But those things didn't bother her nearly as much as they used to. She'd been living alone for a long time now. She had worried that having someone there, having to share her space, would feel suffocating. She also thought she would miss her condo, but that wasn't the case at all. Now that Jess was back home trying again to work out things with Eddie, and Terri had the guest room to herself, she missed sleeping with Nick. And not just the sex, which they agreed would stop the day she moved out of his bedroom.

She'd grown awfully fond of cuddling, and she missed lying in bed with him and just talking. There were so many little things that she realized she'd taken for granted. And she was starting to get the feeling that she and Nick just being roommates might not cut it anymore. Maybe she wanted more than that.

But then she always reminded herself that despite what she wanted, Nick was perfectly content with his life just the way it was. He didn't want to be tied down. And whatever happened with the baby, she knew that in time she would be okay with that. Knowing he was her best friend, and always would be, would be enough for her.

She hoped.

Right now, though, as the date approached when she could take a pregnancy test, she became more and more obsessed about it. She was ultra aware of any changes in her body, any signs of pregnancy. She would check her reflection to see if she was glowing, poke her breasts to see if they were tender. She even started eating foods that she'd read could aggravate morning sickness to encourage signs of pregnancy, but so far, nothing. She tried not to let it discourage her, but she was nervous. Suppose it didn't work this month, or the next, or the next? What if she discovered that she couldn't get pregnant?

Every time her thoughts started to wander in that direction, she forced herself to stay positive. Even if the first try was unsuccessful, it didn't mean the second would be, too. She just had to be patient.

On her way to the dairy section, Terri passed the aisle with the feminine products, and took a detour. Though she had to wait until after her period was late to test, it couldn't hurt to buy it a few days early.

She grabbed the most expensive one—thinking it would be the most accurate—and read the back, both stunned and excited to see that the test could be performed as soon as four days before her period was due, which coincidentally was today.

Heart jumping in her chest, she tossed the box in the

cart. She hurried through the rest of her shopping and paid for her groceries, so nervous and excited she barely recalled the drive home. She forced herself to wait until she got all the groceries upstairs and put away, then she opened the box and pulled out the instruction leaflet.

Her excitement fizzled when she read the line that said to take it with the first urine of the day, which she had flushed away almost *ten* hours ago. *Damn.* If she wanted an accurate reading, she had no choice but to wait until tomorrow morning.

She stuck the test in the cabinet in her bathroom and tried to forget about it, but failed miserably.

Later that night, after the tenth time of not hearing Nick ask her a question or make a comment about the movie that she wasn't really watching, he seemed to realize something was up.

"Is everything okay?" he said. "It's like you're here, but you're not really here."

At least if she told him, she wouldn't be the only one crawling out of her skin. "When I was at the grocery store today, I went down the feminine products aisle."

He frowned. "Is this something I really want to know about?"

She rolled her eyes. "The pregnancy test aisle, Nick."

"I thought we had to wait until your period was due to test."

"So did I, but the directions said you can take the test as early as four days before your period is due."

"When is that?"

"Today. But it was too late in the day, so I can't test until tomorrow morning."

"How early?" he asked, and it was hard to tell if he was excited, or nervous, or really didn't give a crap. His face gave nothing away.

"As soon as I wake up."

He pulled his phone from his pocket and started to fiddle with it.

"What are you doing?" she asked.

"I'm setting my alarm for tomorrow morning."

"For what time?"

He looked at her and grinned. "Five."

Twelve

Nick paced outside the bathroom door, like an expectant father waiting for news on the birth of his child, not the result of a pregnancy test. And what was taking so long? Weren't they supposed to give results in minutes?

The door opened and Terri stepped out, still in her pajamas.

"Well?" he said.

"It's still marinating. I just couldn't stand there watching it."

"How much longer?"

She looked at her watch. "Three minutes."

"Don't worry," he said. "It'll be positive."

"You realize that if it is, that's it. For the rest of your life, it will no longer be about you, you'll always have this person depending on you."

Hadn't they been over this before? Why did he get the feeling she was trying to scare him? Or maybe she was the one who was scared. She had to carry the baby for nine months. The one making the most sacrifices. "I'm ready," he assured her. "And I'm here for you. For whatever you need. No matter what the results are."

"Meaning, if it's negative, you still want to try again?"

"Terri, I'm in this for the long haul."

"For the money."

"Don't you think it's a little late in the game to be questioning my motives?"

She sighed. "You're right. I'm sorry. I guess I'm just nervous."

"We're in this together. If you don't trust me—"

"I *do*. I don't know what my problem is. Maybe I'm hormonal."

She looked at her watch again and said, "It's time."

Here we go.

She took a step into the bathroom, then stopped. "I can't do it. I'm too nervous. You look at it."

"What am I looking for?"

"A plus sign is positive, a minus sign negative."

"Okay, here goes." He stepped into the bathroom and picked up the little stick off the counter. He turned it over and looked in the indicator window for a plus sign...

Damn.

"Well?" she asked hopefully from the doorway.

Damn, damn, damn.

He looked up at her and shook his head, watched her face fall. "Are you sure you did it right?"

"Yes, I'm sure. It's not as if it's the only one I've ever taken."

That surprised him. "Really?"

She nodded. "I had a few scares in college."

"Why didn't you tell me?"

"What difference does it make?" she snapped, and he realized he was being insensitive.

"I'm sorry. Come here." He held out his arms and she walked into them, laying her head against his chest. "Is there anything I can do?"

She shook her head. "The directions do say that I could get a false negative taking the test this early. They say to try again the day my period is due."

"So, you could still be pregnant?"

"There's only a twelve percent chance, so more than likely, I'm not."

"Twelve percent is better than zero percent. You'll test again Tuesday and then we'll know for sure."

Nick tried to keep a positive attitude all day, tried to keep Terri's mind off anything having to do with pregnancy or babies, did everything he could think of to cheer her up. He made her favorite dinner, but she only picked at it. Then he suggested they rent the chick flick she'd been bugging him about, but she looked so lost in thought, she probably hadn't absorbed the plot.

They said good-night at eleven, and it was almost midnight when Terri appeared in Nick's bedroom doorway. "Nick? Are you awake?" she whispered.

He sat up. "Yeah. Are you okay?"

She took a few steps into the room. "Can't sleep. Would it be okay, just for tonight, if I sleep with you? And I mean, actually sleep, not—"

"I get it." He pulled back the covers on the opposite side of the bed. "Hop in."

She climbed in beside him and he laid back down, facing her.

"Sorry about this," she said, shivering and burrowing under the covers. It did seem particularly cold, which meant she had probably been messing with the thermostat again. At her condo, she kept her thermostat at a balmy sixty-three degrees. He could swear she'd been an eskimo in a past life. Or a reptile.

"Don't apologize. I like sleeping with you."

"For years I've managed to fall asleep just fine on my own," she said, sounding disgusted with herself.

"It's been a rough couple of days. You don't have to go through everything alone. We're in this together, remember?"

"For now, but there could come a time when you're not around, and I have to be able to stand on my own two feet."

"Where is it you think I'm going?"

"Like my aunt used to tell me, if you don't let yourself depend on people, they can't let you down."

Nick could hardly believe she'd just said that, that she would even *think* it. He knew she had trust issues but if she really believed that, her insecurities ran much deeper that he had ever imagined.

"Have I ever let you down?"

"No."

Why did he get the feeling there was an unspoken "not yet" tacked to the end of that sentence? "So, who? Your parents? I really don't imagine they *wanted* to die."

"No, but they did."

He sighed. "Terri—"

"I'm not wallowing in self-pity or looking for sympathy. It just is what it is. You never know what might happen, so it's important to be self-sufficient. That's all I'm saying."

"'Tis better to have loved and lost, than never to have loved at all,'" he said.

"And after you lose someone, see if you still believe that."

She said it not as if it were a possibility, but a predestined event. He didn't even know how to respond to that, what he could say to change her mind. If it was even possible to change it. But the real question, the thing he needed to decide first was, did he want to?

Unfortunately, they never needed that second pregnancy test. Terri started her period Monday morning. As long as he'd known her, he'd seen her cry maybe four or five times total, but when she called him that morning at work to tell him the bad news, she was beside herself.

"Do you want me to come home?"

"No," she said with a sniff, her voice unsteady. "I'm being stupid. I knew this would happen, but I guess I was still hoping. I shouldn't be this upset."

"It's okay to be upset. I'm disappointed, too. But we try again in a couple weeks, right?"

"You're sure you want to do that?"

"Of course I'm sure." He'd only told her that a dozen times since Saturday morning. Was she really worried that he would back out, or was *she* the one having second thoughts? "But you realize that means being stuck living with me for an extra month. Think you can handle that?"

"Well," she said, her tone lighter, "you are pretty high maintenance."

He laughed, because they both knew that couldn't be farther from the truth. "So, when does act two start?"

"I haven't figured that out yet. I'll do that later today."

"What sounds good for dinner? I'll make or pick up anything you want."

She paused for a second, then said, "Pizza. From the little Italian place around the corner. With ham, mushrooms and little hairy fish."

"Pizza it is," he said. He heard a knock and looked

up to see his dad standing in the open doorway, and he
didn't look happy. Nick's gut reaction was to immediately wonder what he'd done this time, but that was just
a holdover from his childhood. He didn't answer to his
father anymore, and sometimes he still forgot that, still
got that sinking feeling when he walked into the room.

"Terri, I have to let you go."

"Okay. I...I love you."

"I love you, too. I'll see you around seven." He hung
up and looked over at his dad. "What's up?"

"Sorry to interrupt, but I need to talk to you."

"Come in."

He stepped inside and shut the door behind him, which
was probably not a good sign.

He took a seat across from Nick, his brow furrowed,
far from the happy-go-lucky facade he wore most of the
time. Even if he were smiling now, it would have no bear-
ing on what he'd be doing five minutes from now. He had
a hair-trigger temper and could turn on a dime.

"I've noticed something lately," he said. "And I thought
maybe you knew what was going on. That Tony and Rob
may have mentioned something."

"About what?"

"Your Uncle Tony and Uncle Demitrio."

"No, they haven't said anything. Why? Is something
wrong?"

"All I know is that something feels...off. They hardly
talk anymore, and when they do, it's obvious there's tension. I asked them both individually but they swear nothing is wrong."

Nick debated telling him what Terri had seen at
Nonno's house, but it didn't seem fair to drag her into this.
"I don't know, Dad. Have you talked to Rob or Tony?"

"You're close with them. I thought it would be better if you did."

Nick sighed. Unlike most of the rest of the family, Nick had no burning desire to stick his nose into someone else's business. "No offense, but if there is something going on, I don't want to be in the middle of it."

"I'm not asking for much," he said sharply.

"Maybe they told you everything is fine because they feel like, whatever is going on, it's none of your business."

"If it starts to affect this company it is."

"You're the CPA. Is it affecting the company?"

"Not yet, but—"

"Instead of jumping to conclusions, maybe you should just ride it out for a week or two and see what happens. *Nonni* used to tell us that when you and Tony and Demitrio were kids, you had fights all the time."

"This is different," he said.

"Just give it some time, okay? Then if you're still worried, I'll mention it to Rob and Tony."

He nodded grudgingly. "So, how are things with you and Terri?"

"Good." At least he hoped so. She'd been...off lately. She'd been quieter, more closed up than usual. They used to talk on the phone nearly every evening, and the conversations would sometimes last for hours. But lately, they could be sitting in a room together and she barely said two words to him. Sometimes she was so lost in thought, she would seem to forget he was even there.

Maybe it was that she'd been anxious about getting pregnant. Or they just needed time to get used to living together. Whatever it was, he hoped that she would be back to her old self soon. He was beginning to miss his best friend.

"Your mom mentioned that the two of you are planning to start a family soon."

"When did you talk to Mom?"

He hesitated, then said, "At your wedding."

Why did Nick get the feeling that wasn't the only time? And why would he be contacting Nick's mom? Was he harassing her?

Nick made a mental note to ask his mom about it.

"Yes, we're planning on starting a family, but it looks as if it might take a bit longer than we'd hoped."

"So, Terri really isn't pregnant?"

"You shouldn't listen to gossip, Dad. It's beneath you."

He pushed himself to his feet. "If my son would talk to me once in a while, I wouldn't have to."

Maybe, he thought, as his dad stalked out, slamming the door behind him, *if you hadn't been such a rotten husband and father, I would.*

But those words would mean nothing to him, since the great Leonardo Caroselli took no responsibility for his past bad behavior. It was always someone else's fault.

Nick stewed about it for the rest of the day, and began to think that it would ruin his entire evening. When he got home later with the pizza and a bottle of wine, he went searching for Terri, worried that he might discover her curled up in bed crying. Instead, he found her in her office, so focused on her computer screen and the design she was working on, she hadn't even heard him come in.

"Pizza's here," he said.

She turned, surprised to see him, then smiled and said, "Hi, is it seven already?"

In that instant the stress of the day, with his mounting frustration seemed to melt away until all he felt was... happy. And content. But hadn't she always made him feel that way?

He hadn't fully appreciated that until just now.

"I have something to show you," Terri said. "But first…"

She got up from her chair, put her arms around him and hugged him hard. And damn did it feel good to hold her. So good, he didn't want to let go when she backed away.

"What was that for?"

"For being so patient with me, and for being such a good friend. We've gone through some pretty huge changes in the last month. Everything happened so fast, we didn't have much time to prepare ourselves. But at the same time, in the back of my head, I had this idea that we had to hurry, that if I didn't get pregnant right away, if I missed the deadline I set for myself, it would never happen. I think maybe that's why I didn't get pregnant. I was anxious about *everything*."

"I've noticed that, the past week or so, you haven't been yourself. Like you're here, but you aren't really here."

"I know. And I'm sorry I've been so self-absorbed. But from now on, I'm back to being my old self. I promise."

"Good, because I've missed you."

She smiled, then gestured to the calendar on the wall above her desk. "See that highlighted week?"

She had marked the twenty-third to the twenty-seventh in blue. "Yeah."

"Do you know what it is?"

"Um…Christmas vacation?"

"That's the week I'm due to ovulate."

Nick laughed. "Are you serious?"

She smiled and nodded. "That would be a pretty awesome Christmas present, don't you think?"

"It certainly would."

"I think this time it will work."

"And if it doesn't?" He hated to see her get herself all stressed out again.

"If it doesn't, we try again in January. I just want to relax and let things happen naturally."

"And they will," he said. He had a really good feeling about this.

But just when he thought he had everything figured out, thought he knew the plan, a few days later she threw him another curve ball.

Terri's car was parked in the garage when Nick got home from work a few days later, but the apartment was quiet. He looked in the obvious places. Her bedroom, her office, even the laundry room behind the kitchen, but he couldn't find her, or a note explaining where she'd gone. He was about to grab his phone to call her, thinking she may have gone down to the fitness room for a quick workout before dinner, when he swore he heard the sound of running water from the direction of his bedroom.

He walked down the hall to his room and stepped inside. "Terri?"

"In here," she called from his bathroom, and he heard what sounded like the hum of the sauna jets in the tub. Was she cleaning it, maybe?

The bathroom door was open, so he walked in.

Unless she liked to do housework naked and submerged in the water, she was not cleaning anything.

He stopped beside the tub and folded his arms. The water came up to her neck, and with the jets on high, he couldn't see more that a blurry outline of her body, but that was enough to kick his libido into gear. "Something wrong with your tub?"

She smiled up at him. "Nope."

Okay. And she was in his tub because…

"I've been thinking about it, and if we want to get it right this time, if we really want me to get pregnant, maybe we could use a little more practice."

"If you'll recall, I actually suggested that we practice first. You said no."

"I guess I was wrong."

Though it would be all too easy to pretend that he believed her just to get laid, they were both better than that.

"That's an interesting theory. Now, you want to drop the bull and tell me why you're *really* here?"

Terri should have known that Nick would call her out, that he would demand total honesty from her. And as annoying as it could be at times, he kept her honest.

"It's not like you to play games," he said, looking disappointed in her. "If after twenty years you can't be honest with me—"

"I miss you," she blurted out, hating how vulnerable the words made her feel. "I know I'm not supposed to, that we're just friends unless I'm ovulating, but I can't help it."

"Are you saying that you want a sexual relationship outside of baby-making?"

Honestly, it was all she could think about lately, and she was tired of fighting it, tired of feeling as if something was missing. But maybe he didn't feel that same way. "If you think it's a bad idea—"

"I didn't say that." He shrugged out of his suit jacket and hung it on the hook next to the shower stall.

"I know it wasn't part of the plan," she said. "But I've begun to think that the two of us going nine months without any sex is a slightly unrealistic goal. I like sex, and we do it really well together, so why not?"

"You don't think it will complicate things?"

"Why would it? We both want the same thing—to have a baby without getting tied down."

He closed the lid on the toilet and sat. "I thought you were still looking for Mr. Right eventually."

"Instead of trying to find him, I think I may just sit back, relax and let him find me. There's no rush."

"So what happens with us after the baby is born?"

"We get divorced, like we planned."

"And we start seeing other people?"

She shrugged. "I don't see why not."

He looked skeptical. "It wouldn't hurt your feelings, or make you jealous to see me with someone else?"

"I've seen you with lots of women and it never bothered me before." At least, not enough to impact their friendship. Sure, it might be a little strange at first, but they would adjust. Hell, for all she knew, they could be completely sick of each other by then. Going back to a platonic friendship might be a huge relief for them both.

But considering how long it was taking Nick to respond, maybe he didn't think it was such a hot idea. He had been pretty hands-off lately, not so touchy-feely as before. Even when they slept together in his bed the other night, he hadn't put the moves on her. Maybe he was only interested in sleeping with her when they were trying to make the baby.

He rested his elbows on his knees, his hands folded under his chin. He was deep in thought, as if maybe he was trying to come up with some way to let her down easy.

A knot formed in her stomach, and she started to get the distinct impression she had just made a big ass of herself. But it was too late to back out now. Not without making herself look like an even *bigger* ass. The one time she took a chance and put herself out there on a limb—

"You're sure about this?" Nick said.

She nodded, feeling a slight glimmer of hope.

"*Really* sure?"

"Really sure."

"Because not touching you the past ten days has been hell on earth. So you can't just sleep with me once, then change your mind again. Either you're in or you're out. There's no middle ground. Agreed?"

Whoa. "Agreed."

"Now that we have that settled," he said, grinning and tugging his tie loose, "scoot over."

Thirteen

"Earth to Nick!"

Nick's attention jerked from the notepad he hadn't even realized he'd been doodling on. Everyone at the conference room table—his dad, his uncles, plus Rob, Tony and Elana—was looking at him.

"Sorry, what?"

"Have you heard anything we've said?" his dad snapped, as if Nick were a stubborn child and not a capable adult. Well, maybe not so capable right now, but that really wasn't Nick's fault.

"Currently sales for the quarter are down," Nick said, regurgitating the only snippet of the conversation he'd heard so far.

"Is that it? You didn't hear anything else?"

"Sorry, I didn't get much sleep last night."

"Have you tried a sleeping pill?"

"Leo, he's still a newlywed," Demitrio said, winking at Nick. "He's not supposed to sleep."

Yeah, and Terri had kept him up particularly late. They made love after the nightly news, then at 2:00 a.m. he woke to find her buried under the covers doing some pretty amazing things with her mouth. But starting today they had to abstain until she ovulated. And though he never thought he would catch himself thinking it, he was ready for a break.

Since the first day of their honeymoon, the sex had been great, but this past week she had been *insatiable*. They made love in the morning, either in bed or in the shower, and if he had no meeting scheduled for lunch he would come home for a quickie. Yesterday he'd asked her to bring him a report he'd left on his home office desk, and when she got there, she'd had that look in her eye. Then she locked his office door and he knew he was in trouble.

They did it some evenings right when he got home from work, and always when they got into bed at night. They had done it in the tub, on the sofa, in his office chair and about a dozen other places. It seemed as if every time he turned around, she was poised to jump him.

Not that he was complaining. But, *damn,* he was getting tired.

"We're considering bringing in a consultant," Demitrio told him. "Someone to view our line with a fresh set of eyes. Someone who could help us update our marketing without losing the essence of who we are as a company."

"Who are we thinking of?" Nick asked, noticing that Rob, as marketing director, did not look happy.

"Her name is Caroline Taylor. She's based on the West Coast, and she comes highly recommended. She's not cheap, though."

"Which is why I think we're wasting our money and our time," Rob said.

Nick was sure it had more to do with Rob's bruised ego. If they brought in another chocolatier to develop new products, Nick would be insulted, too.

"Son, this in no way reflects on your job performance," Demitrio said. "It's quite common for companies to bring in outside consultants. We've been talking about a fresh look for the company, and I believe the time is now."

Rob clearly wasn't happy about it, but he didn't argue, either.

"I take it we've contacted her already," Nick said. Undoubtedly, someone had mentioned this, but he'd missed it.

"Yes, and we got lucky," Demitrio said. "She's typically booked up for months, and sometimes years in advance, but the company she was supposed to start with in January went bankrupt. She's all ours if we want her. And I have to give her an answer by the end of the week."

Everyone, except Rob, of course, thought it was a good idea.

"Great!" Demitrio said. "We wanted to run it past everyone first, and the board will make a final decision tomorrow."

Uncle Tony was up and out the door before anyone else had a chance to stand up. Though Nick tuned out most of the meeting, during the parts he did catch, his uncle Tony hadn't said a word. Maybe his dad was right, and there was something going on between his uncles.

Nick knew that his uncle Tony had always followed the rules. He went to the right schools, graduating with honors and worked his way up through the ranks. Uncle Demitrio, on the other hand, had been a hell-raiser, uninterested in the family business, in and out of trouble with the law until he joined the army. Nick had heard his dad mention that while everyone else in the family had to earn their position, Demitrio had everything handed to him. Maybe that was causing hard feelings between Tony and Demitrio. But then, how did Aunt Sarah factor into that?

As Nick walked back to his office, Rob caught up with him in the hall. "So, any baby news to report?"

"First try was a bust."

"I'm sorry. How did she take it?"

"Not well at first, but she's okay now. We're just going to take it one cycle at time."

"Besides work, Tony and I haven't been seeing much of you lately."

"That's married life, I guess." Nick stopped in front of his office door and leaned on the jamb. "Maybe after Christmas we can all go out. Maybe even for New Year's."

"We could do that."

He was quiet for several seconds, and Nick asked, "Something on your mind, Rob?"

"I feel as if I owe you an apology."

"For what?"

"When you told us you were marrying Terri, instead of congratulating you, we accused you of doing something underhanded."

"And threatened to kick my ass, if I recall correctly."

"And it was a lousy thing for us to do. A person just has to see you two together to know that you really love each other, and not only that, it's obvious you're best friends. Which I think is really cool. If only it could be that way for everyone, there would never be another divorce. You really don't know how lucky you are to have her."

"Believe me, I know." And the more he thought of divorcing Terri, the less he liked the idea. He was beginning to wonder if the feelings of love that he'd been having for her were the romantic kind. And he had the distinct feeling that she was wondering the same thing. In their entire relationship he had never felt so close, so…connected. Not to her, and not to anyone else for that matter.

Most of his relationships—the semi-serious ones—rarely lasted much more than a month or two before he started to feel restless and smothered. With Terri, it felt as if there weren't enough hours in the day to spend with her. But at some point, they were going to have to make a decision. In his mind, he was pretty sure the decision was already made.

"Did you get her a Christmas present yet?"

"Not yet," Nick said. "But I have something in mind."

"First Christmas as a married couple. It better be special."

"Oh, it will be," he said, although he had no clue how he was going to wrap it.

On the Saturday before Christmas, which was two days before she was due to ovulate again—yeah, they were both climbing the walls in anticipation—Nick and Terri braved the crowds and four inches of freshly fallen snow to finish up their holiday shopping. They had both been so busy with work, they hadn't had time to get a tree. It seemed silly to go all-out so late in the season, so they picked up a pre-lit, battery-operated tabletop version to set on the coffee table.

She bent and fluffed the artificial branches into what sort of resembled a real tree—a real, *small* tree—switched the lights on then sat back on her heels to admire her work. "Not too shabby."

"What are we going to hang on it?"

She sat beside him on the sofa. "Your mom has a box of stuff that's made for a small tree. She put it aside for us."

"You want me to go pick it up?"

"Would you mind?"

"We're supposed to get another six inches tonight. If we wait, we may not get the ornaments until after Christmas."

"In that case you should probably go."

"Did you want to come with me?"

She sighed. "I can't. I have about fifty gifts to wrap. And if I recall correctly, you were going to help."

"You choose. Decorations or wrapping, which would you prefer?"

She though about that for a second, then said, "Decorations, I guess."

He pushed himself off the sofa. "I'd better go now, before the snow starts again."

She followed him to the door and watched as he put on his coat and checked his pockets for his wallet and keys. "Anything else you need me to pick up while I'm out?"

"Dinner?"

"You don't want to fix something?" He'd been making her watch him cook every night, yet she hadn't tested out what she'd been learning.

"Would you prefer a microwave frozen dinner, or burnt grilled cheese and tomato soup?"

"Fine, I'll pick up dinner. Thai okay?"

"Sounds delicious."

She kissed him goodbye. What shouldn't have been more that a quick peck, lingered. Then her arms went around his neck and her tongue was in his mouth, as one of her legs slid between his.

"Hey!" he said, pulling away. "That was an illegal move, lady. Two more days."

She flashed him a wicked smile. "Just keeping you on your toes."

He opened the door to leave, looking at their pathetic excuse for a tree. "Are you sure you don't mind having this tiny fake thing? You always get a real tree."

"So we'll get a real one next year," she said. "Drive safe."

Nick was in the elevator, on his way down to his car before Terri's words finally sank in.

So we'll get a real one next year....

Did that mean she was planning on them having a next year? That she thought they would still be married? Did she *want* to stay married? He'd been considering bringing up the subject, just to test the waters, but he hadn't yet figured out what he wanted to say. Was this it, handed to him on a silver platter?

And now that he knew she was thinking about it, too, how did he feel?

Nick got in his car and sat there for several minutes, thinking about what it would mean to both of them to make this a real marriage. To spend the rest of their lives together.

That was a really long time.

He drove to his mom's condo on autopilot, but as he turned the wheel to park in the driveway, he saw it was already occupied. *By his dad's car.*

Aw, hell, this couldn't be good.

Hackles up, Nick hopped out of his Mercedes and jogged through an inch of fresh snow to the door. He rang the bell, and when she didn't answer, he knocked briskly. Still no answer.

This was *really* not good.

He used his key and opened the door. He stepped inside, expecting to hear shouting, or furniture crashing. Instead, he heard the faint sound of a radio playing a classic rock song—which his mother favored—then a muffled moan of pain, all coming from the back of the condo.

Oh, hell, they've gone and done it now, he thought, picturing one of them with an actual hatchet in their back. Or possibly missing a limb or, God forbid, some other protruding part.

He rushed down the hall, tracking snow all the way. Realizing the noise was coming from his mom's bedroom, he burst through the partially closed door. And when he got an eyeful of his dad's bare rear end, he realized that no one was feeling any pain. At least, nothing they didn't want to feel.

Nick cursed and covered his eyes, realizing that he'd just walked in on every child's worst nightmare—his parents in bed doing it.

He heard the rustle of the covers and then his mom said, "Nick, what on earth are you doing here?"

He dared move his hand, relieved to find that they had covered themselves, and were in a less compromising position.

"What am *I* doing here? What is *he* doing here? And why in God's name were you..." He couldn't even say the words. He knew the memory of the whole gruesome scene would be eternally burned in his memory, and would haunt him until the day he died. "What the hell is going on?"

"What do you think is going on?" his mom asked, sounding infuriatingly reasonable. "We're having sex."

Ugh, it was bad enough to see it, but to have verbal confirmation was just too much. "You can't do this."

"Obviously, we can," his dad said, looking amused.

"Nicky, we're two single, consenting adults. We can do whatever we want. Within the boundaries of the law," she said, giving Nick's dad a wink.

Nick sniffed, catching just a hint of something that had been burning.... "What the... Have you been smoking *marijuana?*"

"Like you never have," his mom said. "Besides, it's medicinal, for your father's back."

The nightmare just kept getting worse. "You *hate* each other."

"We've certainly had our differences, I won't deny that, but we don't *hate* each other. And though we may have had a bad marriage, we had a good sex life."

He always knew that his mom's mother-earth, hippie-child attitude would come back to bite him. And speaking of that, were those teeth marks on his dad's left biceps...?

He closed his eyes, wishing the vision away.

"Why don't you put on the kettle for tea," his mother said. "We'll be out in a few minutes."

"Sure," Nick said, hoping they weren't planning to finish what they started.

He headed to the kitchen, shrugging out of his coat and draping it across a chair. Then he pulled out his cell phone and dialed Jess's number. When she answered, he could hear the kids screaming in the background, and Jess sounded more than a little exasperated. "What's up?" she shouted over the noise.

"I need to talk to you," he said, keeping his voice low so his parents wouldn't hear.

"What?" she shouted. "You need what?" She paused then said, "Hold on, lemme go somewhere quieter."

While he waited, Nick filled the kettle and set the burner on high. The screaming on the other end of the line faded, and Jess said, "Okay, now I can talk."

"Where did you go?"

"Front hall closet, so it's only a matter of time before they find me or I run out of oxygen."

"I just walked in on Mom and Dad doing it. And they were smoking pot."

She was silent for a several seconds, then said, "Together?"

"Yes, together."

"How did you manage that?"

He explained everything, expecting her to express the same horror he was experiencing. Instead, she started to laugh.

Irritated, he said, "It's not funny. It was...*horrifying*."

"No. It's pretty funny."

"I think you're missing the point. Mom and Dad are *sleeping* together."

"No, I got that. I'm just not sure why you're so freaked out. Would you rather have walked in on Dad chopping Mom into little pieces?"

"No, but...they hate each other."

"All evidence to the contrary. And you should be happy that they're getting along."

"And if he hurts her again?"

"Do you really think she was the only one who was hurt when they divorced?"

That's the way Nick remembered it, but before he could say so, his dad walked into the kitchen.

"I have to go," Nick told Jess. "I'll call you later." He hung up and asked, "Where is Mom?"

"You mother is getting dressed."

Nick's dad walked past him to the sink, pulled down a glass from the cupboard and filled it with tap water. He seemed to know his way around pretty well, which led Nick to believe that this wasn't the first time he'd been here. How long had this thing been going on?

"What the hell do you think you're doing?" he asked his dad.

"Getting a glass of water," he said, taking a swallow. "Would you like one?"

"You know what I mean. After what you did to Mom, what you did to me and the girls, you have no right."

He dumped the rest of the water down the drain, set the glass in the sink then turned to Nick and said, "You're twenty-nine years old, son. Don't you think it's time you grew up?"

The words struck Nick like a slap in the face, rendering him speechless.

"I realize I wasn't the greatest father and I was a pretty lousy husband, but you've been holding this grudge for twenty years. Enough already. Let it go. Everyone else has."

Nick was at a loss. Anything he could say at this point would just come off as immature and petty.

The kettle began to howl as his mom walked into the kitchen, dressed in hot-pink workout gear. "Who would like a cup of tea?" she asked, sounding infuriatingly cheerful. Who wouldn't be cheerful after an afternoon of sex, drugs and rock 'n' roll?

"Rain check," his dad said, then gave Nick's mom a kiss. It was disturbing to watch, but almost…natural in a weird way. They seemed like two people who were perfectly comfortable with each other, and happy to be so.

When the hell had that happened? And how had he missed it?

Fourteen

"Tea?" his mom asked Nick after his dad left.

"Sure," he said when what he really needed was a stiff drink.

"Have a seat," she said, gesturing to the kitchen table. He sat down and watched as she got out the sugar and cream and placed them on the table. When the tea was ready, she set a cup in front of him, then sat down across from him with her own. "So, to what do I owe this unexpected visit?"

For a minute he couldn't remember why he was there, then he remembered. "Decorations for our ugly little tree."

"Well, for future reference, if you ring the bell and I don't answer, come back later."

Yeah, he'd learned that lesson the hard way. "I'm sorry. It was inappropriate of me to barge in like that. But when I saw Dad's car, I was concerned."

"About what? You didn't honestly believe that I was in some sort of danger? That your father would hurt me?"

When she said it that way, it did sound sort of stupid. "I guess I didn't know what to think. Everything has gotten so…jumbled up lately. I don't know what to think about anything anymore."

"Oh, honey." She reached out to cover his hand with her own. "Are you and Terri having problems?"

"Not exactly."

She gave his hand a firm squeeze. "Take it from some-one who knows. Marriage is tough. You have to keep the lines of communication open. You have to really work at it."

"And if it's going *too* well?"

Confused, she said, "*Too* well?"

He should shut his mouth now, since she was never supposed to know about this, but who else could he talk to?

"Despite what everyone believes, my marriage to Terri was never supposed to last."

She blinked. "I don't understand."

"Terri wanted a baby, and she was going to use a donor."

"I know. She and I discussed it."

"Well, the gist of it was, why use a donor and not be sure what she was getting, when she could use someone she knew? Specifically me. That way the baby would have lots of family, and if something were ever to happen to Terri, she knows he will be well taken care of."

He didn't dare tell her about the ten million. He could live with the entire family knowing about their baby ar-rangement, but if his mom blabbed about *Nonno*'s offer, he was a dead man.

"Well," she said stiffly. "It sounds as if you have it all figured out."

"You're angry?"

"No... Yes." She stood so fast her chair almost fell over backward. It teetered on two legs, then landed with a thunk upright.

"Mom—"

"I'm mad. I'm disappointed." She paced back and forth behind him, her puny little hands balled up, as if she might haul off and pop him one. Which would probably hurt her more than it would hurt him. "How could you lie to your family that way?"

"It's not as if I could tell everyone the truth."

That's when he felt it, a firm crack against the back of his head so hard he could swear he heard his brain rattle. She must have been channeling *Nonni* for that one.

"Jeez, Mom." He rubbed the still-stinging part of his head.

His mom sat back down, looking much calmer. "I feel better now."

"I'm sorry, okay? We didn't do it to hurt anyone. You know how much Terri wanted a baby. And you've said a million times that you love her like a daughter. Would you prefer her baby be your grandchild or the product of some random sperm donor?"

"But you two seem so happy, so in love. You can't fake that."

"Maybe we weren't."

"You love her?"

"I think I do."

"And how does Terri feel?"

"That you can never depend on anyone, because eventually they'll let you down."

She sucked in a quiet breath. "Oh, that's not good. But I'm not surprised. She's been hurt a lot."

"But since she said it, things have been really great. And today she was making plans for next Christmas, so I'm thinking maybe that means she wants to stay married, too. I just want to be sure of my own feelings before I make a move, because two years from now, I don't want to wake up one day and realize I've made a terrible mistake. Because I will have lost my wife *and* my best friend."

"Not all marriages go bad, Nicky."

"Mom, you can't deny that our family hasn't exactly had an impressive track record when it comes to successful marriages. You and Dad were a disaster. Jess is miserable."

"There's a reason for that, you know."

"A Caroselli family curse?"

"Nicky, what you have to understand is that your dad and I, we were never friends. When it came to sexual compatibility, we were off the charts, but you can't base a marriage on sex. It just doesn't work. At least, not long past the honeymoon. And your sister, she was so determined to prove that she was different than her parents, that she would never make the same mistakes, she rushed into a relationship before she was ready. And when it started to go south, she didn't have the skills to know how to fix it. Which unfortunately, is partly my fault. I wasn't much of a role model. It's taken me until very recently to get my head together and realize what a real relationship should be. And you know who helped me?"

He shook his head.

"You and Terri."

"Seriously?"

"Maybe you two don't see what everyone else does, but you really are perfectly matched."

"Maybe this is a stupid question, but if your marriage was that bad, and you were that unhappy, why have kids?"

"Because you think it will change things, bring you closer together. And it does for a while. Which is why, when things get bad again, you have another baby, and then another."

Which explained why Jess had four kids of her own, he supposed. "So what you're saying is, you only had us kids to save your marriage?"

"Of course not. I was thrilled when I found out I was pregnant with all three of you. You kids were the light of my life, and sometimes the only thing that kept me going, when I thought I couldn't take another second of being miserable." She reached up, touched his cheek. "You and your sisters always made me happy."

"If you were so miserable, why did you stay married for so long?"

"I came from a broken home, and I wanted better for you. I thought that if I couldn't be happy, the least I could do was give you kids a stable home with two parents."

"Our home was anything but stable, Mom."

She sighed. "I know. But I had to try. And you will never know how sorry I am for what I put you kids through. And so is your father. We were both doing the best we could, or what we thought was best."

"And what you two are doing now, is that for the best, too?"

She shrugged. "All I know is, we have fun together. We talk and we laugh, and he seems to understand me in a way no one else ever has. And the sex—"

Nick held up a hand to stop her. "TMI, Mom."

She grinned. "The point is, right now, he makes me happy. Maybe it will last, maybe it won't. Maybe we both just needed to grow up. Who knows? What I do know is that after all this time, we've finally become friends. With you and Terri, it's different. You're already friends. What you have to decide now is if you love her."

"We've been friends for twenty years. Of course I love her."

"But are you *in love* with her?"

He shrugged. "I guess I don't know the difference."

She looked at him like he was a moron. And she was probably right. Maybe what he needed was another good hard whack in the head.

"Okay, let me ask you this. Who is the first person you think of in the morning when you wake up?"

That was easy. "Terri."

"And when you're not with her, how often do you think about her?"

Lately, too many times to count. "If there was a way I could be with her twenty-four hours a day, I would do it."

"Now, think about when you're with her and find a single word to describe how she makes you feel."

He thought that would be a tough one, since she made him feel so many things lately. But with barely any thought, the perfect word came to him. "Complete," he said. "When I'm with her I feel complete."

"And has anyone else ever made you feel that way?"

"Never," he admitted. Not even close.

"Now, imagine her with someone else."

There was no one else good enough for her. No one who knew her the way he did. Who could ever love her as much...

The answer must have been written all over his face, because his mom smiled. "What do you think that means, Nicky?"

What it meant was, he didn't just love Terri, he was *in* love with her. Looking back, there was hardly a time when he hadn't been. He sighed and shook his head at the depth of his own stupidity. "I am such an idiot."

His mom patted his hand. "When it comes to relationships, most men are, sweetheart."

"What if Terri is still afraid to trust me? How do I convince Terri that I love her, and that I won't let her down? How do I make her trust me?"

She shrugged. "It may take some sort of grand gesture to convince her. But if you know her as well as I think you do, you'll figure it out."

When it came to things like grand gestures, he was clueless. He could barely get his own head straight, and now he was supposed to figure her out, too?

"And while you're at it," his mom said. "Maybe you could cut your dad a little slack. Everyone makes mistakes."

"Some more than others."

"And goodness knows you can hold a grudge. But haven't you punished him enough? Couldn't you at least *try* to let him make amends? Would you do it for me?"

Maybe Nick had been a bit bullheaded—a trait he had inherited from his father, of course—but to be honest, he was tired of carrying around this pent-up animosity. After all his parents had been through, if she could forgive him, shouldn't he at least make an attempt?

"I'll try," he told her.

His mom smiled. "Thank you."

"I'm sorry I barged in on you like that," he said.

"Well, considering the look on your face, it was much more traumatic for you than it was for your father and me."

No kidding.

When he left his mom's condo, he went straight home, still completely clueless as to what he would say to Terri.

With any luck, he would have some sort of epiphany, and the right words would just come to him. That was bound to happen at least once in a man's life, right?

When Nick got home, Terri was sitting on the living room floor amid a jumble of wrapping paper, ribbon and bows.

"I'm home," he said, even though that was pretty obvious, as he was standing right there. He was off to a champion start.

She just looked at him and smiled and said, "How are the roads?"

"Getting bad," he said. "How's the wrapping?"

"I've been doing this every year for over twenty years now, and I still manage to suck at it."

He reviewed the pile of presents she'd already finished, and it did sort of look as if a five-year-old had done them.

"Plus my knees are about to pop." She pushed herself to her feet and watched him expectantly. "So where is it?"

He hung up his coat. "Where is what?"

"The decorations."

"Oh, crap." He'd been so rattled when he left his mom's he'd forgotten to grab the box.

"You drove all the way to you mom's and *forgot* them?"

"I'm sorry."

"I don't suppose you picked up dinner, either."

Dammit! "No, I forgot that, too. But I have a very good excuse. I walked in on my parents having sex."

Her eyes went wide, and she said, *"Together?"*

He repeated the story to her, and by the end she was laughing so hard tears were rolling down her face.

"It is *not funny*," he said.

"Yeah," she said, wiping her eyes. "It is."

"I'm traumatized for life. Did I also mention that they were smoking pot?"

"Like you've never done that," she said. She walked into the kitchen and he followed her. "So what are we going to eat? I'm starving."

"We could order in."

"In this weather, it will take forever."

"I could throw together a quick tomato sauce, and serve it over shells. It wouldn't take more than an hour."

"After shopping all day, then living through the horror of seeing your dad's naked ass, do you really think you have the energy?"

Shaking his head in exasperation, he snatched his apron from the broom closet. "Get me two cans of crushed tomatoes and a can of tomato paste from the pantry."

He tied the apron on and grabbed the ingredients he needed from the fridge. He chopped onions, celery and garlic, and sautéed it all in a pan with olive oil. When the onions and garlic turned translucent, he stirred in the crushed tomatoes and tomato paste, then added oregano, basil and salt. He ground fresh pepper in next, then added the slightest pinch of thyme, which his *Nonni* had always taught him to use sparingly, warning that too much would overwhelm. Nick had learned a lot in culinary school, but the really valuable things he'd learned from her.

"How do you do that?" Terri asked from the bar stool where she sat watching him. "You don't measure anything. How do you know it's the right amount?"

"I do measure it. Just with my eyes, not a spoon. When you make something as many times as I've made *Nonni*'s tomato sauce, a recipe becomes obsolete."

She sighed. "I can't make toast without screwing it up."

"It's just a matter of following the directions and using good judgment."

"Well, there you go, I have terrible judgment."

"You married me," he said, hoping to break the ice. Maybe she would say it had been the best decision of her life.

She smiled at him and said, "I rest my case."

He laughed in spite of himself. He set the burner on medium and took off his apron. "So, I was thinking maybe we could—"

His cell phone buzzed in his pants pocket, startling him. Then it started to ring. He pulled it out and saw that it was Rob. "Hold on a minute, Terri.

"Hey, Rob," he answered.

"Hey, have you got a minute?"

"Um, I'm making dinner."

"It'll just take a minute."

"Okay, sure, what's up?"

"Something kind of weird happened yesterday, and I'm really not sure what to think. I thought maybe your dad said something to you about it."

"You know me and my dad, always chatting."

"I know it's a long shot, but I thought maybe he mentioned it."

"Mentioned what?"

"What's going on between my dad and Uncle Tony."

"Actually he did mention it, but only to ask if I knew what was going on. Which I don't. He wanted me to ask you and Tony Junior if you knew anything."

"All I know is that I stopped by my parents' house tonight and Uncle Tony's Beemer was there. I heard shouting from inside, and when my mom answered the door, she looked as if she'd been crying, and Uncle Tony looked pissed. He left just a few minutes after I got there. When I asked what happened, my parents wouldn't talk about it."

"What about Tony? Have you talked to him?"

"A few minutes ago. He didn't have a clue what I was talking about."

He considered mentioning what Terri saw on Thanksgiving, and that whatever it was, Aunt Sarah was involved, too, but he was a little fuzzy on the details. Besides, it wouldn't be fair to bring Terri into this without first asking her if it was okay.

"I'll ask around and see what I can come up with, but I'm sure it's nothing to worry about," he said, even though that was the opposite of what he was actually thinking. Something was up, and he had the feeling it was bad.

Fifteen

"Everything okay?" Terri asked when Nick hung up, but she could tell by the look on his face that something was wrong.

"I'm not sure. According to my father and Rob, there's some sort of friction between Uncle Demitrio and Uncle Tony. Didn't you say that you heard Uncle Demitrio and Aunt Sarah fighting at *Nonno's*?"

He *remembered* that? She wondered what else he recalled from that night. "I don't know if I would call it *fighting,* but it seemed…heated. But like you said, they used to date, so maybe there are still hard feelings."

"Why now, after thirty-some years?"

She shrugged. This was not a can of worms she wanted to be responsible for opening.

"Do you recall what they were fighting about?"

"I didn't hear the whole conversation, just bits and pieces."

"Like what?"

"Something about telling someone something."

"That's vague."

She shrugged. "She said she didn't want to, and then they walked downstairs."

"You didn't hear them mention a name?"

"No. It was probably nothing. Honestly, I figured you would have forgotten all about it."

"I remember a lot of things from that night." Something about the way he said it, the way he looked into her eyes, made her heart skip a beat.

"Wh-what do you remember?" she asked, her heart in her throat, unsure if she really wanted to know.

"Bits and pieces."

"Do you remember saying anything to me?"

"If I recall, I said a lot of things to you. To what specifically were you referring?"

He wanted her to tell him, so he clearly *didn't* remember. She felt an odd mix of relief, and disappointment. "Never mind."

"Was it when I commented on the stuffing?" he asked. "Or when I expressed my unrequited and undying love for you?"

He said it so calmly, so matter-of-factly, that for several seconds words escaped her. She couldn't even breathe. Then she realized that he was just teasing her. She refused to feel disappointed. "I want you to know that you shouldn't feel weird or uncomfortable for saying it."

"I don't."

"All that stuff about you wishing other girls were me. I know you didn't mean it."

"What makes you think I didn't mean it?"

"Because…" She paused, unsure of what to say next, because he had to be messing with her. It was the only explanation. "Nick, come on. You were completely hammered."

"Just because I was drunk doesn't mean I didn't know what I was saying or mean what I said. In fact, that's probably the most honest I've ever been with you. And with myself for that matter."

Suddenly she was having a tough time pulling in a full breath again, and the room pitched so violently she clutched the counter to keep from falling over.

Nick loved her? *Love* loved her? And didn't she want that?

It was one thing to fantasize about it, but she was totally unprepared to actually hear him say the words.

"Besides," he said. "I'm not drunk now. And I still feel the same way, so I guess it must be true."

A small part of her wanted to jump for joy, while another part—a much bigger part—was having a full-blown panic attack.

Slow, shallow breaths. In and out.

What was *wrong* with her? This was a good thing, right? Shouldn't she be happy? A rich, handsome man who just happened to be her best friend in the world love-loved her. Shouldn't she be *thrilled*?

She should, but why wasn't she? Why instead was every fiber of her being screaming at her to run?

"Terri, are you okay?" Nick looked as if he were getting his first inkling that something was off. Specifically, her.

"I'm just a little surprised," she said. "I mean, this definitely was not a part of the plan."

"Plans change."

Not this one.

He sat beside her and took her hands. "Look, I know you're scared."

She pulled her hands free. "It's not that."

"Then what is it?"

"You don't want to be married. You've said it a million times."

"I was wrong."

"Just like that, you changed your mind?"

"Pretty much."

"And how do I know you aren't going to change it back? That five years from now you won't get restless or bored? How do I know you won't die?"

"Okay, Terri," he said calmly, as if he were speaking to a child. "Now you're being ridiculous."

"Am I? Have you forgotten that you're talking to a woman whose parents have both died? Like you said, they probably didn't want to die. I'm guessing they didn't plan on it, either. But they still did."

"I never meant to imply that I'm not going to die. Everyone dies eventually. And, of course, I'm hoping my death occurs later rather than sooner."

"Why are you doing this now? Everything was going so well."

"That's why I'm doing it. After what you said about Christmas, I figured you wanted this, too."

"What did I say about Christmas?"

"That next year we would get a real tree. Which I took to mean that there would be a next year for us, that you're planning for the future."

How could a few innocent words get so dangerously misconstrued? "That wasn't what I meant."

"So what did you mean?"

"I don't know!" She wished he would stop pushing and give her a minute to organize her thoughts. "There was no hidden agenda, they were just words."

"Terri, I am in love with you. I know what I want, and

that isn't going to change. Not a year from now, not five years from now, not a hundred. As long as I am alive, I'm going to want you."

"I want you, too," she said softly. "But I just don't know if I'm ready for this. If you could give me a little time—"

"How much time? A year, two years? Twenty years? Because that's how long it's taken us to get this far. You can't live your life in fear of what might happen."

"This isn't going to work."

"What isn't going to work?"

"The marriage, the baby, none of it. It's not fair to either of us. You want something from me that I just can't give, Nick."

For a minute he didn't say anything. He just sat there staring at the wall. Finally, he said, "You know what I could never figure out? You're beautiful and intelligent, yet you insisted on dating jerks and losers. Men that I— and pretty much everyone else—knew were all wrong for you. And now I realize that was the whole point. Because for all the talking you do about finding Mr. Right, you didn't *want* to find him. You would rather play it safe by getting into a relationship you knew would fail, or one that was just about sex. Because if you didn't care, they couldn't hurt you. But how many people do you think *you* hurt, Terri?"

She bit her lip.

"How many men really cared about you, maybe even loved you, and you just tossed them away? And now you're doing the same thing to me."

He was right, she knew he was, but she couldn't do anything about it. She didn't know how. Those self-defense mechanisms he was referring to were so deep-seated, she didn't know how to be any other way.

"If you could just give me a little more time—"

"Terri, we have been best friends for *twenty* years. If you don't trust me now, you're never going to." He pushed off the bar stool and started to walk away.

"What about the ten million dollars?" she said, only because she wasn't quite ready to let him go. Not yet.

He stopped and turned to her, his face blank, even though she knew he had to be hurting. "There are plenty of other fish in the sea."

He didn't mean it, she knew he didn't, but as he turned and walked away, his words cut deep. If only he could give her a little more time. But he was right, she was damaged goods and he deserved better than her.

When Nick woke the next morning, when he and Terri were supposed to be trying to make a baby, he walked into the spare bedroom to discover that all her clothes were gone. He walked to the kitchen and found "the" note. She said she was sorry and she would be back in a few days to get the rest of her things. Simple, to the point.

And that was it.

Numb, he made a pot of coffee that he never drank, warmed a bagel that he forgot in the toaster, opened a beer that then sat on the coffee table untouched and stared most of the day at a television he never bothered to turn on. And for the first time in years, he did not talk to Terri. He wanted to, though, which surprised him a little. It felt unnatural not telling her about his day, even if all he did was sit around wallowing in self-pity.

On Christmas Eve, at his mom's house, he told everyone she had to flu, knowing that if he told them the truth it would ruin everyone's Christmas. And since this entire mess was his fault, since he was the one who talked Terri into this, and assured her everything would work out great, he deserved to suffer alone. Although he didn't doubt she was suffering, too. And he wished he could take back some of the things he had said to her.

He told himself he wasn't going to miss her, yet caught himself expecting her to be there, because she hadn't missed a holiday with his family in years. Because she had no one else.

He was miserable, but at least he was with people who loved him. She was miserable, too—he didn't doubt for a second that she was—but on top of that, she was alone. Guilt gnawed at him all evening. He hardly slept. By Christmas morning, he knew what he had to do, what he *needed* to do. And yes, what he wanted to do.

From the outside, Terri's condo was the only one that was bare of holiday decorations. It looked so...lonely. A misfit among units draped with twinkling lights and fresh pine wreathes and nativity scenes. They hadn't exactly gone all out at his place, either, but at least they had their scrawny and unadorned little tree that sat for a couple days on the coffee table looking as lonely and pathetic as he felt.

He trudged through two inches of freshly fallen snow to her door and rang the bell. Terri opened it wearing flannel pajamas, due, he had no doubt, to the sub-zero temperature where she kept the thermostat. She was stunned to see him, of course, just as he'd expected she would be. So stunned that for several long seconds she just stared openmouthed at him.

"It's really cold out here," he said, and she snapped into action.

"Sorry, come in."

She held the door for him and he stepped inside. He stomped the snow from his shoes and shrugged out of his coat, surprised to find that it was reasonably warm. "This is nice," he said.

"Nice?" she asked.

"The temperature. It's usually so cold."

"I decided last night that I'm sick of being cold."

It was about time.

"What are you doing here?" she asked as he walked through the foyer into the living room. Her laptop sat open on the coffee table and the television was tuned to what he recognized as some cheesy made-for-television holiday flick she'd forced him to watch a couple years ago.

"I'm picking you up," he said, making himself comfortable on the sofa.

"Picking me up for *what*?"

"Christmas at *Nonno*'s."

"But…"

"You better hurry. You know how he hates it when people are late."

She stared at him, dumbfounded. "I'm sorry, did I miss something?"

"I don't think so. It's Christmas day, and on Christmas day we always go to *Nonno*'s."

"But…the other day…?"

"I'm really sorry about that."

Just when he thought she couldn't look any more confused. "*You're* sorry."

"What I did to you was really unfair. I basically forced you into doing this, assured you repeatedly that everything would be great, and work out exactly according to plan, then I changed my mind and got angry when you were surprised. I tried to make you feel guilty when it was my fault, not yours."

"Nick, you had every right to be mad at me."

"No, I didn't."

"And now you're here to take me to Christmas dinner?"

"Did you honestly think I would let you spend Christmas alone?"

Tears pooled in her eyes, but didn't spill over. "Actually, I sort of thought I deserved it."

"Well, I don't think so. So go get ready."

"So we're just going to be friends again? Like before?"

"If that's my only option. I won't say that I don't love you, because I do. I think I probably always have, even if I was too stupid to realize it. But you're too important to me to let you go, and if friendship is all you want, I'm okay with that."

One minute Terri was standing in front of him looking thoroughly confused, and the next she was sitting in his lap, arms around his neck, hugging him harder than she'd ever hugged him before.

"I love you, Nick."

Now he was the confused one. "Okay, what just happened?"

She sat back on his thighs and laughed. "I don't know. All of a sudden I just...knew."

"That constituted a grand gesture?"

"A what?"

He shook his head. "Never mind."

"I have a confession," she said. "Something I've been wanting to tell you for weeks."

"What?"

"When we lived together, and you brought girls over, I used to wish it was me in the bedroom with you."

"No, you didn't."

"I *did*. I always wondered what it would be like."

"And now that you know?"

She grinned. "I really like being the girl in the bedroom with you. And the idea of another girl being there instead of me..."

"How would you feel?"

"Like ripping out her throat with my bare hands."

He laughed. "Well, you'll never have to, because there's no one else I want there, either. Because despite what I said, those vows meant something to me. And I was meant to say them to you."

She grinned. "Wow, that was so sappy, I don't know if I should laugh or cry."

"Why don't you kiss me instead?"

She did, and then she started to unbutton his shirt.

He caught her hands. "We really don't have time. *Nonno* is expecting us."

"Well, *Nonno* will have to wait. We have business in the bedroom. We're already two days behind schedule."

He'd completely forgotten that she was ovulating. "Well, just a quick one I guess. If you're sure you still want to. We can wait a month."

"I don't want to wait. I know what I want, and besides, aren't you looking forward to all the money?"

"Oh, well, don't even worry about that."

"Why?"

"I told him I didn't want the money anymore."

Her mouth dropped open. "What? *When?*"

"Right after we got back from the honeymoon."

"Why?"

"It just didn't feel right taking it."

"What did *Nonno* say?"

"Not much. I thought he would be really surprised, but it was almost as if he was expecting it."

"But it's ten *million* dollars! You just gave that up?"

"I'm having a child with you because I *want* to, not because I need to."

She cupped his face in her soft hands. "Have I mentioned that I love you?"

He grinned. "Why don't you tell me again?"

"I love you, Nicolas Caroselli."

"What about that perfect man you were looking for? Are you ready to give him up?"

"I don't have to."

"You don't?"

"Heck, no," she said with one of those wicked grins. "I already married him."

* * * * *

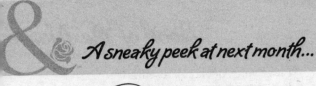

A sneaky peek at next month...

Desire™

PASSIONATE AND DRAMATIC LOVE STORIES

My wish list for next month's titles...

2 stories in each book – only £5.49!

In stores from 21st December 2012:

☐ The Sheikh's Claim – Olivia Gates

& An Outrageous Proposal – Maureen Child

☐ Calling All the Shots – Katherine Garbera

& All He Ever Wanted – Emily McKay

☐ Princess in the Making – Michelle Celmer

& Midnight Under the Mistletoe – Sara Orwig

☐ Whatever the Price – Jules Bennett

& Temperatures Rising – Brenda Jackson

Available at WHSmith, Tesco, Asda, Eason, Amazon and Apple

Just can't wait?

Visit us Online

You can buy our books online a month before they hit the shops! **www.millsandboon.co.uk**

1212/51

Special Offers

Every month we put together collections and longer reads written by your favourite authors.

Here are some of next month's highlights— and don't miss our fabulous discount online!

On sale 21st December

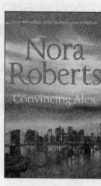

On sale 4th January

On sale 4th January

Save 20% on all Special Releases

Find out more at
www.millsandboon.co.uk/specialreleases

Visit us Online

0113/ST/MB39

The World of Mills & Boon®

There's a Mills & Boon® series that's perfect for you. We publish ten series and, with new titles every month, you never have to wait long for your favourite to come along.

Blaze.
Scorching hot, sexy reads
4 new stories every month

By Request
Relive the romance with the best of the best
9 new stories every month

Cherish
Romance to melt the heart every time
12 new stories every month

Desire
Passionate and dramatic love stories
8 new stories every month

Have Your Say

You've just finished your book.
So what did you think?

We'd love to hear your thoughts on our
'Have your say' online panel
www.millsandboon.co.uk/haveyoursa

- 🌹 Easy to use
- 🌹 Short questionnaire
- 🌹 Chance to win Mills & Boon® goodies